To write *Anshū* the author had to live with the novel's fictional narrator for years of her life, in order to learn and to tell the unspeakable about a subject few if any Americans before Kono have been able to speak about without guilt and revulsion. Anshū, the very word defined by this novel, means an understanding, an apprehension deeper than guilt, deeper than fear, than hate, than love and pity and sympathy, deeper than resignation, deeper than acceptance.

—**Stephen H. Sumida, University of Washington**

Simply put, Juliet S. Kono fleshes out the heroism that defines the miracle of survival during World War II Japan and after the dropping of the atomic bomb on Hiroshima. Kono, through graceful yet unstinting prose, gives us a memorable story of atonement and transcendence.

—**Joe Tsujimoto, author of *Morningside Heights: New York Stories***

Anshū is a courageous and necessary book, steeped in the wisdom of Buddhist cosmology, taking on the large issues of the human condition. Through its rich detailing of the "dark sorrow" of a single human journey, Himiko's story illuminates the relation of each of us to the other, of the very small to the incomprehensible.

—**Sylvia Watanabe, author of *Talking to the Dead***

Also by Juliet S. Kono

Hilo Rains (Bamboo Ridge Press, 1988)

Tsunami Years (Bamboo Ridge Press, 1995)

Ho'olulu Park and the Pepsodent Smile and other stories (Bamboo Ridge Press, 2004)

The Bravest 'Opihi: How Two of Hawai'i's Smallest Sea Creatures Saved the Day (BeachHouse Publishing, 2005)

No Choice but to Follow, linked poems by Jean Yamasaki Toyama, Juliet S. Kono, Ann Inoshita, and Christy Passion (Bamboo Ridge Press, 2010)

D1528468

Anshū

DARK SORROW

Juliet S. Kono

Bamboo Ridge Press

ISBN 978-0-910043-83-0

This is issue #97 (Spring 2010) of *Bamboo Ridge, Journal of Hawai'i Literature and Arts* (ISSN 0733-0308).

Published by Bamboo Ridge Press

Printed in the United States of America

Indexed in the Humanities International Complete

Bamboo Ridge Press is a member of the Council of Literary Magazines and Presses (CLMP).

Typesetting and design: Rowen Tabusa

Cover art: "Transit," 2009, by Stephen Little, acrylic on canvas, 36" H X 48" W

Title page calligraphy: "Anshū" ("Dark Sorrow"), by Reverend Eijo Ikenaga

Author's photo by Rowen Tabusa

Bamboo Ridge Press is a nonprofit, tax-exempt corporation formed in 1978 to foster the appreciation, understanding, and creation of literary, visual, or performing arts by, for, or about Hawai'i's people. This publication was made possible with support from the Cooke Foundation, the Mayor's Office of Culture & the Arts (MOCA), the Hawai'i State Foundation on Culture and the Arts (SFCA), and the National Endowment for the Arts (NEA).

Bamboo Ridge is published twice a year. For subscription information, back issues, or a catalog, please contact:

> Bamboo Ridge Press
> P.O. Box 61781
> Honolulu, HI 96839-1781
> (808) 626-1481
> brinfo@bambooridge.com
> www.bambooridge.com

6 5 4   18 19 20

for Darius

for peace

Contents

If only we had found Nirvana—but he was right who warned us that we were late in this season of the world.

–John La Farge

PART I

HAWAI‘I

1920s – November 1941

All things are impermanent.
—from the Teachings of Buddha

1

Child of Fire

Born of fire,
fire my element,
Himiko, child of fire, my name.
"Don't play with fire!" Mama said. "Do you want to get burned?"
I loved fire. Played with it every chance I could. My parents worried
that I might get hurt, burn the house down, or destroy the cane fields that
took years to grow, and all that the sugar-plantation-camp people had
worked for would go up in smoke. Worst of all, kill someone if not myself.

Early one morning, just after Papa left the house to work in the cane
field to clear the weeds, I took some old Japanese newspapers from a bin
near the wood-burning stove in the kitchen and rushed downstairs to make
a crumpled paper mountain in a corner under the house. That done, I
hastened upstairs to take the box of cowboy matches from the ledge above
the stove, then ran into my parents' bedroom to steal Mama's prayer beads.
Downstairs once more, I struck a matchstick on my geta, the way I had
seen Papa scrape the soles of his boots to light his pipe. No luck. I looked
around and dragged the fat match head on one of the rough beams that
held up the house.
The gritty head caught fire. It rasped, looked close to dying, then
flared. I cupped the flickering head and lowered it to the base of the Japanese newspaper pile. Old and dried, the papers caught fire instantly. With

flames crackling, parts of the newspaper crinkled, rose, then fell into wisps of fragile gray ash, the heat destroying the long thread of ideograms, the stories—curled incantations, old murmurings—going up in smoke.

It was magic. I mumbled *na-man dabs, na-man dabs*, like the bald Buddhist priests at the temple, with the prayer beads I stole from Mama draped over my hands. Fire spoke to me. I clapped my hands, made wild-animal kicks, and scattered dirt into the air. Twirling in the dust like a frenzied death-spirit dancer and placing my hands toward the heel of the runaway flames, I lifted them up to circle the air and, like a child shaman, conducted the spirit forces around me. Fueled, the flames grew into a spindly tree, and the long pointy leaves brushed against my threadbare dress.

I was on fire. I ran out from under the house. I rolled on the ground and shielded my face.

"Mamaaaa, come quick, Hi-chan burning up!" I knew it. Miyo was spying on me again.

"Go 'way, you!" Even with my dress on fire and the house smoldering, I resented my sister's eyes.

"Mama said fo' watch you!"

"No *WATCH*!"

Mama flew out of the house. "What happened? Where's Hi-chan?"

Miyo pointed; Mama spotted me on the ground in flames, the side of the house smoking. With no time to search for a pail, Mama ran to the rain barrel and dropped her long hair into the water. She raised it like a mop and leaped to my side. Whipping her hair about, she unleashed a silver net to douse the flames. Water and hair fanned out to sting me.

Whuuhn, whuuhn. I whimpered dog sounds.

She kept returning to the barrel. She dropped her hair into the water and ran back to me, then back to the house. Spun her head of wet hair at the flames. When the barrel of water ran low, she jumped into the pond, cradled her wet hair, and ran up to the house to keep it from burning further. "UGHHH!" she grunted with each spin.

The fire died, hissing under her vigilance.

I covered my eyes when Mama, lean with anger, stood above me in a long morning shadow, her thin wet body a column of despair. She plucked me off the ground like some half-drowned mutt and pushed me, wailing, ahead of her into the house.

"What's the matter, you. You want to ma-ke?" she asked in pidgin.

"*Ma-ke?*"

"Die."

"Die?"

"No more Hi-chan!"

She twisted her hands across my face to emphasize *no more*, to show how I would be gone, and raised her voice higher each time she scolded me for the near disastrous house fire, my first encounter with such heat.

Dragging me into the house, she stood me in front of the mirror and said, "What kind girl you, eh? Look you. When you going learn?" The more Mama was stern with me, the better her English: "You-want-to-burn-up-in-smoke?"

"No, I no like."

"You-want-Papa-and-Mama-to-suffer?"

"No, I no like, I said."

"Then-what?"

"Don't know, Mama, don't know."

Mama was doubly angry because I had stolen her prayer beads to play with and had burned them in the fire. It was something Papa had given to her on their wedding day, and I had shown neither remorse nor shame for my thievery. Yanking my long braids to rein me in, shaving off my burnt eyebrows, slapping a stinky salve on my scalded skin, snipping off my singed hair were Mama's ways of teaching me a lesson as she spun me, like a merry-go-round, in the cage of her arms.

"Lucky you, this time," she fumed. "Maybe next time, not so lucky," the words, punctuated on my head with a knuckle. I may have been only four, but I already knew how it was to be obsessed by something to the point where the more Mama tended my burns, the more defiant I became. I saw that Miyo noticed it, too. As she whirled around Mama and me, she chanted:

> Ladybug, ladybug,
> fly away home.
> Your house is on fire,
> your children are gone.

15

Miyo watched my face. Narrowing her eyes, she gasped, and upon widening them, she slammed her hands, one over the other, across her mouth. She withdrew in her realization that I wasn't about to stop and had been actually contemplating what to burn next.

"Spooky, you," she said.

"No, I not!" I said, stamping my feet.

Mama grabbed me by the shoulders and turned me around to face her. She said in cold Japanese: "Children who play with matches will someday eat fire; children who burn newspapers will drown in fire; you'll be scarred if you're not careful. Don't you understand? You'll suffer all your life if you don't listen." I gave what must have looked to be an unconvincing nod, for in the next breath, my mother, who was in tears by this time, began shaking me. "Tell me, child, what are we going to do with you?"

The solution came when Mama and Papa decided to use yaito to tame me. They pored over an old apothecary text Mama had brought with her from Japan in 1920 and studied a chart of red dots on the meridian lines of the human body. Left of the tenth vertebra, two thumb widths to the left. Apply the moxa there to control a difficult child. If that didn't work, apply it to the line of the spine. Mama read the Japanese instructions: "Starting from the spine, count . . ." I kicked my feet and beat my hands on the floor.

Papa counted the knobs on my back with his thumb. He felt for muscle bundles, places where nerve channels ran, the bad rivers working their way to my disobedience. Papa made crosses with his fingernail on the skin of my back, then placed the moxa on these evil spots to burn off with a stick of altar incense. I tried to wriggle out from under Mama's body pressed against mine, but she was strong. "Good thing, this," she said. "Make you one good girl."

"Yes, the fire on your back will tame you. Hold still," said Papa, who spoke only Japanese. My parents were desperate to cure my bad habits.

Papa applied the burning incense to the moxa. *Phssst.* Skin sizzled. "Please, Mama, please, Papa, NOOO!"

My cry rose straight up, hit the rusted iron roof, bounced out of the doors and windows, cascaded down the hills past the houses of our neighbors—the Taketas, the Nakamas—and so on down the hill. My parents fought fire with fire as prescribed by an ancient Chinese map, the moxibustion on my back, this torture by fire to make me good, the result of the fire I had set that day. Despite the punishment, I knew that I would do it again, in a minute.

Daily, I was the focus of my parents' late-night discussions. Though they spoke softly, I could hear them talking through the wall of their bedroom, the walls of our home inadequate in holding back sounds, Mama asking Papa in anxious words of Japanese, "Where did she come from?"

"It's all right, Mama. Don't worry. She'll turn out okay," Papa would say and, I imagined, pat her hand to reassure her.

Disappointing one's parents was unheard of in Mama's day; she would never have thought of playing with fire. "Once said, enough said" had been her family's motto. She tried to apply the same rule with Miyo and me, only my sister good about it. Four years older than I, Miyo didn't need reminding, this I thought due to her being born crippled, her left leg shorter than her right. People called this condition fujiyuu in Japanese, muʻumuʻu leg in Hawaiian, or "shot leg," for short-legged in the pidgin we used—we, adept at switching languages. The neighbors would have been quick to notice it, and there were many looks and words for being different. Because he didn't want anyone teasing her, Papa applied a thin, wooden layer to her left shoe and dyed it black, for he had vowed that she would never look different from other children. And no one noticed it, for she could run, hop, skip, and jump, far better than anyone in the school or camp. I was different, though. Unlike my sister, I grew up as wild as the mountain pigs that came to root in our garden.

Both of my parents had come from Hiroshima, the back mountains, from the same hamlet; their families knew each other as neighboring farmers. "Nodding acquaintances," Mama called Papa's family. When Papa had written to Mama's family, to ask if they would allow their daughter to come to Hawaiʻi to become his picture bride, Mama jumped at the chance.

"Being taller than most men, if I had stayed in Japan, I might not have married at all," Mama said, "or would have only been able to marry one of the sake-drinking farmers. I would have had to work very hard, planting rows of turnip seeds or barley rice with nothing to show for it at the end.

At least with your father, I was going to marry a man who made his own way in the world."

"Nnnn," Papa said, smiling at Mama.

"In the picture he sent me, Papa looked so handsome-u," Mama said, causing me and Miyo to giggle at her English in the midst of the Japanese. "He had a nice smile, too, that opened his face like a fan. I was very lucky."

"And Mama was so beautiful that I fell in love-u with her instantly."

"It was good we got together," Mama mused. Miyo and I were able to see how happy our parents were. "My parents' investigation of your papa, who had already been in Hawai'i for several years, revealed his wealth in sugar equivalent to many bags of rice," she bragged, often repeating her around-the-kitchen-table stories. "Papa had his own home and was well supplied with catchment water. He owned a good dog and a sturdy mule. For a dollar a day he worked in the sugar cane fields and had a growing savings account in the Yokohama Specie Bank in Hawai'i. When we got married, Papa strung me prayer beads made of Nāwiliwili seeds to show me how grateful he was. That's the one you took from my room, Hi-chan, and burned."

"Papa can make you one new one," I said.

"You no understand, Hi-chan," she said, returning to pidgin. "Not same."

Mama failed to recognize that she was the product of strong-willed people. Coming to Hawai'i in 1920 on her own had given her a measure of self-confidence unheard of in Japan. It had changed her and, in our time, changed us. My passion for fire was part of this willfulness—the single focus I had on what I was going to burn next.

After my first fire, I was careful about not being caught. I burned my fires in secret: the line of red ants near the outhouse picked off with burning matches; the centipede in the banana patch I drizzled with kerosene, a line of fire on its back; the dog's ticks stacked up like dead soldiers on a nest of burning twigs. And these fires were the best fires, for I knew I wasn't supposed to burn them. My secret fires were like the lure of the locked shed at the back of the house, the irrigation ditch with its slippery sides, the discarded icebox in the cane field, and the sharp machetes. Everything I wasn't supposed to do or touch, I did, I touched.

2

The Fireball

When I was seven, Papa took us down to Hāpuna Beach on the west side of the Big Island. Once there, Papa, Mama, Miyo, and I took a long walk along the shoreline to enjoy the salt-sea air, and we stopped along the way to peer into a tide pool where Papa took me aside and said, "Some of the animals in the ocean carry their own fire—to find their way at night, or where it is dark and deep. They also carry fire upon their backs or in the pockets of their scales. Even on their heads, their tails." Though he winked at me, his expression was serious. "Look closely. Watch. See if you can learn their secret."

"Not good, Hi-chan, watch like that," Mama said, contrary to Papa's urging. Of course what she said didn't stop me. I studied these fires in the tide pools and concentrated on them as much as I did when torturing a stink bug or rubbing two sticks to make fire, the way I saw Indians do it in my schoolbooks.

Late into the night, between retrieving more wood from a pile and helping Papa tend our beach fire, I snuggled in his lap to watch the stars, other fires along the shoreline, and mysterious lights far out at sea. But watching these lights and fires was a mere interlude, for our real place was on the mountain slopes of Kaiwiki. Our life was there, and we had work to do, our feet deeply rooted in the earth, wedded to the surrounding cane, the patches of banana trees, the bamboo shoots. "We are mountain people," Mama reminded us in solemn Japanese. "We were born with dirt under our nails."

As we did whenever he went to work in our garden, Miyo and I followed Papa's long back down a narrow trail of overgrown California and pili grass in the gulch nearby. On one shoulder he balanced a hoe and on the other his walking stick. He had on high, black imitation-rubber Wellington boots from Japan, raggedy sailor denims, and the long-sleeved palaka shirt worn by plantation workers to shield his arms from the fierce sun and sharp cane leaves. Miyo and I wore baggy gingham dresses that rimmed our ankles, the dresses to last us several summers. Along the way, Papa smoked his pipe. He also divided our chores. Miyo carried the heavy jug of drinking water, while I carried the burlap bags for the won bok, sequa, dasheen, fiddlehead shoots, mountain yams, and burdock roots to gather for Mama.

Around the cleared garden plot, Papa fixed the fences to keep out the wild mountain pigs vigorous in their rooting and the cows and horses that pulled out their stakes and wandered from their pastures. After repairing the fences, he put in new poles for the long bean and pumpkin vines, hoed new furrows for planting, and pulled out the thick bunches of California grass that threatened to overtake the place. Miyo broke off some of the hollow grass stalks to make us reed pipes with Papa's pocketknife while we did our chores and waited for him.

Gathering what my mother needed from the garden, we felt the sun beat on our young backs like hourglass drums. Papa, always patient, stopped his work to show me what vegetables were ripe, ready for picking, which ones overripe and to be discarded.

"Just because you Papa's pet, no take his time by asking stupid questions," Miyo slurred from the side of her mouth in her big-sister way. "And no sleep. I gotta do all the work then." But in no time the smell of the heat, together with the sun on my eyelids, made me sleepy. "Eh you, get up," Miyo ordered, kicking me in my side. "Come help. You not tired. S'only because you *lazy*!"

My father finished his work just before dusk; having forgotten the time, he had lingered into the evening. "Hurry," he said, the sun lost over the mountains. "We must get home before dark. I don't have a lantern, and there are no stars tonight. No moon."

Miyo and I gathered our belongings. "Carry yo' own bag," she said, narrowing her eyes.

"No need fo' remind me!"

Up the narrow winding path we climbed. The path wound upward to a cane-haul road, a narrow ribbon of red cinder that eventually led to the house, and it was there, along a sharp bend, that we first heard a faint whooshing sound. It sounded like the movement of wind or the wings of birds in their light rustling, but there was no wind and there were no birds to stir the air in the twilight hush. The waiwi trees around us remained still, no wild-pig dogs stalked from behind, and no crickets chirped. We turned to the unusual sound. We craned our necks to see what it might be, and soon a round light approached us. A blue streak in the dusk.

"It's a fireball," Papa said, dropping his voice as he stopped to look at it. "It's phosphorus from the dead. Sometimes when something dies, their bones and oil give off a blue light."

"Must be Kitano-man's dead cow," Miyo said. "He lost one. Oil, bone, stink gas."

"Or could be one ma-ke man, yeah? Ma-ke, die, dead," I said.

"How you know not one dead cow? You don't know," Miyo said.

"Just hurry," Papa said. "Don't argue. And don't look at the light. People say . . ." Papa hesitated, as if deciding whether or not to complete his thought, ". . . if it follows you, you will die."

My bag was heavy. I could not walk as fast as my sister or my father and still do my share. Surefooted as mountain goats, and assuming that I was following, they walked hurriedly up the path. On her lifted shoe, Miyo could walk in time with Papa as if nothing was wrong with her leg. In no time the distance between us grew, and when the fireball came singing up to my back and began chasing me, I was far behind them.

I ran but was slow. Spinning, the blue light surged forward and looped above my head with a hissing sound. Looking over my shoulder, I shouted: "Go 'way, go home!" With that, I scrambled up the trail as best I could. *I don't need anyone's help,* I said to myself and dug in my toes. But before long: "Papa, HELP! The thing . . . coming after *me!*"

By that time, my sister and father were far up the trail. They turned to look down. The fireball blocked my way and toyed with me; when I advanced, the fireball advanced. With the ax on one shoulder, Papa bolted down the trail to my side. "Run, Hi-chan," he said. "Leave the bag alone. Don't look back, go!"

In that instant, I saw the fireball flash and change direction. It went straight for Papa and lunged at him. I ran up the hill to where Miyo stood watching. Below us, Papa swung his ax at the blue demon ball, but its comet head flashed just beyond reach. They swished like shadow boxers, each trying to outmaneuver the other.

I punched the air like Papa did, while Miyo's voice scratched the surface of the twilight in terrible shrieks. Grabbing Papa's walking stick, I tumbled back down the trail and waved it at the fireball. Miyo followed me, her arms rotating as if beating a taiko drum, but too young and weak, we couldn't do anything to help our father.

"AHHHHH!" Papa suddenly screamed. Miyo and I saw his legs buckle. We ran up and danced around him, and when he turned up his foot to see what had hurt him, the head of a large cane-flume spike stuck out from his heel. We gasped at the size of it. It was huge, like the Jesus nail driven into the Kurisuto's feet on the cross, like the one I saw at Catherine Ferrera's church, Saint Joseph's downtown, Hāla'i Hill.

We stared at it, Papa stared at it; he knew he had to get it out. He couldn't leave it in like the broken arrow we once saw a cavalry guy in the movies leave in his thigh. With all the strength in his stomach, he pulled on the spike. "YAAATS," he cried out in the agony of a wounded animal.

"Papa, Papa!" We screamed at the sight of blood that gushed from his foot in a dark red flow, darker than the coming night.

As if to mock him, the fireball hovered over Papa. With some effort, Papa finally managed to raise himself up to hobble home in his blood-soaked boot. The cold perspiration of pain glistened on his face in the growing dark, and behind him he left a spotted trail of blood, the fireball still following as he made his way up the footpath, its light dancing at his shoulders.

"Papa, make the thing go 'way!" Miyo shouted. She batted the air around her, as if suddenly attacked by a cloud of cane gnats and made crazy by them. Papa swooped her up into his arms to calm her, while I jumped up and down around them.

"There, there, it's all right," Papa said, but my sister was slow to be comforted.

"Miyo!" I yelled, but she wouldn't even look at me or Papa. Her dark, vacant eyes moved past us—somewhere beyond any place I knew—as she picked up the skirt of her dress and brought it up to her mouth to suck.

Before it spun away, the fireball continued circling above Papa, who, by this time, let me lead Miyo home. I pulled her along like a balking dog. "C'mon, Miyo. We go home. We almost there." For once I was soft with her.

Grabbing Papa's flashlight, Mama ran two miles to Maeda Store to call Dr. Minami. When he came to the house, he said, "All Miyo needs is time. Don't worry, she'll get over it." The fireball had scared her so much that she had gone into shock.

Sobbing at her bedside, Mama mewed in soft Japanese, "Miyo-chan, everything's going to be all right. Please, speak to us." Mama repeated this litany while she patted my sister's shoulder for a response. Bending over her, Mama kept smoothing out Miyo's hands and feet, flattening them as if she didn't want anything on Miyo's body curling up like dead leaves. My sister, having retreated to somewhere deep in her mind, just stared straight ahead.

Lest he upset Mama, Papa said little and did little save press his heel with a rag that she had given him to stop the bleeding. "I think I better take a look at that," Dr. Minami offered before leaving.

"It is nothing. Take care of my daughter first. I'll be all right. I've had worse cuts than this before."

I remember the doctor shrugging his shoulders.

Later, I helped Papa bathe his foot in the spring by the house. I played nurse for I was curious about his cut. Using a walking stick, he hopped over to the side of the pond and, as we sat on one of the boulders, he propped his left leg on his right knee. Despite the awful pain I knew he was feeling, he whistled "Hilo March" between his teeth:

Ike houana	We shall see again
ika nani ao Hilo	the beauty of Hilo,
ika ulu wehi wehi	the beautiful
o ka lehua	grove of lehua
lei hoohihi	a lei much fancied
a ike a ka malahini	by visitors.
mea ole i ke kono	Nothing deters the
a kealoha.	the invitation of love.

23

In the low tongue of light from the kerosene lantern, I cleaned off the caked blood and swabbed the copper-green iodine around Papa's heel, then wrapped his tender wound with strips of cloth that Mama had torn from an old kimono. Dark and red inside, the ugly, gaping hole pulsated with Papa's every heartbeat.

In two days my father's foot swelled up like a blowfish. With his foot throbbing, he gnashed his teeth in pain at the slightest touch, even something as light as a thrush's feather could cause him to reel. When he lay still, I held my hands above his leg to feel its heat in the same way I held my hands over fire when they were cold, and unlike having the sweet smoke of a real fire ascend to fill the spaces, the rotten smell of something dead rose from the seepage.

"Papa, we must call Dr. Minami," Mama said.

"No, no, I'll be all right. We don't have enough money to treat me and Miyo-chan at the same time. Don't worry." He resisted Mama's pleas.

The next evening, my father could not get out of bed. Mama had to help him move—to limp with him to the bathhouse, to the bedroom, to the chamber pot. His head rolling on his chin, Papa burned with fever from the blood poisoning, a blue river of fire crawling up his leg.

Mama ran the two miles down the gravel road once more to telephone Dr. Minami from Maeda Store, the only place with a telephone in Kaiwiki Village. Rich as they were, even the Taketas, our nearest neighbor, had no phone.

The doctor came at last. He looked at the horrible condition of Papa's leg and whistled softly. "Your leg will have to come off first thing in the morning," he said. He shook his head as if he couldn't get over Papa's leg being twice its normal size, skin stretched tight as a drum, shiny with oozing liquid. "There's nothing that can be done. I don't have a nurse and Okayama Hospital downtown is closed. You'll have to wait till tomorrow."

My father nodded. "So tomorrow," he said.

"You're young and strong. Nothing to worry about. I'll send a taxi for you."

"Thank you," Papa said, sipping his breath in pain.

That night, I went to sleep at Papa's side. Snuggling next to him, I

24

felt warmed by his fever, warmed by all that was good and sure we shared between us. As a wish for him to get well, I tried to close the distance to where he was traveling by reciting a rhyme learned in school:

> Star light, star bright
> The first star I see tonight
> I wish I may, I wish I might,
> Have the wish I wish tonight.

He patted my head and cooed a bird-soft mantra: "Be good, be good, my daughter, be good." I watched his face as he slowly closed his eyes.

Mama had fallen asleep in the long hours of watching over Papa and Miyo. Deep in the early morning, awakened by a sudden rush of cold wind that swept through the house, she came to check on us, only to find Papa dead. She found me sleeping, trying to get warm, my head nestled on Papa's body that was already turning cold. The morning rain pelted the iron roof like rice; birds chirred in their first stirrings.

The sun had yet to rise.

In the middle of the wake, as the Buddhist priest lit the candles and laid cords of myrrh into the dragon censer for the offering of incense, Miyo sat up in bed under the roof of his chanting. She cried out in delirium: "Papa, where're you?" Mechanically, she turned, startling the people who had come for the ceremony. She pointed her finger at me, and said: "Papa died because of you, Hi-chan. Died, because of you!"

"He neva. Not my fault!" I said and threw my hands over my ears.

"Be quiet—the two of you!" Mama shuffled over to Miyo's side and covered my sister's mouth with one hand. "Don't say that to Hi-chan. You don't know what you're saying. Be a good girl and go back to sleep." My sister obeyed and slid back into bed.

"Not my fault, yeah, Mama?"

"It's not your fault. It is just how it is. No one is to blame," she said in tender Japanese.

Two days later, just before Papa's funeral, Miyo woke up to drink a clear fish-head broth Mama had prepared. "Do you remember—what you said?" Mama asked.

"No, why?" For Mama that was good.

After the funeral at the house, to pay their respects, people in black clothing lined the narrow roadside leading out to the main road. Miyo and I wore our best dresses of white organza, white shoes, small white hats—white the color of death. Mama said that in Japan old people died in white, committed suicide in white, were burned in white.

Waiting for the procession to leave, I heard voices in the crowd: "Too young to ma-ke." "Yeah, too young no? One waste." "Some young the man fo' leave such small children behind, but the wife the one pitiful." People murmured their sympathy and agreed with the voiced sentiments.

Everyone waved the hearse good-bye as it passed the solemn crowd. Mama looked bereft, stiff and tired, in the backseat of Mr. Taketa's car, one of the few cars in our neighborhood, which followed Papa's body to the crematorium. Mrs. Taketa and the Taketas' boy, Akira, stood on the side of the road with Miyo and me.

Mama waved her hand to the crowd that had gathered, and as if it were broken at the wrist, her hand flopped like a long cane leaf caught in the breeze. She bowed, nonstop, to the camp people lined up: Mr. Omuro and his only daughter Betty, Joe Pacheco, Mr. Young the schoolteacher, Mr. Nishimoto, Katsura-basan, the Alvarro family, Nekonishi-man, Buzing the Puerto Rican, Shigeta-lady. All the village people.

At first, I walked behind the small line of black cars; polished chrome flashed light into the humid air and blinded me. After the cars picked up more speed, I began running after them, trying to keep up, and called out after my father: "No leave us, Papa. Please, no leave *meee!*"

My voice dragged his name over the hills, over the cane, over the trees—my body, my voice, making the note of his name into a long sound and letting it resonate in the air. I ran faster. How could I live without him? The sound of gravel stuttered and slurred under my feet.

Miyo, who looked so pale in the bright sun, called out: "Come back, Hi-chan, come back. You going ruin your good shoes."

I continued to run.

Earlier, before the funeral and cremation, because we had the whole view of the town where we lived, Mama said, "Watch where they burn bodies in Hilo. Papa's smoke will rise from the stack, his spirit moving into the sky."

"And where he going?" I had asked.

"His spirit's going to watch over us for forty-nine days before leaving here."

"Then where he going?"

"To a good place, Hi-chan, a good place."

"Sore, when they burn him?" I was interested in what happened to the body before it became a spirit.

"No, Hi-chan. Good fire, so not sore."

Glancing with skepticism at Mama, Miyo pulled me aside by my arm and whispered in my ear, "Not one good fire, you dope. No be fooled. Mama don't know better." She started to walk away, to go back to her sorrow, but I followed her.

"What-chu mean?" I persisted.

"Jes like what I said."

"C'mon, Miyo, I like know."

"You sure? Well, Milton Kohashi from school live whea they burn bodies. One time, he said he'd seen what happens, the face falling off in the fire—like when you burn one book—page after page going up in smoke— *pap, pap, pap, pap*—like when you turning um fast. He said, too, people sit straight up when they burn."

"I no believe you—what you say. That not going happen to Papa."

"See, that's why I neva like tell you. You get your head in the clouds."

But, my head wasn't in the clouds as Miyo suspected. What she told me did not disappear with my denial of what happened to the body. For several days, nightmares of people sitting up as they burned crept into my dreams. Bodies burst into flames and their mouths melted with anguished cries—scream-pitched, like the sugar mill whistle outside.

Every night, from then on, until the end of the forty-nine day mourning period, I tended a large snapping fire near the steps leading to the house, a fire that Mama didn't seem to mind or stop me from making. I made the fire which was supposed to help Papa's spirit find its way back to Kaiwiki and later, when it was time to leave Earth, to use the fire as a point of reference to go wherever it was destined—to worlds beyond our understanding.

3

Loneliness

Not long after Papa's death, Mama went to work for the mill store in Wainaku Camp, another small village between Kaiwiki and Hilo. She walked, rain or shine, six miles every day, six days a week, each time the weight upon her shoulders to support us pulling her tall body down, and she got to looking like a tree bent over by the constant rains of poverty. Weary, depressed, missing Papa with everything in her and her earlier optimism gone, Mama began looking older than her years.

Unlike me, Miyo never gave way to tears. I cried all the time. It got to be where she would say, "No come by me if you goin' cry." So I stayed by myself and learned the harsh bite of loneliness. With no one bothering to tell me to use a handkerchief, the sleeves of my blouses had long streaks, stains from running my dripping nose across them. I missed Papa and didn't know where to find him.

Two years later Mama forced Miyo to quit school and join her at work.

"But I no like go work," Miyo said. "I like stay in school."

"I know, but I can't help this. I can't support you and Hi-chan all by myself," she said in apologetic Japanese.

"But why me?" she cried.

Every day from then on, Miyo wore a long, unapproachable face. She grumbled a lot too. Although I felt sorry for her, I couldn't do anything. Only nine at the time, I was left to my own devices when not in school. With no one around, the hours were endless, and to amuse myself, I sang for good weather every day so I could build my fires. I made teru bōzu—

little weather-god dolls, bald-headed, blind ghost dolls—to hang by their necks on the porch, and strung them up with Papa's old fishing lines, the dolls drifting in the wind like mourning veils. Bitter, spiteful resentment gripping her, whenever Miyo came home, she would take these dolls off the line and hang them upside down, as if this action would cause more rain, hindering my ability to play outside.

"No do that! Mama, look Miyo, look what she doing."

"What, crybaby? What you going do, henh?"

Mama simply shook her head, as if she had given up on us. I knew that she wished that I were softer, interested in the beauty of arranging flowers or sewing like other girls in the village whom I had seen, carrying their embroidery boards, sewing kits, and flower vases filled with anthuriums and orchids, their faces under umbrellas be it rain or sunshine, as they caught the bus at Maeda Store and went to classes on Saturday mornings in downtown Hilo.

"Why don't you go with the other girls?" Mama suggested.

"I no *like*," I said. I didn't want to be like these gentle girls; I didn't know how.

When some of the neighborhood women visited Mama, they stared at me. I saw their fingers making circles around their ears to indicate I was crazy, the women whispering words that shifted in their mouths like abacus beads.

Maybe I *was* crazy. For one thing, I didn't like being left alone in the drafty house with Papa's ashes on the family altar, and sometimes, I could hear the lonely cry of a child coming from the fields, as if left there to die, and I didn't know where to hide myself. I didn't want the bogeyman or obake babies, or the Pa-ke Zaka ghost, or the gypsies or the billy goat troll under Kaiwiki Bridge to get me. Terrified, I wanted my fires to scare them all away.

"I'm obake," my fires said. "Don't come near me!"

On cold, dark nights, when I prayed for sunshine, people could hear my singing—*Teru-teru bōzu, teru bōzu, ashita tenki ni shite okure*—sweep over the rolling terrain as if in a haunting. *Bald-headed one, bald-headed one, make tomorrow a clear day, please.*

Hiro Nakama, who lived nearby, was not allowed to walk home with me because his mother said that one day I would walk with the dead. "I can't talk to you. I'm not supposed to even look at you," he said.

"So, no look. Watch out, Hiro, I going make you disappear."

"Eh, no come by me, you!" he said and ran home as fast as he could. Hiro did not know what it meant to be lonely. He had both parents and a house full of brothers and sisters that stuck together like stinky natto beans.

To help Mama, I built fires to boil the laundry water and cook the food she came home to fix, but I also built secret fires to ward off the evil spirits in the trees, the spring, the outhouse, the pond; fires to chase away the wild animals—like the mongooses, wild pigs, feral cats and dogs that I imagined lurking beyond the perimeter of the yard. I may have built fires to dance around and to cast spells, but these fires of protection gave me no joy.

Mama didn't say anything when she first noticed remnants of these fires strewn across the yard. Too exhausted, she let me do as I pleased. But neighbors in the village began complaining: "What if she start one cane fire? That's all going take, no? We going be ruined."

Sighing, sounding defeated, Mama said: "About the fires, I'm leaving them up to you." I suppose, she either had to give me up to my fires or else go mad trying to control me. She had other, more important things to think about, and I for one was happy to be left alone.

Although Miyo wouldn't admit it, she must have been lonely too, Papa having relied on her, his older daughter, his obedient daughter, to fetch the bucket for the fruits of summer or the hammer for the broken latch to the henhouse or to go with him to the bamboo grove to gather shoots. She must have missed his humming while he worked, but most of all his summoning, the sound of his voice calling her name. And too, were Papa still alive, she would still be in school; she would not have lost her friends.

Angry about her situation, Miyo said to Mama one Saturday, "I not going back work. I quit."

"You know, cannot."

"What about Hi-chan? I bet when she old enough, I still gotta work so she can go school—like most families 'round here. The oldest one gotta work fo' send the young ones to school. I going be stuck in the store— foreva. All my life—you watch!"

"Hi-chan too young fo' work yet. So stop, already!"

Listening to them argue, I volunteered, "I can go with you guys today—fo' help."

"Fo' one day? Easy to talk. Lazy bone, you get all the time in the world. How's 'bout you help Mama when she not home? Who you—one princess?"

"No, I not one princess. I help plenty 'round here."

"Like what, henh?"

"Girls, stop it!" Mama said. Miyo reluctantly put on her dress.

Wainaku Store was a large, open warehouse with long rows of goods stacked on long shelves. Warm air lingered below the high corrugated iron roof as pinpricks of sunlight crept in through the nail holes, with the whole place smelling of molasses, bagasse, and stale men coated with road dust.

Mama took her place behind the cashier's desk, slipped an apron over her plain long dress, wrapped a pair of Ben Franklin eyeglasses around her face, and counted out the money in her cash box. With red-rimmed eyes, she worked in deep concentration over her figures, losing herself in the beads of her abacus that made crisp, clicking sounds when she slid them across the board in order to balance the till.

When she went away for a second, I quickly took the abacus to play with. "Don't do that," she said when she returned and snatched it away from me. I saw that she no longer had patience with me and I saw, too, how much I missed the Mama she had been when Papa was alive.

Miyo put on an apron and hollered. "Hey Hi-chan, come help, if you going help."

She methodically opened boxes of canned fruits and canned meats, some imported from Brazil, and canned vegetables like asparagus and corn, which she wanted me to shelve. I gathered as much as I could in my arms and followed her. Watching her limp as she walked ahead of me, her being crippled something I only saw at home, I realized that she was crippled for everyone else to see since Papa had died. I was so accustomed to her deformity that I had never given it a thought that her circumstances had changed, her whole body, her shoulders and hips, going up and down in twisted rhythm—and this in public! With Papa no longer around, there was no one to fix her shoes.

All day, like a coward, I avoided her figure bobbing between the aisles. I was appalled, for everyone could see Miyo's imperfection in the glaring light of the old plantation store. It was childish I know, but it was also something I couldn't help being—ashamed for her, ashamed for Mama, ashamed for myself because of Miyo's imperfection.

When I was thirteen, with Mama and Miyo gone from the house to work, my loneliness changed suddenly when Akira, the Taketas' boy, started hanging around. Mama didn't mind because the Taketas were my parents' most trusted neighbors. "Better than family," Papa once told me, the Taketas having come from the same place in Japan.

One day, swinging a stalk of purple Hawaiian sugar cane in his hands, he appeared over the rise. As he walked down the hill, I watched him casually peel the cane with his pocketknife and cut it into small bite-sized pieces. Unlike his father who was stiff and formal, Akira, looking so casual in his overalls and straw slippers, had an easy way about him when he swung his arms or tossed his chin up in recognition.

"Here, have some," he said in his perfect English, his first words of offering, no one knowing where or how he had learned to speak so well. Other children called him haolefied, someone acting like a white person with his "haole" English, but he didn't seem to care. I figured that it was how he always used a "hunh" at the end of his questions and emphasized his r's, as in he*rrrr*e, that made him sound the way he did. I grabbed a piece of the sugar cane he held out on his palm and stuck it into my mouth.

"This looks like fun," he said, eyeing the yard, noticing my fires. "What's over there, hunh? And there?" He pointed to different spots in the yard.

I went about poking the fires I had made that day—rattled shells and banged old pots over them and threw in dried leaves to make them flare. My noises, however, did not scare Akira; instead, he leaped up to my fires and followed me as I worked them. What I didn't need was for him to spy on me and take away my secrets—my only possession.

"May I come over one of these days to help you out?" he asked, his question so unexpected that it took me a while to answer him, even as I looked him straight in the eyes. He fidgeted, tapped the fence he leaned on with a stick, and bit his thumbnail.

"Okay," I finally said.

From then on, when it didn't rain or if his mother didn't keep him home, Akira was over at my house. To let me know he was coming, he would whistle and hit a termite-hollowed avocado tree at the head of the road with a guava stick, and thump the old stump repetitively to announce his arrival: *Tan ta ta, tan ta ta, tan, tan, tan.*

And I taught him all about fire. I showed him how I burned leaves, paper, twigs, hair, fingernails, bugs. We used old mirrors on paper and Papa's magnifying glass to burn holes on the matsu, ironwood, Portuguese pine branches, koa, lapa, and ʻōhiʻa logs from the rainforest to test their resiliency. We also gave names to the fires: a horse fire when it raced; a frog fire when it leaped; a monkey fire when it twisted around branches we tossed in. Violet, blue, red, yellow, white flames, logs holding water, logs holding air. Akira learned the intensity of these fires and understood their sounds and their smells. "You're the best teacher of fire, Hi-chan," he said.

For Akira's fifteenth birthday, just before my fourteenth, we celebrated by smoking the old Bull Durham tobacco that I found in Papa's tansu. Miyo wanted me to quit school then and go to work too, but Mama said someone had to stay close to home—watch the house. It made Miyo, who had predicted this would happen, furious; for me, it was cause for a secret celebration. With our backs to the wind, our bodies half-concealed by Papa's tangerine trees, Akira and I rolled the loose tobacco sprinkled from a pouch onto newspaper strips and used our tongues to moisten the paper in the same way we saw the older Japanese women in camp lick their cigarette papers. Just then, busybody Shigeta-lady showed up at the house. "Hey, what you kids think you doing?"

"Nothing," I said, and was quick to crush the lit cigarette in my palm without flinching, my hands behind my back. I quickly dropped the cigarette and stepped into the clearing, Akira following.

"Nothing? Nogimmethat," she said, running her words together, making them sound like a gigantic word. "You guys smoking, I know. Can smell. No try fool me. Where your Mama stay?" she demanded.

"At work. Why?" I said, as if in challenge, then realized that if I challenged her she wouldn't go away. Seeing that I had irritated her, I moderated my tone and said sweetly: "Oh she's working at the store—in Wainaku. Is there a problem?"

"No good, leave you kids alone like this, that's why, and no get cocky with me. You know what I mean? Why—the nerve! And you, Taketa boy-san, you suppose to be home, helping your parents. No good you guys smoke and play fire. You going get burned and not only from cigarettes. You know what I mean?" She laughed, dancing her eyebrows in a cucaracha.

"Yes of course, we know what you mean," I said, smiling pleasantly, using my best school English for respect. I wanted her to leave.

When she saw that we were no longer defensive, she gave up and turned to go. We watched her leave, and when she was out of sight, we went back to our smoking. We had already learned how to French inhale; we were now learning how to do doughnut rings, filling our cheeks full of smoke, tapping our cheeks, puffing uneven spheres from our mouths.

"You think she going tell my Mama?" I said, feeling uneasy.

"Don't worry. Mrs. Shigeta is just nosey. And crazy. She won't say anything unless we burn the house down or destroy the fields. We've been very careful about our fires, so nothing's going to happen."

"Yeah no? We've been careful."

On clear nights, having set up a tent with some old boards, horse rope, and a square of tarpaulin we found in the cane left by some field worker, we camped out in the yard so we could smoke, Mama and Miyo too busy to care. With a nice fire going, we roasted the sparrows and doves we shot out of the guava trees with our slingshots and dry-roasted the persimmons stolen from Mr. Hasegawa's, a neighborhood man's, tree. Baked sweet potatoes under the coals.

We stretched ourselves out to lie in the tall grass nearby and rotated with the earth as we watched the stars and wondered about their fires. "How hot—whatchu think?" I asked Akira.

"I don't know, but it appears to be super hot, doesn't it?"

And we went on, delving into each innocent moment as if this were the only way life could be. We belted out campfire, cowboy, and Hawaiian songs, songs learned in school: "Oh My Darling, Clementine," "On Top of Old Smoky," "On the Beach of Waikīkī," "Song of the Islands."

We smoked, looked at the drawings of old *Saturday Evening Post* magazines that Akira's family subscribed to, and did homework by firelight.

Slept in each other's arms.

4

Cane Fire

Cane fire was the one fire that Akira and I had never started. This was a fire plantation owners deliberately set in their fields to burn away the cane leaves to reveal only the stalks, making them easier to cut—this fire, also tended by seasoned workers only. The plantation luna had always considered us too young and green for the task; besides, no one allowed girls to set them. The summer of my fifteenth birthday, filled with excitement for a cane-fire day that was fast approaching, we had planned to watch it from my porch.

The day of the fire, Akira ran over to where I lived, wearing a faded kabe-silk shirt, old khakis, split-toe socks gripped onto his slippers, and a white headband, with a cane-cutter's machete dangling from his side. He looked like a samurai warrior—lineage cut from men in swinging topknots, sword-fighting men, bodies-close-to-the-ground sort of men. He called out to me in a voice that had the quality of coming from a cave.

"Hi-chan, c'mon, let's go!"

I was on my porch, brushing my hair that was no longer young-girl tangled like Papa's fishing lines, but black and supple like Mama's, which I made sway in waves as I moved its bulk by shaking my head. Earlier, I'd been admiring my reflection in a small mirror Papa had once tacked on the wall. How smooth and glowing my skin! I had grown taller over the summer, too. I was looking more like Mama, just as Miyo, in her plain but sturdy way, was looking more like Papa. Unlike me, she was not intent on

36

her appearance. "Big trouble—to worry too much about how you look," Mama had warned. Danger lurked in the pleasure I got out of prettying myself, but I had to admit, I was pleased by what I saw.

"Didn't you hear me? Let's go," Akira said.

"Go where?" I tipped my head toward Akira's voice, my body bent far over the railing as I let my hair dry in the breeze.

"To help start the cane fire. I'm going to be one of the runners. C'mon, it'll be fun. I'm taking my father's place."

"Why? Where he stay? They not going scold, if I come?"

"No, they won't. Not if you're with me. Everyone here knows you're my partner."

"Yeah, but—"

"My father hurt his back. He can't do it."

"'Kay. Wait, then."

I changed my clothes, my hands shaking, my fingers suddenly clumsy as I buttoned an old sweater, stuffed it into Papa's faded jeans, and knotted a thin rope around my waist as a belt. After tying an old towel across my forehead, I filled my father's canteen with water and strapped his pocket-knife to a belt loop. Before I left the safety of the house, I took Papa's good-luck amulet of gold brocade from the tansu and hung it around my neck.

Akira met me halfway up the steps where he pulled at my hand like an eager groom. I suddenly felt shy, but Akira did not let up on his pulling, almost dragging me out to the field.

"C'mon, slowpoke. You're like Potot's lazy cow," he said. "What's the matter?"

I was crushed. Everything he said that morning hurt with indescribable intensity. My insides churned and my feet felt unsteady. With our fingers intertwined, we ran to the Arruga property, to the house on the thirty acres of cane we were going to set on fire for the harvest that day. The fire lighters were gathering there; they stood around the yard while the plantation boss, Joe Castro, gave last-minute instructions in his heavy pidgin. He said to Akira, "Eh Japanee, you know what fo' do or what? And who dis?"

"She's a good friend of mine—you know, the Aoki girl."

"Bring her okay, but no get hurt, sabe? You guys wait—over dea," he said, pointing toward the mountain. "And wait till you hea Thunda and

Duck-feet guys whistle. Dat's the signal. Fo' now, go help load up the truck befo' you guys go, 'kay?"

Akira and I nodded to the heavy-set gentleman with the wild, curly hair and stale smell and accepted the handful of matches and rag torch soaked in kerosene that he pushed at us. After helping to load the truck with hoes and cane knives, Akira and I marched to our appointed spot without speaking. On a slope overlooking the field to be burned, Akira patted the ground for me to sit next to him. Without a care, he swung his arm around me as he had often done. I could smell his breath, sweet and acrid, the smell of a struck match, something that had come from deep within him, as if from the depth of the earth, and I wanted to breathe and taste it.

I waited with him as if nothing was happening to me. Wind blew down from the mountains and buffeted the cane in long, overflowing sweeps, the fields moving in waves, our restless minds and bodies riding in the crosscurrents of wind. "Soon the whole area is going up in flames," Akira said, as he held his breath, sweeping his free hand over the view before us. "I promise you a big fire, the Arruga property huge. The fires we make are nothing compared to this. I swear you're never going to see a fire like this one again. I'm sure not in your lifetime, Hi-chan. Not in your lifetime."

He then stared at me, and I could feel his eyes like a hot breath across my face. I looked down at my hands.

"Hoi, hoooi!" The man on the Kapoho side of the field shouted as he set the cane in front of him on fire. A lot of whistling sounds moved upward from the fields. Akira jumped to his feet.

"I think that's Thunda and Duck-feet. We'd better get ready."

"Hey, let me light the fire," I said, pushing aside the turmoil I felt inside. As soon as I struck the matchstick on the stem of the torch, the head burst into an unwavering blade of flame. Akira's eyes fell on my face and the fire died out in a gust of wind. I didn't know what had happened; I never let fires die out so easily! My usual confidence crumbled beneath his gaze.

The next time I struck a match, I crouched lower to the ground. I cupped my fluttering hands around the match head and, shielding it the way I had seen smokers bring the stick up to their faces in wind, I watched it light up. I transferred the budding flame to the torch with a swing of my body. The oil rags burned, spitting and giving off a thick black smoke and, wrapped in its smoky turban, I began to cough and choke.

Akira laughed. "Hey, whatever happened to my fire girl, hunh?"

I flinched somewhere deep inside of me; it seemed that my face always flushed whenever he teased me now, his words taking on a different weight and meaning.

Shouting their signals up and down the fire lanes, the fire lighters whistled for us to begin. "There's our signal. Let's go," I heard Akira say, as if from a great distance. I scrambled up after him, my feet made of mud, no longer knowing what was holding me up. Running ahead of me, Akira dipped the head of the torch on the thin leaves to set them on fire. Stopping, he swung the torch over to me. "Here, take it. Place the torch—over there."

I ran to where he had pointed and raised the torch to the silver tassels of cane leaning over in the wind. The tassels crackled then flamed outward in a filigree pattern, the dry crowns sucking the torch fire upward onto the leaves and, in small heat explosions, row upon row of cane burst into flames.

"Move back," Akira said when I returned to where he stood, making a gate with his arms for me to stay behind. "You will get burned if the wind changes directions. And watch your shirt-sleeves, your hair." He turned to see that I was all right. He then stopped, brushed strands of hair away from my face and searched for my eyes.

Small animals and insects—quails, sparrows, rats, crickets, grasshoppers, toads—fled the field in panic. Above us, birds screeched to save their nests, their fledglings. They rose up and plummeted into the heat in the same way I felt myself falling, falling into fire.

Flames climbed the sky, towering above us in a long moving shadow. We scrambled up a nearby hill.

I could hear Akira and myself breathe. During that time together on the hill and setting the fires, I knew that we had crossed the plank, walked over the stepping stones, leaped over the bridge. Somewhere along the way, we had passed from fire to fire.

Akira looked over at me and put his arm across my shoulder. Breathing through my hair, he pressed me into him with the reach of his arm, and I took in deep gulps of the smoke and salty smells that enveloped his shirt, neck, body, as if I couldn't get enough of him. Surprised, my throat went dry; I couldn't speak, suddenly locked in shyness.

After the fire, we walked from the scorched land over to Ice Pond in the back of Kaiwiki School. The pond was part of a river nearby that ran through the pastures, through the gullies, through one side of the village, then down to the sea. We went there to wash the soot off our arms and legs, and waded in knee-deep water that reflected our lean bodies and the trees that surrounded us. Akira splashed water on me. I splashed water back and watched the cool drops slide down his smooth, hairless skin. We then held on to each other's hands so tightly that I thought my fingers would break. It was as if this were the only way we could hold ourselves in, save ourselves, our lives.

Lying on our backs, we chewed on the buffalo grass near the river and dried ourselves in the sun. Most of the smoke from the burning cane had drifted off, and the sky was clear again. I had almost fallen asleep when Akira moved over to place his head on my chest, at which time I shifted slightly and gathered him into my arms.

"C'mon, we'd better be going," he said, quickly retreating from the arousal that burned like wild fire through our bodies. We picked up the towel-headband I had tossed aside, my red home sweater, his split-toe socks; we busied ourselves in this small ritual, moving away from what our bodies truly desired. Our steps slow, we dragged the weight of heat that had descended upon us, and I dared not look at Akira's face. Blood throbbed in my ears. Everything looked luminous: the grass never this green, the sky never this blue.

Akira took my hand in his and pulled me toward him. We walked into the lush growth of grass on the side of the path that shielded us from the afternoon sun. Facing each other, we fell to our knees. We dropped to our sides. Akira's face moved into mine.

Our bodies had nowhere cool to go.

5

Miyo's Money

Miyo sensed the irresistible burning that had been occurring in my young body all that summer. She may have slept with her back to me, but I knew that she was awake and waiting up for me, her eyes wide open whenever I slipped into the house late at night. She wanted to know what it was like, but she couldn't ask directly out of fear and shame.

"Can smell," she claimed as she sniffed the air, her senses heightened by the animal heat, the odor of yeast rising or something like rotting vegetation that came from under my dresses. She must have sensed in me a kind of wildness and freedom she couldn't even dream for herself. Her crippled leg had been back with her since Papa had died, and it had kept her from running, from moving impulsively. She had to be careful or she was in danger of falling. She was ashamed, too, of not having gone beyond intermediate school.

Now, her whole life was centered around the mill store. Her sugar-mill-worker boyfriend was all that she could probably hope for. "I neva going get out of this place," she said. She saw her life stuck between the narrow, forlorn aisles of the store, rows and rows of canned goods to place on the shelves, her life revolving around yet another cane-planting season or harvest, another cane fire, and ripe-smelling fertilizer bins, sour flume mud, and dusty cane-haul roads.

"Eh, where you think you going again?" Miyo scolded whenever I went out at night to meet Akira, the two of us sealed in the lips of the fields or in the darkness of the backside of the house, our backs up hard against the water tank, our young bodies crested in the light of the moon.

"You playing with fire," Miyo said, her body fastened under the tight belt of our futon when I slipped into bed. "Watch out. You don't know whatchu doing." Quick to scold me, that's all she could do.

I was shameless and I suppose Mama was too tired to care or thought that I was still too young to get into *that* kind of trouble. Being me, I flaunted this new turning in my life, never heeding Miyo's words. I watched her watch me as I brushed my hair a hundred strokes and dabbed on some of Mama's lipstick before slipping out of the house. I didn't use much, not wanting Mama to notice that her lipstick was running out faster than usual, but I was lavish in my looks toward Miyo's way whenever I put some on.

"You mean and cocky," she said.

"No fair," I heard Miyo say. I was pregnant with Akira's child, and Miyo's voice was close to hysteria. "So no fair!" she said, as she slapped the table with her hand. I agreed with her, but what could I do?

Mama told me earlier to stay out of it, that she would talk to Miyo. She knew my sister would only get angrier if she saw me, especially since Mama wanted all of Miyo's money for my use. Huddled with my shame, all I could do was to stay behind the wall of my room where I could hear them argue.

"That's my money. I saved long time so Hiromu and I can marry."

"I know it's your money," Mama said, everything that day said in Japanese to better express herself.

"If you know, then why? Why I should I give my money to her? She's neva nice to me."

Miyo went on, presenting her side, and Mama let her rant. I didn't know why at first, but Mama seemed to be agreeing with everything Miyo said. She also talked in this low, slow and easy manner, almost soothingly, to placate Miyo. I could see what she was doing. She was tearing down Miyo's objections one by one, for it wouldn't help if Miyo were unreasonable about my situation. Mama required her cooperation and, in the end, her money. But she wanted Miyo to give it up, willingly. I knew Mama desired Miyo to *come from her side*. Mama wasn't going to be satisfied until

Miyo accepted Mama's understanding of my situation.

"I need your money to send your sister to Japan. No one expected this to happen," I heard Mama say.

"My eye, she knew! I wen warn her every time she went out with Akira. No excuses, her. No one can say she neva know."

Mama returned to my defense. "Excuse or no excuse, what I'm saying is that it can't be helped. It's over now, done with."

"So, we going let her go, jes like that?"

I saw what Mama was doing. She had to make sure that both of her daughters would come back to her, that the family, no matter what, was not going to break apart on my account, and to ensure this, she had to let Miyo have her say. I had never seen Mama more determined, except for the time I nearly burned the house down.

Miyo, however, kept pleading her case. "What about *me*? I like marry too!"

"You're young yet, you can get married later."

"All my life . . . I even gotta give up marrying, fo' her. Why?"

Miyo had known Hiromu Ouchi for about a year. Once, they had gone to the theater in town to see a Japanese movie; once, he had taken her to the Hilo County Fair; once, he had brought her some anthurium flowers from his family's backyard; once, he had kissed her. The few times he came to our house, it was with Fat-boy Obata, and Miyo had to sit, squeezed between them on the bench-seat of the car when going out.

Hiromu worked for the Hilo Sugar Mill watching the cane presses and had met Miyo when frequenting Wainaku Store, both he and Miyo with little education, both having to help their families. In that way Miyo thought they were well suited for each other, especially in their determination to give their children the education they themselves had not received. They had it all worked out and this was probably Miyo's only chance for a different life.

"What kind is this? My money, right? I the one who went quit school and work—so we can eat, right?"

As Mama and Miyo argued back and forth, I wanted to go to them, reach out, ask for their forgiveness, especially of Miyo, but I was too proud to do that—a hard core that even my predicament could not tear down.

"How come Akira no can marry Hi-chan?" Miyo asked.

"Marry? They're too young. Hi-chan made fifteen not long ago. Don't you feel sorry for your sister? It's not all Hi-chan's fault, you know. Just how it is. Papa wanted to believe that we and the Taketas were just like family, but when it comes to something like this—well, that's altogether a different matter. You can't blame anyone."

"What kind guy him, anyway?"

"I don't know. All I know is that Hi-chan can't stay in Kaiwiki if she's not married. We have to send her away." As if she had thought it all out, Mama sounded like the old confident Mama I knew. "People can be cruel, and Hilo is a small town. People will talk behind our back, and we can't have that. I wrote to my brother, Shiichi, and his wife, Harue, in Tokyo and asked them to let Hi-chan live with them for a while. Papa would have wanted it that way, too. To spare her. Later on, she can come back. I'm sure people will have forgotten what had happened by that time."

"I guess I don't have a choice!" Miyo said, resigned. With that, she pushed back her chair, scraping the floor in giving in, the bottom having fallen out. "Go ahead, take my money. Give it to her!"

Not long after Mama's and Miyo's lengthy discussion, we received a hasty letter from Mama's brother, Shiichi Uncle:

> . . . My deepest apologies. It's not that we don't want Hi-chan here, but we question if it is wise of you to send her here at this time. Japan is at war with China, and there are rumors of an even bigger war. We don't know what will happen with America. Food, too, is very scarce. I'm sorry to say we don't have very much. Hi-chan is not used to this kind of hardship. . . .

Mama wrote back that same day:

> Please take Hi-chan. She can't live here. It would be too difficult for her to deal with the shame. You know how it is for girls in her condition. I'm sure she'll be all right in Japan. No one knows her there. I will not neglect to send you and Harue money every month, and food and clothing whenever I can—for her keep. I'm sure what I send you will be helpful. . . .

Shiichi Uncle consented despite his reservations.

Akira and I made an attempt to see each other one night before my going to Japan. I slipped a note to Restituto Albao, a neighborhood classmate of ours, to pass on to Akira in school. Through our hurried notes, Akira and I arranged to meet near a shallow gully between our houses.

Being that Akira no longer took the Hawai'i County school bus into Hilo like the rest of us but was being driven to school by his father, the change happening without anyone noticing, it eliminated the only way we had of seeing each other. I was still at Hilo Intermediate School, Akira at Hilo High School across the street, and Waiānuenue Avenue that divided the schools was like a large river we dared not cross.

The night I arrived at our meeting place, it was already dark with no stars, not even a fingernail moon. A small fire blazed in the corner of the clearing, where I thought I saw Akira's silhouette and ran to embrace him. To my surprise, it was Akira's father, Mr. Taketa, who emerged from the shadows. I jumped back, disoriented by the wall of cold air that met my face.

"You, you," Mr. Taketa said in a slow but fierce Japanese, as he wiped his forehead and looked at me straight in the eyes. He shook a finger in my face, while words sputtered out of his mouth with sprays of saliva. He quickly took a swipe across his mouth with the back of his hand and said, "You made me spy on my son. You made me tackle him down so I could tie him to the tree. You made me gag him so he can't talk. You made him *hate* me. Do you know what this does to me? You have any idea?" He moved into my face. He then thumped his fist on his chest in an agony that seemed impossible for him to express. "Do you know what this does to me?" he asked again. I stared at his wild face, unable to speak.

"I told your mother, when we had the meeting between our families, that you two were never going to see each other again. We all agreed. And yet you dare cross me by disregarding what has been settled, but I would sooner tie up my son, forever if I must, than have him go to you, you understand? You are never to see him again. I don't want you coming around!"

"But this is Akira's baby."

"I don't know that, do I? Neither does Akira."

"How you can say that?"

Mr. Taketa turned his body away to dismiss me. In a low voice, in a muttering close to growling, I heard him state under his breath: "You and your stupid fires."

Nearby, I heard movement coming from the old rose apple tree. Akira was tied to it. He mumbled something from under a cloth that covered his mouth, but I couldn't see his face. All I could see from where I stood in the lighted clearing were his hands, moving in a wild way beneath the rope that restrained him. I could see him twisting his wrists and hitting the tree.

"Akiraaa!" I shouted and moved forward.

Mr. Taketa moved in quickly to block my way. "Don't," he said, stopping me in my tracks. "Please—" lifting his hands, he clasped them together as if he were praying to me. "I'm trusting you to do this. Please leave us alone."

Surely Akira would come to me, I thought, after the incident. But he never did. A few days later, as I got off the bus, I saw Akira walking to his high school. I raised my arm and waved wildly to catch his attention. I didn't know if he saw me. He appeared to be looking right through me, as if through glass, and his face looked blank like one of my weather-god dolls—my teru-teru bōzu, my teru bōzu—with no eyes, unable to look anywhere, unable to see anything.

Along the beach, there are many fires, not only those that Papa told me are on the backs or fins of fishes or those blinking along the shoreline.

In the backwash of receding waves, in the white sand, lights move about as if they are iridescent fireflies. I catch these sparks of fire in my cupped hands and run to show them to my father. I often never reach him before these tiny specks go running out with the water. I have to run back and forth many times, first down to the tide line then back up to the sandbank where he sits, waiting. At times, his eyes grow watery, as if he is weary and his insides have been sloshed by waves. I don't know how he can feel sad when we are having such a good time.

"Look at the stars in my hand," I say if I get to him with the phosphorescence, the bone fuel of dead sea animals, still glowing in my palms. Patting me on the head, he peers at the specks of blue firelight then throws back his head to laugh, his silver teeth shining like fish darting in his mouth.

I sailed from Hawai'i to Kobe on the *President Coolidge*, early November 1941.

PART II

TOKYO

November 1941 – March 1945

All emotions are pain.

—from the Teachings of Buddha

6

New Family

On the eighth day at sea, a yellow butterfly fluttered its way above my bunk. Trapped, it was far away from its home of mock orange hedges, soft sunlight, and lift of winds and flower heads. Like the Chinese man in a story who dreamed he was a butterfly but didn't know whether or not he was a butterfly that was dreaming he was human, I too had trouble telling the difference. After a time I began to feel I was the butterfly, its wings folded, hanging upside down on the ceiling just above my head. I felt the struggle of its wings in the ceaseless motion of the sea, each wing-spread moment a wave carrying me further in to sleep or toward a kind of distant dreaming future I was too weak to think about. Soon the waves stopped and I had passed on to some other dream, another land, past my first fires, past water. The sea was as calm as Hilo Bay on a June evening, and the yellow butterfly was gone. When I looked out of the porthole, the purple island of Honshu loomed on the horizon in the twilight. We would be disembarking early in the morning.

As the ship approached land, though still far off, I could smell the deep draft harbor—what was woven into the stale air—filled with diesel fuel, rotting sewage, decaying fish, and seaweed. I recoiled from the bad aftertaste and gulped down a rush of saliva that filled my mouth. The going was slow, the reach to the harbor barely passable, as tug boats, sampans, sailboats, troop ships, and ocean liners, like the one I rode, vied with each other for their share of sea.

In the morning darkness, I followed others down the gangplank, went through immigration, and waited at a receiving platform, everything huge in my eyes. My thin white dress and straw hat, out of place and unsuitable for the harsh wintry climate, provided little protection against the biting wind. When Mama outfitted me for the trip, she had forgotten how cold November days in Japan could be. I must have looked shabby, drawn, and worn down since I hadn't used a mirror for days. I had lost weight, my body shivering from eight days at sea, the cold deep in my thin, blue bones, now useless as burnt matchsticks. Whatever heat I was producing wasn't much, unable to light even the smallest of fires within me or give even the least bit of warmth or measure of comfort. For eight days I had shivered in my cubbyhole of a berth—homesick, lonely, miserable—and had suffered, acutely, from morning sickness. I worried for my baby in my weakened condition.

To meet me in the morning and bring me back to Tokyo, Shiichi Uncle and Harue Auntie had to come the previous day from Tokyo and stay at a ryokan for the night. I dared not move from where I thought I was told to wait. Standing in the cold, I watched people move with intense purpose all around me. I could see only a handful of foreigners in the crowd. With rifles on their shoulders, young soldiers, either disembarking or boarding troop ships, pressed past me in badly fitted, wrinkled khaki uniforms, puttees, and monkey caps. They looked so young, these eager Japanese boys, smooth skinned, clean featured, with shiny coal eyes and soft mouths. I heard a loudspeaker blare: *Notte kudasai! Manchukou!* A group of soldiers sitting nearby picked up their sacks and, in orderly fashion, worked their way to the steamship going to Manchuria. Each one of them looked like Akira. I wanted to stop each face, bring it up to mine with my hands, and breathe Akira's warm breath of sunlit leaves and moist grass. Of lush flowers.

I had never seen anything like it—hundreds of people milling about. I had to take out Mama's instructions several times to make sure I was waiting at the right place. I grew frightened. What if no one came? "Please. I need some help," I said, trying to get someone's attention. "I just came off the . . ." and I pointed toward the ship that I had been on. People stared at me warily and did not respond. I must have looked strange—Japanese but so tall and darkly tanned—blabbing in a language they knew little of.

Out of nowhere a tall, lanky man, with puppet-loose appendages that swam in a dark suit and short woolen coat, appeared and walked over. In his late thirties or early forties, he was the right age to be my uncle, but I wasn't so sure, until the man approaching, I saw, had a slight but familiar limp—a handicap like Miyo's—and looked like Mama, even as his face bobbed in and out of the crowd. The resemblance was unmistakable; he leaned forward in his gait because of his height in the same way that Mama did! Mama had told me her brother understood some English, having that small connection consoled and reassured me.

"Shiichi Uncle?" I said in a loud voice.

Behind him, with a baby strapped to her back, stood a short, round-faced, severe-looking woman with a tight bun low on the neck, who immediately swung her head about to look at people's reactions after I had called out to my uncle, all too loudly I suspected. As soon as the woman caught me looking at her, she turned her head and lowered her eyes.

"That's right," my uncle said. He gave a formal bow followed by a smile of relief when he raised his face. I immediately felt at ease. "So you are Hi-chan. Welcome." I listened carefully, trying to follow every word said.

Mama had instructed me to use a more formal greeting for my first meeting with the family, and I had practiced the greeting several times with her. I reciprocated my uncle's bow with an awkward bow of my own, my face stuck out, my chin forward, and said, "I . . . I put myself in your hands . . . in this our first meeting," stumbling over my poor Japanese.

The smile on my uncle's face widened, and I was never more relieved to see a stranger's smile; his face, I realized, one that I had seen all my life in serious photographs, photographs that Mama had tacked in a lopsided way on the wall above her bed. Those photos had given him a stern look, but in reality, he seemed nothing of the sort. I liked him at once.

"Hi-chan, I want you to meet Harue, your auntie." Shiichi Uncle turned and bowed slightly towards the short woman in a gray kimono behind him. I bowed to the woman, but since she said nothing and did nothing, I thrust my hand out to shake hers, but immediately felt clumsy when she recoiled at my outstretched hand. "The baby is Yuki-chan," Shiichi Uncle continued, gently patting the head of the child sleeping on his wife's back. "And that's Sā-chan behind her."

I hadn't noticed the young girl until she emerged from the crowd behind her mother and baby sister. She had a Dutch boy cut, and thick sheets of hair swept forward on either side of her face as she made a slight, perfunctory bow towards me. As she did this, I could hear her mumble to her mother and say something like ". . . so tall . . . too dark . . ." but I was unsure of some of the words. In contrast to me, Sā-chan was petite. When she turned to say something to her father, he had to lean in to catch her words.

Uncle went on to tell me about my other cousins, the boys—Norio and Iwao—who were waiting for us at my new home. But I was only half-listening, for I had turned my attention to the homely-looking baby who lay asleep on Harue Auntie's back. Despite her charming rice bowl haircut and soft red cheeks, I secretly wished my child less plain. It startled me to think that Akira's baby would be only a bit younger than this child. She must have been Uncle's and Auntie's "late baby," as Mama had commented, the other children—Sā-chan, Norio, and Iwao—much older and closer to me in age. Because she was about Mama's age, Harue Auntie could have been my mother too!

"So how was your trip?" Uncle asked.

Stammering in poor Japanese, I said, "It was fine, I guess . . . but seasick, I got."

"Oh, really?" Sā-chan said, looking smug. "I've sailed many times and was never sick." I understood enough, but said nothing. An awkward silence followed Sā-chan's remark.

By then, we had fallen into a single file behind Harue Auntie—even Shiichi Uncle—and she headed our group as if she were a field sergeant. She didn't follow my Uncle's lead like I believed Japanese women did. With a determined sense of command, Harue Auntie cut smartly through the crowds and guided us to the baggage area. I went in the doors to go through customs.

After my return, as if he couldn't wait, my uncle asked, "And how's your mother?" He went to a rack that a man had put my luggage on, took the larger one, and handed the smaller one to me. His rough hands brushed against mine, the hands of someone who did hard labor. "How I miss her. She was always full of fun," he said, and a shadow suddenly dimmed his face. "It's too bad about your father. I hope your mother didn't suffer much when he died. They were a happy couple."

Something about what Shiichi Uncle said triggered Harue Auntie to turn her head towards him sharply. I had gathered from Mama's earlier conversations with Papa that her brother's arranged marriage had not always been a happy one, but I was still young and hadn't cared about or listened to all the reasons. I was guessing at the moment, having heard only bits and pieces about their situation, but thought that it had something to do with Harue Auntie being jealous of my mother. I remember Papa saying something once about knowing Harue Auntie before he knew Mama. Was Harue Auntie resentful when he didn't ask her to go to Hawai'i and, later, when he asked Mama to marry him, though she was already married to Shiichi Uncle? Harue Auntie caught me looking at her and stared me down with a glare.

My teeth began to chatter again. "Terribly cold, the sea trip . . ." I said, groping for the right words. What I couldn't say was that I was cold because I had lost Akira, my monthly blood, the goodwill of my mother and sister, my childhood, my baby fat, my fires, grass in my hair, and now, cold because I was afraid of my new auntie whom I followed with my clumsy bag.

"I've never been on a long sea voyage like you," Sā-chan said, interrupting me once more, "but I've sailed often." She tossed her head, coquettishly shaking her chin-length bob. "And once, we went by boat to Hiroshima, right Otō-chan?" She turned to her father for his reply, but he paid her no attention. "Everyone said that I was a good sailor."

I smiled but said nothing, wondering if I'd be able to like her. Sā-chan looked at me up and down then pitched her head upward in a snub that indicated her dismissal.

Not long into the walk, we came to the curbside of the pier. On the street, there were many odd-looking cars passing by, of strange makes I had not seen before. There in the cold, a line of people jostled one another while waiting for taxis that oddly seemed to be powered by steam.

"We have to stop your teeth from chattering. Otherwise, you'll get sick," Shiichi Uncle said, looking at me and handing me his coat. It was true. I had never experienced such cold. "Here, put this on. Big change from Hawai'i, isn't it?" I nodded and felt a surge of hope, his obvious concern for me an unexpected but pleasant surprise.

We were finally assigned a taxi by the dispatcher. My uncle strapped my suitcases on the top of the car and held the back door open for me.

"Wait," Sā-chan said and swept past me to sit next to the window on the far side.

"Sā-*chan*, Hi-chan is our guest," Uncle said.

"Okā-chan said she's not."

"What?"

"Okā-chan said that she's not a guest. She has to work like everyone else does."

"Stop it! Today she's our guest."

"Leave her alone," Harue Auntie said, interrupting.

"It's all right, Uncle," I said, speaking to him in English, which must have raised Sā-chan's and her mother's ire further because of the looks they exchanged.

Sā-chan, I could see, while taken aback, quickly recovered and acted as if she understood what I'd just said; she was astonishingly accurate in her response. "Well good," she said. "Then you can sit in the middle, next to me."

Though the fumes from the taxi were light, they still nauseated me; sitting by the open window would have helped. But because I still wanted to please my new family, I held my anger and my tongue, which was, in any case, not an easy thing for me to do.

The taxi dropped us off at the Kobe Train Station where we boarded a train that would take us to Tokyo with many stops along the way—Nagoya, Toyohashi, Shizuoka, Yokohama—and other places unfamiliar to me. I was told we would reach Tokyo in the late afternoon.

I wasn't prepared for the fine dust, the smell of coal, latrines, and food stalls, the hard seats, the press of bodies, the watchful eyes, and the many young-looking soldiers who boarded with us. Dressed in curry-brown uniforms, subdued and serious in manner, they took their seats in orderly fashion. I wondered where they were going.

By this time, my summer white dress had become striped with soot. I was hungry, too, but said nothing; I was no longer at home, had no idea of my rights, and was unaccustomed to no longer being the center of attention. For the train ride, Sā-chan, Harue Auntie, and I sat crammed on one train bench—Sā-chan again at the window—I, in the middle and Harue Auntie on the aisle, the train packed. I had never seen so many people—and all Japanese!

After serving Sā-chan and Yuki-chan a small snack of rice crackers, Harue Auntie gave me the leftovers. This time, I was able to catch her eyes, and I forced a smile. She, in turn, gave me the effort of a half-smile but was quick to change her position by turning her head to look across the aisle through windows on the other side. From where I sat, I watched the countryside, its flat terrain, as we slid snake-like across it: the large rice fields that had been harvested—cleared and waiting for the coming frost—shallow running streams, smoking stacks from thatched houses, people raking leaves and brush, young children carrying siblings on their backs, and with each clackity-clack, hearing in the monotony, the mother of my childhood saying: *Come to me, come to me. Let me carry you, let me carry you!*

When we finally reached Tokyo Train Station, we took another taxi, I again cramped between Sā-chan, my auntie, and Yuki-chan. I had to fold my legs under my seat and suffer once more the smell of burning coal and the suffocating heat. For someone small, Sā-chan made a lot of room for herself; whenever I got close to her, I had to move away from her squirming.

I tried to ignore her and studied the city filled with people everywhere we turned. In one area we passed grand-looking buildings, which lined fancier streets, and in another, whole blocks of stone buildings that looked like government buildings with their closed facades. While some structures were mere hovels and out of place, I caught glimpses of ancient structures that had slipped out of time—palaces or huge temples with heavy gates, surrounded by high stone walls and wide moats. Most noticeable: the display of Japanese flags everywhere.

Suddenly, the taxi driver pulled over to the side of the road.

"What is it, what happened?" Shiichi Uncle asked.

"I have to put in more coal," the driver said. While we waited, a convoy of soldiers whizzed past us, a dozen or more of these trucks, spewing dirty clouds of burning oil.

"We see more and more soldiers these days," Uncle said flatly. Near us, pedestrians on the street stopped and took out tiny flags to wave, and those who didn't have flags, lined up on the edge of the street and bowed as the trucks passed by.

We moved on, and in other not very prosperous-looking areas, I saw blocks of monotonous, flimsy appearing two-story houses that packed the low, flat plain. Mama would have called these tinderbox houses made of bamboo, mud, wood, and paper, "cracker-box houses," the colors muted, the white glass squares on windows providing the only glow. Tokyo was nothing like the rolling green cane fields I had known on the slopes of the Hamakua coast. How bleak everything was.

Kimono-clad workers and shoppers swarmed among the cars, the bicycles, and the jinricksha in crowded, confined streets, which the taxi driver expertly wove through. As he maneuvered the car, I caught sight of my auntie's weary face, the moon of it appearing, disappearing, and reappearing in the rearview mirror. All before me, a dreary ocean with no bright colors to be had, everything gray, dark blue, black, or brown. Wrung out, drab.

I thought we would reach the house soon, but Uncle leaned over, looked to his right, and from what I could gather, said to the driver: "Please stop in Nihonbashi. I want to go to Sumida Shopping Street."

"Why do we have to go there *now*?" Harue Auntie asked, moving forward, gripping the front seat between the driver and Shiichi Uncle, her eyebrows knitted together.

"Hi-chan needs a jacket."

Auntie turned away and said nothing.

We soon stopped in front of a small silk shop, which was wedged between a small stationery store and dishware store. Were I by the window, I'm sure I could have almost touched the buildings, the taxi that close to them in the narrow streets. After we stopped, Shiichi Uncle signaled Sā-chan and me to come along with him. He looked to Harue Auntie who shook her head and lifted her chin, her eyes not meeting his.

Le Soie Boutique, The Silk Shop, Kinu-ya had its name carved in French, English, and Japanese on a plank of dark pine just above the doorway. When Uncle parted the curtain to go in, a small bell chimed. The high ceiling, the old and dark cypress boards, and the light grain of the pinewood trimming gave the room an elegant sheen, but for all its refinement, the store was empty of both patrons and goods.

"Welcome!" An older woman, with a regal bearing that matched the quiet elegance of the room, called out and glided towards us in an astonishing purple kimono. "It's been a long time since I've seen you," she said to Shiichi Uncle.

"It's been a long time, Kimata-san," my uncle said, making a deep bow.

"Yes, too long. Please do come in, this way, this way," she said, and showed us to a circle of zabuton to sit on. Once on the floor, I didn't know where to put my legs. Nonetheless, I was happy to find that I could follow the seamstress's words for she did not talk as fast as others I had encountered thus far, her speech languid, fastened perhaps to an occupation marked by the serenity found in the texture of the fine silks she designed into jackets, pants, and kimono.

"Where's Harue-san?" she asked.

"She's in the car," Sā-chan said.

"Oh, you must be Sā-chan." Kimata-san bowed slightly to Sā-chan. "Run to the taxi and tell your mother to have tea with us."

Sā-chan looked up at the ceiling. Watching her, I concluded that she was obstinate with anyone who inconvenienced her.

"Go on," Shiichi Uncle urged. "You heard her." Sā-chan stood up, clenched her mouth, and raised her right foot, as though she were about to stamp it on the floor, and turned quickly to leave.

"And who is this?" she asked, turning to me.

"This is my niece, Hi-chan, my sister's daughter. She's come to live with us."

"She's come, now?" Kimata-san gave Shiichi Uncle a quizzical look. "Oh my, what a bad time." When I didn't say anything, she turned to Uncle and changed the subject. "So Shiichi-san, how is business?"

"I had to sell it in 1939." He shrugged his shoulders, slightly. "Two years into the war with China, and gradually, things got too bad for Harue and me. That's why we stopped buying silk from you. We both work for the government now. I tack shoes and Harue sews staple cloth."

"I had wondered what happened. So many changes, aren't there?" Kimata-san glanced at the barren shelves of her store. "There's talk of a big war. People are afraid. I don't know how much longer I can keep my doors open. I keep only one worker now. Imagine, once I had ten!" Calling out to someone in the back she said, "At-chan, some tea please."

"Yes," responded a woman in an extremely high register.

In the echo of that voice, Sā-chan popped back in, breathless from running. "Okā doesn't want to come in," she said. "She'll wait in the car. She said she's tired and asks Kimata-san to release her." She quickly sat down to receive her tea and cookies.

"So, how may I help you?" Kimata-san asked my uncle.

"I've come to buy a jacket for Hi-chan. She doesn't have the proper clothing for this weather."

Kimata-san carefully set her teacup down, rose, and crossed the room. She began taking kimono jackets out from a large tansu against a wall in the back of the room. She lifted and laid out pieces, layered and wrapped in clouds of handmade mulberry, hemp, or Edgeworthia paper, as if in an elaborate ceremony. For protection against moths, each item wafted a strong smell of camphor. I swallowed hard, fighting back a wave of nausea.

"Ahh," Sā-chan exclaimed, lowering her jaw with each jacket pulled out.

The fine silk ran through my fingers when I touched the jackets Kimata-san brought to me—of flowing rainbow-colored waterfalls of birds, leaves, flowers, and butterflies—as if colors missing in the outside sur-roundings had been gathered into these garments to brighten people's lives.

"The red color is best for a young girl like her," Kimata-san said.

"Yes, I agree," my uncle said and held a red jacket in his hand, as if weighing it.

Although willing to accept the selection Kimata-san and my uncle made for me, I liked the blue one better. As I had not been asked, however, I guessed I had no say in this transaction.

"Some money . . . I have," I said, my Japanese sounding brittle in my ear. "The jacket . . . I can help to pay for it."

"Save your American dollars. Let me pay for your jacket. It's my welcome gift. Don't worry, silk is inexpensive," Shiichi Uncle said under his breath, so Kimata-san wouldn't hear. In a louder voice he said, "Go on, put on your new jacket."

I slipped the jacket on and felt the material move on me like cold wa-ter. Kimata-san had retrieved a floor mirror from a shelf in the corner and set it down in front of me. My stomach was not yet showing, so my new jacket looked splendid on, but it was my face that surprised me most for I hadn't seen it up close since leaving Hawai'i. I looked beautiful, so grown-up, and loved the image I saw despite my thinness. Mama, had she seen me, would have had plenty to say about this display of vanity, especially for someone in my condition. *No wonder you got yourself into trouble!*

"Otō-chan, I want a jacket too," Sā-chan said. "Like hers."

"You have enough jackets. You don't need another one, understand?"

"But they're not as beautiful as Hi-chan's. If she uses her own money, you can buy me one, right?"

"Sā-chan, I'll have none of this. Your insistence on coming today had been an added burden. You know we have to be careful about our money."

Sā-chan pouted, rose up, turned on her heels, and stalked out of Kimata-san's place without a good-bye.

"I apologize for my daughter's poor manners," Shiichi Uncle said after Sā-chan left.

"It's no problem. It's hard on the young these days."

"Yes it is, but that's no excuse." Shiichi Uncle sighed and looked my way. "I think we'd better be going. Harue's waiting."

Shiichi Uncle and Kimata-san took their leave of each other, my uncle thanking the seamstress, each vowing to see the other again soon and wishing one another good health, especially in these uncertain times.

"You sure it's all right—about this jacket?" I asked again, walking toward the car.

"Yes," Uncle said. "You need to keep warm. Besides, silk is much cheaper than cotton. No one wants our silk. It's been boycotted, you see." I nodded, although I did not completely understand. The world beyond Kaiwiki Village had been closed to me; I knew nothing yet of the *greater* world.

"What took you so long?" Harue Auntie said, mumbling something else under her breath, as my uncle and I settled in the taxi. I couldn't understand what she said because it was so quick, but Uncle must have caught it. He started to speak, but then, because Harue Auntie had turned away from him, he said nothing. In my new red jacket I rode toward a new home in the middle of their awkward silence.

Like two hostile guardian dogs, Sā-chan and Harue Auntie had their faces up to the cold wind that rushed through the car's windows. In my discomfort I looked straight ahead and dared not move.

During the great depression that swept Japan in the 1920s, the poverty was so extreme, Mama said that her brother, Harue Auntie, and their families nearly starved. How Mama had wished her big brother would come to Hawai'i! For a while, it seemed that Shiichi Uncle had indeed thought of moving, but, according to Mama, Harue Auntie had strenuously opposed it and that was that. Instead, the two moved from Hiroshima to Tokyo where they opened a small business, my uncle weaving bamboo and my auntie sewing children's clothing.

In Tokyo, Shiichi Uncle, Harue Auntie, and their four children, Norio, Sā-chan, Iwao, and Yuki-chan, lived on the outskirts of the Honjo area. Called Mukōjima, or Yonder Island, the place lay northeast of the Sumida River. A poor workingman's district, a low-lying area jammed with small factories and crowded houses, crisscrossed with polluted canals, squalid and prone to flooding, it was home to the city's rag pickers, the indigent, and the untouchables.

Mukōjima was nothing like places in Hilo that I knew. The way Mama had described the district, I thought it would resemble an area known as Villa Franca back home, with its tiny but sturdy, well-kept houses; this place was more of a slum. It looked, however, as if my uncle and auntie lived in more decent quarters than those around them, their house appeared sturdier and in better shape when we approached it. As Harue Auntie was to say, later, "Your uncle fixed the house because of his 'Hiroshima industry.'"

Inside, the small downstairs level had a tiny kitchen with a hard-packed dirt floor, a wood-burning stove for cooking, a deep washbasin, and a narrow, long table for food preparation. A raised dining and living area covered by rush mats opened to a busy yard, which someone had tried unsuccessfully to make into a decent Japanese garden. Upstairs, up a steep and narrow stairway, there were two small, low rooms for sleeping that ran along a claustrophobic hallway at the end of which hung a long mirror on the door to the water closet that had pots to squat over and relieve oneself.

59

That night, I was placed in a room with my two boy cousins, Norio and Iwao. My coming to the house had disrupted the sleeping arrangements. Where once all the children slept together, they were now separated, with me sleeping with the boys, my uncle and auntie with the girls, Sā-chan not wanting to sleep where I was sleeping, I learned later. I took an immediate dislike to the paper-thin walls that separated the rooms and, as I was to soon learn, they didn't hold back anything: no cough, cry, scold, or passing of gas.

My oldest boy cousin, Norio, a tall, skinny boy who was a year or so older than I, backed himself into a corner of the room to sleep, his face to the wall. Although I tried to be unobtrusive, I was too tall and clumsy to be graceful. Iwao, the nine-year-old, was less concerned. To him, I wasn't as much of a nuisance. He placed himself between his brother and me and gave me the spot nearest the door. "Girls have to shi-shi at night—more than boys," he said in a practical voice.

For the first time in my life, I had gone to bed without taking a bath. By the time we got to the house and had eaten, I was too tired, cold, and scared to ask my new auntie about where I was supposed to bathe.

Having just settled back on my buckwheat pillow, I heard Harue Auntie's voice on the other side of the wall. I may have missed parts of what she said but understood the gist: "She could have done without the jacket. We have things here she could have used. Even of the boys'."

I couldn't hear what my uncle said in answer. After a while their voices stopped. Still, when I thought everyone else had fallen asleep and I was the only one awake, I heard their voices again. This time, Uncle's voice was louder, punctuating the end of his sentences with "understand?" I then heard what may have been a sob or wheeze.

I fell asleep, waiting for my auntie's reply.

7

Neighbors

The next day, a Saturday, I awoke with the sun streaming on my face, and for a moment I didn't know where I was. Suddenly, understanding my predicament, my hands wandered to my belly. I felt sad and sorry for myself. I began crying until I heard Harue Auntie's voice downstairs, at which time I promptly stopped sniffling. Looking around the room, I saw that the boys were already gone and had put their bedding away. Because it was my first day there, I supposed I was allowed to sleep in. I thought of home and wondered what Akira was doing. While still in bed, I heard Harue Auntie send Sā-chan on some kind of an errand. I listened carefully in order to understand what was going on. "Go over to Hamada-san's, Toma-san's, and Omoto-san's and ask them . . ." my auntie said loudly.

Before going out, Sā-chan came up to my room. "So you're finally up. About time! My mother wants you downstairs, so you don't have time to change or to eat. We have guests coming." I learned later that Hamada-san lived in the house to the right of us, Toma-san to the back, and Omoto-san across the alley. When they arrived, the women uniformly dressed in dark clothing with their hair in buns, I was just coming down the stairs. Sā-chan showed the women to the low dining table on the floor, but she let me find my way. The women stared, and if they had questions, no one said anything.

As soon as I sat down, Harue Auntie ordered me into the kitchen. "Make the tea and put the tea cookies on the tray with the teacups. Tea's on the shelf." All eyes followed me as I got up and moved toward the kitchen.

Unlike the other women, my auntie had on a stylish green jacket over her dark winter kimono. Her hair looked different, too, her bun combed up higher than the day before, her neckline showing, which made her appear more youthful. I was tempted to pull her bun down.

"My, my, Sā-chan, you're growing up to be such a pretty girl." The voice of one of the women carried back to the kitchen where I fumbled about—searching for the utensils, trays, pot, and cups—in making the tea.

"Yes, she is, isn't she?" Harue Auntie's voice sounded higher, lighter than when she spoke to me. Lifted with pride, I imagined.

She came to the kitchen where I sat waiting after having made the tea. She began dividing, into several small paper bags, the brown sugar Mama had sent with me as a gift to the family, then took three of them out to where the women sat. "I want to share this with you," she said.

"My goodness, what is it?" I heard one of the women say.

"It's sugar."

"Sugar? How special! But from where?"

"Hawai'i," Sā-chan said.

"Oh, thank you *so* much!"

"Don't fuss," Harue Auntie said in that clipped tone of hers. "Thank my husband's niece, Himiko Aoki." She called to me. "Hi-chan, come out here and bring the tea with you."

Rushing into the living area from the poorly lit kitchen, I clipped my head on a low support beam and nearly dropped the tray. I heard Sā-chan giggle. Disregarding her, I walked over to the low table, and managed to set the tray on it before Harue Auntie introduced me to the women. As if orchestrated, they darted their eyes up down my body, then looked to Harue Auntie, and that I gathered was because I was still in my new red jacket and the dress I had traveled in. From their scrutiny, I could tell they thought me strange, but I didn't know if it was because they also guessed about my condition—in either case, their looks were filled with judgment.

"From Hawai'i? Such a far place to have come from." While she stared at me, the woman called Toma-san said, "One day, you must tell me about your trip."

"I will," I said without enthusiasm.

The youngest of the three neighborhood women, Hamada-san, turned to me with her head down. "I'm forever indebted to you," she said. "Sugar is so scarce and my children have been without it for so long." Her voice vibrated with feeling. She pointed her body toward me like a compass needle and bowed with her hands thrust forward, touching the floor with her head, and when she finally lifted herself, she gave me a warm smile. I was startled by her pretty face; breathless, I clung to her eyes. Miyo often said that I had a tendency to befriend only those who were attractive. She said that I would not have been her friend had she not been my sister, with her limp, plain features, and all that. Of course, I always denied it, but it was true; I had this girlish, childish compulsion—like playing with fire—to be beguiled by the beauty of others.

Toma-san spoke to me once more. "How was the boat ride?" So taken was I by Hamada-san that I didn't know Toma-san had said something to me.

"Didn't you hear that?" Harue Auntie said.

"Huh?" I said, confused.

Toma-san looked at me strangely. "How was the sea crossing?" she asked again, slowly, deliberately.

"Oh, fine," I said, still finding it difficult to tear my eyes away from Hamada-san. She reminded me of my once beautiful mama, whom I was missing deeply at the moment, needing her guidance and good sense in wending my way through my new experiences.

Peering into her package of sugar, Omoto-san said, "My, this sugar is strange, isn't it? It's brown."

"Brown?" Hamada-san asked.

I turned to her and apologized in poor Japanese. "I'm sorry it's not white sugar."

"Why is it brown?" Toma-san asked, and to her I said nothing again, this time not knowing how to explain in Japanese that white sugar was expensive and that brown sugar was unrefined, therefore cost less. However, my not answering her made it seem as though I had dismissed her. She turned her face toward my auntie, who picked up on it.

"Today, she only cares about what Hamada-san thinks, don't you,

Hi-chan?" I felt hot and my palms grew sweaty. I may have smiled but there was fire in my veins. "Yesterday, her attention was focused on Shi-ichi-san, and she ignored me," Harue Auntie went on to say. I wanted to say that it wasn't true but couldn't think fast enough and find the words. Besides, Toma-san was *plain*.

The women put their heads down and stared into their tea; no one spoke or looked at Harue Auntie or me. After a while, Omoto-san said in a tentative voice, "The price of thread is up again."

"Yes, fish, too," Toma-san said quickly.

"And fresh vegetables. They're never in the government food depots," Harue Auntie said.

"Things will change for the better," Hamada-san said.

"You're young and optimistic," Omoto-san said.

"But I'm sure of it," Hamada-san said.

I studied her sincere expression as she spoke, how she dipped her head to one side. Watching her, I liked her ladylike manner and how she carried herself.

"My son wrote me recently from China," Toma-san said. "He is opposed to the war there and hopes it doesn't come our way. He'll be glad to hear that I have some extra sugar. He's been worried about our starving."

"Did you hear the news?" Harue Auntie said. "Satsuma-san and several of her children died of starvation. Terrible, isn't it."

"Yes, it is . . . saa, with that, I think I'd better be going," Toma-san said. "I have to cook something for my in-laws. They've come to live with me after my husband was sent to the Dutch East Indies and our boy to China."

Soon after, Omoto-san also excused herself. Auntie saw Toma-san and Omoto-san to the door, and when she returned, Hamada-san made a move to go. "Please don't go yet," I said, clearly out of turn. "We still have some sugar left, don't we Auntie?" When my auntie said nothing, I went to the kitchen and came back with another small package. "Here, take more with you."

"Oh my, but you don't have to," Hamada-san said.

"I know, but I want to." I smiled a smile that I knew looked cute, something I had practiced many times in the mirror. Of course, Harue

Auntie couldn't say anything in front of a guest, but I did see her pull herself in at my audacious move.

When Hamada-san excused herself, as if no longer wanting her body and thoughts to be a burden on us, she slipped away from the house as if she were a leaf taken up by the wind into the skies. I would have given anything to be that graceful.

All day, I clung to thoughts of Hamada-san, her soundless moves, her water-soft gestures, her startling grace and charm. I couldn't seem to let her go, but I said nothing of this to Harue Auntie. It didn't matter; I sensed she saw right through me.

8

Sā-chan and Harue Auntie

"Hurry, get up, stinky," Sā-chan said, charging into my room the next morning. I was dreaming that I was with Hamada-san when my cousin awakened me. It seemed as if I had just gone to bed; also, I had not taken a bath again—an unspeakable sin for a Japanese.

"What time is it?" I asked, my words unsteady across my lips.

"It's already five o'clock."

"Five? Why so early? Isn't this Sunday?"

"It doesn't matter what day it is. We get up at five every day. You better get used to it. Yesterday my mother let you sleep, but no more."

I wanted to kick my feet on the futon in frustration. I even thought how satisfying it would be to kick Sā-chan in the shins. Back home, I could sleep as late as I wanted to when school was out, and even on school days, I could roll around in bed until the last minute.

Sā-chan stood over me. "Mama wants you to help with the breakfast."

I put on my jacket over the same dress I'd been wearing and went downstairs. I didn't feel especially dirty because it was so chilly. Breakfast was already set on the low dining table in the living area, and I could smell the steam from the miso soup and the hot rice, the salt of the pickled vegetables. There was a dish of tofu and a strip of dried fish on a small white plate. "Sā-chan?" I called out. No one answered; no one seemed to be around. Hungry, I sat down and picked on the dark green, minced tops of white radishes with my fingers. Was this all they ate for breakfast? No eggs? No milk? No bread? Why, at home . . . I made comparisons, felt homesick, and nearly vomited.

"Hi-chan, where's your manners? Don't you know you're not supposed to eat before Otō-san sits down? And with your fingers, too. How disgusting!" Sā-chan's voice came from the kitchen; like Miyo she had been watching me all along.

"I was hungry," I said, slowly pronouncing every word.

"That's no excuse. You just have to wait. You didn't even change your clothes or wash your face."

"I have nothing else to wear and I don't know where to wash my face. No one told me." It felt silly to change into my muʻumuʻu.

"Why didn't you ask? My mother left a stack of old clothes by your bedside."

"I didn't know that," I said, struggling to control my temper and find the right words.

"Oh my," Sā-chan sighed. "I guess I have to show you everything, like Okā-chan said I would."

"Wait till you go to Hawaiʻi," I said in English.

Without another word, I stomped upstairs and hurriedly dressed. I didn't know, nor cared if I put my kimono on right. I wanted to wash my face, but like bathing, I didn't know where this was done; no one had said anything and once, when I did try to ask, Sā-chan ignored me. After that, I was too proud to say anything. I checked the water closet upstairs once more, but there was no washbasin. Puzzled, I went downstairs. Only after I had seen, through a small side window, Iwao slip out of a side door just outside the kitchen, did I see the washroom. I ran into the tiny room that housed a basin and two enamel squat pots with covers, like the ones I used upstairs. Someone had cut squares of newspapers for us to wipe ourselves, but still no place to bathe.

I washed my face quickly, resenting the need to hurry, for at home I'd done everything at my own pace, in my own time. Because Mama said before I left, "Try to do things for yourself and not bother others. Don't be noticeable or lazy," I was trying hard not to be "noticeable," but their eyes were trained on me like knives. I know I had promised to be good, but I was finding it hard to do.

When I emerged from the washroom and went back to the kitchen, I saw Shiichi Uncle and my boy cousins across the way, seated on the floor, waiting for Harue Auntie to serve them their first rice. Sā-chan was still in the kitchen area, her right hand reaching for a small bowl on a higher shelf. "I can get that," I said, going to her, trying to be helpful.

"Don't bother. I've done this a thousand times. Just because you're tall . . . ahh," she grunted as if to give more length to her torso while on tiptoes. Losing her balance, she knocked down a plate already on the counter with her trailing kimono sleeve. "Now see what you've done?" she shouted after the crash.

"What's the matter?" Harue Auntie rushed into the small kitchen.

"She's so clumsy, Okā-chan," Sā-chan said in an exaggerated voice.

"Iie . . . I didn't do it!" I said, half in Japanese, half in English. "She did," I said, pointing to Sā-chan.

Harue Auntie didn't listen to a word I said. "We don't have many dishes to spare. For that, you should eat from the floor," she said and walked out.

"Clean it up, Hi-chan," Sā-chan said in a sing-song way that indicated she was thrilled at the idea of seeing me on my hands and knees.

"Yeah, yeah, you big trouble-maker," I said in English, knowing she didn't understand the words but would catch the sarcasm.

Afterward, my arms up to the elbows in dishwater, Sā-chan said, "You shouldn't use that much soap. And when you're done, my mother wants you to come with me."

"But," I said, "I promised your father I would show him some of my mother's pictures that I brought with me."

"Forget it. We have a lot to do today. I have to show you where the public bath is, so you can bathe. We don't have a bathtub in the house." That explained why everyone had bathed except me; I surmised that not showing me where to bathe was a form of humiliation and a way to keep me in line. "You also have to know where the bread store, the tofu store, and the food depots are for our ration of staples."

Sā-chan led the way down a crowded alley near the house. The roofs of the houses extended over it, which made it seem as if we were walking through an archway. Her talk and walk were brisk. I could hardly keep up, my feet in a pair of geta that didn't fit me. "That's all we have," Uncle had said earlier, in his gentle, apologetic way. "Soon, I'll get you something that fits."

When Sā-chan and I emerged from the alleyway, the crowd thickened around us like stew. I fastened my eyes on her small back, afraid I would get lost. Soon we came to the bathhouse that the family frequented. It looked like any of a million little establishments on that street. "This is where you will bathe. Okā-chan let you go the first two days, but you can't sleep without bathing any more. I don't know why you didn't ask."

"Why you didn't tell me!" I said in English.

As we walked along, Sā-chan chattered away about the people in this shop and that shop. Since I knew neither the shops nor the shopkeepers, her gossip didn't interest me, but I was surprised at how kindly people greeted her, some even affectionately. Because she was so sweet and easy going in front of these people, I began to wonder if she were two different people.

When we finally reached home, I felt drained and unhappy, my life topsy-turvy. I said, "I'm going upstairs to lie down for a while."

"What do you mean? No one sleeps during the day unless you're ill. Only Yuki-chan takes a nap. We have dinner to start. The rice has to be cooked by the time Okā-chan gets home, and I have yet to show you where we stack futon and air them outside. Okā-chan said that I should also teach you how to use the stove and the brazier in the living room."

Later, while washing the rice, I made an effort to be pleasant. In halting Japanese I said, "Thank you for showing me around. Everything's so different in Hawai'i."

"Don't thank me. You need to know where these places are and how to start the fires because from now on, you're going to have to do all of the shopping and cooking. Take over my chores. My mother expects you to do them all, now that you're here. I have so much school work; it takes up most of my time."

It was easy to see that Sā-chan was the privileged one, the blessed one, Harue Auntie's favorite child. To make it clear from the very beginning, my auntie, the enforcer of the rules in the family, had my name first on her tongue for any chore to be done. As soon as she came home that day from her clothing factory, she said, "Hi-chan, go outside and fetch the wood. Then set the table. Also, don't forget to boil the water. Go on, go on."

After dinner that evening, I saw Harue Auntie and Sā-chan getting ready to go to the bathhouse. I saw them by the doorway, clothing rolled in logs and tucked under one of their arms. They had their other arm curled around a small washbasin, each filled with a washcloth, soap, and brush.

"P-please wait for me," I said. "I'd like to go with you."

"No, you can't. You have to watch Yuki-chan. From now on you will have to go to the bathhouse by yourself. You still have dishes to wash and food to put away. Go later," Harue Auntie ordered.

"But . . ." I was afraid I wouldn't be able to find the place and get lost.

Overhearing the conversation, Shiichi Uncle looked up from where he sat on the floor reading the newspaper and said, "Harue, let her go with you. I can watch Yuki-chan and take care of the dishes. Hi-chan can go by herself from tomorrow."

"How's she going to learn? How's Yuki-chan going to get used to her?"

"She can learn from tomorrow and you don't have to worry about Yuki-chan. Why are you rushing Hi-chan, anyway?" Uncle's voice was sharp when he rose and moved up to us. My auntie's eyes blazed with anger, having been put in her place. She and Sā-chan moved toward the door to wait for me to gather my things.

"Don't mind them," my uncle said to me softly before I left. "Enjoy your bath. You can go alone from tomorrow."

"You are very kind," I said. "Thank you for understanding." He gave a wan smile. I was already a lightning rod between these two unhappy people; it was not a comfortable position to be put in.

9

Trapped

"Senso daaa!" Someone shouted as he ran down our crowded alleyway with a Japanese flag fluttering in his hand. "We just bombed Pearl Harbor!"

Mama, Miyo, Akira! With no one at home, I ran over to Hamada-san's house and pounded on her door, but when she didn't answer, I ran over to Omoto-san's house. "What does this mean?" I asked when she came to the door.

"I don't know, but you'd better stay in the house," she said, staring at me coldly. Before shutting myself in, I ran out to a shopping street near our area to see if I could learn anything more and saw people gathered in small groups, talking about how great Japan was in keeping the attack a secret. Large block ideographs were already splashed across newspapers in the small tobacco stands and bookshops, which I saw announced the sinking of American battleships, hasty drawings showing columns of smoky fires rising in the harbor, the ships apparently caught by surprise. Photographed faces of triumphant Japanese government officials confirmed the Japanese Imperial Navy's actions and America's defeat.

Uncle said to us that night, "Japan is crazy. What does she think she's doing?" I was surprised at what he said.

"Tō-san, don't say that," Harue Auntie said, folding her arms, defending her countrymen. "You should be proud of what we did."

"Proud of what? It's a terrible situation, don't you see? It's people like you . . ."

71

"People like me, what?" Harue Auntie said.

"Do you think I can go back to Hawai'i?" I asked, uncaring about their argument. I wanted to go home.

"We should check at the Mukōjima Ward office," Shiichi Uncle said. "Maybe they'll give you permission to go home."

The following day, Shiichi Uncle took some time off from work and we went to the ward office, a place that kept records of people living in the area. Many foreigners were waiting in line, but I didn't dare speak to them, thinking I might hurt my chances.

"I'm from Hawai'i, and I was wondering if I could return," I said in my best Japanese to the immigration officer assigned to me.

"It is not permitted for you Japanese traitors to leave our country," he said from behind his cage, my uncle translating, "at least not until the war is over." He slowly shuffled and reshuffled my papers like a deck of cards and toyed with the stamp in his hand that could release me. "Don't worry. In no time, the red sun of Japan is going to rise above your country." Smirking, he shoved my papers back to me under the protective bars of his window.

Japan detained and ordered foreigners to work in factories or for the government, some while under house arrest. It depended, too, on how old you were and the circumstances under which you were in the country. While those who were bilingual did translations for the Japanese war effort, I was luckier, the immigration official able to see that I was not well educated, therefore unable to help, and too, because my condition was beginning to show, the government released me to my auntie and uncle.

As usual, I fixed the dinner that evening, for by this time, Sā-chan's name was the last to be called. Even Iwao's name came dashing out of his mother's throat before his sister's. Being a boy and younger than Sā-chan gave him no favored status in this household. My place in the family was thus firmly established, my life relegated to that of a common housemaid, a role everyone took for granted as right and proper. I was a wipe cloth, mop-up person. Already my hands were cracking miserably from all the work I had to do, mine the lowest status in the house.

While I did want to do my chores nicely that night, I banged the pots and pans deriving great satisfaction from the release it gave me. Though I didn't want to be troublesome and was indebted to my uncle's family for taking me in, I gave in to this childish behavior, for every new day felt as if another knot was being tightened around my will and now, to make matters worse, I wasn't allowed to go home.

When I finished my kitchen chores, I took my darning to the living area and sat with the family. "Otō-san, will you fix my geta?" Iwao was asking when I sat down.

"You don't need a new pair if that's what you're thinking of asking Papa for," Sā-chan said. "Your straps always break because you're so rough."

"No, I'm not. Tell her, Norio."

"Sā-chan, Iwao's not rough," Norio said disinterestedly and lifted his head from a book, hair in his eyes. I had rarely heard him say anything since I had arrived. That evening, his deep voice matched the shyness and moodiness I had noticed earlier.

"Everyone, quiet," Shiichi Uncle then said. "I have something important to discuss with you—to caution you about. Times are going to be difficult from now on, and I don't want you calling attention to yourselves. We are at war, so you have to be careful about what you say. It's easy to get careless." Uncle regarded us with great seriousness. "You have to watch out especially for the Thought Police. They're the ones who can come and take you away."

"The Thought Police?" Sā-chan said.

"Yes, of the Kenpeitai."

"What's the Kenpeitai?" I asked.

"The government police," Shiichi Uncle said.

"It's all Hi-chan's fault," Sā-chan, said. "That's why we have to be careful."

"No, everyone has to be careful," Uncle said.

"But who's going to say anything bad about the government?" Iwao said. "Not us!" He couldn't believe anyone would do such a thing.

But Sā-chan was right. My coming from America had obviously put the family under suspicion.

"Just do your work and don't say anything, understand?" Uncle said.

Late that night, under my thick winter futon, I grew cold at the thought of them, these strange police. I dreamed of them coming for me, dragging me out of the house, scooping my brains out, spreading my legs wide open and snatching my baby out of my body. I was afraid I wouldn't be able to stop these baby stealers, these mind stealers, these body stealers from destroying my thoughts and memories, and I would not be able to remember Akira. I would not be able to remember his face. I would not be able to remember my father, my mother, or Miyo. I would never know my baby's face.

Not long after my uncle's warnings, Iwao shouted, "They're here!" He was preparing to go to school one morning and came running downstairs. "I spotted one of them from the window."

"What are you talking about?" I said.

"The Thought Police of the Kenpeitai."

"They've come for Hi-chan," Sā-chan said, clapping.

"Stop it," Norio said. "That's not funny!"

We all moved up to a small window in the front and peered out. At first I couldn't see anything. "There's no one out there," I said.

"Look closely, by Omoto-san's doorway across the alley, in the shadows," Iwao said. The man that Iwao pointed out had on a dark suit and cape and looked different from the other men in the area, those who wore work clothes or civilian government uniforms.

Norio saw him too and quickly withdrew from the window. "What would he want with us?"

"Like I said, it's Hi-chan they want," Sā-chan said.

The man cased the area for a few days, looking with suspicion at our house. After school each afternoon, Iwao would change his clothes and follow the man. I spotted Iwao on the rooftop of Toma-san's house on one occasion and Hamada-san's house, another, as he looked over toward the Omotos' home where the man could be seen watching our place. Light, agile, and full of purpose, Iwao wove through the shadows and moved like the wind between the close houses, the man having no idea he was being watched.

A week later, Iwao reported, "He's gone. The dark alleyway swallowed him to Jigoku."

"Good, Hell is where he should be," Norio said.

"Iwao's so full of purpose that even the Kenpeitai would have to respect him, had they caught him following them," Auntie said to Hamada-san soon after the incident. Flashing a rare smile, Harue Auntie was braced against the flimsy bamboo gate that divided the houses when she said this. I could hear her talking to Hamada-san in a loud, animated voice from where I sat in the kitchen. It was as if she wanted me to hear what she was saying; too, it may have been her way of flaunting her relationship with Hamada-san, knowing how much I liked our neighbor but had been unable to see much of her. "Being purposeful, however, is nothing compared to how well he can sing. Did you know that his voice is clearer than a nightingale's? I'm sure you've heard him before."

I'm sick of your bragging, Harue Auntie. Sā-chan this. Norio that. Now Iwao is the greatest singer. If he's such a wonderful singer, why haven't I heard him before?

With the day's stew simmering, I took Yuki-chan off my back and went with her from the kitchen to the living room to sit and patch one of Norio's shirts, the sliding doors open to the garden and afternoon light. By now, my stomach had grown visibly fuller, and I had been worried about carrying Yuki-chan so much. Harue Auntie had come home early from work that day and, after having spoken at length with Hamada-san over the fence, had been checking her plants. I watched her trim a few wayward, leafless azalea branches that had asserted their way into a cluster of bamboo. At this time, Iwao came downstairs and sat on the wooden walkway just outside the sliding door. Seeing him there, Harue Auntie called out and said. "Iwao, why don't you cut some bamboo and trim a propeller for Sā-chan. She would like that."

"I'll get my knife. I'll make one for Hi-chan too."

Harue Auntie shook her head. "Hi-chan doesn't need one."

Iwao came into the house and took hesitant steps when he neared me. He looked at my face then ran upstairs to get his pocketknife to cut a bamboo stalk and avoided me when he came downstairs.

No longer interested in watching him whittle a toy for someone else, I put my head down to concentrate on my own work. *I'd like a bamboo propeller toy,* too, I thought—it would act as a diversion—and my stitches went crookedly across the length of the material. I sighed, pulled the running stitches out, and started over.

It was then, while he was in the garden among the bamboo that Iwao began to sing. He started in a soft swelling a capella, and after a few notes, his voice grew loud and strong. I saw several people in the neighborhood look out from their upstairs windows. I had heard the song before, and it triggered such a great sadness in me that I began to cry, Iwao's voice a wind that lifted the seed of the song and planted it in my chest in a spasm of longing for home:

Shina no yoru.	What a night in China
Shina no yoru, yo	What a night in China
Minato no akari,	Harbor lights
Murasaki no yo ri	Deep purple night

Toma-jiji, Toma-san's father-in-law, called out from his back window. I couldn't see him, but I heard him say, "Iwao, at least we can enjoy listening to you sing, that's still free. I think you should enter our ward's songfest. You're sure to win it—a little money too."

Iwao's singing must have taken Sā-chan away from her studies and caused her to drift downstairs. I hadn't noticed her until she was practically at my side. "Oh," I said, jumping.

"What are you crying for?" she asked, her eyes roving my face.

"Nothing."

"You can't just cry for *nothing*. Everyone cries for something."

"Not me!"

"You're crazy then. Wait till I tell my mother."

"Tell her, see if I care. And if I *were* crying for something, I wouldn't tell you anyway!" I stood up, threw my sewing down, and kicked it into a corner of the room. Yuki-chan began to cry. I stormed into the kitchen, my hands trembling as I took down the teacups and plates.

"I'm going to tell my mother about what you did with your sewing! And what about Yuki-chan?"

"What about her?" I said, anger making my Japanese sound clearer, as it did with Mama and her English. "You watch her for once, and you tell your mother anything you want!" I said, all the while hearing my mother's voice about being deferential. After having released my anger, I wished I hadn't acted that way. I kept on breaking my promises to Mama.

That night, exhausted and cold and the last one up, I turned off all the lights, made sure the embers in the stove were dying, locked up the house, and dragged myself upstairs. I changed my clothes in the room at the end of the hallway and went into the bedroom, the boys already sleeping. I sat on my bedding. Looking out into the dark, I couldn't hold back my tears. I covered my face with my hands, but couldn't muffle my sobbing. I didn't want to wake anyone, so I reached over to the side for my pillow to raise it to my face, but felt something strange and rough inside of it. I instantly withdrew my hand. Back home, rats sometimes came into the house, and I thought it might be one. After I went over the object, I choked on an intake of breath and felt a hot stab of joy. Nestled in my pillowcase was a small bamboo propeller.

Shiichi Uncle and Harue Auntie both worked in damp and dirty factories for long, monotonous hours. Before the sun was up, they set out for their workplaces. For the rest of the day, I heard Harue Auntie's voice, in a remnant of sound, go round and round in the fabric of my mind with her list of chores: do the dishes, feed Yuki-chan, sweep the house, wash the socks, fold the bedding, cook the rice, darn the holes in the boys' shirts, wash the seaweed, cut the carrots.

Goods were in short supply and I had already given up my oxfords for the war effort. Of my sacrifice, Sā-chan said, "I think it's funny that you gave your shoes to Otō-chan, especially when he'll use the leather to make shoes for Japanese soldiers. What about your Americans?"

"I did it for your father," I told her, which was true. I had heard that factory workers were being pressured by the government to find what leather they could.

Like the shoe leather I had given away, cotton was in short supply, unlike silk which was abundant and used in winter and for formal wear, and because I had very little to wear those first months in Japan and Sā-chan was outgrowing her wardrobe, early that spring, my uncle gave us money to buy the cotton material needed for our summer kimono from a small yearly bonus he had just received. It was easy to see it was an extravagance; nonetheless, my uncle was insistent, and my refusing the money made him more adamant. While Yuki-chan would inherit Sā-chan's clothing, I was an added expense—another wedge in my uncle and auntie's relationship.

On a rare time off for both of us, Sā-chan and I took a trolley ride to Nihonbashi. While there, we went to several shopping streets, long narrow alleyways filled with shops having little in them. In one of the establishments, we came across rare bolts of cotton material, similar to what we'd been searching for. Sā-chan stopped and took her time looking at them.

"I think we should go, Sā-chan," I said, after surveying the offerings on the table. "They're too expensive."

"Wait, let me look. You're always in a rush."

"We should do as your father said and go to see Kimata-san. She would know a place with reasonable prices."

"Is that all you think about?"

"No, but . . ."

"They're pretty, aren't they? You never get them this pretty anymore. There's almost nothing in the other shops."

"I wouldn't know. I've never shopped for material before."

"Yes, I guess you wouldn't know, would you? Well, I'm telling you that this place looks like it has the best cotton goods."

Sā-chan began lifting various fabrics to see how they looked against her. She soon came across an indigo-colored kasuri with small dainty red designs delicately interspersed, which she immediately liked.

"Let's go," I said, for it did no good for us to remain there.

"But I truly desire this," she said, ever so sweetly but close to whining, looking at me with hopeful eyes. Admiring herself in the mirror, the material pressed up to her chest, Sā-chan moved her head this way and that, her silky black hair swinging like a rope. "It's so pretty."

"I know, but it's really too expensive."

"Even soooo," she said, swishing her body all the more in front of the mirror, and I understood what she was driving at. "You can let me use part of your share of the money, can't you?"

I said nothing. *What if I don't give you the money, what are you going to do?*

"Well, can't you?"

"Here, take it," I said. I removed money from my kimono sleeve, counted out the necessary amount, slapped it into her outstretched hand the way Miyo had done with me, and handed her a portion of my money.

I settled for something inexpensive in the store and barely had enough to pay for it. After the transactions, a burning sensation in my throat and stomach made it difficult for me to thank the patient clerk properly.

The side-eyes glare I gave Sā-chan made no impression. "Okā-chan will be very pleased at what I bought for myself," she said. She twisted her handbag in school-girl fashion and walked down the street. I was silent all the way home.

The next day, Hamada-san saw me and said, "I heard you and Sā-chan bought some summer kimono material. Your auntie said that you picked out a beautiful piece of yardage for yourself. Bring it over. I'd like to see it, and let's have some tea."

"Yeah, thank you—can't today," I said and hurriedly dismissed myself.

10

Hamada-san

It was bitter cold by the time 1942 rolled around. At first I could hide my pregnancy with all the clothes I wore to keep warm. But soon I was the object of neighborhood gossip and could do nothing about it. Now that it was apparent that I was pregnant, the reason for my being in Japan no longer idle speculation, people in the neighborhood began staring or whispering to each other whenever I walked by. I saw that they were trying to make me feel ashamed of my condition, but Mama had been right. I would have felt more ashamed were I in Hilo. She so much as said that because I didn't know the people in Japan, I would be okay. And I was. I held my head up and went about my business.

Although she didn't say it, Harue Auntie was grumpy about the gossip. My kindly uncle, oblivious to it, reminded me to rest whenever I could, and at the dinner table, offered me a little more fish or vegetables that should have been his portion. As for Sā-chan, she complained about the attention directed towards me, while Iwao was full of curiosity about the baby. Norio didn't do much, only hugged himself tighter to the wall in the bedroom as my stomach grew larger. I was younger than he was but already pregnant, and he acted as if I had something contagious. I was certain he had little experience with girls.

Early one morning, I was out throwing rice water on a dying sacred bamboo plant in front of our house when Hamada-san came rushing out. "Yes, rice water may save it," she said.

"That's what my uncle told me."

"Listen, I'm glad I caught you. You still haven't come for tea, and I have yet to thank you for the sugar."

Whenever Hamada-san had seen me coming home from the factory with Yuki-chan or out hanging the clothes or sweeping the walkway, she would invite me in, and up until then, I had refused her invitations. "Also, bring the fabric you bought with you. Your auntie said that you picked out something pretty." *Yeah, sure, something pretty.*

This time, despite the abundance of chores, I said, "Thank you, I'll be right over," but left the fabric at home.

That day, I entered a surprisingly orderly house, this only because it was unimaginably bare, as if Hamada-san had had to sell everything in it, the only things visible the low table and zabuton. In her mid-thirties, married, and looking years younger than her age, Hamada-san had an older husband whom I had yet to see. I also knew that she had one boy and two girls at home, with one boy, called Jun, in the regular army. Surprised to see the younger children at home, I found them to be nondescript, despite their pretty mother; what stood out about them was that they were withdrawn and passive, lacking in energy—a telltale mark of hunger. Hamada-san, as though sensing what I was thinking, said, "My children weren't feeling well today," and as if on cue, the children, with eyes to the floor, not once even glancing at me or bothering to greet me, retreated into the shadows.

Hamada-san and I sat on the bare floor, only a red lacquer tea tray between us. On it, were two teacups, a small flower arrangement, and one pink bean cake on a leaf-shaped plate with a thin bamboo spatula. "Please," she said, showing the palm of her hand.

Without thinking, I took the bean cake and shoved the whole thing into my mouth. Only after biting into the bean filling, did I realize that I should have shared it with her by cutting the cake in two with the spatula. "I'm sorry, I didn't . . . for you . . ." I managed to mutter.

"It's all right, don't worry," she said and began laughing with a hand over her mouth.

"What's wrong?"

"The beans are stuck to your teeth and you look so funny." She laughed harder, and I joined her, both of us suddenly released by the laughter and the feeling of friendship that rushed in.

"Neh, it's nice to see you happy for once," she said after straightening the neckline to her kimono. "You always look so serious."

"I guess I've been busy."

"And worried, I suppose."

"Yes, worried—mostly about my family."

"I would be, too." She hesitated, then added, "Unlike you, however, my father and mother are no longer living so I don't have to worry about them."

Dead! It struck me like a blow to the stomach that Mama and Miyo might be dead. Until that moment I had never considered the possibility. I began to sob, and when Hamada-san reached out to touch and console me—"What's the matter?"—I jumped up and ran out of the house.

Feeling foolish, I went to her home the next day to say, "Hamada-san, I'm sorry about yesterday, but I have no idea what's happening in Hawai'i so that scares me. I'm nervous about my family and friends, especially to think they may be dead."

"Don't worry, I'm sure everyone's fine. According to the papers, I don't think we bombed your island."

"Oh, how I dislike being here in Japan," I blurted, no longer able to suppress my true feelings. "It's so cold, yeah? Too, everything's so strange—the food, the smells, the way people talk. The way they look at me."

"You'll get used to things. You're just homesick, you see, and I'm sure your father is taking care of things back home."

"My father? But he's dead!" Thinking about how disappointed he would have been in me, I began to cry once again.

"There, there," Hamada-san said and moved toward me to pat my back. "I feel terrible about your father. I'm sorry, I wouldn't have brought it up if I knew. You're young to have lost a parent."

"Listen, I think I'd better go. I seem to be forever crying."

"It's all right. Stay, rest awhile."

"I have chores to do."

"They'll still be there. A few more minutes aren't going to matter."

We sat in silence until I was calmer. When the opportunity seemed right, when I no longer seemed so sad, Hamada-san said, "May I ask you something?"

"Of course," I said, curious now.

"It's nothing—almost silly and I don't mean to be impolite—but what do you mean by 'Yah' at the end of your sentences? It's bothered some of us."

"Oh," I laughed. "You mean *yeah?* Sometimes, I forget that I'm in Japan. We use it in Hawai'i. It means *isn't it so?* or sometimes 'yes' as in the expression, *neh,* that you all use. Your *neh* is tricky too because it can mean other things like 'hey' or 'listen'."

"Oh, is that what *yeah* means? It sounded so strange," she said, breaking into a broad smile. Right after my explanation, I tried using "neh" in my sentences and Hamada-san, "yeah" in hers. Because our renditions sounded so strange and we laughed so hard, I had to hold onto my stomach, and Hamada-san, clamp her mouth with her hands.

From that day on, it was not just bean cakes and tea. Like a whale, I spouted everything that was in my heart to Hamada-san. I even asked her to keep my deepest secret. "No one knows this, but the name of my baby's father is Akira Taketa," I revealed. "I'm sure Harue Auntie and Sā-chan are dying to know this."

Hamada-san was surprised at my candidness. "Americans are different, aren't they?" she said.

From then on, having found a confidant in Hamada-san, I couldn't stop myself. I was talking too much. "I know I should be more appreciative," I commented, "and I am grateful to my uncle and auntie for taking me in, but sometimes it's difficult. Shiichi Uncle and Harue Auntie always argue, I don't get along with Harue Auntie, and my cousins puzzle me. Take Norio—he does weird things like pressing himself against the wall when I pass by him in the hallway so my stomach wouldn't touch him—or Sā-chan, who snubs me for no reason. Iwao's by far the most normal." I inflated my cheeks, blew out the air, and said, "I hate it here. I don't fit in. Japan is so strange. People are always watching me. Watching, watching, watching!"

"Yes, Japanese people are like that. That's the way we keep each other in line," she said and gave a smothered laugh. And while she often laughed at her own remarks, she never laughed at my mountain of complaints.

At the time of my growing relationship with Hamada-san, the other women, Omoto-san and Toma-san, began keeping to themselves. Noticing the change, I asked Harue Auntie about their behavior: "Do you know why Omoto-san and Toma-san don't speak to me?"

"It's not hard to understand," she said cockily, the way she spoke to me most days now. "It's because you don't include them when you and Hamada-san go shopping or take tea or go to the park. They feel hurt. Don't take people cheaply, Hi-chan. It's bad luck." Harue Auntie was right, of course, but since it came from her, I balked at what she said. I thought the women small and silly in their ways, anyway.

At least once a week, Hamada-san and I, with Yuki-chan strapped on my back, took the streetcar to Asakusa to shop; later, we would cross over to Ginza to stare in the windows at goods we couldn't afford. If they happened to be outside of their homes, tending their makeshift gardens or hanging the wash when we walked by, Omoto-san and Toma-san would stop what they were doing to watch us pass. They would bow out of habit but never say anything. I ignored them, content to have Hamada-san all to myself. It was nice having a close woman friend, a new experience for me.

I was so involved with Hamada-san that I disregarded my auntie, too. However, when I happened to grumble to Hamada-san about Harue Auntie, about her wanting me to bind my stomach with a long piece of soft cloth to hold it up, to my surprise, Hamada-san said, "You should try it." I had to admit Harue Auntie was right. The sash that lifted my stomach did make me feel better. "You should bind your breasts too," Hamada-san said in response to another of Harue Auntie's suggestions. Up until that time I had also disregarded the idea, but with Hamada-san's prompting, I did what my auntie had said. During this time, Harue Auntie didn't say much; she just watched me. When she saw me using the stomach bindings and later the one for my breasts, she smirked, then shot one of her eyebrows up in obvious disdain.

Sensing my auntie's growing resentment, Hamada-san said, "Why don't you come over only when your auntie's not home. I don't want to upset her."

"Why? I should be able to visit you at any time that I'm free," I said.

"And why would you want to do that?" She cocked her head to one side, her look skeptical. "Maybe you need to change your ways a bit. You can please your auntie but still have your way by trying not to go against her, you know?"

"I do, but I can't help it."

"That's because you don't want to, neh."

I often thought Hamada-san wise in her dealings with people, and I wanted to listen to her, but my resentment of Harue Auntie had grown deep roots. In this short time I could only see my auntie as yamamba or a witch woman, who in old Japanese stories ate the children of villagers. Before bedtime, Iwao at my side, I sometimes shared stories of yamamba that my mother had told me. Soon tiring of the few stories I knew, he said, "Why don't you tell me stories about Hawai'i instead?"

"Sure, I don't mind," I said as Iwao curled up close to my stomach. Norio was also in the room, but as usual, he faced the wall. Before beginning and in great ceremony, I spread my red jacket over my lap as if it were a storyteller's cape.

"Kaiwiki, where I come from, is a splendid place," I began. "In Hawai'i, there are so many different colors—like on this material." I smoothed my hands over the spread of my jacket in nostalgia. "You won't believe this either, but we have bright-colored sea creatures that even make their own fires—to light their way through a deep, dark world."

"You're making that up," Iwao said.

"Oh no, it's true. My father, when he was alive, showed this to me."

Later, I told him about Mama and Miyo. I even told him a little about Akira. "My best friend, a very nice boy, lived over the hill and . . ."

"He must be the father of your baby," Iwao said, knowingly.

"Who told you that?" I asked in a sharp tone.

"Sā-chan did, but I don't care."

Did Hamada-san reveal my innermost secret to Auntie who repeated it to Sā-chan? I felt betrayed and a surge of panic overcame me. I guessed then I couldn't trust anyone. Perhaps, inadvertently, Mama, in the early exchange of letters to her brother and sister-in-law, told them about Akira, in which case, what I thought had been a secret was no secret right from the start.

"But others care," I said to Iwao.

"They're just narrow-minded," Iwao said. "I'm different."

"That's because you don't know any better," Norio said from his corner.

I was startled by his remark that he was not sleeping but listening to us.

"I do, too. I'm not like you," Iwao said and kicked his brother.

From then on whenever I talked of Akira, Norio stirred under his futon, making exasperated sighs, sounding disgusted like his mother, and I dismissed his attitude as unimportant. After all, wasn't he still a schoolboy? Akira, the same age as Norio, was about to become a father, and perhaps this knowledge bothered Norio. Akira had already lived so much more in the few years of his life, whereas Norio had not begun to live at all. I felt sorry for him.

We were restless that night. I woke up feeling warm and felt an incredible pressure on my side. I thought something had gone wrong with the baby, but it was only Norio and Iwao who had migrated in their sleep in the cold, their dark heads pushed up against my belly. "Norio, Iwao. Hey, you're sleeping on my stomach!" I said and shook them both. Iwao groaned and rolled over to his place without opening his eyes. Norio, realizing what had happened, looked up at me sheepishly. He picked up his futon, wrapped the heavy covering around his body, and slunk away like a scolded animal.

I didn't go back to sleep right away. I heard an argument coming from somewhere, and I knew it was not between my uncle and auntie, who argued far less in their bedroom these days since the girls began sleeping with them. I strained to listen. The noise was coming from Hamada-san's house. I heard a dish break and what sounded like someone being thrown to the floor or against a wall. "Please, Otō-san," I heard Hamada-san plead, her voice high and trembly. A child began to cry. I wanted to go to her, *but did I really want to do this after feeling betrayed by her?* And what if I *did* go to her? What could I do? In the end, immobilized by a sudden silence that overcame the neighborhood and my indecision, I stayed beneath my futon.

"Did you hear the commotion last night?" Sā-chan said at breakfast.

"What you heard is none of your business," Shiichi Uncle said.

"She's only saying what everyone heard. It's nothing new," Harue Auntie said.

"Even so," Shiichi Uncle said. "Mind your own business."

After Shiichi Uncle left for work, Sā-chan followed me into the kitchen with her father's rice bowl and teacup. She said, "Hamada-san's husband is nothing but a common drunk who beats up his family. That's one reason

Okā-chan doesn't want you going over there. It makes us look bad. We should stay away from people like them."

One part of me said, *all the more—we should be Hamada-san's friends*, the other didn't want to care. I shoved my hands into the hot dishwater and, with extra vigor, scrubbed the tea stain that rimmed Uncle's cup.

For several days after that, I did not see Hamada-san. Her house was dark and quiet as if no one lived there. But she was once again her usual self when I next saw her. The argument with her husband must not have been too serious. She made no mention of it to me, and I did not ask, her face inscrutable to any suffering she may have undergone and, like most Japanese, holding on to the idea that no one should burden others unnecessarily. I also said nothing about Akira and that I suspected her of revealing my secret. With everything left unsaid and hidden, we went on as if nothing had happened, though now, we both had things to hide from each other, an underlying strain evident. The only thing I did was to promise myself never to tell her anything more about my life. I suspected that the conversations she frequently had with Harue Auntie over the bamboo fence between the gardens may have included mention of Akira. That made her dangerous in my eyes. While I had to be cautious, I concluded that I needed her company and friendship; she was still the closest—no, the only real friend I had in Japan. Nonetheless, the suspicions I had about her began spreading in me like unchecked fire.

I stuck close to home. I minded Yuki-chan during the day while others in the family went to work or school. With her strapped on my back, I tended the fires in the stove and brazier, cooked the rice gruel, patched the boys' pockets, darned the girls' socks, and waited in long lines for our rations of rice, vegetables, and fuel.

In the tedium of my chores, I often thought of Akira and home. "Do you think I should continue writing to my family back home even though no one answers me?" I asked Shiichi Uncle.

"I think you should keep trying. The government may lift their restrictions at any time. You never know about these things."

"It seems so useless. Everything I write comes back censored. Look at this!"

I showed Uncle how my letters came back, stamped with large red seals of authority and the disapproval of someone's emblem, the sanction of ivory chops, big red blocks of Chinese characters that I couldn't read or understand.

"That's terrible. You'd think personal letters like yours would go through. I guess there's no feeling when it's wartime," Shiichi Uncle said.

I cried each time a letter was returned. After a while, I stopped writing. If the Japanese government was strict about us writing overseas, I guessed that letters from Hawai'i never made it to me. Discouraged, I reasoned that if I were having a time writing letters home, Mama and Miyo must have been suffering the same ordeal. Maybe their situation was worse in that they didn't dare try.

One afternoon, I was in the living room seated on the floor, turning the uncooked rice over and over with my hand in a pot, picking weevils from the grain. Iwao was beside me on his stomach, reading a section of the *Asahi Shimbun* on the floor when Uncle and Auntie came home from work earlier than usual. Auntie put down her shopping bags in the kitchen and walked into the living area where we sat; Uncle also came to sit with us. Both my uncle and auntie took parts of the paper to read.

Illiterate in Japanese, I said to Iwao, "Please read me something. You can practice reading the Chinese characters."

"Sure," he said, and read me a couple of very short articles. "Wait, here's something interesting. Otō-san, if I come across a hard word, will you help me?" Uncle nodded. Iwao began reading an article, which stated that the U.S. government was rounding up the Japanese in America like cattle and horses and placing them into concentration camps. Uncle and Auntie lay down the sections they were reading to listen to Iwao.

"Why would the Americans do that?" he asked, when he was finished.

"I don't know," I said. *Oh, Mama, Miyo, Akira—what's happened to you?*

"I think the Americans are going to kill them all," Harue Auntie said.

"You be quiet," Shiichi Uncle snapped. "Are you crazy? What you say is extreme. It could be my sister you're talking about!" Auntie ignored him.

"Do you think the Americans would do that?" I asked.

"Nobody knows, Hi-chan. But this is war and . . ." He shrugged his shoulders. I began to weep softly. Iwao plucked on a loose string sticking out from the weave of the rush-mat flooring.

Irritated, Auntie said, "Iwao, stop that! And Hi-chan, don't be silly. Nothing's going to happen. So Hi-chan, isn't this when you would get up and run to Hamada-san's home, looking for consolation? What happened to your best friend? I don't see her around much. She's not good enough for you, too?"

"Shut up," Shiichi Uncle said to Harue Auntie, and to me, "Hi-chan, you mustn't let your spirits fall. Your mother wouldn't like that, and don't mind your auntie." He snuck an exasperated look at his wife.

I nodded, gathered my things, and went upstairs to my room. Iwao followed me up.

"I'm sorry," he said. "My mother doesn't always mean what she says."

"You don't have to apologize for her. Go on outside and play with your friends!"

11

Akira's Baby

In my fifth month, Akira's baby began fluttering in my stomach like the butterfly above my berth in the steamship to Japan. In my sixth month, Akira's baby began kicking my body, shaking me, as in the small earth tremors under the unsteady palm of the Kanto Plain.

"Come feel this, Iwao," I said to him from the kitchen when Akira's baby first began moving, Sā-chan and he studying on the small low table in the main room.

He came running over and put his hand on the shelf of my stomach. "Yaa!" he exclaimed. "It's a miracle."

"I was home from school first," Sā-chan said in a loud voice, her bottom lip protruding in a pout as she rushed into the kitchen. "Why didn't you call me to feel your stomach?"

"Here, feel it now. The baby's still moving."

"I don't want to anymore." She stamped her foot and walked out.

In the days that followed, Akira's baby began somersaulting in abandonment. Buoyed in its world of water, it stretched its arms and legs to grow. It tumbled in its confinement, awakening me to new and strange sensations in my body as it slid past different organs.

Many hands around the neighborhood reached out to touch my stomach for luck and to make guesses about the baby's sex. "A stomach rounded like a pumpkin means a boy," Hamada-san had said. These days when we did talk, it was focused on the mundane. "And a stomach more elongated, flat like a summer melon, means a girl."

But my stomach proved puzzling. Neither very rounded, nor wide and flat, it made the guessing harder. Small bets for matchsticks or incense sticks flourished in the neighborhood over what I carried. Hamada-san had cautioned earlier: "Don't let too many people touch your stomach. And watch their faces. A hard face can leave an angry spirit with you and the baby." I knew that what she had said was only a superstition, but I didn't give Harue Auntie any opportunity to touch my stomach for, deep in my subconscious, I must have associated her with a bad spirit.

I heard Harue Auntie complaining bitterly to my uncle about this. They may have been in their bedroom, but I could hear her low rumbling, clearly: "Hi-chan's mean. She won't let me touch her stomach."

"It's all in your head. Why don't you ask her?"

"Can't she offer?"

"You're being petty."

"Me, petty? What about her?"

"Yes, I see. You're both wrong. If my sister was around, she would know exactly how to handle you two!"

"You always talk as if your sister is better than me, and you're always on Hi-chan's side. I'm sick of your sister. I'm sick of Hi-chan. She's nothing but a troublemaker." Auntie's voice rose. "Can't anyone see it? You and Iwao are blind. My neighbors are blind. They all want to be in her good graces—even if she shuns them."

To my auntie, I was not a person of virtue. No matter what, though, I couldn't let her touch my stomach. I just couldn't.

In a surprise move, Norio came to talk to me one day after school. He was still dressed in his black school uniform, his overcoat draped over his arm, his other hand carrying a book satchel. A rare sun out, spring breaking through, I had been sitting on the steps by the kitchen door of the house, patching a hole in one of his shirts, my head down in concentration. Up to this time, Norio had rarely spoken to me, merely grunting at my presence or saying only what was necessary. This time, he took off his cap and gave me a big smile, his flat, slanted eyes sparkling in his strikingly smooth-skinned face. He was clearly trying to reach out to me and, after some hesitation, he said, "I wanted to ask you . . . um-ahhh, is it all right for me to touch your stomach?"

"Of course," I said, puzzled, placing my sewing to my side.

He was shy at first then slowly put a warm hand on my abdomen. While his touch was tentative and full of reserve, it grew firmer after a short while. "I think it's a girl," he announced, looking up and blinking his eyes in deliberation. "I'm sure of it."

Norio's gesture admittedly took me by surprise, but I saw that he just wanted us to be friends, and from that moment on, he seemed more relaxed in my presence. Perhaps it was Iwao's saying that he was narrow-minded. Perhaps it was his awareness that I was the one who ironed his shirts and pants and washed his socks, that I was the one who pickled the vegetables and went to the food depots so that he and his brother and sister didn't have to pick up our household rations.

"It will be good to have a new baby in the house," Norio said. "It will soften my mother. She likes babies, you know. And she's not as hard as you may think. I've watched her change over the years because of so much hardship."

His touching my stomach left a good, quiet spirit with me, and because of what he said and did, I resolved to be nicer to Auntie. That evening, while cooking beside her, she, fanning the fires and stirring the pots, I said, "Auntie, I want you to make a guess about my baby."

"Who do you think I am?" she turned and said, her eyes drilling a hole in me. "You let everyone touch your stomach. Only when you have no one else to play your silly games, you come to me. I wouldn't touch your stomach even if you paid me!" She lifted her head and one shoulder, dropped the chopsticks she was cooking with, and walked out.

Placing the food on serving dishes and leaving the kitchen-fire stool, I went to sit, away from the smoke and heat, on the bench by the preparation table in the crowded kitchen. Akira's baby tumbled in my stomach, as though some trauma had been passed on to it, and in reaction it made wide sweeps, pushing the curtain of my belly outward with its hands, leaning with its hip into my side, and somersaulting. It was in such a hurry to show itself, to be released, I thought. I wondered if Akira's baby sensed Harue Auntie's resentment or if it cried when it heard Auntie and Uncle's words of disagreement. I didn't know what was going to become of Akira's baby. This life was promising it so little. I had nothing much to give: no star, bird, flower, or hope.

Being pregnant did not stop me from trying to earn my keep, however. Skilled in starting my fires with the Boy Scout flint and steel (tools brought with me from Kaiwiki), I was able to save the six matches per person, per week, allowed by the government. Soon, I began teaching other women in the neighborhood how to use flint, which was abundant in the cutlery shops. I taught Hamada-san first, and she referred me to others.

Whenever I went out to help someone with her home fires, Harue Auntie wrinkled her nose as though she smelled something rotten and muttered, "A useless thing to do." But I kept my mouth shut and my appointments. Earned a few cents for this menial work.

Despite having distanced herself from me in the past, Toma-san asked Harue Auntie if I would teach her, her son's wife, and her mother-in-law how to save on fuel. Necessity triumphed over how they felt about my having ignored them earlier. That day, Harue Auntie made Sā-chan follow me for the afternoon appointment.

When we showed up at Toma-san's home, the three Toma women greeted Sā-chan first. Toma-san's daughter-in-law said, "It was nice of you to come and help, Sā-chan."

"Mmm," Sā-chan acknowledged, her lack of enthusiasm apparent. The Toma women looked at each other, discomfited by Sā-chan's curt reply.

When Toma-san greeted me, her in-laws, who were in the back of her, covered their mouths to giggle; they couldn't seem to help themselves and I tried to ignore them. "Come on in," Toma-san said. "It's been a long time."

The women looked embarrassed for me, perhaps because I was tall, gawky, unladylike, a girl waddling about with a fat stomach—a funny sort of Japanese—especially when I bowed before a totem of paper and sticks that I had made and brought with me in respect to the god of the hearth and fire. I had seen those looks made by other women I had taught.

Back home, while growing up, I never paid much attention to the pine and bamboo Mama put up around the house for good luck or the porcelain earth-gods on the shelf or by the doorway, but now paying them respect began to matter. Maybe it was the new life in me that made me more respectful of the earth-gods. Maybe it was a growing awareness of how vulnerable life could be. Whatever it was, before my lessons on fire, I paid my ritual respect to the household god of fire in order to shake loose the disagreeable and disabling spirits. To send them on their way. I offered them oranges and dumplings; I lit beeswax candles; I clapped my hands three times in obeisance. Houses were filled with spirits and I wasn't taking any chances. I remembered Mama warning me before I left: "Be humble in front of fire. Don't play with it. Find good uses for it. If you aren't careful, something can happen to the baby."

Sā-chan fidgeted throughout the long lesson, while the women and I giggled at their attempts at striking the steel and flint to produce sparks, and later to get the kindling going through our shared exhalations. *Wheow, wheow, wheow.* We did this over and over again. "Go on, go on," I encouraged, despite the looks of disgust Sā-chan gave us; bored, Sā-chan did not join in the laughter but continually rolled her eyes at the women's timidity.

Nonetheless, the women worked until they were successful. Once started, the fires danced on the women's faces in generous ways, smoothing away some of the strain and trepidation inserted into their lives by the war. I deliberately prolonged my stay and watched with glee Sā-chan's face grow impatient; I knew I was wrong, but I enjoyed frustrating her.

As we were leaving, the women gave me a small gratuity that I refused sufficiently in feigned attempts: "Oh, you shouldn't have . . ."

"No, no, take this" attempts on their part, and again the "I'm humbled" and "You're too kind" comments on mine, before I took the money that came with a thousand bows, this interaction making it more palatable in accepting the money. This was all a shibai—an act, a lie—when what I really wanted to do was to take the money and run.

Once outside, Sā-chan said, "Okay, hand it over." I stared at her but said nothing.

She went on. "From now on, Okā-chan wants to make sure that all of it goes to her. You can't keep anything for yourself."

"I've always given your mother more than half of what I earn."

"Okā-chan wants it *all*. She will give what you need. C'mon, hand it over."

"I'll give the money directly to your mother, not you."

"Do what you like, but don't blame me if you get scolded for not do-ing what I say."

"All right!" I said. "You want the money? Go on, take it!" In the same instant that I threw the envelope at her, a wave of guilt about Miyo's money swept over me. It was a different matter, I tried to rationalize, which, deep down inside of me I knew wasn't true.

"You just wait. I'm going to tell my mother." She threw the envelope back at me and ran into the house.

I tucked the money into my kimono sleeve and hurried after her but was stopped short by Harue Auntie who stood just past the entryway with her hand out. Not an inch submissive, I straightened my back and looked right at her. I fumbled for the envelope from deep within my sleeve and handed it over. She quickly checked to see if the seal on the envelope was broken and, when satisfied that it was not, that I had not taken any of the money, she said, "Help with dinner," and turned away.

I wrapped my arm around my stomach to shield it.

12

Languages

Our rice bag grew lighter with each passing week, although I was earning and conserving as much as I could. Our rations had been cut so gradually, such that no one noticed it, but soon we were down to two meals a day. Because we had growing children to feed, I stretched what little we had. I thought of Mama often those days, how the color of her face had changed when Papa died—remembered that her eyes were constantly rimmed with tears, as she agonized over what little she had to feed us. I realized it was crucial for me to learn to speak better Japanese in order to obtain more food; I had to be able to bargain like a Portuguese fish woman back in Hilo.

I seriously began to listen to how people talked to each other. It was easy to see that the Japanese I spoke slipped crookedly down my tongue, shamelessly American, the words slithering out of my mouth like Hama-matsu eels. No wonder people found me weird. Without knowing, I was speaking to both men and women in unacceptable ways: *Oi, mizu kure*. "Hey you, give me water." And because I didn't know any better, my tone made me sound crude, impolite, someone of low status.

When I told Hamada-san about my difficulties, she loaned me some of her children's books. But they were difficult for me, I, a slow learner of the Japanese ideograms. I studied them between my work and at night before going to bed and even approached Sā-chan for help. She was the only one in the family who seemed to have time on her hands, Iwao and Norio having chores of their own to do, but she said, "I'm too busy. Ask Iwao. He has nothing to do." I should have known better than to ask. I soon found, however, that I could learn by listening to people talk and, as it turned out, pressured by necessity, I quickly mastered the spoken language, though remained slow in reading and writing it. After a few humbling weeks, I was able to use the proper honorifics and became proficient at switching from high to low language; I learned the necessary idioms, words of demand, and the inflections found. The *o* of effacement. Without these renewed skills, I could have starved the members in our family to death; they depended on me, and I couldn't let them down.

Although Harue Auntie poked fun at me when I first started going out for food at the depots, saying, "Because you don't know how to bargain well, you're no help to us," her taunting stopped, having recognized that I had learned how to barter, as well as anyone, with the merchants and street-side vendors.

Shoyu kure! or "Give me some of your soy sauce!" turned into "May I have some of this soy sauce, please?" on one of the first days I ventured using the more polite language I had learned, the shoyu vendor whom I had patronized regularly giving me a broad smile.

"Oh, yes!" she said.

"How much is it?" Before this, when thinking in English and repeating it in non-standard Japanese, I would probably have said *Ikura?* or "How much?" and sounded offensive.

"It is thirty sen."

Totemo takai desu neh? "That's a bit expensive, isn't it?" I said, no longer reverting to "Expensive, eh?" my old way of speaking.

Now, the soy sauce shopkeeper and I were able to barter like regular people. I bought the gallon of soy sauce for twenty sen that day, the vendor nodding, smiling, and encouraging me through our exchange.

I learned to work with the best of the vendors. I still dropped an occasional "yeah" here and there in my speech, but they seemed to disregard it as a peculiar habit.

Watching me learn Japanese, Norio said to me one day: "Please teach me English." Back home Mama had indicated that he was terribly bright and serious, and I recalled her saying something about him wanting to go

97

to the university to study math and other languages.

Each day after his request, I gave him a word to practice before he went to work at his school-turned-wartime-factory. "Norio, today the word is train."

"Tsu-rain."

"No, Norio. It's chu-rain, chu-rain. Train."

"Chuu-rain. Chuu-rain. Chuu-rain."

"That's better."

Norio practiced the sounds and repeated the words I gave him in a loud eager voice that became a pitch higher in his excitement to learn. These lessons kept me in touch with my first language and home, just as they, I suppose, kept Norio's mind off his hunger. Naturally, Harue Auntie disapproved of our arrangement and scolded Norio: "English is the enemy's language—for sissies. I don't want you using or learning English in this house. This is Japan, not America."

In response, hiding in our bedroom before school, I began giving Norio two words a day, even three. "Norio, today, the words are tree, sun, flower. You hear? Tree, sun, flower!" And off he went repeating the words: "tsu-ree, sun-u, frower."

By this time, my auntie and I were too tangled in each other's im-placable pride for me to care. I wished she would just leave me alone and that I could leave her alone, but the house was too small for us to coexist comfortably. Our bad feelings vibrated in the very house boards.

One morning, Sā-chan came around the corner to the bedroom where Norio and I were seated. "Ha, caught you," she said. "You wait and see. I'm going to tell Okā-chan."

"Don't you dare," Norio said, reaching out to grab her. He missed her sweater.

"Who's going to stop me?"

"You'd better go to school," I told Norio. I quickly hid the tablet of words I'd been using, but was too late. Harue Auntie, who had gone out earlier in the morning, stepped back into the house, probably having forgotten something, which was not unusual for her. As soon as she came in, I heard Sā-chan running up to her and tattling on us.

"Okā-chan, Hi-chan is still teaching Norio English. I was going to tell you tonight, but I'm glad you're here."

Harue Auntie came upstairs and all puffed up she said, "What did I tell you before?" She threw her clutch bag at me. "Not in this house!"

While only a year separated Sā-chan and me, she seemed so much younger. She was also obsessive about her looks. She studied her features in the mirror every day, admiring the many pouts and smiles she created, and moved her head from side to side like a flower swaying in the wind. Watching Sā-chan doing this in the mirror down the hallway, I had to admit, I must have been insufferable back home when I did the same thing in front of Miyo.

In my own childish way, I complained about Sā-chan to Hamada-san, who knew how much I hated my cousin's enviable position. I also no longer cared if Hamada-san repeated what I said to my auntie. After having told Hamada-san about Akira, I had no more secrets worth keeping. Regardless of our own situation, regardless of the tension between us, Hamada-san and I kept in contact and she kept reminding me, "You just can't compete with the daughter of the house."

"I know I can't . . . but she's nasty."

"You have to be mindful of yourself, not drag yourself down," she said. "You have a baby coming; you can't be a baby yourself."

Over time, it was because I had so little control over Sā-chan and my auntie, and everything else around me, that Mama's animistic as well as her Buddhist rituals, something I had ignored back home, became of greater solace. Every morning, to maintain some kind of balance for myself, I thanked all the earth-gods—of the water, trees, mountains, and seas. I clapped my hands three times to call them. I thanked the earth and household spirits; I bowed to the altar guardians; I kept the ancestral candles lit beside the mortuary tablets for all the souls who had come and departed and for those who would reappear. I asked that everyone on both sides of the Pacific Ocean, living or dead, be well. I asked for what was lacking inside of me: compassion and moral growth, better self-awareness, and deeper understanding of Sā-chan and Harue Auntie.

13

Sumie

Cold rains of March and April 1942, and we entered some of the bleakest days of our humdrum existence, days when cracked skin drew closer to our bones and fire was the only cheerful thing, as it danced on our walls. On fair days, once released from my chores, I played outside in the alleyway in front of our home with my cousins and the other children in the neighborhood.

While still joined to me, I wanted Akira's baby to hear songs, the shouts of children, the words of poems. Through me, I wanted my baby to feel a lightness of spirit, for already there had been too many rivers of tears flowing through my womb. Akira's baby knew sorrow more than it knew joy, and knowing that, I struggled for happiness, this baby making me look at things differently in my life; I saw that I couldn't only think about myself, but of the baby and others as well. Thinking about others remained challenging.

The war continued. I knew little about what was going on. I couldn't read the newspapers and was too busy to be overly concerned. We were far away from areas of actual conflict, and I didn't know enough to ask about the war. Uncle or Norio also had little time to explain the war to me. The only connection to the war happened when, for two days a week beginning that April, Harue Auntie began volunteering her services at a Japanese Imperial Army Hospital nearby.

In discussing Harue Auntie's work, Hamada-san said, "I hear she's very successful in dragging many of the wounded soldiers out of their gloom, men who've been to Manchuria, China, and French Indochina, men who bang their heads against the walls or look out from the windows day after day, men who scream in their sleep, seeing nothing but the terrible things that they did or what had gone on."

"What did the soldiers do? How does she fix that?" I asked, curious to know what good my auntie was ever capable of doing.

"I don't know—but it must be something so terrible that they can't forget," Hamada-san said.

The raw iciness continued into early May. Fresh food was scarce because of the prolonged cold, everything we ate pickled and salty. One evening, when everyone was home, I surprised the family with fresh-roasted chestnuts. As soon as I brought them out from the kitchen after dinner, the children plunged their hands into the large hot bowl, quickly retrieved a nut, and blew into their hands to cool it.

"Hi-chan, give some to Yuki-chan," Harue Auntie ordered. "See if she likes it." I shred the casing of the nut with my teeth, broke off a small section, and gave it to Yuki-chan, who was sitting on my lap. She chewed the meat of the nut several times and swallowed it.

"Please, more," she said, lifting one hand out.

I took another piece and gave it to her. This time, to my amazement, she chewed it but once, then swallowed the whole thing, which immediately caused her to choke.

"Look what you did," Auntie said, rushing over to us. She snatched Yuki-chan away and began patting her back in a flurry. Yuki-chan quickly coughed up the piece.

"You gave her too big a piece. Look at it. What kind of mother are you going to be?" she said as she thrust the regurgitated piece of chestnut into my face.

"I didn't . . . it wasn't," I said and suddenly doubled over. A wave of pain washed through my body. I was in labor.

"You're too young to be having a baby, your hips still young-girl narrow," the midwife said. "I'm not going to lie to you. It's not going to be easy."

I shut my eyes tightly and held my breath in the unbearable pain of the contractions. The mid-wife's challenge? Turn the baby around that was trying to come down feet first. "But don't worry, trust me," she said. "You'll be just fine, I've done this before. Your baby's trying to come out feet first, because it wants to walk." I smiled feebly at her attempt at humor.

I thrashed on the floor in pain. "Akiraaa!" I called out in anguish, Mama not having prepared me for the pain's intensity. I felt as if I were burning inside, once more feeling the heat of the cane fire back home.

Harue Auntie, who wove in and out of the room with this and that the midwife requested—more blankets, more towels, more water, more petroleum oil—was not the least bit sympathetic, upset that everyone had to sleep that night in her already crowded bedroom because of my labor. Watching her aggrieved face, all I wanted was for her to disappear, leave the midwife and me alone.

I did not want my auntie to see me at my weakest. I didn't want her to see the shield of my hair or the baby's crowning. But she came into the room anyway, curious to see my sex, curious to see me at my most vulnerable. Maybe then I wouldn't seem so frustrating to her, and my beautiful mother, whom Shiichi Uncle talked so much about, wouldn't seem so mysterious. Every time I shifted position, she craned her neck and moved in closer. Once, when I moaned loudly, she said, "Be quiet. Hold back. Japanese women don't cry out for little things like this!"

That was all I needed to hear. From then on I did not make a sound. I refused to moan even when the midwife pressed on my stomach. Instead, I gripped the futon until it slipped from my hands and my nails dug into my palm. *Akira, Akira, Akira,* I chanted to myself, his name a lifeline to hold on to and lead me through this birthing.

My labor dragged on. "I think I have to call a doctor," the midwife finally said to my uncle and auntie.

Harue Auntie's eyes narrowed. "Why? What for? We've all gone through this without trouble. It costs money to call a doctor. A doctor, indeed! This girl's nothing but a weakling."

"Hush, woman, don't say things like that. It's bad luck," Shiichi Uncle warned.

"Bachi? I don't care. Send Hi-chan to the orphanage. That way, we wouldn't have to care about her."

"You'd better care! She's part of the family, my sister's daughter."

"Oh yes, your *sister's* daughter!"

"How dare you! You don't just throw people out because it suits you, understand? If we throw her out now, we'll suffer the fate of the Hungry Ghost. You'll send us straight to the fires of hell—all because of your hard heart!" Shiichi Uncle said, reminding my auntie of her afterlife while he argued for me.

I didn't believe my auntie was afraid of anything except this, her own salvation. At whatever cost, she had to take care of her chopsticks and rice bowl. Having been reminded that her rice bowl could burn for eternity did not sit well with her and made her desist.

I was lucky to have Shiichi Uncle at home that day to help in my defense. Though he tried to intervene in our spats, he was often working and away, the few times he was around he did what he could to create harmony. Too, I was beginning to understand my uncle and auntie's relationship better. On things Shiichi Uncle felt very strongly about, his *was* the final voice of order in the household. He put on his coat to go out and call the doctor.

"Wait," the mid-wife said. "Before you call the doctor, let me try again."

With her help pushing the baby out, I struggled through the startling throes of the end of labor, Akira's baby sliding into this world in the heat of Uncle's and Auntie's voices. I named her Sumie.

After giving birth, my body refused to produce milk; I blamed that on having had very little to eat for so many months. Sumie had sucked me dry even before her birth, eaten my flesh from the inside out like a fig grub. By the time she was born, my body had nothing left to give. Even so, she sucked my nipples, hard, trying to draw a little nourishment. A brown substance appeared at first, but it was a useless trickle. When sucking, Sumie grumbled over my nipples. "Mmm, mmm," she murmured, then letting go of my nipple in a snap, she threw back her head and cried in lusty howls; frustrated in these early and futile attempts, she fell into periods of restless sleep. In my lack of experience, I knew little of what was happening to my body. I could only hold Sumie close to me and rock her. Ease our pain.

Waaaa! Hungry, she woke up and wailed like a child left in the cane fields to die. She nuzzled my body like a blind, hairless, pink, cane field rat, poking its nose into the ground, mouth wide open. Agitated, she slid her body up and down against mine, her strength a miracle, for hunger does strange things to people, even babies.

"Here, eat this," said Shiichi Uncle, who brought hidden morsels of food for me in the sleeves of his old haori, the coat he wore over his work clothes to keep warm. He wanted me to gain strength. "Have some chick-peas, rice cakes, dried persimmons, pieces of bread." He spilled them out as if by magic into my waiting hands.

"Thank you," I said, faintly.

Desperately hungry, I gobbled the food, while Shiichi Uncle picked up the yowling Sumie and rocked her in his arms. "Yoshi, yoshi," he said to console her. Those first few days, as she began losing weight and power in her voice, he sang songs to her.

Hello, hello my turtle . . . "You can't give up now, understand?" . . . *In this wide world, your home* . . . "Your life is the most precious thing, hold on to it. You can't die on us—after all, it took you this long to swim to us." . . . *At least you* . . . "Hang on, you understand?" . . . *So why are you so slow?*" At every chance, he sang and talked between the sag and lift of his rocking. To test Sumie's grasp, he wove his little finger into her fist. "That's the way. You'll survive," he said, his eyes a shattered glass of tears.

By turns, Norio and Iwao came upstairs to talk to Sumie, to push her along in this life by the flow of their voices, the living stream of their strength and breath. More curious than sympathetic, Sā-chan came along with her brothers, once, to see what was going on with the baby. "Look at her," she laughed. "She looks like toothless old Mihata-san down the street. How come you don't have any milk, Hi-chan?" Oddly, her words did not have the usual bite; she seemed curiously deflated, puzzled, perhaps, by this new life.

"We don't want to have to pray at the shrine for children," Iwao said to Sumie, ignoring Sā-chan. "We never needed a Jizo Bodhisattva before. We don't want you to be the first."

"Don't say such things," Norio snapped.

However poorly phrased, Iwao's sentiment came from the right place, and I could not fault him. No one wanted to pour water over the guardian of children to pay their respects to my dead child or to have to clothe the Jizo's statue with a red apron, Sumie's name sewn on it.

"Well, I for one can't see why people keep bringing her beautiful little things. Look at all the socks, mitts, shirts they make for her," Sā-chan said.

"Is that all you care about?" Norio asked. "Gifts? Go away. Don't talk like this in front of Hi-chan. You're my sister but I don't want to look at you."

"I'm going to tell Okā-chan how you talk to me."

"Go ahead," Norio said with disgust.

"Don't mind her," Norio said, after Sā-chan left. "She's just jealous because you have all the attention and gifts from people in the neighborhood. You know how she is. She wishes they were for her."

A thin film soon clouded Sumie's eyes and filled me with panic. I thought I was going to lose my mind in watching her grope as she tried to see through the shadows around her. It was as if she wanted to know who brought her into this world to suffer. *Who are you?* her eyes seemed to ask. *Why have you exposed me to all this hunger and pain?* She sucked my dried-up breasts with a vengeance until they were raw.

Hungry, always hungry, she took to rubbing her gums with her fist and gnawing on her knuckles until they cracked open. Soon she began sucking her own flesh. With almost no patience left, she waited for a stream of nourishment to come. Waited to pounce on my nipples like a starving animal. But nothing happened, nothing helped, and having grown useless, my breasts, instead of swelling with milk, flattened like rice paddies. Sumie flailed her fists on my body and wailed in painful hunger.

On one of his visits to my room, Iwao asked, "Why did you name her Sumie?"

"I gave her that name because . . ." And while Iwao waited for me to go on, I couldn't explain any further. I wanted to say that I had named her Sumie because she was going to be the last, my one and only child. To end having any more children or sumu, as in the name Sumie, had been my idea. I never thought that she might die.

In her third day of existence, Sumie's stomach grew hot. It bloated like water-soaked beans as I waited for my milk to appear. Weak now, she could only whimper and stretch her mouth in yawns. I passed water from my mouth to hers and let her suck on my tongue.

"We have to help Hi-chan," my uncle said to Harue Auntie. "We can't let this child die."

"But we have no money for milk!"

When Hamada-san did not come to see me and Sumie, I had assumed that she had been through another episode with her husband. I had not seen her since before giving birth, so I hadn't expected her at all when four days later, she finally appeared. By this time, Sumie was listless and not very responsive. Hamada-san herself looked pale and unwell. "I'm sorry. I would have come sooner, but . . ." She gave a long drawn-out sigh, shrugged her shoulders, and looked at me with a line of pain etched between her eyes.

"It's okay," I said, noticing a faint yet unmistakably yellowish discoloration under her right eye. Relieved to see her and, because of past patterns, quickly forgetting that she might have had problems of her own and a need to unburden herself, I blurted instead: "Hamada-san, can you help me? I need milk for my baby. My body isn't making any."

"Saa . . . let me see . . . I do know someone who may be able to help you . . ." was all she said, her visit short. Later that day, she sent me a note with a name to contact. Through Hamada-san I found Kato-san, who lived around the dense block of our neighborhood.

"Look at me, I'm a cow," Kato-san said, laughing like a deva, a heavenly being, when I brought Sumie over to see her. "I have lots of milk for Japan's children. See how full my breasts are? Yes, this is my contribution. The government wants us to have many children, so I'm having lots of them. Besides, they increase my rations every time I get pregnant."

I circled Kato-san with my limp, yarn doll of a daughter in my arms. She peered at Sumie and said, "She's too young to be so skinny, dried up, and wrinkled like an old woman. Look at this poor thing. But don't worry, give her to me." Happily, I handed Sumie over. "Here, let me feed you," Kato-san said, as she plopped her nipple out of her kimono and into Sumie's oval, receptive mouth. Sumie clamped the nipple with her lips. She gulped down the milk between large, exhausted gasps, and drank in long, cheeks-pulled-inward sucks.

I had found my milk bodhisattva. Thankful, I gave Kato-san a gold locket and tortoise-shell comb, gifts to me from Mama when I left home, and a cowrie shell Papa had found on the seashore when I was a little girl. Shiichi Uncle supplemented my tokens of appreciation with a small fee. Kato-san fed Sumie well, and in a few days her sallow color turned pink and her stool changed from hard, dark-brown pebbles into feces that were coiled and golden. Sweet smelling. For once I could gloat; I had done something without Harue Auntie's help. She tried to avoid me during this period by slipping into her room after coming home from work, but I made sure that she heard my clucking over Sumie's cooing sounds, made sure Sumie's happiness radiated to every corner of the house and every quarter of the neighborhood. I wanted to make it clear in Harue Auntie's mind that I would be a good mother.

As Sumie grew stronger, I felt myself growing weaker, until one day, I couldn't stand without feeling faint. I could barely take Sumie to Kato-san's to be fed or wash her diapers for the day. "Where's your fire, Hi-chan?" Harue Auntie jeered whenever she came into my room to see why I wasn't downstairs to start up the breakfast or do the laundry.

"Leave the girl alone," I heard my uncle say. "You don't know what's wrong."

"She's just lazy, doesn't want to work. 'Not feeling well.' 'Can't eat.' 'Must lie down.' All these excuses, every time, every day." She sounded like Miyo.

During my pregnancy, I had given a share of my food to Norio and Iwao, whose rib cages began showing. To Yuki-chan, who lost the color of her rose-spun cheeks and some of her hair, I had given my share of beans. I had eaten too many sunshine meals of rice with their red plums stuck in the center resembling the Japanese flag—a diet lacking nourishment, and now, I couldn't get up. Every time I tried, I would wobble then fall over, as if someone had taken a machete and whipped it across my legs to cut me down. I finally lay sprawled on the floor like a bunraku puppet.

Not long after hearing Harue Auntie grumble, I heard a shuffling of feet and Iwao running from the house, my cousin answering with a snappy "hai" to meet some request made by his father. Harue Auntie slid a shoji door shut with an angry bang and the whole house shook.

Shiichi Uncle had gone ahead and sent Iwao to fetch one of the few doctors in the area, the war having taken most of them to other countries. At the same time, Sā-chan came upstairs to my room with a long face because she had been ordered by her father to take Sumie over to Kato-san's to be fed. "Here, hand me your crybaby," she said, avoiding my eyes.

The doctor finally arrived and my auntie paced up and down before the latticed door of my room, her feet dragging on the straw mat in a rushing sound while the doctor examined me. He finally slid open the shoji and popped his head out to announce his diagnosis to the rest of the family. "Hi-chan has beriberi!" His tone was grave.

"Beriberi!" Harue Auntie said, opening the shoji to my room wider. I then heard her following the doctor down the stairs, her body a stream, a constant flow of questions directed at him: "Tell me, where do you think we're going to get the money for her medicines? Who's going to take care of her? Who's going to do the shopping?"

"She's a very sick young woman," the doctor said. "You must do your best." I heard the front door close, his quickly retreating steps sounding relieved.

With me ill, Harue Auntie could no longer go to work. Every day that she was home, I sensed in her the rage of a caged animal. With the two of us alone in the house she came dashing into my room one morning. "Get out of my house," she said. "You're good for nothing."

"What did you say?" She had aroused me from sleep.

With no one to stop her, no doctor or husband or children in the house to keep decorum, I knew she felt free to scream at me. "Weak and useless, from the first time I laid eyes on you, I knew it would end up like this. Take your crybaby and get out of here. You can't work. You can't do anything. What do you think this is, eh, charity?"

"Please, Auntie. I can't help being sick," I said. I patted Sumie's back to reassure her when she began whimpering because of Harue Auntie's angry tone. Seeing Sumie settled, I covered my ears and shielded my face from my auntie's words that stung it in the wrath of bees.

Harue Auntie ripped off my futon. My hands scrambled after it, as she flipped it aside. She moved toward it before I could get to it and flung it even farther from me. I wrapped my body with my arms as if I were naked and totally exposed, totally vulnerable.

"Why are you doing this?" I asked, shielding Sumie with my body.

"*Why?* Because you've been nothing but trouble."

Grabbing both of my wrists, she tried to drag me out of the room. I imagined myself being hauled away in the same way that Papa and Akira's father in Kaiwiki had hauled out the wild mountain pig they had killed in the rainforest. But I must have been heavier than she realized. She tugged at my body but could not move me very far.

Huffing between pulls she said, "You've ruined everything. You're no help. We only spend money on you. Where's the food money your mother was supposed to send? Where's the needed clothing? My children get skinny. Yuki-chan's losing her hair, Iwao, his teeth. All because of you. It's maddening. Get out of here. I want you *gone*." She pummeled my curled body with her fists.

I then heard someone running up steps to the second floor. It was Norio. "Okā, stop it. Don't do this!" he shouted.

Harue Auntie lifted her head, whirled around, and threw up her hands. She glared at Norio and stormed out of the room.

"Thank you," I said in tears to Norio.

"Don't thank me," he said, heaving, his words clipped by the shears of frustration and anger. "You must excuse my mother. She has a lot on her mind."

After a long pause—as if we both had to let out all the air we had been holding—I ventured to say, "Aren't you home early from school?"

"My instructor asked me to deliver some papers for him, so I thought to drop by."

Just then, Harue Auntie banged her broomstick onto the ceiling below my bedding. "Go ahead," she screamed. "Tell Norio everything. Make me look bad."

Norio ran downstairs. "Just stop it, okay? You have no right to treat her this way," he said, with his father's sternness and sense of fairness. I imagined them both breathing hard, staring at each other in the ominous silence that followed.

Not long after I became ill, I heard Uncle say to Sā-chan in their bedroom. "You can't go to school anymore."

"But why?" Her voice was sharp with disbelief.

"Hi-chan's sick, your mother has to work, and this is wartime. We must give what we can to the soldiers fighting for us. This is one way you can help, understand?"

"Well, I just don't understand. I don't know why we have to sacrifice so much." Her voice began to tremble. "It's not fair. Why can't Norio quit, or Iwao?"

I lay in my room and held Sumie close to me.

Later I heard Harue Auntie going after Shiichi Uncle. "The children must stay in school," she shouted. "I don't want them to be like us—nothing but factory workers or farmers. And why should Sā-chan work so hard on account of Hi-chan?"

"If you can figure out a better way, we will discuss it," Uncle said coldly and left the house.

From then on Sā-chan went out to pick up the rations, minded Yuki-chan, took Sumie to be fed by Kato-san, and ran the family errands so that my auntie could return to work. From the upstairs window, on days I could get to it, I saw her carrying her sister or Sumie, plus the wood, plus the rations, to and from the house. Sā-chan's expression was shuttered, devoid of emotion whenever she came into my room to pick up Sumie and take her to Kato-san's to be fed. I didn't blame her for being angry; in her position, I probably would have reacted the same.

Sā-chan said one day, "You're lucky you got sick. Now you don't have to do anything. Papa even put in a special tub for you to bathe. But you can't have something for nothing because things don't work that way. What if I said I'm not going to take Sumie to Kato-san's unless you give me something of yours. What are you going to do?"

"I guess I would have to give you something, wouldn't I?" Sumie had to be fed after all, so that day, without hesitation, I gave Sā-chan my rancid red lipstick.

The next day, Sā-chan extended her hands, one lapped over the other. "C'mon" was all that she said.

"Take my nail polish, then."

This extortion continued until I had only my teru bōzu left. "I can't give you this doll. It's Sumie's," I said. It was my only reminder of Akira. "Looks like I have nothing left."

"Oh yes, you do. What about your watch? I don't have one, and I need one since I'm the one who's working."

I had forgotten about my watch. From what was by now a very skinny wrist, I reluctantly removed the beautiful silver Bulova, which once belonged to Miyo who had given it to me as a going-away present. She had worked hard for it as an investment of time, restocking the shelves, mopping the floors, attending customers, and helping Mama at Wainaku Store. Angered by her nerve, I dropped it into Sā-chan's cupped hands.

"Thank you," she said. She snapped the watch on her wrist and extended her arm to admire it. "It looks nice, doesn't it?"

"If you say so," I said, between clenched teeth. *Whatever you think, it's still mine; you stole what really belongs to me!*

Spinning on her heels in renewed happiness, Sā-chan went off to do her chores.

14

Starving

Not long after Sā-chan was forced to leave school, Norio decided to quit. He had not been attending many classes after his school had been converted to a brass and pipe-fitting factory where he worked part-time. "You shouldn't quit school," I told him when he announced what he had done. "What about your dreams of becoming a math or language professor?"

"I can do that later. Right now, I need to help Sā-chan and Mama. You too. I told Naito-san, the headmaster, about our predicament, and he agrees with me. When you get better, I'll go back to school. I promise."

"No, you have to go back to school *now*," I said. "I *am* better. My legs are coming back to me. I'm crawling, already, see?" I made a shaky attempt to crawl from my bed to the sliding door. Norio watched me with amusement. "You're moving like a caterpillar," he said. "Don't worry, I can go to night school. Lots of my friends do that. Besides, your getting well isn't going to take that long."

Shiichi Uncle and Harue Auntie continued their work at the government factory. For the rest of us, our job was to make sure we had food to eat. Every morning from then on, whenever I felt reasonably well, Norio wheeled me around the food depots in a pushcart, a wheelbarrow-like contraption that he and my uncle built to carry our goods and me. Norio strapped Sumie upon his back after her morning feeding at Kato-san's, and Sā-chan carried Yuki-chan on hers.

"I don't want to go," Sā-chan said every day that we went out.

"You have to!" Norio said.

"I hate this, and I hate you!" she said to Norio, tossing her head back to let her hair fly up, as if she were above this effort.

At the ration counters in our neighborhood, we stood in long lines to wait our turn. Sometimes, I would see Hamada-san, and while she politely nodded at us, she did not stop to talk. I could see the struggle in her face.

In a small reprieve because of my condition, the doctor's prescription brought us extra food rations. This small blessing softened Harue Auntie's temper; it made up for what she spent on my vitamin B injections. It also made Sā-chan happier. She was able to coax a few sen from her mother and buy the neck scarf or hairclip that she had been wanting.

Nineteen forty-two had gone by swiftly with Sumie's birth and my illness. The spring of 1943 started out slowly with many of the cherry trees dying as people stripped the bark for tea and something to eat, but once the trees that were left untouched began to bloom, they budded fiercely as if to compensate for those that had been violated.

Norio, Sā-chan, and I made a good team looking for extra food, especially since I was getting stronger. Although Sā-chan continued to grumble, she knew she couldn't get away with it, Norio quick to put her in her place. When Norio and Sā-chan got tired of carrying the children—Sumie about nine months old at this time, Yuki-chan almost two—they sat with me in the crowded cart, unmindful of splinters and nail heads under the mat. They were extremely obedient and rarely fussed, as though they understood the seriousness of what we were doing. Occasionally, Sā-chan would run off by herself on some indulgence, but those carefree moments became fewer and fewer as time went by.

As with most people, the search for food and money-raising schemes became our main preoccupations. At the ration depots, we piled staples into the cart—wrinkled eggplants, squishy tomatoes, small skulls of head cabbage, crooked radishes, chunks of pumpkins, ten cups of rice, later, down to seven for the week—for *all* of us. As the war progressed, rice and meat became scarcer, and the ration stations carried little. Japan's cupboards were bare. Together with thousands of other citizens, we roamed the streets like a pack of ancient hunters, searching for things to sell. Norio, Sā-chan, and I (even Iwao when not in school) learned to bark like the other black marketers. "Come on over, see what we have," Norio called out, yelling out prices for my collection of matchsticks and cigarettes in order to buy a potato here or a radish there, a fish or two.

Those days we would cross Etai Bridge that spanned the Sumida River and travel as far as Asakusa where the black market flourished. Pushing and shoving our way between people and stalls, we sold high, we bought high.

In the late afternoons, as we hurried home after our tasks, rays of light filtered through a dusky sky, hazy with smoke and dust. The sky had an otherworldly pinkish afterglow of celestial fire as we wove in and out of the streets among the shops and buildings, temples, shrines, and houses. The soft ripple of twilight and deepening shadows cooled our faces and tired feet, and we were suddenly transformed, as if our silhouettes had suddenly risen out of the history of the place, its ancestral tombs, promises, songs, and chants. I imagined that we looked resolved and ancient as our ancestors as we moved across the city, over the bridges with the wind-shimmering water below us in the rivers, the reed grasses swaying. Our broken-down grocery cart, lopsided and shabby, became my black-lacquered palanquin, the babies my dark-haired mascots, the older children my loyal retainers who ran alongside me as my guards.

And I became a court lady in red. Straight-backed and lean, my guards marched with their spear-stick legs pumping high as they led the way into the Eastern capital, banners fluttering in the wind. Ripples of intrigue, the music of lutes, the recitation of poems, the call of courtesans, the blaze of torches, and the men of the court accompanied my daydreaming. Our spirits had been lifted, our heartbeats as if from another world, and we were transported.

I knew I was dreaming those days, but it took me away from Sā-chan's pouty face and constant groans, away from the worry over the children's health and my illness, away from Harue Auntie's recriminations, and it blunted my despair over the growing distance from home, the light of it flickering, close to disappearing.

Putting our rations of briquettes up for money, we gathered pinecones in the park for our home fuel. At night, Norio and Iwao went around scraping the cement walls and the crook of trees filled with nightingale droppings, a natural urea whitener for women to use for their makeup. One day feeling an unfamiliar surge of strength, I strapped Sumie on my back and went to a small temple park with Sā-chan to gather the pods of honey-locust trees to mix with lye for washing clothes. When we found some bran meal in a bag on the side of the street, near the remains of a house that had been partially razed, I wondered out loud, "Now what can we do with this?"

"You can do a lot," Sā-chan said. "Follow me."

We moved through a maze of dark alleyways. Like us, everyone walked quickly, their heads down. I had not been in that section of Mukōjima before and nervously looked up and down the path we were on. "Shhh. Be quiet. Make sure Sumie doesn't cry." Sā-chan pushed open a gate. "Quick, come in. Close the gate behind you."

"What are you doing?"

"Be quiet I said! You want to get us arrested?"

Sā-chan slid the front door open and bounded up the stairs. I followed slowly, clinging to the banister, the full moon shining through the slats of the house and showing our way. Sā-chan knew exactly what to do. She rummaged through one tansu, then another. She quickly took something from one of the drawers and said, "C'mon, let's go."

Once out on the street, I asked, "What did you take?" Giving her a dirty look, I said, "You're nothing but a burglar."

"Yes, but so are you. You were with me. And if you want to know, I took some old socks left in the house, that's all. The whole family, Satsuma-san and her children, they died because they were stupid like you. They didn't know how to stay alive. You clean the bran since I did all the work so far."

"No, you help me. I'll tell Norio if you don't."

Afraid of her brother, she complied. Just as Sā-chan used her mother to get me to do things, I used Norio. Grudgingly she helped me pick out the weevils from the bran and mixed brick straw into it. Together we filled the socks with this mixture and made scouring pads for pots and pans. We would sell them to the rich women who paid good money for such luxuries.

Just when I thought I was getting better, I had a relapse and took to bed. Perhaps because I was ill, the war felt far away and home felt far away.

To help, I had Iwao bring discarded magazines retrieved from the nearest train station upstairs to my bedside, and together we cut the pages into strips and rolled dried, crushed eggplant, persimmon, or tomato leaves with tobacco bought at the black market. We cut, measured, and rolled our special mixture and, on the sly, we sold them to gentlemen who had run out of their own supplies and were dying for a smoke. "Sā-chan's good at spotting them," Iwao said. "They're the ones who are always tapping their top pockets. 'Tabako?' Sā-chan would say and wink at them. You should see her."

Yes, I had seen her making believe she had a cigarette between her fingers, putting it up to her lips like a cute whore. Hard-pressed to satisfy their addictions, men would nod their heads, then fish into their pockets for loose coins.

Old buttons, leather, anything aluminum to sell to the government were on our list of things to find. When a call for brass came, I hobbled to the small Buddhist temples in our area to pray for my well-being and to ask for any brassware the monks could spare—bells, incense burners, beggars' bowls—and they were generous. We needed everything we could get our hands on.

Desperation was acute, as when Omoto-san ran over to the house one day, crying with abandon. "Where's Harue-san? Is she around? I must speak to her!"

"She's at work. Why, what happened?" I asked.

"It's my son . . . he sold the baby, my grandchild. I want Harue-san to talk some sense into him. Maybe it's not too late to get the child back." She wailed and tore out of the house.

When Harue Auntie came home that evening, I told her what Omoto-san said. "I know," she said. "Omoto-san came to the factory, but it was too late. Her stupid boy had already used some of the money. Fathers sell their daughters and their babies; mothers become prostitutes in Ginza. You better work hard, Hi-chan. We might have to sell Sumie or you might have to sell your body if you don't find enough to feed us." While she did laugh, anything was possible with her.

Feeling better that evening—after putting Sumie to bed, after going out to canvass the neighborhood for goods—I helped Auntie cut patterns for robes used in overseas hospitals. She bought bolts of silk and also made underwear for the volunteer nurses to take to the front, the net of boycotting countries ever wider, no one buying silk from Japan, silk going for prices cheaper than dirt. At first, the sewing was Sā-chan's duty. Like her mother, she was a skilled seamstress. Of course, Sā-chan complained. "I hate doing this," she said whenever she went to the machine. "I never have time for my friends."

"Shut up, Sā-chan," Iwao said. "Stop whining and do your job. Everyone does theirs." He was busy cleaning the bird droppings, which he had collected with Norio, pulling out feathers stuck in them. "You want Otō-san to sell you? You're lucky Otō-san and Okā-san know how to make extra money. Otherwise, we'd all die."

"You Iwao, shut up," my auntie scolded and, as if scripted, Sā-chan got up and left. "And you, Hi-chan," throwing a piece of cloth to me, "start sewing."

I dared not grumble. Out of desperation she might decide to sell Sumie, especially if she had to choose between her daughter and mine. I had to protect Sumie at all cost. From then on, under my auntie's ready gaze, I sewed silk robes and panties; every night I pumped the treadle to the sewing machine with extra vigor and blistered my feet.

Getting into the act, Shiichi Uncle made bootleg liquor out of sweet potatoes; people called it his pig wine. But whatever it was called, people came to the house in secrecy to buy the liquor with the big kick. It was a popular item. "Give me the bombshell drink," they ordered. I got dizzy just smelling the strong, raw brew whenever my uncle opened the wooden vat he hid under the floor.

Hamada-san's husband banged on our door late one night. "Oooi. Give me what you have," he shouted. "Tomorrow, the army is shipping me to the Philippines. I don't know why they want someone old and useless like me, but I have no choice."

"To the Philippines?" my uncle said. "It's bad, isn't it?"

"Yes it's bad, so bad that they have to take me. They need cooks and barbers like me. Does this mean that all the cooks and barbers have been killed?"

Uncle gave Hamada-san's husband a free bottle of sake, after which Hamada-san sat cross-legged on the ground in front of the house and drank it down.

A short while later, I looked out from the kitchen window and saw him swaying as he sang out: "I'm drunk, I'm drunk!" He continued sucking the long-necked sake bottle like a hungry baby its milk, though nothing was in it. He soon shouted for more, but before my uncle could bring it to him, he stood up and in a second passed out on our doorsteps. Uncle dragged him out of the cold and into the entryway of our home and left him there to sleep.

Early the next morning, I heard Hamada-san's voice. She was talking to her children. "Hurry, come with me. Help me bring your father home. He needs to leave soon. They'll come and arrest him if he doesn't report for duty."

One day, just before Iwao's summer break in 1943, with the face of a stubborn dog, he refused to go to school, and in spite of my coaxing, he was resolute: "I'm staying home. That's final!" That's when he became our lookout for the Economic Police.

Only ten, Iwao proved excellent for the task. Skinny and light, he could go places no one else dared venture. Sometimes, I'd see him up on the rooftop of a building or jumping from housetop to housetop. To signal Norio, Sā-chan, and me of any danger, he would whistle with two long fingers stuck in his mouth, or caw like a Tokyo crow. Upon hearing these prearranged signals, we would scatter with our goods. We couldn't afford to be arrested or have our goods confiscated.

As fuel and foods grew scarcer, more and more Economic Police roamed the streets. We were small operators with very little money, so we just couldn't risk being caught and having to pay the heavy fines the government would have levied against us. We would be ruined. On one such foray, near Asakusa, we heard Iwao signal *Caw, caw,* but it was too late.

"Stop right there," an Economic Police officer said, running toward us. "I want to check your cart." We complied, jerked to a stop. No one spoke.

He looked at me strangely. "Why are you on the cart, like this? Are you hiding something?"

"I can't walk well," I said, hoping he would pity me. "We have only what belongs to us."

"Mmmm that so?"

"Here, have some candy. Give this to your children." I shoved a handful of sweets into his hands, making sure that they overflowed his cupped palms.

As the officer bent over to pick up the candy that had scattered into the street, Norio said, "Let's go. Run!"

"Hold up!" the officer shouted and blew his whistle, but he didn't chase after us right away. Looking back as we ran, I saw that he was more concerned about the candy on the ground and ran after us only after having pocketed every piece.

"Head toward Asakusa Jinja," shouted Norio.

"C'mon, Sā-chan," Iwao said, running out from his lookout position to help Norio push the cart; I bounced high on it, barely able to maintain my balance while I held on to Sumie and Yuki-chan.

"In here," Norio yelled, the milling crowd at the shrine swallowing us whole.

"That was fun," Iwao said after we lost the policeman. He grinned and dusted his hands in a good riddance.

"No, it wasn't," Sā-chan said, grabbing her side and grimacing. "We're just common thieves. That's what we've become."

None of us took Sā-chan seriously, but we had learned our lesson. We moved with extra caution from then on.

In the city, people planted vegetable gardens with onions or carrots on every square inch allowed in the parks or on the sides of the streets. We rarely saw rats, cats, dogs, or birds around anymore. Every so often, the boys would trap a dove or starling, and I would boil the bird into a thin soup, together with some radishes and wrinkled carrots, for a feast. Though we wanted to, we couldn't keep chickens or rabbits because we had no feed. On a rare occasion Harue Auntie brought home a small chicken. In our first meal we ate all of the meat and sucked on the bones for their juices. Auntie saved the bones on our plates and boiled them (which we cracked then sucked for their marrow), creating a watery soup mixed with vegetables for the next meal.

Reduced to eating stews made of grass—a mixture of thistle, mugwort, chickweed, almost anything edible found on the ground—we suffered from upset stomachs, frequent cramping, constipation, diarrhea. I stretched the rice and beans by adding a little to these stews. After a time, the revolting ingredients of a pudding made of fried wheat flour and rice bran took the place of rice on the ration counters.

"I can't stand it anymore. I want rice! I can't eat this horseshit," Norio cried out in disgust, spitting out in a spray, the nukapan, the rice substitute we had been eating. "When is this going to stop? Smells like horseshit, tastes like horseshit! Can't the government give us anything better?"

After Hamada-san's husband left for the Philippines, she stopped by to see me and brought along something to eat, which is customary when visiting someone, but I said to her, "You shouldn't do this. Save the food for your children."

"It's hard to visit someone empty handed. It's not easy to break the habit."

"Well, I'm different; I wouldn't have cared," I said, noticing that she was close to tears.

It was not long after her visit that I heard the news of Hamada-san's husband's death. Everyone had lost weight because of the war, but I wasn't prepared for what I saw of her family at the funeral. They all looked half-starved. Hamada-san's loose fitting kimono fell away in tatters, although she did her best to hide it; the children looked like sticks, their clothing shabby on their lean frames. I remember telling her to take care and her dropping her head in response, not bothering to look up and meet my eyes.

When her eldest child, Jun, prepared to leave the following day for his base, I could hear him sobbing, asking his mother if she would be all right. They were talking outside by his army truck, and their voices rose to my bedroom. "I'm not going back. I won't go," he was saying, his voice cracking, heavy with emotion. "How are you going to support yourself . . . and the children?"

"You have to go," Hamada-san said in her sure, calm voice. "Your country needs you." Although I felt uncomfortable eavesdropping, I couldn't help myself. "You'll be in big trouble if you don't return," she continued. "You will be jailed for desertion, and it would bring shame to the family. Besides, it's only for a while longer. The war will be over soon. I will find work, and we will make it. Believe me."

As the autumn of 1943 rolled around, I was stronger despite frequent relapses and the lack of food. Looking into the mirror, I saw that the whites of my eyes no longer looked as green as that of children harboring tapeworms, and while my legs still shook under me, as in a small earthquake, and I was still slow in getting around, I could walk better and barely needed help.

Things were looking up. At sixteen months, Sumie was a happy child, and even on her limited diet she was growing and seemed strong, her plump arms and legs like sections of lotus roots. Although I boiled a rice stew mixed with tofu and salted vegetables every day, I worried that this was not enough. She needed more solids. I scrounged, begged, and bargained for more aburage, fish, or meat to give her. I agonized over her bones, watched for the plague of soft teeth.

Akira would have been proud of her, Mama and Miyo, too. She was a good child—sweet in disposition and not very demanding. She had my high cheekbones and long legs and frame, and Akira's warm but alert eyes. You could already tell that she was going to be tall. I wished my family could see her now, growing faster than Papa's Kaiwiki cane. I promised myself at the time that whatever I did, I was not going to spoil her in the same way Harue Auntie had spoiled Sā-chan.

Around this time, Harue Auntie stayed home from work because of a sprained ankle. Hearing of her misfortune Omoto-san and Toma-san came to pay her a visit. Both women looked thinner, their skin gray from lack of nourishment.

"Hi-chan, we haven't seen you for a while. At least you're well now," Omoto-san said when she walked in. "Oh my, Sumie's so cute. You're lucky you have her with you. I miss my grandchild. And you," she said, scrutinizing my face, "you've become even more beautiful. Being a mother must agree with you."

"Please, I'm not beautiful at all," I said, feeling my face get hot. "You shouldn't say things like that. You embarrass me."

"Why should you be embarrassed?" Toma-san put in. "You're a rare bird and you know it, don't you?"

"Hello, it's been a long time," Harue Auntie called out to her two friends. She was seated at the low table in the living room, one bandaged foot sticking straight out. I placed zabuton down on the mat for our neighbors, then went into the kitchen to make some tea. From where I was in the kitchen, I could hear their conversation. At first it was small talk. Toma-san and Omoto-san asked Harue Auntie about the condition of her foot, the children, the weather, the war, the food situation.

During a lull in their conversation, Harue Auntie asked the two women, "Tell me, what's going on in the neighborhood? I don't know anything that's happening, these days. Shiichi and I have been working hard, so we don't . . ."

With that, the women started whispering. After a moment I heard exclamations of disbelief from my auntie: "No, are you sure? That's funny, what happened?"

Curious to learn what they were saying, I walked out with the tea tray, but everyone fell silent when I dropped down to my knees to place the tray on the floor next to the table. They squirmed and looked at each other.

"Well, do you think we should tell Hi-chan the news?" Harue Auntie said, with a snide laugh.

"What news?" I said.

"It's about your friend Hamada-san," Omoto-san said, straightening the kimono under her folded legs by rocking herself.

"Is she ill?" I asked, perking up.

Harue Auntie laughed. "You can call it that. Very ill, I would say. It seems that . . . ha ha ha . . . your good friend has turned into a . . . a prostitute."

I stared at her, then at the others.

"I saw her with my own eyes," Toma-san said. "She was on Pigeon Street in Asakusa, and I saw her when I went to fetch my father-in-law from a nearby bar. All dolled up in a short red American dress, her hair twisted in the back, she was laughing with some man before they walked arm in arm into an inn."

"I don't believe you," I said. "You have no business saying things like that about her."

Omoto-san smirked and said, "Everyone's talking about it. See for yourself!"

Challenged, I enlisted the help of Norio that night. "Please go with me to Asakusa—to Pigeon Street," I said. "The women are saying bad things about Hamada-san, and I want to see if they're true."

Norio said nothing when we started out. He walked lightly in his geta, and having pulled himself in, he stooped in his school jacket, his hands deep in his pants pockets. He had grown taller and even more serious since I had first known him.

And what the women had said was true. There she was all right, leaning against a wall of one of the shops on the street. The man with her whispered something in her ear, and she answered with a high unfurling of laughter. He put his hand on her thigh and she lifted her leg up, her heel on the wall; a slit exposed her flesh. The man and she linked arms and walked away together. When she passed under a dim light, a silver ornament shimmered in her hair.

I pulled Norio angrily away, and we walked home alongside a malodorous canal. Scraggly matsu moved in the slight breeze, and their shadows brushed up against our feet in the pathway as if to sweep us along.

"Why didn't she say something?" I said, more to myself than to Norio. "We could have helped her." Disgust came in a visceral reaction of betrayal. "No wonder her children look well fed these days. So, this is how she's been living. She's nothing but a cheap, no-good mother. She's ruined her reputation and her children's name."

I must have listed some pretty awful things about her on the way home. After listening to me rant, Norio finally broke his silence. "Really, how did you think she could go on living? This is what war does. She's doing this just for the sake of her children." I was surprised at Norio's defense of Hamada-san.

Lacking understanding of her predicament and wanting nothing more to do with her, I withdrew myself from Hamada-san in the days that followed. I had no leg to stand on, but in my thinking, being a prostitute was far worse than someone having a child out of wedlock, like me. After seeing her on the streets and in commiseration with the other women, I said nasty things about her to Omoto-san and Toma-san when they came over to gossip with Harue Auntie.

"Yeah, she's two-faced, isn't she?" I said. "To think that all this time she acted like an oku-san when she's really no better than an untouchable."

My auntie became friendlier toward me, now that we had something in common to gossip about. "For once you think like I do," Harue Auntie said. "You surprise me." We were getting along and, I believe, I actually made her happy.

15

Norio

It was around October 1943. With me fully recovered from my illness, Harue Auntie said to Iwao, "You can't stay at home any longer. Your father wants you to go back to school."

"I'm through with school," a belligerent Iwao said.

"Let *me* go back," Sā-chan pleaded.

"If I had my way you could, but you stay out of this," Harue Auntie said, in a rare scold directed at Sā-chan.

"Yes, let *her* go back," Iwao said, "and let me stay home. I don't want to be polishing aluminum for airplanes with Kazu and Tets. That's all school is now."

"What they're doing is for Japan, Iwao. You also have to listen to your father. He wants you back in school."

"I know, but I want to stay home and help."

The next day Harue Auntie dragged a reluctant Iwao back to school.

A few days later, when we were alone, I asked Iwao how school was going. "I hate it," he said. "We have classes in the mornings and that's okay, but they later march us single file to the cafeteria where they play this loud music—'Lay Me Beneath the Waves'—while we work. It may be a patriotic song but I'm sick of it. Can you talk to my mother and tell her that this is ridiculous?"

A week or so later, I walked in on Norio, Iwao, and Shiichi Uncle seated around the living room table and could immediately sense the tension. I put my vegetable bag down in the entryway and swung Sumie off my back. I guided her up the steps into the main room with Yuki-chan following.

"But why?" Uncle was asking Norio.

"It's just time," Norio said, not meeting his father's eyes. Sumie ran to Shiichi Uncle, who unconsciously put her on his lap. Yuki-chan sat next to Iwao, and I sat in the back of everyone.

"You have a deferment, so why volunteer now?" I heard Uncle say. "We need you at home."

"I know, but this is a way I can help. Besides, I'm just one more mouth to feed."

"Hi-chan, please make us some tea," Uncle said, distractedly. I could tell that my uncle was deeply distressed for he seldom asked me to do anything for him. Before going to the kitchen, I sat and studied his profile as he talked to Norio. He looked suddenly very old; he had lost more of his hair and his face was crisscrossed with the lines and wrinkles of a hard life.

I learned that Norio had volunteered to train in the Air Fleet of the Japanese Imperial Army. Besides his love of languages, his exceptional skills in math and science made him a prime target for solicitations to become a flight trainee. Japan needed more men like him. His good physical condition, his tall bearing, and tough leanness had made him desirable.

"You should become a poet and be a professor at Tokyo University, right, Otō-san?" Iwao said. "What good would it do for you to fight?"

"Shut up, Iwao," Norio said. "You don't know what you're talking about."

"Yes I do—as much as you!"

Biting his lower lip, Shiichi Uncle said, "I guess it's inevitable. Though we're all in the army, the government is looking at older men and younger boys to recruit into active duty. If the war keeps up, soon it will be Iwao. Even me," he said, forlornly.

Norio had made up his mind, and there was no stopping him.

Much talk of an invasion by the Americans prevailed. My uncle, Toma-jiji, and Omoto-san's father coordinated the bucket brigades and the defense of the community in our area. One night, when they came back to our home after teaching the older neighborhood boys and girls how to fight with bamboo spears, since I was still up, I made tea for my uncle to serve to his two elderly friends.

"I tell you, we're losing," Shiichi Uncle was saying as I brought the tea to the low table, then retreated to the kitchen. "No one talks about this at our meetings, but the Americans have been gaining on the Japanese Imperial Armed Forces with their better equipment and planes. Boys from Japan are easy targets."

"Yes, very easy targets," Omoto-san's father said in a worried voice. "I know because my oldest grandson is on the aircraft carrier, *Zuikaku*."

"Is that so? I didn't know your grandson was at sea," my uncle said.

"Well, I don't think we're losing the war," Toma-jiji said, adamant. "If we all stick together, we can win this war. We must fight to the bitter end!"

"Then we'll all be killed and that's stupid," Omoto-san's father said. "We're sending our children and grandchildren to slaughter. Personally, I don't believe in the war anymore."

"It's people like you who are hurting us!" Toma-jiji said, his voice rising. "That's treason!"

"Hey, hey, calm down," my uncle said. "This is only talk, but I'm with Omoto-san's father here," my uncle said.

"Don't you understand? This kind of talk is no good!" Toma-jiji said and banged his fist on the table. Upon hearing their raised voices, I stood up from the kitchen table and saw Toma-jiji head out the door, his eyes and lips narrow in anger.

"I'm sorry," Omoto-san's father said to my uncle after Toma-jiji left. "He comes from the old school."

"It's not your fault. He believes strongly."

"We *all* believe strongly."

The next morning Harue Auntie said, "I heard you and our neighbors talking. I'm with Toma-jiji."

"It figures you would be. And we'll all be killed—will you be satisfied then?"

"But Shiichi, we *have* to make a stand. We can't have foreign invaders coming into our country. They'll torture and rape our children."

Shiichi Uncle and Harue Auntie argued for some time.

I worried for myself and Sumie and wondered how the Americans would treat us if we fell into their hands. Had I turned so Japanese that they would not see me as anything else, let alone an *American*? Would it make any difference were I to say I was from Hawai'i? I couldn't even guess.

Having made his decision to enlist and go to war, Norio grew gloomy, as if he were just trying to puzzle things out. "I know I volunteered," he said, "but it's a useless war. We're losing, isn't it obvious? Even I can see what's happening." He and I were sitting and talking on the stoop of the house, a place where we could be honest and by ourselves, away from the children and adults. Hands clasped between his legs, arms on his thighs, shoulders drooping, Norio confessed that he was afraid he was going to die. "And, I'm not sure I could kill another living soul even if my life depended on it. What kind of a soldier is that?" I put a hand on his shoulder, which he quickly brushed away with a shrug. "C'mon, let's go in," he said.

I knew that Norio had volunteered because he did not want to seem like a coward, boys his age all going to war, and too, because he felt he was a drain on our meager resources. But his decision didn't come from recklessness or a resolve drawn from the heartbeat of his country; it had come from long hours of hard thinking, motivated by wanting to protect, aid, and relieve us from our burdens. If I had accused him before of not being as grown-up as Akira or thought that he was still a boy, he had far surpassed all of us by this time.

"Okā-chan. Norio doesn't want to go to war. He doesn't want to help the Emperor, " Sā-chan said during dinner, several days before Norio's call date.

"What? You should be proud to go, Norio," Harue Auntie said. "It's your duty, an honor to fight for the Emperor."

Norio looked down at his plate. "You and your duty," he mumbled.

The day after this exchange, Harue Auntie hung an even larger picture of the Emperor in the house. From his horse, the Emperor of Japan looked straight down at us no matter where we were in the small living space. "Look what Okā-san bought," Sā-chan said. "Isn't it grand?"

In early November, shortly before Norio was scheduled to leave, Sā-chan came running up to my room and said, "Hamada-san is here to see you. She said she wants to leave some money for Norio—for us to offer at one of the shrines."

"Tell her I'm sick and thank her for me," I said.

"Oh no," said Sā-chan. "You say that yourself. I'm not going to lie for you."

I didn't want to see Hamada-san. All I could think of was the makeup on her face and her seductive behavior. The thought that she might actually be enjoying herself on Pigeon Street made matters worse. Shamed by Sā-chan's refusal, I went downstairs and opened the door just a crack, my face a mask.

"Hi-chan?" Hamada-san said.

"I'm sorry," I said, "but I have a bad cold."

"Oh, I just brought an offering for the temple—for Norio." The look she gave me was searching and sad.

"The family thanks you for your kindness," I said curtly, taking her envelope.

In the awkward air, Hamada-san said, "Well, I must go. Please give my regards to Norio and your aunt and uncle. They've always been kind to me."

"I will," I said and shut the door. I expelled a deep sigh. *Why did you betray me and yourself? You were my one friend in this lonely country. How could you?*

For Norio, I visited several roadside shrines and gave coins to the Jizo Bodhisattva, guardian of children and travelers. The coffers at the shrines overflowed with coins, so many boys in our district going off to war.

Later, I made Norio, Sā-chan, and Iwao go with me to visit several larger shrines, the first, Mimeguri Jinja, where we left an offering of Hamada-san's coins. There Sā-chan said, "Look at this. The shrines are making a lot of money because of other people's misfortunes. Let's hope they're giving some of this money to the poor families, especially helping those whose fathers had to go to war."

"Why wouldn't they?" Iwao asked.

"Because it's human nature to want to keep the money," she said.

"Your nature, maybe," Norio said. "Not ours and maybe not theirs. Not everyone thinks like you."

"Well, at least we don't have to worry about Otō-san," Sā-chan said.

"That's true," Iwao said. Norio nodded in affirmation.

It was true. It would have been disastrous for the family if Shiichi Uncle had to go to war. Handicapped like Miyo, Uncle had been born with one leg shorter than the other, and so far, that had given him a dispensation from serving at the front, and while his age also made him exempt from serving outside of Japan, that appeared uncertain as the days went by. Hadn't Hamada-san's husband, about the same age as Uncle, been ordered out much earlier?

At the Fox Shrine, I tied white fortune ribbons to a tree to carry my wishes of goodwill for Norio and watched, at length, the ribbons flutter in the wind. Later, at yet another shrine, because I wasn't about to take any chances with Norio's life and though he protested, I brought him to the Temple of Long Life to be cleansed of bad spirits riding his back. He remained silent throughout the ceremony and stood with his eyes closed as the priest waved his paper wand over Norio and recited an incantation of exorcism.

"I want you safe," I said. "Help protect you." I also insisted that he wash his hands and drink the bubbly water from the temple's constant spring. Although he did everything asked with good humor, he uttered a sigh of relief when the rituals were over.

When in battle, Norio would be wearing the Japanese flag on his body like all of the boys would be doing; he'd also be wearing a white stomach band of protection. In place of Harue Auntie, who was too busy to do it, I went around the neighborhood asking women to sew Norio a red knot stitch of luck. I needed a thousand of these stitches for his sennin bari, the scarf of a thousand needles done by the hands of a thousand women, to wrap around his body. I needed the strength of a thousand warriors, from ancient times to the present, to make him a thousand strong and for him to feel the beat of drums and the flutter of warrior banners in his fighting spirit.

I went from house to house or stood on street corners, calling out to patrons from under my umbrella, feeling the coming winter wind in my teeth. "I beseech you," I said, bowing, repeating my wishes to any woman who stopped. "My big brother is going off to war, so please join me in bestowing him with many blessings for his mind and spirit." Women hurriedly put down their shopping bags to make a quick stitch and went on their way. Norio needed all the help I could give him; he was so young, so sensitive, so certain he would not survive the war. I worked nonstop to finish the scarf before his departure.

For as much of a celebration as we could muster for the occasion, we held a small party for Norio on his last night at home. Holding back our sadness, we kept our faces cheerful in front of him. I fried some rice cakes that I had preserved in water to keep from molding and cooked a block of fish bought at the black market for a "dear price," as Mama would have said for something that delectable.

"Where do you think the fish came from?" Sā-chan said, her round, young and flushed face leaning into the pot, staring at the fish, as I cooked it in a mouth-watering sugar-soy sauce. There was something about the sauce's rich smell that made one pine for a time when life held so much promise and our stomachs were filled with crabmeat, fish roe, and all the rice we could eat. This may have been what prompted Sā-chan's next question: "Do you think the fish swam all the way to Japan from as far as where you lived in Hawai'i?"

"Tuna are strong and we do have them," I said, and because it was Norio's going-away party, for this once, I buried my grievances with Sā-chan and answered her questions without irritation.

"So it's possible," she said, also unguarded.

For that evening's tea, I crushed dried potato leaves and mixed them together with some pine bark chips to make a bitter but robust brew. The meal was quiet, everyone eating with deliberation, as if lost in thought, the clicking of chopsticks against the chipped lacquer bowls almost plaintive; the sips as we drank our tea were meditative but weary. Even Harue Auntie appeared subdued, her head bowed over her food, her rice bowl close to her face, almost covering it.

After the meal, everyone gave Norio a small going-away present. Sā-chan gave her brother a "fire rock," a small piece of Chinese flint and a steel rod to strike it with. "You might need it," she said, "if you get lost." They smiled at each other with a warmth I had rarely seen between them.

Yuki-chan was next. "Yuki-chan, go ahead," I said and encouraged her to hand over the red beanbag she and I had made to give him, she having gathered the beans and I having sewn the bag.

Iwao gave his brother a handkerchief. "You sure it's clean?" joked Norio.

"No, I just blew my nose on it," Iwao said. The brothers laughed, looking at each other without wavering. They then cast their eyes down and lowered their heads.

"Saa," Shiichi Uncle said and cleared his throat to steer his sons away from their sadness. He extended his palm outward and gave Norio his old but useable pocketknife. I had seen Uncle trim his nails, shave the calluses on his hands, and cut dried cuttlefish slices for the children with this knife. I had never seen him without it. At first, Norio shook his head. "I can't take it, Otō-san."

"But I want you to have it."

Norio and his father exchanged deep, clear-eyed looks of understanding.

Norio never expected the comb, the handle adorned with specks of mother-of-pearl shells, when his mother handed it to him. He choked back his tears as he thanked her. Then, she extended her hand toward Norio in an unexpected move, and Norio laid his hand on her palm. "Norio-kun," she whispered in endearment, tears spilling down her face in two long streams like columns of wax.

As for me, I gave Norio my papa's amulet, the one he never wore. I had worn the gold and red brocaded charm around my neck ever since Akira and I had been in the cane fire. Now, it belonged to Norio.

"Maybe it's going to snow tonight, after all," Norio said, turning his attention to a high window behind him as he blinked back tears.

"I wish it would," I said. "I've never seen a real snowstorm." It had snowed in the city, but only lightly over the time I had been there.

"Never seen a real snowstorm? I can't believe it!" Norio said.

"In our part of Hawai'i, it never snows."

Norio turned back to the window to look out once more. "It's the most beautiful sight, the white flakes having a light in them. It's something you'll never forget. Even if you die, you'll remember it."

To change the subject away from death and its possibility, my uncle said, "Hi-chan, there's no question you're fire's child, like your name. You come from a place where it burns underneath, but with a difference. It stays nice and warm where you're from and it doesn't get as cold."

I wrapped my worn, red silk jacket tighter around me. What Uncle had said reminded me of how much I missed sunlight. I wanted it on my face, its rays to seep into my skin, and I wanted to take the lush, fruitlike heat into the core of my body. The thought of snow and more cold made my teeth chatter.

After dinner, Shiichi Uncle brought out some of his pig wine. Holding back the sleeve of his blue coat, he poured the liquor with great ceremony into tiny sake cups for the adults. For me and the children, he poured tea. We held the cups up and made a toast: "Kampai!" Norio scrunched his face and bravely drank the harsh liquor in one gulp, his face and ears quickly reddening.

Uncle played shaky songs on his shakuhachi, everyone's favorite, "The Sound of Deer Calling to One Another." In one corner, Yuki-chan and Sumie, getting silly, held hands and spun in dizzying circles with their heads thrown back while Sā-chan clapped her hands in time to the music. Auntie retreated into a corner to do some hand sewing; every so often, she lifted the thread to her mouth to cut it with a gnash of her teeth.

Iwao soon stood up and said, "I'm going to sing a going-away song for Norio that I learned in school." In a young boy's falsetto, he began:

| *Aogeba too toshi* | It is with honor and gratefulness |
| *Waga shi no oon* | That we pass before our teachers |

"Enough!" Norio said after a few bars. He rose from his zabuton and kicked it aside. "That's a graduation song and I'm not graduating. I'm going to war!"

Everyone was stunned by his outburst. Sumie and Yuki-chan came running to me, their tiny feet pattering across the mat like a sudden rain hitting the tiles on the roof. Sumie scrambled up my lap, and Yuki-chan huddled behind me. "What happened?" Yuki-chan said in a soft voice.

"I'm going out for a walk," Norio said. We watched him slap on his jacket and walk with anger toward the front of the house. We heard him shovel his wide feet into his slippers and leave, banging his body into the flimsy walls that seemed to hold him back. He couldn't get away fast enough.

As soon as he left, Harue Auntie said, "Too many dreams in the head. Crazy that boy!" She threw her sewing down and turned to Uncle. "It's because you put too many silly things in his head."

"Shut up!" Uncle said, putting his hands on his kimono belt and giving it a sharp tug downward. Everyone stared at the floor, not used to seeing him so angry at Harue Auntie. We were frightened to look up at him.

"Otō-san, did I do anything wrong?" Iwao asked. "Why is everyone angry at me? I don't understand."

Choked by what appeared to be frustration and an unfathomable sadness, Shiichi Uncle was unable to respond.

"No one is angry at you, Iwao," I said to answer his questions and fill the quiet that had settled in the room. "It's just that your brother doesn't want to go to war."

"Then why's he going?"

"Because he has to. His going out had nothing to do with your voice. Your voice is beautiful. You'll make a good singer one day."

I began gathering the dinner dishes and piled them into small blue stacks, and by the time we all went upstairs to bed, Norio had not yet returned. I heard him enter our room early in the morning.

The next day, the whole family went with Norio to the Hikifune train station where he was to rendezvous with other recruits. The boys would then catch the train to Tokyo Station and, from there, go on to the army flying school based in Mibu. On the long platform, as we waited for the train to arrive, Norio patted Yuki-chan's head when she came to hold his hand. He then turned and bowed in the most formal manner—first to his mother, then his father. Auntie heaved. Her whole body shook as she poured tears into her hands.

To Sā-chan and Iwao, Norio said, "You're in charge now. Mind Okā-san and Hi-chan." Turning to me, he picked up Sumie who had wrapped herself around one of my legs. "You've grown big. Much heavier, since . . . when was it—yesterday?" He tickled her around her stomach, and she giggled, fingers in her mouth. Looking straight at me as he held her, Norio said, "Thank you very much, for everything." He handed Sumie to me and stepped back to give me a short, snappy bow. I saw my father's amulet, dangling from his neck. I lowered my head, my heart reaching out to embrace him.

The children ran after the train, which belched steam and gray soot. At the end of the platform, they waved slowly, in wide arcs, until the dark line of cars receded into a pinpoint, the line of track and horizon converging at the vanishing point.

16

Learning to Fly

In early 1944, in the first months of his training, Norio was stationed at a base somewhere in Shizuoka from where he wrote us long letters that the government censored. Iwao put the first letter we received that January from Norio up to the light to see if he could decipher any of the blocked-out passages. "They did it with coal ink. Can't see a thing," he said.

After his stay in Shizuoka, the army moved Norio to a base in Kagohara not far from Tokyo. "I miss home" was all he could tell us. Not long after, Shiichi Uncle learned that Hamada-san's oldest boy, Jun, was also at the base and worked as a cook's helper. He came into the city about once a week to transport and pick up goods. I often saw him arriving at Hamada-san's house where he would stay for an hour or two, then dash off to his base in a brown flatbed truck, with its mountain of goods under canvas covers that flapped like old sheets and bounced his young helper with every rut encountered.

"Jun is going to forward Norio's letters to us," Uncle said, after having made some kind of arrangement with the boy, which meant Norio's letters would bypass the government censors. The first of these letters was addressed to his mother. Harue Auntie, happy to be the center of attention, read it aloud to us with great ceremony, and, as if to say he hadn't forgotten the rest of us, Norio's subsequent letters were addressed to his father, with shorter letters coming to me and the children. This change did not please Harue Auntie. I thought that she was particularly jealous of his letters to me because she would give me curious looks whenever Jun handed me an envelope.

"He can't be writing anything important," Auntie would say. "I don't see what he has to tell to you." Perhaps she was hoping I would reveal something of its contents in these letters home.

In his first letter, dated February, 1944, Norio said:

> *Dear Big Sister (I hope you don't mind my calling you this),*
>
> *Japan is truly a beautiful country. When I traveled inland to my base, the snow began to fall, and I thought about you because you said that you had never seen a snowfall. They say this year will be cold. It will soon snow in the city too, and you'll feel a big snowfall for the first time, if you haven't already. How I envy you—this new discovery, its first moment. I wish I could be there to see the joy on your face. Did you know that snow burns, too? Pay my respects to the god of snow when you do your morning prayers.*
>
> *I hope that you are getting along better with my mother these days, and that she doesn't scold you too often. Please take care of everyone for me. You're in charge now.*
>
> *Norio*

"I wish Norio were here. He would know what to do with her," Harue Auntie was saying to Uncle one day in the late afternoon, as I stepped into the house from the public bathhouse, with Sumie and Yuki-chan in tow. When Uncle and Auntie saw me, they lowered their voices. At first I thought they were talking about me, but then Uncle went upstairs to talk to Sā-chan.

A week later, I returned from chores in town to find Harue Auntie yelling at Sā-chan. They were in the kitchen. "You are not to do that again, you hear? Without Norio around, do you think you can do anything you want to? Your father may be useless, but I'm still in charge here. I know everything that goes on in this house!"

Sā-chan's head was down and her whole body was shaking with sobs. When she looked up and saw me, she hissed from under the sweep of her bangs, "Go away, this is none of your business."

I glanced at her and turned away. "Come with me, children," I said and took Yuki-chan and Sumie upstairs.

"Okā-chan is always scolding Sā-chan, isn't she," Yuki-chan said. "She scolds Sā-chan in our bedroom at night."

"I know, but shhhh."

For several days, Sā-chan came home from visiting the black market, deposited the food in the kitchen, and went straight to her room. She didn't emerge to help me to prepare dinner in the evening; if she ate, she picked on something in the food safe after we had finished our meals.

One day, Sā-chan did not come home as expected. "Where is she?" Harue Auntie asked my uncle when they came in after work.

"I don't know, but don't worry. She's not a child anymore," my uncle said.

"Not a child? But she's still a girl. She's supposed to tell us where she is. No young girl ever does this kind of thing. A shame . . . and it had to be Sā-chan! How can she do this to us—and where were you?" Her voice was heavy with accusation.

"You have to be patient. She's probably out with her friends from school. She misses them. I'm sure she'll be back soon." My uncle paused. "It's really because you spoil her."

"So, it's my fault! Is that what you're saying?"

"Oh, Harue . . ."

Sā-chan did not come home that night. Every so often, I heard Harue Auntie get up and go to the window when she heard a sound. The next morning, I heard her debate whether or not to go to work.

"You have to go to work. She'll come home," Uncle said. "You'll see."

Sā-chan didn't show up for two nights. On the third day, she tiptoed into the house after Shiichi Uncle and Harue Auntie had gone to work. "You better not say anything," she said when she saw me in the kitchen.

Her harsh tone obliterated any sympathy I may have had for her. *What is there for me to say?*

"You haven't seen me, understand?" Sā-chan hurried up to her room.

That afternoon, Iwao sauntered in from school and dropped his schoolbooks on the floor. "Did Sā-chan come home?" he asked. He looked worried.

137

I nodded. "We're not supposed to know this," I whispered. "But she's upstairs in her bedroom."

Iwao sighed with relief. "She was with Jun's brother, Tadashi, again," he said. "Everyone's talking. They've been staying in the empty house—the one where the Satsuma family died of starvation."

""I know the house," I said.

"How could she do that? Okā-san is going to kill her. Give her yaito!" I remembered when Mama and Papa put moxa on my back when I almost set the house on fire.

As soon as Harue Auntie walked in that evening, she asked, "Has Sā-chan come home?" Iwao lowered the paper he was reading and lifted his eyes toward the ceiling. Auntie rushed upstairs.

"Okā *please* . . ." I heard a slap and Sā-chan cry out.

"Don't you dare do this to me again, you hear?"

"I only wanted to have some fun. I never get to do anything. I never get to go anywhere. I hate this life!"

"Fun—with Tadashi? You're no better than his mother."

"How can you say that? I'm *not* like Hamada-san!"

Not long after their conversation, Harue Auntie flew downstairs. I heard her clatter into her geta and run over to Hamada-san's house, knock on her door, and enter. I heard no more. Whatever happened at the Hamadas, whatever was said, no one knew. All we knew was that Tadashi and Sā-chan no longer saw each other after that day.

At that time, we were hearing all sorts of war rumors about invasions and bombings. Sā-chan said, "The Americans are not here yet, but if they come with their bombs, as people are predicting, maybe it's better to be killed by a bomb than to starve to death. I don't want to starve and look ugly."

"Mmm, yes, I don't know which would be worse," I said. And I had seen those suffering from malnutrition—what Uncle called, *shinda yooni aruite iru hito,* the walking dead—those with the sunken eyes, the bloated stomachs, the gaunt looks. More and more people, disoriented and bewildered, had collapsed and died in the streets from starvation. Children of some families looked so emaciated as they sat in front of their houses that they were unable to jump rope or carry their younger siblings, and looking at them made me want to scream with rage and frustration because I knew our own situation was precarious. By the early summer of that year, the mad scramble for food accelerated, and we began hoarding food in earnest. I had to wonder if Mama, Miyo, and Akira were suffering in the same way.

But then again, there were those like Kato-san, now pregnant with her eleventh child, who kept reassuring me that she would continue feeding Sumie because she had more than enough milk. With nothing much for anyone to eat, I never understood how she managed to stay fat even when she wasn't pregnant. Other women speculated on this mystery. Harue Auntie said, "While the rest of us are starving, she's cheating on her rations. She's the kind of woman who gives the war a bad name. While boys like my son are fighting hard, she's getting fat."

Kato-san was indeed *not* like the walking dead around us. She radiated happiness, her eyes clear, her mouth dancing with humor, her cheeks flushed, her lips full, despite the hardship around her. What the answer was, no one knew.

In June of 1944, I finally received another letter from Norio.

Dear Big Sister,

Azaleas will be in full bloom soon at the base. Then the hydrangea. Summer will come along, and the government is rushing us in our studies. They need men to fight. As for myself, I wish I were outdoors, taking a walk or feeling the sunlight on my face. I work every day but my thoughts are lazy about the war.

I hear that a lot is happening outside. Morale, however, remains high where I am. (Only I seem to be having trouble with mine.) Things are picking up in pace for us, too. Japan has little time to train more men. Speaking of time, I'm sorry the snows did not come as you had anticipated. Maybe they'll come at the end of this year or the beginning of the next. Certainly something for you to look forward to.

These days, I see city folks carting and trading their treasures for some fresh fruits and vegetables, under the elms. I watch them bartering their goods with the farmers near our airfield. It just goes to show you how desperate people are, how worthless everything is in these times. The only thing people worry about is where their next meal is coming from.

But I don't worry about you. You've always managed to find ways of helping the family. You can fly a kite of steel, as Otō-san used to say.

You've taught me a lot. I can still see the profile of your face in the shadow of the firelight whenever you meditated in front of the altar. I always felt secure with you there.

All is well with me, knowing the spirit of your fire burns in our home.

Norio

It was also a time when the Japanese government decided to accelerate moving more children out of Tokyo. Boys and girls like Iwao were being gathered and sent into the country because of the potential danger.

"Is this what they did in America—to the Japanese?" Iwao asked when ordered to go.

"Absolutely not, it's a different thing. The Japanese in America were under arrest. You're not."

"Then why do I have to go? I don't want to," he protested.

"You don't have a choice," Harue Auntie said. "The government arranged it."

He didn't grumble much to his mother, but he complained to me. "So how come Sā-chan doesn't have to go? Why not Yuki-chan?"

"Sā-chan is old enough to stay back and your mother wants Yuki-chan with her."

"But I don't want to go!" he said of being sent to a school in Narita, farther north, away from the city.

"You have no choice," I said.

In the end, he knew it was useless to fight the inevitable. I found him an old Gladstone bag I had picked up at the black market and helped him pack. Later, I took the tearful, skinny Iwao to the bus station to join the rest of the children. His black school uniform looked too tight on him, his legs shooting out of his shorts like bamboo stalks.

"Don't forget to write," he called out from the bus.

"Don't worry, Iwao, it's not going to be so bad. There'll be many children there."

"It's not going to be bad? It's going to be awful!"

The day I sent Iwao off, I received another letter from Norio. It was a strange letter, neither addressed nor signed.

> *Whenever I'm in the sky, I found—above the drone of the plane—what the reverend at the base calls peace and tranquility. When I try to explain my feelings to my fellow officers, they laugh and say things like I have my head in the clouds rather than on my shoulders. I guess I'm a dreamer. I don't mind, though, that they don't understand.*
>
> *I recently got lost in a cloudbank. I wasn't afraid of the silence or not knowing where I was. I felt serene even though I could spin out of control if in it too long. It doesn't take much. The silence was so clear at that moment that I thought I had gone to the Pure Land. That's what it must be like. Above me, the skies were blue, of a blue I had never seen before, and while it was cold, I didn't feel cold. I could have gone on forever.*
>
> *I didn't want to leave the cloud cover, but the clouds soon parted and I could see the sweep of land below me. I wasn't eager to get back to earth and feel its heat. I didn't want to land in the dust. There was a vastness in my feelings for all things, as if I no longer needed to hold onto myself. I wanted to keep flying forever. It was a strange feeling and even stranger that I had to land on a spot on earth when the sky was so much more beautiful and infinite.*

Suddenly, in late November of that year, we began seeing large American planes flying overhead, but they were flying so far above us that we felt unconcerned. We could hardly see them in the bad and cloudy weather and wondered how they could see us below. The Japanese government, however, began to step up their air raid drills, and most of the neighborhood women and I did little during the American's poorly conducted flyovers of the city. Occasionally, we heard of a bomb or two being dropped, but they were often duds or fell into the rivers or canals. Seeing this to be the case, the women and I never sought shelter. People in the drills lacked resolve, the drills more like social gatherings with women chattering away with their friends and families, eating their tiny lunches packed in small wooden boxes.

"I don't know why I go," I told my Uncle. "The drills don't make any sense—having us go to the parks. They're too open."

"I guess you could go to the shelter."

"The shelters are too dangerous. You can get trapped in them and die."

The government, however, soon became heavier handed. Having no alternative, my neighbors and I marched to and from our houses to the parks with extra clothing, our sleeping mats, and food whenever the sirens sounded. I followed the crowd in the coming cold, but I felt vulnerable with the children out in the open.

In the coming weeks, I began to notice American planes were flying in our neighborhood with ever increasing frequency. By the end of 1944, more and more planes covered the skies of Japan.

"The Honorable Lord B has come to pay us a visit again," Shiichi Uncle would say of the B-29s flying over.

Out on the street one day, when I rushed out with Sumie and Yuki-chan to look at the planes, Toma-jiji had one of his grandsons with him. They were also looking up into the cloudy sky at the bombers flying over the city. The little boy ack-acked the American planes down. "That's the way. Kill the bad Americans!" Toma-jiji said and patted his grandson's head.

At night, holding onto Sumie in my arms, I had nightmares of bombs falling and blowing us up.

17

Divine Wind

Early 1945. Small Japanese fighter planes flew straight into the American bombers in kamikaze fashion and crippled them in flight or burned them up in their spin. Missions of the Divine Wind.

"Otō-chan, I don't think Norio is brave enough to be a kamikaze pilot, don't you think so?" Sā-chan asked Uncle one day.

"Let's hope he's not a kamikaze pilot," Uncle said, a dead expression in his eyes. "And you be careful what you say about your brother."

I also wondered if Norio was connected to these special forces. I grew suspicious when we heard almost nothing from him as time went by. I knew too that Shiichi Uncle went about his work dazed with worry. Every morning, photographs of bright, young fighter pilots who had sacrificed their lives for Japan appeared in the newspapers with a list of their names and wasted ages: Inoue Fujiro, 22; Ohashi Samaji, 20; Maeda Daizo, 21; Kitamura Tamori, 19; Ueno Satoshi, 23; Fujii Nobuo, 25; Ishii Osamu, 21; and so on. I scanned the faces, searching for Norio's among them. I didn't trust the Japanese government to contact us immediately if something had happened to him.

After a long silence, I finally heard from Norio after the New Year holiday.

> *Dear Big Sister,*
>
> *My squadron was recently assigned to a special force. But because we have so few planes right now and not enough petrol, I'm going to be grounded to study maneuvers. I don't know*

when I will be flying again.

I am keeping fit by exercising, and for recreation I play cards with my fellow officers. Sometimes my best friend and I sneak out into the village to trade cigarettes for early fruits. I feel bad, thinking that I'm unable to share them with the family.

Hi-chan, if I don't make it home, do me a favor. Please place my ashes in one of the temples in Kyoto—a small place would do. I know it's far and expensive to go there, but do it as a pilgrimage. Make it a holiday. (This is something special I am asking of you. Tell my father and mother about my wishes only if something happens to me.) By the way, it was good to see them both when they came to visit last month. I was surprised at how thin my mother is.

Also, please ask Iwao to forgive me for getting angry the night before I left. Tell him I am not angry with him. How is he doing in the country?

I have a book of Japanese poems by Saigyo that I want you to have. It's in the bedroom, in my drawer. A bookmark marks my favorite poem.

Norio

Not long after Norio's letter, the temperature plummeted; it was one of the coldest days on record. The cold knifed its way into our bones and twisted itself. In anticipation, people kept looking upward into the sky. To keep them warm, I bundled Sumie and Yuki-chan and made them sit under the futon covering the brazier. They waited for the snow while eating rice crackers and sipping hot tea.

No planes flew at the moment and all seemed excruciatingly quiet, as if the earth had laid its head on its arms to rest after all this craziness. Then it began, like soft music, part of earth's magical dance—the snow had finally come. It was heavy, as if to make up for the sparse snowfalls of past years.

For one pure moment, falling in thick, heavy white flakes, they cleansed the world of evil and death. I opened the latticed doors overlooking the garden and watched as the flakes fell in an ethereal lace on the barren ground, covering it layer upon inexhaustible layer.

"Hi-chan, listen. I hear music in the snow," Yuki-chan called out, white notes floating in the air. Sumie clapped her hands in time to the imaginary music and made surprise sounds from deep in her throat. Drifting in like clouds, snowflakes got caught on the thin bamboo gate, the momiji, the scrawny brushwood hedge. A white miracle, it was as if the snows had come to renew the hope we found difficult to hold on to.

The children and I watched a rare dove sing as it hopped along the fence, the cold newness under its feet. "Ahh," the children exclaimed, their mouths open, fingers creeping up to their lips, the light from the snow brightening their faces.

I put on my jacket and my geta to step outside. I sank into the drifts and the snowflakes falling on my face felt soft and gentle. "Look, Norio," I cried out. I tilted my head and raised my face to the white light of the snow as I spun myself, my arms above my head, the flakes settling on my eyes, nose, lips, and cheeks. I closed my eyes for a long moment and saw the light of the snow coming through my lids. It was that bright. I went round and round in my dance.

Suddenly, lightheadedness overcame me. The air in my lungs seemed to compress then congeal, and when I opened my eyes and took a deep breath, I was unable to breathe, the cold air unbearable. I wound my hands around my neck and gasped. I couldn't seem to recover. Stricken by some unknown fear, I scrambled into the house. My face, once covered with a light snow, burned with an intense and frightening cold.

That evening, as the snow continued to fall, I removed from Norio's dresser drawer the book by the poet Saigyo that he had given to me. The marked page read:

Negawaku wa　　　　　Were I to die
hana no moto nite　　　I wish I would
haru shinamu　　　　　in springtime
sono kisaragi no　　　　under the flowers
mochizuki no koro.　　and moon.

When I heard the knock on the door two days later, my hand shook when I opened the door to a tired-looking army officer who had come to the house and who, upon entering, acknowledged my aunt and uncle with a deep bow before making a formal statement from the government. Then less formally, he said, "Your son died with great honor in the service of his country. He slammed his plane into an American bomber, both planes crashing into the low mountains back of Koshigaya City. He fought with uncommon skill and gallantry and did not suffer in the fiery crash."

Clearly out of turn, I asked the officer if anyone could know of someone else's suffering. The tired-looking officer, the weight of many deaths on his shoulders, ignored me and directed his remarks to my auntie and uncle: "Norio's good work means one less bomber for the Americans and another step toward victory for Japan. You should be proud of your son."

Auntie covered her face completely with her hands; Uncle cried into his forearm.

Presented to Shiichi Uncle and Harue Auntie soon after: Norio's ashes in a wooden box; a mortuary tablet with his Buddhist name, Soku Sho, Instant Enlightenment, inscribed on it; the Japanese flag; and his blood-stained scarf stitched with a thousand needles by two thousand hands, that was taken from his body. And articles from his dresser: his wallet, his parting letter, a red beanbag, a piece of flint, Uncle's pocketknife, and the ebony comb his mother had given him—all of this delivered later to the house by two very young and weary-looking boy soldiers who couldn't have been more than fourteen. I assumed Papa's amulet had been burned with Norio when it was not returned.

"Not even a thousand warriors behind Norio could save him!" Harue Auntie cried out. Like her loud scolding of Norio once upon a time, her crying trailed like a scarf out of our home and into the neighborhood.

The Japanese Army made boys like Norio write their parting letters before they went into combat. His letter was written back in October of 1944.

> Otō-san, Okā-san,
>
> Although I have not written to you for a while, I know that you are well and in good spirits. Marvelous autumn is here and the momiji in the mountains look so beautiful from where I sit at my desk. Soon it will be winter. Then early spring. The seasons do go on.
>
> I wish I could have done more for you, but there is always regret in life, so I hope you forgive my shortcomings as a son.

146

Also, take care of the children. Tell them to mind you. If I have one regret, it is that I won't be able to see their faces once more.

Thank you for everything in my life. I will carry its remembrance with me wherever I go. Someday, my spirit will come back to this place—to see the beautiful leaves upon these trees.

With all my gratitude,

Norio

Upon reading the letter, Harue Auntie let out a wail, full of a mother's desolation. "This is not how it was supposed to happen." She pounded the floor with her fists. "Not now, it's too soon!"

Shiichi Uncle stopped his own keening to glare at his wife. "Did you think that Norio would come out of this alive, a hero? We sent him off to die, don't you know that? And what did you say? 'Be proud to fight for the Emperor, fight with honor!' What honor? It was only a matter of time."

"Oh, but not so soon, not so soon!" she said and shrank into a fetal position.

We called Iwao back from the country to attend his brother's funeral. "I knew this would happen," he said as soon as he saw me. He repeatedly slapped his cap on his thigh as he sat with me in the kitchen and cried. "I should have been here, at home, not in the country."

"I don't think that would have helped your brother," I said. Still a child in many ways, Iwao seemed to think that if he had not been made to leave home, Norio could have been saved. "Norio would have died no matter what we did," I said. "Like most of the young men sent to fly, he had no chance of coming back."

"It's like we killed him, then," Iwao said. "He didn't have a chance."

"But it was his choice," I said.

"I don't think he had any!"

We tacked a black mourning ribbon on our door for Norio and held a small Buddhist funeral over ashes at the house. Everyone, in a drone of voices, recited the *Sutra on the Buddha of Infinite Life*, and later the presiding Reverend read the "Sermon on the White Ashes" by Rennyo Shonin in a voice coming from the depth of his waterlife:

In silently contemplating the transient nature of human existence, nothing is more fragile and fleeting in this world than the life of man. . . . There is nothing more real than this truth in life. . . . By so understanding the meaning of death, we shall come to fully appreciate the meaning of life which is unrepeatable and thus to be treasured above all else. . . .

Only a few people came to chant Norio's passage to Nirvana, sorrows of their own pinned to their sleeves, every family busy with its own burials. As in the parable of the poppy seeds—where the Buddha said that he would bring a grieving mother's child back to life if she could bring to him two or three poppy seeds from any family who had not experienced death—she could find no one, in any household, untouched.

"I'm finished with the country," Iwao said with determination once the funeral was over. "After Otō-san, I'm the head of the family. I'm taking Norio's place."

"I'm too tired to argue, Iwao. Stay home, then," Shiichi Uncle said.

"Japan is crazy. We're killing all our young."

Harue Auntie could not be consoled after Norio's death. She slept little, she ate little, she drank little. Whenever she had a chance, she dashed out of the house and into the streets when the bombers flew over us. "You killed my son," she screamed. "You beasts! He'll never come back to me."

"Yes, Norio's never coming back," Uncle said to her. "You have to stop this madness." My auntie wailed, swore, fell to her knees, raised her arms to the sky, and rocked herself as she cried.

"Mama, please," was all that Sā-chan could say.

In sympathy, Omoto-san came over to the house to bring some fruits for Harue Auntie. "Harue-san, you need to rest," she advised. "You'll get better as the days go by."

"Get out. How dare you come and tell me these things? You don't know how it feels!"

"My own son was killed. How can you say that?"

"Get out! Just get out!" she screamed at the poor woman who had come to console her. Omoto-san shook her head and left.

Harue Auntie pushed everyone away from her, except Sā-chan; she wouldn't allow anyone to come close to her in her pain. Our neighbors, who tried to help, soon dismissed her as crazy and went about their business. Whenever she began screaming in the streets, Sā-chan, Iwao, or Uncle would go out to bring her back into the house, but this was all they could do. Once, when I went with Sā-chan to fetch her, Harue Auntie said, "Don't touch me!"

"I just want to help," I said.

"I don't want your help. *Stay away*. You're an American!"

I must admit that I was ashamed of her behavior. No Japanese woman dared show her emotions the way Auntie did; it was unprecedented. Even to talk too loudly was not something Japanese women did in public, so everyone was startled by her yelling, and Shiichi Uncle, more peaceable and restrained by nature, didn't know what to do.

A week after Norio's funeral, Uncle came home at midday looking for Harue Auntie. "She's supposed to be at work," he said, looking worried. "Have you seen her?"

"Not since this morning," I said. "I thought she went to work."

I went out, saw Omoto-san in her tiny garden, and called to her. "Omoto-san, have you seen my auntie?"

"Harue-san? Ahh, I did see her early this morning. She was saying something about going to Yasukuni Jinja."

"Yasukuni Jinja?"

"Yes, in Chiyoda-ku."

Instead of going to work, Harue Auntie had run off to pray at the Shinto shrine where the spirits of the departed soldiers were said to return. I reported this to my uncle.

"Get Iwao and Sā-chan and go to the shrine. See if you can find her there and bring her home," Uncle said.

Iwao, Sā-chan, and I took the streetcar down to the shrine, and we moved along with hundreds of other people in a slow moving tide toward the towering gate, the scuffing of geta on the rock pavement sounding like the incessant *tap tap tapping* of a snare drum. Rows and rows of dark-clothed people sat in the open area and faced the main entrance of the building, which housed the shrine of the earth-gods. The three of us waded

149

through the ocean of these men and women who came, rain or shine, to sit and mourn before the earth deities. A light rain began to fall, which made it all the more difficult to search for her; hundreds of black umbrellas shielded the participants' faces. "Please excuse us," we uttered, looking under these umbrellas.

Iwao spotted her first. "Come, Okā-chan," he said to her, tenderly. I had never heard him take this tone with his mother before. "It's time to go home. Norio wouldn't want you out in the rain like this."

Her whole body shaking, she sobbed, nodding her head. Her hands trembled on her knees. I sat quietly beside her, Iwao, and Sā-chan, and Auntie acted as if I were invisible to her. After a while she picked up her purse and her zabuton. Her face was swollen from crying.

"He's not coming back? Can't you go and fetch your brother?" she asked Iwao.

He shook his head. "He's not coming back, Okā-san."

Since Auntie wouldn't let me touch her, I had Iwao take her to the low table and sit with her until Uncle came home from work. I brewed a pot of tea and had Sā-chan serve it to her mother.

"You find her?" Uncle asked as soon as he stepped into the house.

I nodded from my place in the kitchen. "She's with Iwao and Sā-chan," I said.

"Is she okay?"

"She's been quiet."

My uncle took off his neck scarf, hung it on a peg near the entryway, and walked into the living room.

"Don't do this, okay?" I heard him say. "You worry us. You can't do this to yourself."

"*Nnnnn, nnnnn,*" she sobbed.

"It'll be all right," Shiichi Uncle said.

"No, nothing will be right ever again. Kill me. Just kill me. Life is not worth living. Norio, Norio!" she said, crumbling in anguish, pounding the floor.

"She's escaped again!" Iwao cried out, early next morning.

Uncle said, "I can't look for your mother. I must report to work or I'll lose my job. You must find her, Iwao, hurry! It's not good for her to grieve like this. It only makes her sick. I'll be back at noon to check on things."

Iwao and Sā-chan ran off to the shrine, but this time I did not go with them. I would be of no help.

It took the entire morning before they found their mother and could coax her back to the house. "Don't do this *again*," Iwao was scolding when he brought her in.

When Uncle came home at noon, Sā-chan said, "Otō-san, Okā-san is really not herself. No one can control her; she's going crazy. She just cries and screams. You have to do something, please." She sat erect before her father, sobbing and wringing her hands on her lap.

"She's not crazy, only grieving," Shiichi Uncle said. He finally called a doctor's office; the person there sent a nurse instead because of the shortage of doctors.

"She'll be better after I give her a sedative," the nurse said.

That evening, Harue Auntie stopped crying and finally rested. Freed from her hysteria, the house returned to its usual quiet pattern. I could hear, once more, the sparks in the brazier snap, the dull buzz of the planes overhead, the children's high voices as they played.

On a long scroll called the Gōshimeibo, the shrine's scribes wrote the names of the war dead, their places of death, their permanent addresses. They did this around the clock with so many boys dying. We got word that Norio's name was soon brushed among them.

The day Norio's name appeared on the perpetual scroll, I went up to our family altar where his ashes were and put my hands together in the Oneness of all Life with the promise: *I will take you to Kyoto.* Unrolling his bloodstained band of a thousand stitches, I lifted it to my face and cried into it.

18

The Firebombing

Sumie let out a scream when the bomb exploded, the light of a fire outside dancing behind the squares of our windows and paper-latticed door, making menacing ghostly patterns on the wall. Nearby, several houses went up in flames, and the frantic voice of a man pleaded for his children to be saved from the growing fire, but the terror in his voice made his appeals sound confusing, guttural, more animal than human, the only words recognizable in his plea: "Save us, please!"

Toma-jiji rallied the neighborhood squad: "Ho-o-o-o-i, come out and fight the fire. Saito-san! Iwao!" I heard my uncle and Iwao rush out. In the background, children continued screaming. I cupped my hands around Sumie's ears; I didn't want her to hear their horrible cries.

I learned the next morning that Kato-san's husband and ten of their children had perished in the flames. When the firebomb fell, an anomaly really, the occasional bomb never hitting their targets, the heavy tile roof of the Katos' house had collapsed and trapped them. A small explosion of a shallow gas line killed the whole family, except Kato-san, who, due to complications in giving birth, had been in the hospital with her newborn. When I saw her later, Kato-san was but an elongated shadow of herself, and she was carrying her new baby like a dishrag on her arm. Sumie did not recognize her as her wet nurse and hid her face in my kimono when Kato-san made a move to pat her.

Kato-san looked at me in a way that pulled me straight into her sorrow, at which time she cried out: "Oh, Hi-chan, everything has ended for me. There's nothing left!"

"Kato-san, I'm so sorry, so very sorry," I said, crumbling to the ground and chanting my grief at her feet.

A couple of days later, the Americans dropped leaflets asking Japan to surrender. One such drop contained leaflets with a picture of, by this time, Japan's former (something the Americans didn't seem to know) Prime Minister, Tojo Hideki, and other military officers with a caption in Japanese that read: "Military leaders of Japan, can you convince the people that you are able to defend the soil, the waters, and the sky of Japan?"

The day those flyers fell, the children and I, Shiichi Uncle who had not yet gone to work, and all our neighbors gathered outside to read them, my uncle reading it aloud for me. "This is just another way," Toma-jiji, said, "that the Americans are trying to sway us away from the right path for Japan."

"Maybe, but I'm not convinced Japan is able to defend us," Shiichi Uncle said.

Toma-jiji shook his head and said, "You have no right to say that!"

"You are deluded," Shiichi Uncle said and walked away.

The children and I gathered as many of these leaflets as possible for they could be used for toilet paper and fire starters. What was left over, we cut into squares to roll tobacco and dried potato leaves into cigarettes.

A rumor that the Americans were dropping a new kind of bomb that drizzled gasoline—a much more potent kind of firebomb—circulated, and after the air-raid sirens sounded one night, a low-flying bomber dropped a burning streak of an unknown substance onto the ground. The bombing was in our ward, so I went out to see if I could help. Leaving Sumie at home with Shiichi Uncle, so he didn't have to go out to fight the fire, Iwao and I walked to the target area where we saw that those caught in the wake of the explosions glowed, as if with a blue-red halo. Flesh melted and sizzled, as pieces of the gelatinous mass dropped by a few bombs that evening burned off the bodies like morning mist. Walking along the roadside, I later came upon the form of a crumpled child, her hand melting away and glowing from within, the substance like coal; she screamed as it ate into her flesh. People came to her aid, but washing the substance with water did very little but prolong her agony.

After helping to throw buckets of sand on a fire raging in the target area, I left Iwao with the others and roamed the streets nearby to assess the damage made by this substance. As I wandered through the alleyways, I saw many stretchers emitting an eerie blue light as people were carried away to the hospitals. Where the substance burned on isolated pieces of wood, I poked the small puddles of the burning element with a stick, the glow reminding me of the blue bits of phosphorescence on the beach that I had once carried out to show my father. Whatever it was that fell looked like the same material from the fireball that had chased Papa, but in reality no one knew what this substance was or how to stop its deadly power.

On the night of March 9, 1945, I noticed an unusual stirring in the streets. People with worried looks on their faces were rushing to their homes, ordering their children to stop playing and gathering them inside. I rose from the table where Sā-chan, Iwao, Yuki-chan, Sumie, and I had eaten an early supper. Looking out of the window, I said, "I want you all to put on your air-raid outfits." To my relief, Sumie did not protest, the urgency in my voice apparent. Yuki-chan, obedient, watched my every move, her eyes serious as an adult's.

"What's happening, Hi-chan? Why are you making us dress in our air-raid uniforms? And you never turned down the fires in the brazier before. You scared of something?" an impudent Sā-chan asked.

"Yeah, yeah," I said. "Just do as I say."

She gazed at me defiantly and ran upstairs to see how she looked in the mirror with her fire hood on, ambivalent about wearing it, if it looked good on her or not. On her way downstairs, I heard her say, "I hate the hood. It looks so ugly on," then decide, "I'm not going to wear it. No one can make me, not even the government!"

Oh stop it, I wanted to scream. *Don't you know this is serious?*

Turning to me, she said, "Nobody's that afraid of the bombers. What's happened to you?"

"It's just a feeling I have. I can't explain it!"

Later that evening, after my uncle and auntie came home from work,

I said, "Shiichi Uncle, it doesn't look good. It's a clear night, a bad omen." He looked at his hands and rubbed them.

"You're right," he said with an anxious face. "Harue-san, get your things ready."

I placed some beans and rice crackers into a cloth wrap and shoved it into my pants pocket. Next, I pulled down our emergency basket hanging from the ceiling and took out the money and identifications, and stuffed them in the folds of the sash that held up my pants. Iwao blew out the altar candles; I smothered the incense into its own ashes.

The usual air-raid warnings sounded at ten-thirty. For the first time since I had lived in Japan, it felt prudent to smother all of the fires in the house and leave nothing burning. I raked the coals in the brazier one last time, closed the damper, and dropped on the heavy lid. Before shutting the door to the family altar, I paid my respects to Norio's ashes. Wind fluttered the blue doorway curtains. The tattered breezes rattled the doors and lifted loose ashes around the burner. I rubbed prayer beads between my palms.

Sirens went off again. Planes appeared to be flying lower than ever before. I looked out of the window and saw in the distance, in that black-crystal night, the shadows of the long planes, the B-29 bombers, flying in the light of the stars. The land was dark in the blackout; I saw only a flicker of light here and there. Far off, on and off, I heard the low *thud, thud* of anti-aircraft guns, the inadequate coastal guns protecting the area, the city's first and only line of defense, as searchlights rotated and crisscrossed their beams in the sky.

The planes—some say as many as three hundred—were flying in to drop their bombs. I ran upstairs to look out. I watched as a small lead plane, not like the bombers, swept down into our part of the city and dropped a strip of flames. The fire, fueled by a steady wind, moved upward like a river of fountaining lava. Fire bells clanged in the streets. Another low-flying plane dropped a strip of fire that crossed the other one at its center. Fire rose along this new line, brightened the night sky, and dissolved the stars and shadows. The houses that fell in relief looked dark against the sudden light.

"What's happening?" Sā-chan asked, her eyes wide and darting. "Okā-chaan!"

At that moment, I realized in horror that Mukōjima was the target—a fiery X marking the spot—the American bombers after the factories and plants in the area. I woke the children up, then banged on Shiichi Uncle's door. He hitched the packed bedding to his back and Auntie swung Yuki-chan across her shoulders.

"Hurryyyy, let's gooo!" Uncle shouted and we rushed into the night.

Looking up as I ran, I saw thousands upon thousands of incendiary devices drifting in. They made strange whistling sounds—whine after whine—with no let up. Planes and their bombs darkened the sky.

"We're not going to stay here to fight the fires," Uncle exclaimed.

"But Shiichi . . ." Harue Auntie objected.

"Don't be crazy, Harue," Uncle said. "We'll all die if you do what the government wants." Around us, other families already had hoses and shovels in their hands. Unlike us, they were compliant and ready to fight the anticipated fires.

"Run—to the river, not the shelter!" Shiichi Uncle commanded.

We had not gone far when a series of blasts moved the ground beneath us. We dropped to the street and covered our heads; our bodies rocked with the impact of the bombs. Harue Auntie was the first to react and stood up. Stunned, the rest of us staggered about, unsure if we were still alive. My head clearing, I heard Harue Auntie cry out, "Norio!" and saw her run back to our house that was already in flames, Auntie wanting to get back inside to retrieve his ashes, but Shiichi Uncle reached for her and held her back by her kimono collar. "Let me go," she said, twisting. *Let me go!*

She fell to her knees, and without reason, we all followed her in reflex. She cried as she pounded the ground with her fists: "Oh, to be burned twice by fire. How cruel! Norio, is there no mercy?"

With a look of panic on her face, Sā-chan crawled toward her mother and kept yelling: "Okā-san! Okā-san! Okā-san!" When we got up to run once more, we saw people throwing away their shovels. Like us, they saw the futility of fighting the fire and, like us, began running for their lives.

In the firestorm generated by the firebombs, Sā-chan, who kept screaming for her mother, seemed to be losing her mind. I also thought I was losing mine. I wanted to drop Sumie so that I could move on; I wanted

156

to leave her like a Bodhisattva statue on the roadside. In the press of people, the strong pushed aside the weak and plowed into and over them, our family no less guilty in our selfish struggle to live. Like the throng of people around us, we moved by instinct, like rats, to get to the river. With thousands upon thousands of others, we dodged flying debris, smoke, splintered wood, and glass. Clouds of glowing gases spun in tornadoes on the side of us and behind us—the fire whooshing; it sucked up bodies that exploded in the heat. Reaching the river, we saw to our dismay that it too was on fire. We saw floating bodies twisting their blackened arms and legs toward us and Sā-chan screamed again, so Uncle signaled us away from the increasing panic of the crowds and directed us south.

Tied onto their mothers' backs, sagging as if sleeping, children smoldered, their mothers unaware that they were dead. I saw so many of them as I ran. Eventually, they burst into flames and burned like torches. Because Yuki-chan's and Sumie's clothing kept catching on fire, Iwao and I whacked the children. He also helped with Sā-chan by calming her down. I spat and pasted saliva on Sumie's face and hair until my throat was so dry I could hardly swallow; I rolled her hot feet in my mouth to snuff out any possibility that they might burst into flames, and I shoved her hands into the cleavage of my kimono to shield them. "Sore, Mama, sore," she whimpered. I carried her high on my chest for I wasn't about to let her die without my knowing.

Strange black figures came at me and receded. I shoved and screamed at people who wanted to breathe my air. I could no longer see well, and it was as if I were moving through a dream, my body in hell's air. My arms began speaking to me in their need, *put Sumie down, put her down, save yourself*; I wanted to be free of her living weight for she was choking me to death with her frightened arms. Sā-chan kept falling behind and I could no longer wait for her. It was like carrying two children: Sumie and a whining Sā-chan.

We ran and ran toward what seemed to be an area of less fire, but we were soon hampered in our escape route, trapped by a wall of flames that towered before us. Iwao, thinking quickly, saw that the other side was open and clear and leapt through it. He ran back through the flames to where we stood and shoved his reluctant mother to the other side. His father, who had Yuki-chan by this time, having thrown the family's bedding on the street, took leaping strides to the other side of the flames, shouting at Sā-chan and me to follow. When Iwao found we weren't behind his father, he rushed back to where I waited with a hesitant Sā-chan.

"You must run through the fire," he commanded his sister. "What are you waiting for?"

"I can't," Sā-chan said. "I just can't."

"Why not?"

"Going that way looks safer to me," she said, pointing in another direction. "I'm too scared to go through the fire!"

"You, scared? Since when! You're only trying to be difficult! C'mon!" Turning to me, Iwao said, "Talk to her, Hi-chan. Make sure she comes with you."

"I'll *make* her come. Don't worry."

"You promise, right, Sā-chan? To do as Hi-chan says?"

Sā-chan nodded. Looking at me, Iwao grabbed a wailing Sumie out of my hands, and holding her high, he dashed through the flames to take her across the fire.

But Sā-chan stalled. Her body was leaning toward the direction she wanted to go; I couldn't let her get away from me. "Come on!" I screamed at her like Harue Auntie would have screamed at me. I was screaming at Sā-chan, her mother's golden child, the recipient of her mother's kindness and gifts, the spoiled child, her mother's favorite. I stood there thinking how much I hated her and her mother.

By this time, I had no patience for her contrariness, the flames growing fierce. "How can you be so selfish?" I said. "You're putting everyone in danger, can't you see that? We're doing our best to help you! C'mon, let's go!"

"I can't, and you can't make me go!" She held her wrist protecting my watch, which must have been burning hot.

"I hate you," I screamed.

"I hate you too," she said. "What do you think about that?"

I reached out and slapped her across her face.

"Oh, Hi-chan," she said, surprised.

"Go, go to hell," I shouted and went after her. Enraged, I grabbed her by her shoulders and pushed her into the fire.

"HI-CHAAAAN!" she screamed as she fell, flames engulfing her.

"Get up! Get up!" I cried. "Get up and run!" But Sā-chan couldn't hear me anymore.

PART III

KYOTO
March 1945 – June 1945

All phenomena are illusory and empty.
—from the Teachings of Buddha

19

Aftermath

If remembering is hell, then I was in hell. Sā-chan falling into the fire. Sā-chan staggering and in flames. Me leaping into the fire and going after her. Sā-chan howling and trying to get away from me. Sā-chan running past her parents and Iwao. Iwao and me scrambling after her to stop her. Saachan never stopping. *Oh no, what had I done?*

She seemed possessed, as if by demons. Swarming crowds blocked our way as Iwao and I ran as fast as we could to catch her. We hollered for her to stop, but she never did and, by the time we got to her, she was lying on the street in a smoldering pile, parts of her body like charcoal, some of her clothing still burning. Iwao took Sumie's carrying cloth off my back and smothered whatever spots continued to burn.

"How can she keep on burning?" Iwao asked, his face fierce as he patted his sister's body. "She has so little fat."

I could no longer see Sā-chan's face. *Oh, what had I done?* It had happened so quickly, the fire hungry, gnawing at her flesh. One eye was burnt out, and a glob of tissue hung from the socket, as if her eye had simply melted away like butter. I had the urge to push the hanging mass back in, to make her face look whole again, but I couldn't move my hands to do it. Teeth protruded where the soft flesh of her lips had burned away.

Sā-chan suddenly sat up without effort, in a kind of frantic movement that had taken over her limbs, as if she bore no pain. "Try to stay still, Sā-chan," I said. She popped open her one good eye as if surprised to hear a coherent voice above the persistent roar of the fire that surrounded us. "Oh, Sā-chan, I'm sorry, I'm so sorry," I cried out. She turned, and following my voice, she looked at us with her good eye and, at *me*, with so much tenderness it was agonizing. Unendurable.

"I tried to catch her," Iwao said, crying openly, tears flowing down his cheeks. "But she had such crazy strength, I couldn't stop her." He turned to look at me. "Why, Hi-chan? Why didn't she stop?"

"I don't know," I lied. Despite the heat around us, I began to shiver, my teeth chattering. I had no control over my body. "She was . . . she was probably just scared," I managed to say.

"But don't you see? I was the one who forced her to jump through the fire!"

I couldn't tell him that it was my fault and not his. I still couldn't believe what I had done, let alone admit to what had happened. Although my throat burned at its depth and was scorched by guilt, I buried the truth by swallowing it and said to Sā-chan, "Everything will be all right. Your mother's coming." How I could say those words was beyond me. I promised myself I would talk to Iwao later, the honorable Iwao who had taken the burden of guilt upon himself.

When the rest of the family caught up with us, Harue Auntie threw herself over Sā-chan's body. "First Norio, then you. What have I done to offend the gods?"

Yuki-chan, who came to my side, stared at her sister, and Sumie began to wail, the same way animals wail when they know that one of their kind is dying. I took her from Uncle's arms and swung her on my back to calm her.

Seeing that Sā-chan was trying to say something, I knelt over her. "Water . . ." she managed to whisper.

"I'm sorry, Sā-chan," I said, "but there's no water. Sā-chan . . . ?" I gripped her arm, everything in me wanting to say something, but I couldn't. A sticky fluid oozed from her body. "I, I . . ." I tried again, desperately wanting to explain what I did, but I couldn't find the words. She tried to say something, too, her voice a frothy gurgle.

"Sā-chan, why didn't you listen to me? You should have listened," Iwao said between sobs, his shoulders shaking with grief. Sā-chan held up her hand and waved to silence her brother, as if to say it was all right and that he was not to blame.

We had to move on. We had no choice but to leave Sā-chan lying on the road. The fire was turning into a hurricane; hot winds gusted with extraordinary force. "Leave me here to die with her. I can't abandon Sā-chan, my child, my daughter," Harue Auntie said. Shifting her gaze at me, she said accusingly, "And you, you were the last one with her . . . What happened?"

Giving Yuki-chan to Iwao, Uncle lifted Harue Auntie up from Sā-chan's body, but she pulled away and dropped to her hands and knees. When she didn't move and remained on all fours, Uncle gathered her in his arms and dragged her along to run with the rest of us. As we fled, I looked back on the small, twitching figure, what remained of Sā-chan. I was too shocked by what I had done to even cry. *She's dead because of you, Hi-chan, dead because of you*, the words, *because of you*, exactly what Miyo said to me when Papa died.

As we ran, Sumie's clothing kept igniting in beautiful red blossoms. Iwao came up to me and beat her clothing with his blistered hands to put out the sparks. I kept seeing Sā-chan's face in front of me, smiling, telling me to come with her even if she were already dead. She moved backward; I moved forward. She was telling me she was already dead and chanting a nonsensical children's rhyme:

Cho-chi, cho-chi
a wa wa
kaikori, kaikori
atama ten ten.

"Hi-chan," yelled Iwao, his face up to mine. "Pay attention. Stay awake. You're going to die like Sā-chan." *Cho-chi, cho-chi a wa wa.*

I nodded but the lethargy I had fallen into was profound. I deserved to die.

"Follow me, come, come," Sā-chan beckoned. "The flowers here are beautiful." She was spinning her hands, tapping her head: *Kaikori, kaikori, atama ten ten.*

"Hi-chan! Snap out of it!" Iwao yelled.

Oh, what had I done?

The open plaza of Ryōgoku Station saved us and thousands of others. Somehow, we had managed to go as far as the station, the large open area serving as a firebreak. Exhausted, I fell asleep on the gravel with Sumie in my arms.

The next morning, the air was dry and cold, carrying on its breath the smell of cooked flesh, old lumber, and bomb fuel. I shivered and pulled my jacket around me, now full of holes from the sparks. Though groggy, I managed to climb on a train platform to survey what had happened to us, with the memory of what happened to Sā-chan and my part in her death stunning me. My whole body began to shake, uncontrollably.

After a while, I gained enough composure to survey the miles and miles of scorched ruins that lay with its uneven perimeter of half-burnt material and low structures, in the same way that waves along a shoreline washed up debris. In the center of the firestorm, almost everything was gone but the stir of ashes. The scene, beautiful in its desolation, its mute gray coloring with outcroppings of destroyed buildings jutting here and there, looked like the devastation of a huge volcanic disaster. Man had succeeded in outdoing nature in wreaking havoc on earth. Soon Iwao was at my side, followed a moment later by Shiichi Uncle, and like me, they were astounded by the spectacle before them.

"We should try to find Sā-chan—to bury her," I said after a long while of looking at what lay before us. "The place where she fell did not have much that would burn. Perhaps part of her is left. Then we must go back to the house."

Uncle, Iwao, and I went back to where Harue Auntie sat with the children. Sumie and Yuki-chan, now awake, were hungry and whimpering. "Stop it," Harue Auntie scolded.

I checked on the girls; I found their burns not very severe. "Yes, stop your sniffling, both of you," I said, sternly. "Listen to Harue Auntie. She's right. Crying's no good. It just makes it hard on everyone. You have to be strong."

I had a package of what was now a handful of smashed beans and crumbly rice crackers in my pocket, which I gave to the children. Iwao looked on with hungry eyes but said nothing. If the adults weren't eating, he wasn't going to either. He was different now; he had traveled through fire and emerged on the other side. "Listen, maybe I can find something to eat," he said, running off, glad to be doing something. I nodded. I found it hard to look him in the eyes.

Before we headed out to find Sā-chan, Iwao came walking back with an egg, a drooping cucumber, and some water. "I'll get more, later," he said of the water.

Staring at the egg and cucumber, I began laughing and crying at the ridiculous look of them, which must have struck the woman next to me as funny too, because she began laughing as well. Iwao and Uncle smiled. Harue Auntie stared at the woman and me with irritation. Seeing her angry face, I laughed all the more and louder. Close to hysteria, I was really crying for myself. *Oh, what had I done?*

"So, what happened back there?" Harue Auntie said, after my laughter dwindled to tears.

"What do you mean?"

"You know what I mean—with Sā-chan."

"I, I . . ."

"Stop it, Harue. Leave the girl alone!" Uncle said, intervening. "What are you trying to do? This is not the time. Sā-chan is dead and we have to find her."

Auntie stared at Shiichi Uncle with clenched fists and teeth. A second later, she dropped down to Yuki-chan's height to check a burn on her daughter's cheek, which she quickly patted with saliva.

Without asking, I left the children with Harue Auntie while Iwao, Uncle, and I walked alongside the Sumida River filled with logs of dead people, a line of solemn men along the banks and walls already hauling out bodies with long poles and ropes. Occasional shouts echoed through the burned city, and gusts of warm air, spun from the ground, bathed our feet. On the streets, stacks and stacks of charred bodies. Entire families had huddled together to die. For most, reaching the river had been impossible, thousands upon thousands stacked up against the river walls or the bridges, and those who got there were crushed by others or frozen by the cold water or burned by the fires on the water.

Between coughs, Iwao recited the names of the streets we passed: Yokozuna, Kiyosumi, Mito Kaido. I didn't know how he could tell what direction he was going, but reacting to an internal gyroscope, he moved with certainty.

"It was around here," he said, sweeping his arms over the area like a priest giving a blessing. The utensils of daily living, inert and scattered, connected to nothing now—rice paddles, whisks, wire egg baskets, knives, spoons, chopsticks—lay in small, discrete piles. Here, however, everything had not been completely burned; I felt we had a good chance of finding Sā-chan's body.

"I know this is the right area," Iwao said. He then called out, "Look. Over here, these bodies—I'm sure one of them is Sā-chan."

"We don't have much time to find her," I said. "The death wagons are already here to pick up the bodies." In an incredible move by the citizen army from areas of Tokyo untouched by the fire, the dead were being hauled away.

"Otō-san, how are we going to tell if it's her?" Iwao asked.

"I don't know, but somehow we'll know," Shiichi Uncle said with conviction.

We walked up and down the streets. Aid stations had sprung up in areas along the river with lines of people appearing as if by magic. Where everyone had come from, what terror they had encountered and survived, none of us knew.

An eerie hush filled the surroundings. People bowed when passing and said softly, "Excuse me, excuse me," and we acknowledged them. How they, we, could be so polite was beyond my understanding, when only the night before, all of us were part of a teeming, screaming, clawing mass of rats. I wanted to scream: *Have we all gone mad?*

Not much later, Iwao and I came across a body that by size and shape could have been Sā-chan's, but we saw that it was scorched beyond recognition by flames. It had no face, no feet, no clothing. The upper arm had fallen away from the body's shoulder and sagged on a thread of ligament. Only the hand holding the other at the wrist did not appear burned. Intestines were spewed out, the odor fierce, and Iwao and I gagged at the sudden flux of bad air. Flies swarmed, excited by the smell.

"It's disgusting!" Iwao said. "This body's been cooked like Murata-san's pig." He squatted, punched his fist into the ground between his legs, and gave out a yell as he sprang up.

"Don't say things like that in front of the dead," reprimanded Uncle. "This could be Sā-chan."

"It's important to your mother and father that we find your sister and give her a proper burial. At least we have to try," I said, Iwao nodding gravely.

As we looked at the bodies in the area, I became more and more convinced that the one with the torn shoulder was Sā-chan's. It had to be hers. While it may have been wrong to claim her if we weren't sure, it didn't seem to matter, seeing that there were thousands of bodies no one would ever search for or claim.

"What shall we do, Uncle?" I asked after we had searched throughout the area and had come back to look at the same body. "Can we say this is Sā-chan, take her away—give her a proper burial?"

"I don't know. I wish there were some way to identify her. What if we took it and it was someone else's brother or sister? This person's spirit would never rest."

Weary of the smell of flesh, weary of death, I sat on the ground and put my head between my knees. In truth, I no longer knew who we were, what we were as people, or what we were as fellow human beings. *What I was as a human being.* I didn't know how we were all connected anymore. To our enemies in the air, none of us on the ground mattered. We were just numbers, without faces, without identity—a mass of scurrying rats to be destroyed by fire. Then again, I thought, this could have happened in America, to my family, to our towns. Wasn't it the case with Pearl Harbor? And all the boys I knew, even Akira, could be fighting in the war. Just then, some American planes flew overhead. What a strange thing it was—my looking up at planes from my country that had bombed me. Which side was I on? Then again, how could I hate *either*?

"Hi-chan," Iwao called out. "Come here! You must see this."

He stood over the body and said, "It's Sā-chan for sure."

"How can you tell?"

168

"Take a close look."

I examined the body carefully, but I noticed nothing that would suggest it was Sā-chan. Iwao handed me a long piece of metal he had found in the area. "Pry under her hand, the one covering her wrist."

I understood. Underneath her hand was the face of my watch, the time 2:15.

"Do you think she died at that moment?" Iwao said after a long silence, just staring at her body.

"I don't know, Iwao. What made you look at her wrist?"

"I just thought it was strange, the way she was holding her hand. I wanted to know what she was protecting."

Uncle dropped to his knees beside Sā-chan. He didn't make a sound but clasped his hands together near his forehead. Large tears covered his cheeks as he murmured something unintelligible. I could do nothing for him; I also had to get away from him. Glad that Harue Auntie was with the children, I motioned Iwao to come with me.

"Where are we going?"

"I want to go back to the house; perhaps we'll find something."

Since we were fairly close to where the house had been, I decided that we should take a look at the area, leaving Uncle to grieve. A thick layer of fine gray ash covered the ground where our house once stood; beneath it, the still warm, scorched earth. The only thing I found was a shard of our broken mirror, its edges no longer sharp but melted down. I slipped it into my pocket. Then, I dug a hole with my hands, scooped up some of the soil, placed it in the center of my handkerchief and tied this into a ball.

"What's that for?" asked Iwao.

"This is Norio," I said, "to give to your mother."

"It's not Norio. It's only dirt." Iwao spat in disgust.

"It may be dirt, but it's also Norio. We come from dirt and we return to dirt," I said and cradled the cloth to my chest. "At least we have something of him."

"War is stupid," Iwao said squatting, watching me look for things in the ashes. "Because of the war Sā-chan, Norio are dead. We're all crazy to support a war like this!" he muttered scornfully, and cried.

Before we left, Iwao scooped up two handfuls of ash and dirt from the

169

ground and flung them high and wide into the air, the mixture falling like a spray of water hitting the rocks along the seashore, after which time he ran off into the haze, his protesting lungs hacking away.

We decided to cremate Sā-chan and gathered what was left of her into a blanket Iwao found. He also searched for large pieces of unburned wood, and he and Uncle then hauled them and Sā-chan on a flat wheelbarrow that they had borrowed from a government worker picking up bodies and brought her to a pyre near the Sumida River. I watched as her body burned. In the dying embers her bleached bones resembled the white coral on the beaches back home.

The next day we held a short roadside service to consecrate her ashes. "Would you please chant the Junirai, a song of adoration, instead of the usual funeral sutra?" Uncle asked the itinerant priest. "That was her favorite." I remember thinking that even upon their death, we continue to learn new things about people.

This is how we sent Sā-chan to the kalpas, to infinity, the ninth verse fixed firmly in my mind, this smattering of words that got caught in my throat, these words of ashes:

> *Sho u mu jo mu ga to*   All life changes like the dew
> *Yaku nyo sui gatsu den yo ro* We have no permanent self

For days after the ceremony, Harue Auntie carried Sā-chan's urn under her arm wherever she went. She also tied the little pouch of dirt of Norio that I had taken from the house on a piece of string and hung it around her neck.

Not a roof tile or teapot or garden leaf remained, every house within sixteen square miles had disappeared in the firebombing, and Tokyo was nearly gone with a hundred thousand or more people dead. Sharing a burnt-out bus with four other families and fighting others off, we came to live next to an old military barracks on the outskirts of the city near the Edo River. The government was slow in providing food or shelter, and dysentery, scabies, and cholera reached epidemic proportions. Rats ruled. Iwao whittled bamboo spears—rat killers—to distribute among the older children, the bamboo taken from a stand near Shinobazu Pond in Ueno

Park. I was watchful for signs of coughing and unusual body aches in the children; vigilant about it, I checked for hair and body lice. Much time was spent in long lines for ointments and bandages to cover our burns, for syrups to fight our coughs and congestion, and for food that I had, earlier, dreaded so much to stand in line for, all of life's necessities in shorter supply than ever before. Even the black market had disappeared.

People in the lines were secretive, distrustful of everyone else. We couldn't meet each other's eyes, and we tried to avoid any recognition or contact, as if each of us harbored some dark, hidden secret because we had lived. We were alive, breathing and eating unlike the dead, but survival had come at a terrible price. Many of us had committed secret acts of violence in order to save ourselves in the firestorm. We were alive, but none of us, as written on our faces, was able to share in the joy.

Four days after Tokyo was firebombed and destroyed, I received a postcard from Miyo through the Red Cross. A letter of compassion, it was called. Iwao had been in the area of our neighborhood, looking for what he could find, when a Red Cross volunteer appeared and said, "I'm looking for Aoki Himiko. Do you know anyone by that name? Do you think she died in the fire?" Iwao, bringing her over to where we lived, told me later, "I thought it might be you—though I had forgotten your real name."

In her short note Miyo said, "Mama is very ill. Do you think you can write home?" The postcard, postmarked in late September of the previous year, nearly six months before it had reached me, had red marks authorizing its delivery. I looked at the letter and realized I couldn't remember Mama's face. Nor Miyo's.

Though I wondered in passing what Mama's sickness could have been, I never wrote back. Cancer? A stroke? Whatever it was, I couldn't do anything about it. Even if I'd had a pencil, guilt about surviving, guilt about Sā-chan's death had overpowered my life; answering a letter six months after it was written seemed utterly unimportant. I couldn't begin to list all the suffering I had faced.

20

On the Road

The smell of dead bodies lingered everywhere, but when human ashes began falling into his bits of fish and small scoops of rice, Shiichi Uncle decided that we had to leave Tokyo. Ashes entered the seams of our clothing, fell into our hair, and lined the rims of our noses, ears, and eyes.

Shiichi Uncle's and Iwao's coughs were worsening under the poor conditions that surrounded us, my uncle blaming it on the ashes, Harue Auntie, on the smoke. Both Uncle and Iwao began having more difficulty breathing, their breaths coming and going like the sound of reed pipes. Too, the drone of airplanes continued and drove everyone crazy with fear. We held on to our children. Huddled and cowered like small animals in their burrows.

Only a week after we found the bus to live in, Uncle announced that it would be best if we moved out of Tokyo. "I know Hiroshima is where we come from and that my brother is there, but I don't want to be a farmer again," he said. "Also, I know Harue doesn't want to move far."

Earlier, when Norio had died, I told my uncle about Norio's wishes—about his wanting his ashes placed in a temple in Kyoto. After a day of pondering, Shiichi Uncle made a decision. "Listen, let's just do what Norio wanted and go to Kyoto. We can always come back here when things get better," he said.

The day before we decided to leave for Kyoto, Hamada-san appeared at the bus. "Excuse me please, is anyone around?" she called out. I was seated on the iron floor, on a small piece of futon, patching the children's clothes, when I heard her voice. Uncle and Auntie were out hunting for food and Iwao was on one of his explorations; the girls were playing under a scorched tree with a group of other children. Yuki-chan was now four years old and Sumie close to three; young as Yuki-chan was, I could depend on her to watch Sumie.

I went to the open bus door to show Hamada-san in. She looked well, her kimono and coat looking very becoming and, next to me, she was the height of elegance in subdued blue silk. I wrapped my badly burned jacket tighter around myself.

"Please forgive me," she said, her head bowed. She did not look at me. "I waited and watched the bus for a while. I was unsure what to do or how you would receive me. I'm sorry to barge in on you like this."

"There's nothing to be sorry about. Hurry, come in, the dust is bad outside." I showed her to an area with a small mat and two cushions on the floor. "We can sit here," I said. "I'm sorry but I can't serve you any tea. As you can see, we have almost nothing."

"And I couldn't bring something to share."

"That's no problem. In other circumstances, it would have been different. You had been all too generous before," I said, thinking about the dried beans, candy, and crackers she brought over whenever visiting, deeply ingrained cultural customs holding sway despite her family's poverty.

I looked at her tiny frame seated across me and nearly cried, my feelings for her having softened, feelings that the fire had changed profoundly. I had been through one of the largest fires in the world and had killed someone in my anger and moment of poor judgment. How could I not be humble, how could I not feel connected to this woman? All the anger I once felt for her had dissolved.

"I don't think that any of my children made it; except perhaps Jun," Hamada-san gushed, as though she had kept this all to herself and needed to break the dam that held back a cascade of tears. At that moment I wanted to hold her in my arms but was afraid it would only make matters uncomfortable and worse for her.

"I was with a client at the time of the fire," she admitted. She suddenly looked old, her eyes sunken in dark circles. "We had gone out of the city.

I . . . I've been searching for my family ever since. I heard from someone that you and your family were here, and I wanted to know if you had seen any of my children."

"I'm sorry, Hamada-san, but I haven't seen anyone," I said.

Her shoulders shook as she cried. "What have I done?"

"You didn't do anything. You were trying to live your life. Feed your children."

"The night of the fire my daughter said, 'Okā-san, don't go out tonight. Stay at home with us.' It was almost as though she knew something was going to happen. I scolded her and called her selfish." Hamada-san covered her eyes with her hands. "There is no excuse for me, no excuse at all!"

"You can't blame yourself. No one knew this would happen."

"My client and I had taken the train out to the hot springs in Nikko. Selfish, I wanted to go somewhere that would take me away from my suffering for a while." She removed her hands from her eyes and stared at me, her eyes burning into mine. "You knew about me, didn't you? That's why you withdrew yourself."

"I was being childish. I was angry because I thought you told my auntie my secret—about Akira. I thought you were responsible."

"I didn't . . ."

"I know, but by the time I saw you on Pigeon Street, the weight of what I thought had been your betrayal fell upon me. It was a case of selfish thinking on my part, but by then, we had been pulled so far apart that it was hard to get back together as friends."

"Earlier, I had wanted to tell you about what I was doing, but I couldn't confide in you because I was ashamed and you had closed off yourself."

"I might not have understood."

"Yes, that's true. I needed money so badly; I didn't know what to do. The men—I closed my eyes to them. But I was able to feed my children. Can you understand that?"

"Now I can," I said.

"Jun would never have forgiven me, you know, having been born with a powerful sense of virtue. If he had learned the truth he would have hated me. It's best that he never found out."

"Whatever he may have felt before . . . I'm sure he'd have come around."

Hamada-san shook her head. "I don't think that would have been possible."

"What if he's still alive? He'll go on searching for you."

Hamada-san reached out and took my hand. "I have to make sure he doesn't find me. If you ever see him, promise me you won't say anything. He's a young man with the world ahead of him, so his heart will mend. It's better that he remember the mother he once had than see me as I am now." She rose and moved to the door. "I'd better be going. Please extend my regards to your uncle and auntie. Say hello to Sā-chan, Iwao, and the girls too."

She was slow in gathering her scarf and handbag. I said nothing to her about Sā-chan.

"But you really don't have to go. Why don't you wait for my auntie and uncle to return?"

"I don't want them to see me," she said.

She quickly walked away, taking strides as long as the confines of her kimono allowed as she made her way through the ashes and debris. From the door of the bus, I watched her walk into the outskirts of the gray landscape of the city. Perhaps, had my situation been desperate enough, I would have done for Sumie what she had done for her children. Could I have been as brave? I could no longer blame her.

When Shiichi Uncle and Harue Auntie returned, I told them nothing of Hamada-san's visit.

Despite their malaise, to prepare for our journey, Shiichi Uncle and Iwao made a sturdy pushcart from parts found in junk heaps dotted around the burned-out city, the cart much like the old one we had wheeled about in the black market. We piled on a futon, two small pots, a few items of clothing, and pieces of wood I had salvaged in my wanderings. On the top of the pile, we perched what little food we had, along with Sā-chan's urn and "Norio's dirt," as Iwao began calling it. At the last minute, I put "Norio's dirt" into a small bronze incense burner Uncle found in the rubble and used it as a substitute urn.

We began our journey to Kyoto by avoiding the packed trains, following loosely the path of the old Tokaido Road between Tokyo and Kyoto, Shiichi Uncle, Harue Auntie, Iwao, and me helping to push the cart ahead of us, the trains whizzing by. The firestorm slowly receded into the background. Planes flew over us every day and, at first, though we scrambled for any bit of shelter, we soon began paying less attention to them. Big cities were what they were after. Shiichi Uncle said, "If the bombs come, the bombs come. Let's not worry. Besides, I don't think the planes are interested in us. There's no need to scramble for shelter out here, no need to be afraid."

All the while, Harue Auntie commended the Japanese for their tenacity. "The Americans may have bombed out the city and many of its railroad tracks," she said, "but look at the Japanese. They're already rebuilding them." The Japanese did work quickly, much as in the frenzy of red ants repairing their nests in the cane fields after Akira and I had set their anthills on fire.

On a lonely stretch of road that we had been following, a farmer in an old truck gave us a ride. The truck bed was cramped because of the cart, but we managed to cover some distance before he dropped us off. We passed the broken spine of many coastal towns, and along the way, we sang nursery rhymes, recited poems, made riddles, played number games. Harue Auntie was determined that even if the children did not go to school, they were going to learn something: "a, i, u, e, o, ka, ki, ku, ke, ko, sha, shi, su, se, so . . . Hey, pay attention," she said.

There was little sign of war in the country. Rabbit-ear irises in the sleeves of their leaves emerged in spots along the way, water reeds swayed their velvet heads next to the streams, snipes called from the waterways for their mates, and an occasional cicada rubbed its wings. At night, we slept under the stars and the *neep neep* of the frogs. Longbills made an appearance about that time, and by day a few grebes dotted the ponds.

The children no longer woke or screamed from nightmares, and Iwao began singing again between captured breaths "Tokyo Ondo," one of his favorite songs. Even the children could sing the refrain. They raised their little hands to clap them and jumped up and down to shout the "yoi, yoi!" parts.

"Sing it again, Iwao, sing it again," Yuki-chan said.

"Yes, sing it again," Sumie said, copying her cousin.

"Sā-chan would have liked this trip and to sing like this," Shiichi Uncle said, reminiscing. "I can still hear her in her high voice, her much-about-nothing talk." While it was good for him to talk about her, I could not bear to listen to what he had to say. Whenever he talked about Sā-chan, I thought I would die, thoughts about her excruciating to remember. This time, I went over to the children and walked along with them.

In its own strange way, it was nice to hear Harue Auntie grumbling to Shiichi Uncle, bringing a sense of normality back into our lives. "We should have stayed in Tokyo," she was quick to complain. "I don't know why I agreed to do this."

"Enough! No matter where we went, you would not have been satisfied," Uncle said.

At night, we found shelter under the eaves of a farmhouse, by the side of a large boulder, in abandoned houses, or under the brow of the trees. It felt good to be part of the countryside, to disappear into its low skirt line at dusk, to build small snapping fires to heat tea and boil the radishes and cabbages we scavenged for our evening meals. Generous farmers along the roadway gave what they could.

One morning Harue Auntie braved the sting of honeybees living in the stump of an old tree in order to retrieve honey for the children. Although she cried out with each sting, she was rewarded with the children's smiles as they lapped the honey that dripped from the wax into their hands. Auntie had grown even more severe after Norio and Sā-chan had died, but that day she was smiling at the children without the usual harshness in her eyes.

Iwao did more than his share in feeding us. He caught birds in a small trap he had made of bamboo or loaches in a stream for our dinners. No one talked while we inhaled the meat of the tender fish that I had broiled over the fire, Shiichi Uncle exclaiming: "It's so rare to eat like this. There's still so much to be grateful for."

After finishing her portion, Sumie cried out for more. "Still hungry, Mama," she said. Before I could say anything, Harue Auntie slipped a piece of her own fish onto Sumie's plate. With her face a blank, there was no way of my thanking her without feeling rebuffed.

We were anonymous travelers through this war-torn land. People wanted to be kind but did not want to get to know us or about our hardship. They would give us a ride, extra produce, whatever they could spare and, for once in this country, we could take things without feeling guilty or beholden. Without the usual formalities, we accepted lifts on people's truck beds for as far as they were going. We would then get off and walk again until someone else came by to take us a bit farther. Having the children with us helped; people always felt sorry for the children.

Near Hamamatsu, Iwao went into the cold water and caught some eels in a roadside stream. Later that evening, I heard Harue Auntie waking Shiichi Uncle up. "Iwao has a high fever," she said. "Wake Hi-chan up. Tell her to get some water from the stream."

After I fetched a bowl of water, I watched Auntie wring out the towel and lay it across Iwao's forehead. She and Uncle sat next to each other, watching over Iwao with worried frowns on their faces that the firelight accentuated.

Late the next day, near Ashima just outside of Kyoto, we had to stop at a roadside inn, Iwao too sick to go on. Luckily, the money I had put in my waistband just before the fire was still intact.

"Stopping here is like entering Nirvana, isn't it? We could use the rest," Shiichi Uncle said.

There we had our first hot bath in days, the girls and I overstaying our welcome in the soothing water. Awaiting her turn, Harue Auntie hollered: "Hey, get out from there. You're taking too long!"

The food at the inn was also surprisingly good. The owner, Mikami-san, was an excellent cook, and prepared eggs from a couple of chickens she kept hidden in a shed and succulent vegetables from her backyard. The next day the children ran up and down an embankment near rows of early carrots and white radishes, while I stretched out under the trees to meet the sun. Though the winds were brisk, the air was warm.

Harue Auntie gifted Mikami-san with some of the honey she had found, which put us in great favor. In return, the woman gave Harue Auntie a few yards of extra silk material so she could sew some clothing for the girls. In one day, Harue Auntie whipped up two vests.

"Sā-chan would have liked this," Yuki-chan said.

"Sā-chan would have liked this," Sumie said, imitating Yuki-chan.

"Nice, yes," Sumie kept repeating, the two girls comparing their new vests, moving their heads back and forth like Sā-chan when she used to admire herself in the mirror. "Sā-chan would have liked this! Sā-chan would have liked this!" the two chanted.

"Stop it," I said sharply to the children, puzzling them.

Just before leaving, Uncle had the bill reduced by giving the woman a hand with some of her chores. "My husband is dead and my two sons are in the war; there's no one to help me," she said. Although Shiichi Uncle was tired and still coughing, he chopped some wood and fixed her broken water tank.

"Thank you," she called out and ran after us when we left. She stopped on a small rise, and we could see her bowing and waving us on.

When we left the inn, Iwao, weakened by his fever, rode on the cart while Uncle, Auntie, and I helped each other push and pull the odd contraption that was full of squeaks and groans. The girls, clutching their rag dolls, ran back and forth like restless animals, aware that we were close to our destination.

That day, we spotted Mount Otowa to the east, and far off, near Uji, rose what they called the Hill of Gloom. We were nearing Kyoto. "Children, don't get silly," I reminded, to quell their giddiness, but I myself was feeling light, floating inside. As Shiichi Uncle had promised, the early buds of cherry and plum blossoms were beginning to bloom in a pink and white haze across the landscape and, dreamlike, the hillsides of Kyoto were covered with filaments of this translucent veil. I was used to seeing red, raging fires, landscapes of dark, hot radiant colors—the reds, yellows, purples, greens of things ablaze or tropical. Too, I was used to smelling strong, hot, and heavy fragrances, nothing as subtle as the scent of these blossoms that dappled the air. In spots along the road, the pink and white flowers on the trees looked soft and forgiving and put us all into a reflective mood, the children quieting down when we passed stands of these trees. They were subdued by the softness of the flowers around them.

21

Anshū

The old capital of Kyoto had been barely touched by the war. Temple bells greeted the city's visitors, couples strolled along the Philosopher's Walk, the Golden Pavilion scattered its light on the trees. The serenity of Kyoto veiled our bad experiences, almost as if the firestorm in Tokyo had never happened.

Shiichi Uncle and Iwao were growing weaker, their coughs incessant, deep. Uncle began raising his arms to his chest to contain the pain of his coughing, his face etched in agony, his legs weak under him. It was clear we couldn't go on traveling. Uncle talked of finding a job, but I knew that it was impossible for him; he needed rest.

Upon our arrival, we walked to the far side of the Kamo River and rested under some willow trees that lined the banks, which were close to the Kyoto Train Station, and once there, Uncle and Iwao flopped down on the stiff grass to stretch themselves out in the sun like how Mama left laundry out to dry on the bushes surrounding our Kaiwiki home. With Harue Auntie watching the children, I stole away to see what was available in jobs or places to stay.

I walked toward Umekōji Park, a park I had heard of, whereupon I came across a lonely vendor on the street. "It's a nice day, isn't it?" I said.

"Yes, isn't it?" the woman said. She may have thought I was a customer, at first, but had changed her mind, seeing that I looked like a beggar. I fingered the purses she had for sale.

"Excuse me please, I'm looking for anyone needing help in cleaning their houses or doing odd jobs in return for rooms," I said. "Would you know of any such jobs?"

She glowered at me as though I were crazy, her eyes traveling up and down my body *snap, snap* with no attempt at discretion. "Go up Kawaramachi-dōri," she said, using her chin to point the way. I turned away and walked back toward the river and up the street that she pointed out. Geta clacking, hair flying, I boldly stuck my head into the establishments along the way and made humble appeals for work. I felt as though I were back in Tokyo during my first days there, luckless, with people full of suspicion and anxiety about my manner. I failed to find work. That night, we stayed under a tree next to the riverside—in the midst of the murmur of water and the rustle of old willow trees—and moved about like shadow people.

Uncle having worked briefly in Kyoto as a young man knew enough to give me some directions for the next day, and I wandered up and down the streets to knock upon the heavy doors. "Please," I said, begging, "I need your help." Small women, hugging the doors to their machiya, peered out, stared at me, and said, "We're sorry but we have nothing for you," and quickly closed their doors, clicking them shut. *Did they lean their backs to the door? Did their hearts beat in fear?* I looked down at myself. Feral from fire, I was no more than a human mongrel; I could have been a beggar, a thief, a prostitute. Or even a murderer. So why should they have trusted me? It was all very clear that I was not from Kyoto, my speech different from their dialect and my voice too assertive. Too, had they known my other secret—that I was an American—they would have been equally appalled. But, being dogged, I went to the next house and the next, and continued my search into the late afternoon. By that time, the responses were the same, the faces the same, the polite shutting of the doors the same.

I knew we couldn't go on living among the trees beside the banks of the river or under the bridges much longer. It was unthinkable to be without a place to live, especially in a society that frowned on those they thought to be less than industrious or diligent of purpose. I had to find work and a place for us to live.

"I'm sorry," I said when I returned to the family waiting by the river. "I couldn't find any work today."

"Don't worry, it can't be helped," Uncle said. "We just have to be careful of the police."

"Yes, the police," I said. I did not want to contend with them again.

That night, we walked up river to a spot that was less noticeable. In the morning, we followed the river back down, stopping frequently, but even so the strain on Uncle and Iwao was considerable. Uncle said, "It's important not to be run out of the city before we place Norio's and Sā-chan's urns in a temple."

The following day, close to despair and about to give up finding a place to work and live, I was leaning against the wall of Sanjusangendo Temple, where I had stopped to ponder what I should do next, and was staring at the walkway stones when I saw a pair of tiny feet in black geta and white toe-socks stop next to mine. I slowly lifted my eyes.

"Are you all right?" the woman asked.

I peered at her white-powdered face; she was unusually tiny. "I'm all right," I said, in hesitation. "Thank you for your concern."

"You look hungry. Here, have some candy," she said, reaching into her bag.

"Oh, thank you, thank you." Overwhelmed by her kindness, I couldn't stop from crying. "I'm so sorry for crying like a baby."

"There's no need for that," she said. "Can you tell me what the matter is?"

Shamelessly, in an outpouring of words, beginning with having very little to eat and the Tokyo fires, I told her what had happened to our family, why we were in Kyoto, and that I was in desperate need of a job and place to stay.

"I see," the woman said when I finished my story. She seemed to be lost in thought, and after a while, I took her reticence to mean she couldn't help me.

"I'm sorry for taking some of your time," I said, ready to leave.

"Wait a minute. I know just the person who can help you. Let me write you a note."

"Oh, thank you," I said, fighting to hold back another bout of tears.

Her note referred me to a Reverend Hara. "I heard that the government had taken the reverend's regular cook away and that he has been looking for help."

I thanked the woman and ran to the address she had given me—a small Buddhist temple on a narrow side street off Takatsuji, the west side of Kyoto. The temple compound took up a large corner of the block and was surrounded by a thick white wall with three cherry trees in full bloom at its entrance. The courtyard had a more traditional look with its sculpted Japanese garden—stone lanterns and a small fishpond against one side—momiji, Fujian flower trees, camellia bushes on the other. A moderate-sized main temple, a long structure that resembled a dormitory building, and other smaller buildings were scattered throughout a maze of dark gray, river-stone gravel walkways.

"Good afternoon," I called out into the tidy surroundings. "Is anyone around?"

A young man of average height, dressed in black trousers and a white shirt, soon appeared. His head was shaven, revealing two small white scars near his right temple that moved when he wrinkled his brow in inquiry. "May I help you?" he asked.

"I'm looking for a Reverend Hara. I have a note for him—about a position?"

"Ah, it's good you came," he said, sounding relieved. He ran into an office on the side of the temple and soon a short, portly man in black robes appeared.

"Are you Reverend Hara? I have a note for you," I said extending my hand.

He took the note while scrutinizing my face. "Mmm," he said and hastily read it. "You've come at the right time. When can you start?"

"Right now," I said, and quickly told him about my circumstances, including the fact that I was an American.

"Is that so?" he said, looking up at me for a while.

"Is it all right?"

"I see no reason why not," he said, breaking into a smile.

"Oh good. I will go and tell . . ."

"No, wait. Let me show you around first. You might not like it here," he said, laughing easily, and guiding me to the main temple. Upon entering, it was very dark and cold inside. "I suggest that everyone come to the services I conduct every morning to start the day. I also want you to take care of *all* the fires in the compound—for the cooking, the bathhouse, the trash. The boys are careless sometimes and don't do a very good job. You think you can do that?"

"Why, yes!" I'd be working with fire again.

"Your duties," he said, moving up toward the altar, "include the lighting of the candles and burning of the incense in the censer for the five o'clock recitation of the Shoshinge every morning." The Shoshinge was Shinran Shonin's Gatha of True Faith and his treatise on gratitude. When I was young, the reverend in Kaiwiki said we should be grateful that we had something to eat, that we had parents who took care of us.

At this point, I thought to myself, I had very little to be grateful for. Call it resentment, call it arrogance, but it was hard for me to be *truly* thankful, for what was there to be thankful about—the poverty, my empty stomach, the deaths of Norio and Sā-chan, the fires that destroyed our lives? "Oh," I uttered, suddenly, having forgotten where I was for a second.

"Anything the matter?" Reverend Hara said as he turned to look at me. I quickly shook my head. The reverend, though looking puzzled, went on to light a few more candles so that I could see the entire hall. A warm glow filled the quiet room. I felt the peace found in the centuries-old dark wood, in the soft drift of the cherry blossoms falling in the courtyard, in the candlelight on the altar in the silence. Peace was something I hadn't felt for a long time. As Norio once described: *I wasn't afraid of the silence or not knowing where I was. I felt serene . . . The silence was so clear at that moment that I thought I had gone to the Pure Land.* Yes that's what it was like, I thought.

In exchange for several rooms in the compound, I was given the responsibility for cooking and cleaning after the reverend and five novice priests. According to the reverend, although the novice assigned as the cook had done a fair job, he had heard the boys muttering among themselves about the terrible food; the boys tired of eating the same gelatinous mountain yams and rice gruel. "I was in desperate need of help when you showed up. One day, not too long ago," he confided, "the boys refused to take a bath. On another occasion, they struck back by going on a hunger strike. When the boys didn't eat their food, I couldn't account for what was being wasted, and though no one would have known what was happening, it still hung on my conscience, especially when so many people are starving." He looked embarrassed to admit that the boys were spoiled.

"Young men love to eat," I offered, surprised at his ready confidence in me.

"I keep losing all my help to the war. The last cook left in such a hurry and since then, we've been without help. I'm sorry I can't give you much— only food, a small stipend, and a place to stay." He stood up, pressed his hands together, and bowed quickly. "Your uncle and cousin can help, too," he said, his black robe swishing around his short, plump body as he rushed off, in a hurry to attend to the next task.

I ran back to the river. Shiichi Uncle's eyes welled with tears when I told him of our incomparable good luck. "That's wonderful," he rasped, the only response he could give. Iwao closed his eyes as if he had been spared to live another day.

I soon had everyone settled in rooms of the compound. Uncle and Iwao had one room that was attached to the dormitory, Yuki-chan and Auntie another, and Sumie and I had a room across from the kitchen. In addition to what I had seen before, the premises had a library and study close to the main temple, with one of the smaller buildings containing the kitchen and dining areas where I would spend most of my time. Hidden down a path adorned with bamboo stood the bathhouse, and beyond that, the outhouse.

The Takatsuji Temple, I learned, had been in Reverend Hara's family for more than eight generations. His wife, having died young, left him childless, and he welcomed student-priest aspirants to study at his temple before they went on to the Headquarters of Jodo Shinshu nearby to complete their training in Pure Land Buddhism. I gathered that he also had these boys stay at his temple to save them from going to war; he secured deferments whether or not they had a calling for the priesthood. He knew that the boys were oftentimes not serious about their studies, but if they were willing to keep up appearances, he wasn't concerned. He didn't question the families' motives for wanting to keep their sons with him.

"Maybe they will learn something from the experience itself," he said. "I was also wishing to find someone to give my temple to. Until recently, I'd been unsuccessful in finding a successor, but now, I have a boy in mind. His parents sent him here a year ago, but he was orphaned when they died in

185

the bombing of Nagoya, right after Tokyo. He's the one who came to get me when you arrived. His name is Teruo. Someday, I'm going to adopt him."

I settled into an easy routine. I hurried through the kitchen chores every morning, rushed over to the temple to chant the morning blessings, fed the reverend and boys their breakfast, fed our family, and raked the courtyard leaves. If my pace was manic in the beginning, it slowed down after a few days. At the stroke of noon, I served lunch, the leanest meal of the day and, however small the meals, at least we were eating three of them. During this time, keeping busy helped me to take my mind off Sā-chan.

Early in the afternoons, I would look in on Uncle and Iwao, then take Yuki-chan and Sumie to one of the small parks in the area. I could get away because Uncle and Iwao were doing poorly, and Harue Auntie stayed with them much of the time. She demanded little of me. Auntie also decided to wait until Uncle and Iwao felt better to hold services for the placement of Norio's and Sā-chan's urns in the temple.

During the dead spaces of our days, the girls and I wandered around Kyoto and went as far as we could walk if rain did not drive us back. On cooler days, the children huddled under the futon with me to sing and recite children's poems, and although I found some books at the temple to school them, they grew bored with my attempts at instruction. "Do we have to?" Yuki-chan would moan. One day I read the children the story "Urashimataro." Written in a simple Japanese that I could muddle through, the story was about a boy who was rescued by a turtle, but Sumie fell asleep on her crossed arms and Yuki-chan kept asking me, "Do you think Sā-chan can come back on a turtle, too?" I said nothing.

Evenings, after my chores, Reverend Hara and I began talking over matters regarding the running of the temple—about how much food was left, what staples were needed, what I had to buy. During the two hours of our first talk, Reverend Hara said, "The boys are young in their thinking. Too, they may go to war and never come back. I haven't done this before, but I now feel the need to share the temple's records and finances with someone and, American or not, I feel I can trust you. Teruo is still grieving for his parents and the others are childish," he said. In subsequent days, our conversation regarding the temple flowed over into talking about our lives.

The war compressed time in such a way that it accelerated the need for us to trust and confide in each other on many different matters and levels. Of course, I never talked about Sā-chan.

On rainy days, when the dreary sound of water dripping on the walking stones and the leaves of the spring trees marked the hours, I took the children to the small study so that I could listen to the sutras Reverend Hara and the boys recited in mellifluous tones, the girls sitting on the floor and drawing pictures on old magazines with their blunt pencils. Seeing the girls, the novices took a break from their studies to play with them. Finding him free, I talked with Reverend Hara about the sutras—he, chanting excerpts and explaining the Buddha's teachings, as if I were one of his novices. Over Sumie's and Yuki-chan's heads and voices, I asked: "What do these things mean—that all emotions are pain or that all phenomena are illusory?"

"Mmmm . . . there's no easy answer . . ."

"Tell me, is happiness also pain?"

"That is so . . . even being happy is filled with pain."

"You're confusing me."

"Yes, it's confusing, but think about it for a while."

From then on, with every chance I had, I went running to ask him about words or phrases in the sutras recited in the mornings that I did not understand. *What does this mean? What does this mean?* became my impassioned cry in my search for answers about my behavior toward Sā-chan.

Reverend Hara stopped me one morning and said, "Hold it. These concepts are not easy to explain. Take them one at a time. Let them seep into your being. In the first place, what is your *real* question? Why are you in such a hurry to understand what takes most people a lifetime?"

His asking me this was like a slap in the face, my real question: *Why, Sā-chan? What was wrong with me that I did such a thing?* With that, I understood. I realized that I could not go on asking questions without an understanding of what had truly happened between Sā-chan and me. This brought an abrupt end to my inquiries. In the short time, however, I did learn one thing: the Buddha's call had been *entrust in me and free yourself of all attachments, even the attachment to your secrets, your lies, your guilt.*

I could not.

One evening after going over the books with Reverend Hara and talking about the family and the war, I went back to my room after our meeting but was unable to sleep. After making sure that the girls were all right, I walked out and leaned against the side of the building to look at the full moon. While watching the clouds, a wave of sadness drifted through me and I began to cry. I don't know how long I stood there crying, but when I looked up, Reverend Hara was across from where I stood and sitting on a bench in the garden. Looking my way, he raised his hand and beckoned me.

I walked to him like a wayward disciple.

"Sit down, sit down," he said when I reached him.

"Thank you," I whispered.

Not saying anything for a while, he finally said, "The war has been hard on you, hasn't it?"

"I suppose so, but everyone carries something of its burden. Some more, some less."

"Then your burden must be large. I heard you crying from the depth of your being."

"You heard me crying?"

"Nnnn, I heard you. I was gazing at the moon when I heard you."

"I'm sorry for having disturbed your enjoyment."

"No, I'm sorry for not being more helpful—about whatever it may be."

I nodded my head and began to cry softly. At that moment, I desperately wanted to confide in him, but I was ashamed and unable to face his judgment.

"Look at me. I wear the uniform of war when the government orders me to do it; I carry a sword, but I'm not a willing fighter. I wear the robes of a priest, yet I can't help what is troubling you. How powerless I am." He dabbed his broad brow with a handkerchief he took out of his sleeve and continued thoughtfully: "Sometimes, I think we have to go back to the old words to understand what is happening to us in the present."

"Old words?"

"Yes, old words. They somehow seem more fitting in defining the predicament we face. Japan has truly entered the 'valley of darkness.' This is a time of 'dark sorrow' for us—of anshū."

"The word sounds so sad, doesn't it?" My shoulders sagged.

"Oh, don't mind this old man for the gravity of the words he places on you. I've said too much, already. Really." Reverend Hara dusted his robe and rose from the bench to dismiss himself. "You're young and I'm nothing but an old priest who knows little about life. The only thing I'm sure of is that life doesn't last. It's the melancholy that swims in my heart, that makes me prone to share these ideas."

"I suppose in all of us."

"I apologize for being morose; I get into these moods and it doesn't help anyone. I guess it's in the makeup of a man getting old. I hope I didn't unsettle you."

He turned to go but stopped when I said, "That ancient word—about sorrow?"

"Anshū. Dark sorrow."

"Anshū."

After Reverend Hara left, I sat in silence for a long while, looking out at the garden—the lilies, irises, hydrangeas, azaleas—all in early bloom and muted in the dark. The cherry and plum blossoms had already fallen, the tiny new leaves above me stippling the ground of the courtyard under the perimeter of the tree's canopy and moon's light. I felt confused, sad, scared, and guilty, as if there would be no spring or summer, ever, for me, the leaves and flowers never again to be part of my life or my eyes. Strong, sudden breezes swept down from the mountains, and as they passed through, they stripped the cloud covering, leaving an openly blue-black sky with orphan clouds here and there that drifted, as though lost.

Anshū. Anshū. I made it slip over my tongue, and though Reverend Hara had meant it for the war, I took it as something more personal, for that *something* so deep and sad that I had been feeling about all I had done to others, especially Sā-chan and Iwao. Anshū was mine, for my condition, the sadness and guilt for what ate at my heart. Now, I had a name for it.

Papa and I had gone under a falls once, in the stream near his garden, and we had watched the rush of water going over us. That night in Reverend

Hara's garden, I was no longer merely watching water go over me in a roar, but I was in it, its crush. I was falling with it, pitching forward because of its weight, tumbling with its force, submitting myself to its source of power—the power of my *anshū*.

Shiichi Uncle and Iwao began having prolonged coughing spells that stopped their breathing. Their deep coughs sapped their strength and what little energy they had in reserve. Spittle laced with small spots of blood appeared on their handkerchiefs like the scattering of sparks from a fire. When a doctor's assistant finally came to the temple, he confirmed what I had suspected. Shiichi Uncle and Iwao had tuberculosis. Harue Auntie fainted at the news and Reverend Hara, not at all shocked, told us that we could stay at his temple as long as we needed to be there. The doctor's assistant posted a warning sign on their door in dark, ominous, bold characters: **Quarantine**. From then on, Auntie took a room by herself next to Uncle and Iwao's room, and Yuki-chan came to stay with me.

Sumie didn't understand the changes, and being that she was growing older, she was becoming more demanding. "I want to see Iwao and Uncle. Why can't I play with them like before?" she asked when I found her crying in front of Uncle's door soon after, pounding it with her tiny fists, begging them to let her in. "I want to show Uncle and Iwao the butterfly I caught."

"Hush, Uncle and Iwao are sick. You can't bother them." Just how much Sumie understood, I couldn't say, especially since she had just played with Uncle and Iwao with no restrictions the day before.

When Yuki-chan asked her mother why we didn't get sick too, Harue Auntie said, "I've been praying at the Ichihime Shrine for Women's Well-being and that's what's saving us." She brought out a porcelain, gold-painted Kwan Yin from her purse for us to see. "Sā-chan is looking over us, too. The men aren't as lucky, not having such guardians."

Nonetheless, Harue Auntie made sure the girls never got near Uncle and Iwao and washed their hands and faces at the least hint of contact, also making sure that those in contact with Uncle or Iwao wore masks and washed their hands and faces frequently. She also burned the rags they coughed into. And if she didn't get sick, handling all of their sputum, I regularly thought that it was because she was *too mean*.

Later, thinking of her this way made me feel small, for in the evening of the butterfly incident with Sumie, Harue Auntie brought over some rice crackers for her. Someone in the congregation had given them to Harue Auntie as a payment for sewing some children's clothing, and she in turn had given them to Sumie. Before I could say anything to thank her, she slipped away into the evening shadow.

22

Kazuo

One afternoon, before cooking dinner, I was sitting on the floor, folding a stack of the children's laundry in my room.

"Is anyone around?" someone called out. Placing Sumie's slip on the floor, I went to the door.

"You the new cook here?" A young man in a soldier's brown khaki work uniform stood before me. His whole demeanor looked intrusive, as if he were about to burst into the room like a bullet. I opened the door wider as he eyed me up and down.

"You sure you're the cook? Young, aren't you?" he said and placed the heavy, large box on the ground. "Some fresh fruits and vegetables for you. My mother had some extras so she said to give it to the cook. So here I am. Will you at least help me unload this stuff and not just stand around? I have to report back to work. I'm not supposed to be here."

"This is not the kitchen," I said. "This is my room. You can't unload the things here. Please take them to the kitchen across the way." I pointed to the kitchen entrance. "And, yes, I am the new cook."

"I do you a favor by bringing these goods and you want me to bring them to the kitchen? You're the cook, so you take it. I can't do it now, I have no time." He pushed the box toward me with his foot and turned to go; his whole back dared me to challenge him. Before I could say anything, he bounded out from the courtyard and into the street where I heard a reluctant truck sputter, then leave.

I learned from Reverend Hara that the young man was Ogawa Kazuo, whose mother was a wealthy patron of the church. "Through her connections, she has been able to give us extra food." Reverend Hara did not think to question its source. I suspected that to be ungrateful toward the Ogawa family by questioning how they got the food was unthinkable.

A few days later, I found Kazuo in a corner of the courtyard holding a shovel and using his foot to shove the blade into the hard-packed soil. "Stop!" I cried out, rushing to his side, lifting my kimono to shuffle my feet along faster. "What do you think you're doing? You're destroying the plants. Who gave you permission to do this?"

"No one. I'm starting a garden, so I don't have to bring you extra food," he said, his tone once more a challenge.

"Well, don't bring the food. We can do without it if that's the way you feel."

With a jerk, Kazuo stopped what he had been doing. He began to laugh, and uprighting his long-handled shovel, he leaned his long body forward, the chin of his handsome face touching his hands that were mounted, one on the other, upon the handle. "You tell *that* to the Reverend. I dare you. Maybe you can do without the extra food, but the boys can't. I bring this food so you don't have to go out and scramble for food at the government depots that carry nothing. Don't you know a good thing when you see it?"

Harue Auntie stuck her head out of her room. She shouted at Kazuo, "Don't you dare speak to anyone in our family like that." She came out, fumbling into her geta, crunching her way through the gravel walkway and shuffling her hands against her sides in an "I mean business" gait. "You hear?"

"You speak clearly enough," he said.

Continuing to scold, Harue Auntie rocked Kazuo back on his heels; clearly he was not anticipating anything like this from a woman. For her, no stranger was going to interfere with anyone in the family. He finally interrupted her heated monologue by shrugging his shoulders and walking away.

After this encounter with Harue Auntie, it appeared that Kazuo was not going to continue with the garden he had started. For several days I watched for him. Harue Auntie kept an eye out, too. Rain beat down on the furrows and water settled in the trenches he had dug, and seeing that nothing was going to be done, my auntie took over the garden and began planting vegetables for pickling. Concerning to Reverend Hara, however: if Kazuo remained angry and did not show up with food from his mother, we would all starve. "You don't need to worry," Harue Auntie assured him. "His mother is not about to let her spiritual destiny change course by giving up her good work. I know people just like her."

Harue Auntie was right. Soon Kazuo was back with a boxful of eggs and vegetables. He shrugged his shoulders and said something rude under his breath. As for the garden, Auntie seemed content in having taken it over, Kazuo, in having relinquished it.

In the days that followed, when I was not in the kitchen, I left the front door to my room half ajar to let the air in, the weather warming considerably, and my ears keen to the sounds outside—for the children for one thing—but also for Kazuo. Although I didn't care for him much, a part of me still listened for his truck, his low voice, or the crunch of gravel when he walked toward the kitchen with his box of goods. The children on the other hand were always delighted to see him. After all, he brought them sweets and little trinkets. If after a day or so, he had not appeared, Yuki-chan was quick to ask, "When is Kazuo Uncle coming?"

In turn, Sumie would look at me in inquiry, "Yes, when?"

When he did appear, he and I remained antagonistic. The children picked up on it, and one day, with hands on her hips, Yuki-chan mimicked both of us in front of Kazuo: "What are you doing here?" Turn. "It's none of your business." Turn. "Oh really?" Turn. "Yes, really!"

Kazuo threw back his head and laughed. Were Kazuo and I really no better than children? It seemed so as I listened to our banter from Yuki-chan's mouth.

Kazuo's visits grew more and more frequent—two or three times some days. He was a distraction and made it hard for me to do my chores and make the food stretch.

"What's this all for—salting the cabbage, making the vegetable preserves?" he mocked, rubbing his hands together, watching me carry the heavy buckets of turnips and cabbages in brine. "You're only prolonging your agony. We're all going to starve. Don't you know that?"

He baited me this way into talking to him when I really wished to ignore him. "Look, just drop the food off and leave," I ended up saying one day. "We don't need your help, yeah, so I don't know why you linger around this temple if everything we do here bothers you!"

On his next and following visits, he left boxes of shriveled vegetables at my door. "Why are you doing this?" I asked, perplexed.

Unable to contain his laughter when I called him on it, he said, "You're wrinkled and dried out; these vegetables remind me of you." And to annoy me further, he left drooping flowers at my doorstep on two consecutive days.

"They're here again," Yuki-chan said of flowers in Kazuo's arms on the third day as she ran out to meet him, Sumie skipping her way to him from behind. While Yuki-chan, being older, was aware of Kazuo's teasing, Sumie saw him only as a kind person who brought her a piece of candy or a toy whenever he visited and clung to him like 'opihi on the rocks back home.

"Why are you always bringing these flowers?" I heard Yuki-chan asking.

"It's because Hi-chan is an old lady. She is shriveling up and looking more like someone's grandmother," he said.

"That's not true," Yuki-chan said in my defense. "She is beautiful. She's not old!"

"That's what you think," he said.

"Don't listen to him, Yuki-chan," I said. "He's hardly a soldier. He doesn't have anything better to do."

"Listen," Kazuo said, coming up to me after several days of this dueling. "Let's be friends. After all, we're working toward the same goal, right?" There was an air of offhandedness about him that showed me that he was unwilling to let go his pride altogether.

"And what might that be?" I responded.

"To get out of this war alive. So . . . I've been thinking."

"You mean you think?"

"Be fair. Give me a chance. I've been thinking long and hard about this."

I was about to argue again but relented. "I guess you're right," I said with a loud sigh. "It's not good for the children to see us like this, always squabbling."

A few days later, to celebrate our "peace treaty," Kazuo suggested we take the children for an outing to Nijo Castle. "They'll have fun, walking on the nightingale floors that squeak in warning at someone's approach. I also want to show you the Crane and Tortoise Islands of Longevity in the garden."

"You really don't have to . . ." I said, which he took as a "yes."

"See you on Wednesday, then. At one."

Overwhelmed by the change in Kazuo's attitude, I ran over to Reverend Hara's quarters that evening to ask him what he thought of Kazuo's idea. As we sipped tea, I explained what had been happening between Kazuo and me.

"You were saying you didn't like each other very much," Reverend Hara murmured, rotating the tea bowl with its design of scattered maple leaves in his hands.

"Do you think Kazuo is sincere, that he wants us to be friends?"

He closed his eyes and pondered my question. "You must understand that Kazuo has been spoiled all his life. But he means well. Go out with him and see for yourself. I believe he's sincere. As for his teasing, he just wants your attention." Reverend Hara smiled, amused at this turn of events.

"I'm sorry, but I need one more favor. I was wondering if you know of someone who would donate an old dress or kimono to me. I have nothing nice to wear."

"I understand your predicament. The church has several patrons whom I can look to for such a favor. Don't worry, I'll come up with something. When will you be needing this?"

"I didn't know of this outing until today. This doesn't give you much time, but it's in two days."

"I see. You've grown fond of him in spite of yourself, haven't you?" he said. "I will try my best to find you something suitable to wear."

"Thank you." I bowed and retreated.

The morning of my outing with Kazuo, I found a package by my door with my name on it in Reverend Hara's fine hand. I tore open the package. The simple, off-white linen dress, although a bit loose, fell on me in a nice way when I put it on, and the calf sandals looked hardly used. At the time, Japanese people looked down on you if you wore Western dresses, the government suggesting women wear nothing but Japanese clothing, but I didn't care. I was tired of wearing a ragged, scorched kimono or other drab government-issued apparel that smelled of camphor, stale food, and home fires.

That day I dressed with care. I pinned a camellia blossom into my hair, the brittle stem held up with several pins, and thought of Sā-chan with a flower or trinket often in her hair. As I always did before going out, I went to see Shiichi Uncle and Iwao in their room. Too, Uncle had sent me a note saying he had something that he wanted to discuss.

I walked into the warm, humid room that smelled of fevers and medicines and immediately went over to open the windows to let in the restorative air from the Higashi Mountains. I straightened my facemask—Auntie insisted that everyone wear facemasks—and pulled up my zabuton to sit next to Shiichi Uncle so I could rub his back.

"You look nice today," Iwao said. Lying down next to his father, he followed me with his eyes.

"I'm going for an outing with the children and Kazuo," I said.

"Really? You're lucky. I wish I could get out of this room."

"I'm sure, soon," I said.

"Hi-chan," Uncle interrupted, his voice gloomy. "I'm thinking that we need to go to Hiroshima after all, we are putting a strain on Reverend Hara. It will also get unbearably hot and humid here, more than in Hiroshima. But this means we have to move again."

"I don't know what to say, Uncle. We have a place to stay, I have a job, and I've saved some money. And what about Tokyo?"

"Yes, what about Tokyo?" Iwao demanded of his father. "You never wanted to go back to Hiroshima. I heard you say so yourself. For me, Tokyo is home."

"I know, Iwao, but as much as I like Tokyo, I have to rely on my family in Hiroshima to help us. We can't go on obligating ourselves to others."

"Reverend Hara says it's all right, doesn't he?" Iwao looked at me hopefully.

"I'm sure he's okay with our staying, but your father must do what *he* feels is right. It's a burden to be obligated."

Iwao looked up at the ceiling in disappointment. I faced my uncle. "Sumie and I will do whatever you ask," I said, bowing to the floor.

"You make it easy for me . . . but we can talk about it again. Perhaps *you* can stay here."

"If she stays, I want to stay too," Iwao said.

It was a nice thought but I knew that it was impossible. Much as I wanted to stay in Kyoto, I knew I had to go with the family. Harue Auntie would need my help. "As you said, Uncle, we can talk about this again. Well, I have to be going," I said and dismissed myself.

I went back to my room and dressed the girls in their good vests, the ones Auntie had sewn at the inn in Ashima. I walked them out, near the sidewalk fronting the temple, and waited for Kazuo to appear.

While waiting, the girls played alongside the hedge. Yuki-chan spotted a quail that was hurt or ill, hiding in the sacred bamboo bush. The two girls pulled my hands to take me to where the puffy bird sat panting.

"Hi-chan, can we take it home?" Yuki-chan asked, tilting her head to look up at me as she squatted before the bird.

"No, Yuki-chan. I don't think it's a good idea."

"Why not? Aren't we supposed to help? Sā-chan would have."

"I know, but we can't help everything we see suffering."

"But it's only a bird. It won't eat much."

"I know, but we still can't keep it. We can't travel with it all the way back to Tokyo. It's best to leave it here." The girls knew nothing about the possibility of moving to Hiroshima, so I wasn't about to change the story until I learned for certain what Uncle planned to do. I didn't want them confused or asking questions.

"Are you going to cook it, then?" asked Yuki-chan.

"No, I'm not going to cook it. There's no need for that. Reverend Hara shares his vegetables and rice with us, isn't that so?"

"Yes . . . but . . ." Yuki-chan said.

"Uh hum," Kazuo said and cleared his throat. "Going back to Tokyo, eh?"

The children turned at the sound of his voice, quickly forgot about the bird, and ran to him. How long he'd been standing there I had no idea, and I hoped he had not heard our conversation about our having to eat birds, wanting to hide the ugly parts of my life from him. His obvious refinement made me aware of how different we were.

"I'm sorry I'm late," he said. "I had some errands to do." He doffed his hat and pushed his hair back with a sweep of his long fingers. He appeared so young and pleasing to the eye in the early afternoon light that I felt heat rise in my face. Kazuo then looked at me and my dress in an approving manner, as if he'd had something to do with choosing it. *Did he?*

"Come with me to the car," he said. "I have some gifts for the children. And I want you to meet my mother."

"Your mother . . . right now?"

"Any objections? She wants to see the cook she's been giving her vegetables to."

I bit into my lower lip and called the children to my side before I walked to the car. Packages of clothing, toys, and candy boxes were piled high in the front seat, the presents rising in tiers like a large, layered wedding cake. The children and I had never seen so many gifts before. Neither had Sā-chan, I thought.

Above the girls' squeals, Kazuo introduced me to a slender woman in the back seat of the limousine. The car itself didn't seem to be running on charcoal but petrol, an extravagance reserved, I suspected, for the privileged. The woman inside the cab sat tall and straight on one side of the car, her body pressed up against the door away from us. She had on a stiff-collared, red satin-lined black coat, which she held around the neck with one hand, black leather gloves, long woolen serge slacks, and patent-leather shoes. Tons of white makeup. Jet-black hair. A swan's neck. She looked European. As she lifted her chin to gaze at us, I was struck by the sternness etching her features and the surviving traits of true beauty. I suddenly wondered if I were wearing her dress and sandals for we looked about the same size; I tried to shake off that uncomfortable thought.

I bowed in formal greeting when Kazuo introduced us. After greeting her, I said, "I wish to thank you for all of the food that you've given us. We are greatly indebted."

She dropped her head to one side to acknowledge my presence. And that was all.

After talking to his mother for a moment, intensely, in a whisper, Kazuo unloaded the parcels and sent the chauffeur and his mother on their way.

Through the Chinese moon gate, through the great squeaky halls, we walked into Nijo Castle, a sixteenth-century fortress built by Iyeyasu, first shogun of the Tokugawa Period. We explored the old rooms. Once outside, on a pathway in the gardens, I finally summoned enough courage to say, "About your generous gifts, even though they're for the children, I wish you would take them back."

"Look, just take the gifts. We're friends now."

"I just don't feel comfortable, taking things from you. I can't reciprocate . . ."

"Ah, a woman of principles. Think of my gifts as a peace offering."

We walked in silence for a while, until Kazuo began asking me questions about my life. Although I told him about Sumie and that I was not Uncle's daughter, Kazuo found my being an American from Hawai'i the most surprising and interesting part about my background.

"It does pose a problem, doesn't it?"

"A problem—my being American?"

"I am an officer of the Japanese Imperial Army. My friendship with you could be questioned and my position compromised if they find out you're an American. But I'm willing to take my chances." He grinned and jokingly said, "I can't turn away from your fast talking."

"So you're not afraid to be seen with me?"

"No, I'm not afraid." I expected that he would tempt fate.

In silence, we walked farther down the path; the children, whose vests of bright red silk hid the faded patchwork of their clothing beneath, skipped ahead of us and clutched small white and blue flowers that they had picked while weaving through the willow trees along the banks of the castle's river and its meandering waterways.

When we came across a park bench, Kazuo said, "Do you mind? I'd like to rest a bit." He sucked in breath through his teeth like someone in pain and sat down.

"Are you all right?" I asked.

"Oh, I'm fine. It's just that I was wounded in my leg and sometimes it bothers me."

"Wounded? I didn't know that. I'm sorry . . . I thought you were in Kyoto on furlough, and not because you were hurt."

He laughed. "Furlough? There's no such thing in the Japanese Army."

I apologized for my ignorance about military matters, even though I felt more angry and irritated about his laughing at me, the truce we made still very much a touch-and-go affair.

"Don't worry," he added, sensing my discomfort. "You couldn't have known about my condition."

I nodded but did not respond verbally, having to fight a volatile mix of anger and excitement in my feelings for this man.

We sat for a few moments longer, watching the children at play, then continued walking the circular path around the centuries-old buildings. He scrutinized for long periods of time the scrolling and carving upon the walls and doors, appreciating them with a depth of knowledge I could not even hope to understand. We soon chose another spot to sit and view the garden. Color from the vegetation around us spilled from everywhere, piling onto itself as if the air were aroused by its own feverish heat.

"So why is it that you are really here in Kyoto?" I asked.

"I'm here, I think, because of my father's influence. One day they transported me out of China, carried me on a stretcher into the hold of a ship, and sent me here with a satchel of important papers in my bedding. They then assigned me as a temporary liaison officer for the Army. There is talk, however, that the government will close this office and go to Kyūshū, the first line of defense. Perhaps I'll be lucky and end up in Shikoku." He added: "I'm also here because of my mother. Her real home, Tokyo, is in a state of confusion. She came here to live although she says she doesn't like this city because it's too old for her taste, being that she considers herself *modern.*" Kazuo's smile was wry, as though he loved his mother but didn't completely approve or know what to make of her.

Leaning forward, placing his elbows on his thighs, and clasping his hands together under his chin, he looked pensive, like a lost child. Self-involved, he continued talking as if I were no longer there. "There's another reason my mother doesn't like this city—my father lives here with his girlfriend. I don't know why she even cares. She has her own boyfriend, her own car, her own apartment. Sounds crazy, doesn't it? I wish it were simpler."

"Nothing is simple."

"I guess not."

"I'm sorry about your circumstances."

"There's nothing to be sorry about," he said and gave an exasperated look. "You have to understand Japanese men. They have affairs and expect their wives to be faithful. Divorce? It was out of the question; my mother took a lover instead."

"It sounds complicated," I murmured. "Are all Japanese men like your father?"

"Too many of them are," he said. He was silent for a moment then added, "Because of him, my parents were always fighting. There was little peace in the house."

"My experience has been very different. My sister Miyo and I fought, but we were sisters and young. Aside from the problems with the father of the boy I planned to marry, I've been fortunate." I avoided mentioning my many fights with Harue Auntie and Sā-chan.

"It sounds like you had a happy childhood."

"My mother and father got along well, but my father died young— when I needed him most, I suppose."

Kazuo stretched his leg and stood up, and we walked through a green overhang of wisteria vines. "Right now I'm on 'unofficial' medical leave," he said as he tossed a small pebble into the water. "Due to my father, I'm sure." We watched the water swallow the stone and the ripples widen. "Soon, I'll have to go back to my regular duties. I have only a few days left to spend in Kyoto so I was wondering—would you spend them with me?"

"You want to spend them with me?"

He spread his arms, smiled, and said, "Who else? I asked *you*, didn't I?"

"I would like that," I answered, although I didn't know how to take the sarcastic *who else?* remark. Kazuo was a mystery to me. I wondered if he was a mystery I would ever learn to solve.

23

The Promise

Before leaving, for his last evening in town, Kazuo invited me to a Kabuki performance, a special showing at Minamiza, a theater in Gion, featuring a rare troupe passing through; it was a treat for anyone, most programs by that time having been suspended because of the war. Harue Auntie consented to look after the children and seemed pleased that I was dating Kazuo with some regularity. "Maybe he'll marry you," she said the day I told her of my plans. "I must say you're pretty good for used goods. You may be useful after all, maybe pay us back. Go on, enjoy yourself, even if your uncle and cousin are close to death's door. You have no pity, but why should you care, being selfish at heart!" Mama had often said I was wagamama.

I suppose Harue Auntie could not help being confrontational given the chance, though I must say she had been quiet of late, busy caring for Shiichi Uncle and Iwao. And she went on, her hand poised across her forehead in a self-pitying way: "I guess this is not new. This is something I've known from the first time I laid eyes on you. Now, fire is burning between your legs." She threw back her head in unbridled laughter.

You're nothing but a nasty old woman! I did not say this to her, trying to be less retaliatory. I was, after all, still indebted to her and I wanted to remain respectful for Mama's sake and, above all, for the sake of the secret I kept about Sā-chan. I simply stared at her.

"Oh, I see. Now the girl is arrogant, too. A few days spent with some rich man in Kyoto and it all goes to her head. You think a gentleman like this Kazuo fellow is ever going to marry you? I don't think so. Do you want to know the truth? You come from different worlds. You have no money, you have no class. You're nothing but an uneducated peasant, a fool from America with two strikes against you." She moved close to my face. "And if you're thinking of love-u, American-style, there's no such thing."

"Who's talking about getting married? Or love?"

"I am, because you're going to want to get married. I know your type. You're feeling the fire, it's burning up inside of you. You can't help it, you're stink, *stink*!" She said and fanned herself with her hands. "I can smell you, your sex. Your chitsu is rotting between your legs."

"You're a crude, dirty old woman!" I finally said, not able to help it.

"What, you calling me names? How long has it been since you've had a man, eh? Tell me."

It was useless to argue with Harue Auntie. Besides, she had forced me to face the truth; I *was* feeling intensely attracted to Kazuo. Even the remote possibility of marrying him someday had crossed my mind. In her coarse, dirty-minded way, Harue Auntie had once again cut close to the truth.

The play that Kazuo and I watched was called *Love's Messenger on the Yamato Road*. It was a story about a desultory lover and dilettante, Chubei, who took a wrong turn in life and was forced to face the consequences. He had used the money entrusted to him by his patron to buy Umegawa, the woman he loved, to release her from the Floating World. When his deception was discovered by the police, he and Umegawa decided to get married and use whatever was left of the money to enjoy themselves until such time they would have to commit suicide to atone for what they had done.

Chubei entered along the flower road in loud geta steps and called out to his lover. Loud applause thundered through the hall. The play had begun. Kazuo leaned closer, brushing my arm. I did not pull away. He then took my hand into his, and as the play went on, he slid his hand toward my wrist and rubbed my childhood scar of a crescent moon that I thought was lost to my childhood home I once set fire to. I kept my eyes forward, and my body, so aware of his overwhelming presence, grew unbearably warm.

The lovers, quaking in fear onstage, cried and draped themselves on each other and vowed to be together even after death. Nothing could tear them apart. When Chubei told Umegawa about the money, Umegawa said she was only too happy to join him in death because of what he had done on her behalf. In their love for each other, they quivered like lost snowbirds on a cold night, and a short time later, realizing that they had no choice about their future, they felt serene in their resolve to live every moment with joy. With that knowledge, when discovered, they could and would kill themselves. A dance that signified the lovers' deaths concluded the play. My question that evening: *Was anyone capable of loving me that deeply? Was Kazuo?*

The stage assistants hit the wooden clappers in diminishing sound, the curtain closer cried out, and the black curtains drew together. The crowd applauded with vigor. Faces in the audience glistened with tears when the house lights went on, and an aviary of white handkerchiefs fluttered in the theater above the sound of muffled sniffles, the audience, quite affected by the play, slow in leaving their seats.

Kazuo and I walked out into the cool, clear night. The stars were out, the moon, the first fireflies. We walked over to a small teashop on Pontochō-dōri where we had some thick green tea and sweets. In the middle of eating, hoping he wouldn't notice, I wrapped a piece of my cake into my tea paper.

He frowned at me across the table—I, never more humiliated. "Eat it all. Don't save it. I will buy some for the children."

Wrapping scraps of food to take home made me feel cheap, poor, so *country*, a typical Kaiwiki girl without class. I was grateful to the waitress who brought us more tea.

After lingering over our cups, which eased my embarrassment somewhat, Kazuo bought some fancy rice cakes, an extravagance in my eyes, for the children. After paying for our tea and the cakes, he steered me through Gion, and we looked into the windows of the tiny shops with their meager displays. While there were no lights on the streets, the moonlight was enough for us to see and make our way.

"There's not much of anything, is there?" Kazuo said, appearing surprised, as if he knew nothing of how people had been really struggling to live all these years of war and destruction.

At the end of a long walk through the quiet streets, we came upon the Shirakawa-minami Canal lined with cherry trees showing their lush leaves and tiny nubbins of fruit. As stars sparkled through their branches, we wove around the trees like grade-school Maypole dancers and dodged the low-slung boughs, bending ourselves under them, then straightening up between the trees in silent, contemplative rhythm. I tried to visualize Akira's face but couldn't remember it.

"I'll be going to Kyūshū, tomorrow," Kazuo said out of the blue night.

"So soon?"

"Ehh, my leg's better so I've been ordered to move out. They need men in the south. We lost the fight in Okinawa."

I hadn't been paying much attention to the war. So the front had moved close to Kyūshū; the Americans were that close to my home in Japan. "I guess we'll be moving along, too," I said. "My uncle has decided to go back to Hiroshima. He's very ill, and he has a brother there who will take care of us. It was a difficult decision for him to make. I plan to stay with my auntie and uncle for a while, but now that Sumie is older, I was thinking of working in the city. That way Harue Auntie no longer needs to get upset with me. I can help repay the family, too."

"You've been conscientious and resourceful. I've seen that. I don't think your uncle expects anything from you in return." Kazuo's tone had softened in the past few days, no longer so guarded. Something had changed between us.

"I still feel obligated to them," I said.

"Of course you do. That's only natural."

Kazuo stopped walking and turned to face me. Reaching out, he suddenly gripped my shoulders with both hands. Startled, I held my breath, which only seemed to make him hold me tighter, as if I were a fish about to leap out of his hands. "Hi-chan, will I see you again?"

"I don't know."

"I don't know how much time I have and . . ."

"You mustn't say things like that."

"But it's true. And Hi-chan, there's something else." I held my breath, both frightened and excited at the same time by the earnest look in his eyes. "I like you very much," he said, barely above a whisper. I opened my mouth but no words came. "Say something," he said, looking embarrassed.

"I don't know what to say," I stammered.

"Say if you like me or you don't like me . . ."

Releasing me from his grip, he reached above me and pulled down a tree branch, and with a snap he let go of it and watched it spring into the air. He leaped like the branch and grinned at me boyishly—too boyishly, I thought, to be in the war and baring all that was in his soul to me.

"You must think that I'm crazy, don't you? I know you do. But I've finally said what I've been wanting to say all this time."

I leaned against a tree trunk. I tried to think of Akira just then, but his face appeared unclear, overshadowed by the strength of Kazuo's features and his presence—Kazuo who circled dizzyingly around the tree and me.

"I wanted to be smooth, but I guess I've bungled it," he said. "Oh, I know it's sudden, but I want to know if you feel the same way about me. Please say something."

I nodded and said slowly, "I feel the same way about you."

Looking relieved, he stopped circling the tree and gazed at me intently. "Hi-chan, I'm so happy. With that, I'll be able to fight with fire in my heart. I'll be able to kill all the American snakes."

I wanted to remind him that I was an American too, but couldn't; instead, I bit down on my lower lip until it bled. I didn't want to bring him down to earth.

"We'll see each other as soon as we can," he said. He held my hand and regarded me seriously. "I have a confession to make. Do you know why I was so nasty when I first met you?"

"No, why?"

"I was scared, scared of what I was feeling. But now . . . will you write to me?"

"Of course, I will."

"You promise?"

"I promise!"

"I hear your young man left," Reverend Hara said as he approached me soon after Kazuo's departure. "Let's hope nothing happens to him. Japan is losing all of its good men."

I had been working that afternoon in our garden of late spring, these days Harue Auntie and I taking turns in tending it: Auntie in the mornings, me in the afternoons. Better this way. Dusting off my gritty hands, I bowed to the reverend and swiped the back of one of my hands across my nose to relieve an itch and to push the perspiration-soaked hair away from my face. It was getting warm in Kyoto. He walked over to a bench under one of the trees, his head down, his hands clasped behind his back while taking slow, measured steps. I followed and sat next to him.

"I hope nothing happens to Kazuo, too," I said, "but he's a soldier and . . . he's going to Kyūshū. The Americans are running Japan out of many countries, I hear. Is that true?"

"That seems to be the case."

"I'm hoping Kazuo remains in Japan. He'll have a better chance of staying alive."

"Then, let's hope he stays."

"This morning I prayed hard that Kazuo be saved."

"Ahh, but you should know by now that you can't ask that people be saved. We can't petition for life; it doesn't work that way. Our deaths are out of our hands, having no control over them. We cannot will someone's death not to happen, for surely it will happen whether it be now or later. Things happen in ways that we cannot predict."

"I want to think that we have some control over our lives. It's too hard for me to think of having no control." *After all, didn't I have a hand in someone else's life? Wasn't I in control of that?* Sā-chan's burnt face swept before my eyes. *Look what I had done to* her!

"You must trust the Light. You can't ask, for asking means that you want to be told the answers."

"I guess I don't know how to do that. I'm a poor believer." When I first came to the temple, I remember Reverend Hara saying: *When we entrust ourselves to the Inconceivable Light, we will dwell in the stage of the truly settled.* This much I knew: I would never be among the truly settled, never free from my anshū, as long as I was disbelieving of the Buddha's Wisdom and remained in what Buddhists call the realm of indolence and pride.

I got up from the bench, left Reverend Hara to his moments of reflection, and walked toward my room. I felt confused. It was difficult to think that things *just happened.* And yet it seemed that they did—to the old, the rich, the merchant, the rice farmer, the Kato family, Hamada-san's family—yes, even Sā-chan. And did they all not ask to live? Had they all not prayed, but died nonetheless? I reached my door and turned to look back at Reverend Hara. He was looking at me from the bench, a hand perched on his bald forehead.

Later that day, thinking about anshū and repeating it to myself, the word reminded me of the English word *anxious*—anxious in the way it ran over my tongue and ran through my life like a slippery shoe. I wanted to scream and scream, not stop screaming, for I saw that my anshū—in its gravest meaning—had kindled something further, a strange hopelessness, a constriction in my chest, in my throat, in my heart, in my very being so that I began to feel a great anxiety for Kazuo, the boys in the compound, Sumie. All of us.

"You have something you wish to tell me?" Reverend Hara asked, finding me in the kitchen a day or so later. "I saw your note on my door."

"Yes, it's about the family. We decided to move, so we'll be leaving soon. My cousin and uncle . . . we need them settled in Hiroshima as soon as possible. Uncle wanted to go back to Tokyo, but because he's so sick, it appears impossible."

"I understand. You've taken good care of your family. I can see where they rely on your strength. You have a sensible head on your shoulders." He lowered his head and voice as he spoke. "We'll miss you, Hi-chan. You brought order to this place. The boys have cleaned their ears and washed their socks, and we've never eaten better. You've always managed to find something special to put on the table in this time of intense rationing. We still have canned goods left on our shelves."

"Kazuo's mother helped." We fell silent, dropping our heads.

"Look," Reverend Hara said after a while, "your aunt's garden does well, and the nearly dead chestnut tree thrives again. You and the children have brought such joy to these otherwise drab quarters and fussy boys. What we'll remember most are your fires. About this, I'm sure the boys will agree. Fires in the stove and in the braziers or on the altars—there was a difference when you tended them. They looked inviting, soothing, even gracious. When the boys made the fires, they let the flames jump, the sparks fly." He chortled in recollection. I thought of Papa and me on the beach and the soft fires we tended.

"Thank you, Sensei. You've been most kind and generous to our family. I don't know how to repay you or thank you enough."

"You're always welcome here, Hi-chan. If you ever need help, you have a place to stay."

"I'm obligated as it is, but I do have a request. I'll be writing to Kazuo here, and I was wondering if you'd forward my letters to his mother so she can send them to him. That is, until I find a place for Sumie and me. I will send you my new address."

"You plan to live by yourself?"

"Yes, once Uncle and Iwao are settled."

"I'll be glad to help in any way I can. One last thing before you go. I've been meaning to tell you this. Do you remember your first days here, reading in the scripture room, with the children napping and the rain banging over our heads outside, how you struggled over the Teachings, asking for the meanings of this and that? I want you to know that it was good for us—for me."

"Deep listening, it takes deep listening," he had said at the time. By now, I knew enough that it meant listening deeply to the Teachings of the Buddha in order to understand oneself. It was more than asking about how to be *aware*—deep listening meant learning how to be aware from *within*. So far, I hadn't dared to listen deeply. I was afraid I was going to find something about myself that I couldn't face. "Yes, I remember," I said after a pause. "I hope I wasn't a bother."

"No, not at all. I will miss seeing you listening to the boys' chanting in the dim light of the study. Your curiosity was infectious. There I was, in this business of guiding people, and yet, I still felt like a novice. It was only after I watched you that I realized I had stopped listening, stopped learning, stopped reaching out."

"But all I had were questions. It's because I didn't and still don't understand anything." *I still didn't dare to talk about Sā-chan to anyone.*

As if he understood my angst, he said, "Maybe, it's because you don't want to. But in reality, I think you understand much more than you realize. I wish you well, Hi-chan. Take care, continue to find yourself, live long."

Anshū. The word circled in my head.

Life at Reverend Hara's temple had been so filled with activity that our three-month stay seemed longer. Almost forgetting why we were in Kyoto, we held a short inurnment service for Norio and Sā-chan. In the temple before the altar of the standing Buddha on its lotus dais, I lit the candles and murmured words of gratitude—the words of gratitude Reverend Hara taught me—even for my cousins' deaths. I didn't understand what that meant—to be grateful even for death—but it was soothing to repeat the running-water words in the ocean of life: Namu Amida Butsu, Namu Amida Butsu—*the self in oneness with the Inconceivable Light.*

Reverend Hara recited a short sutra, gave a short lesson from the Teachings, and Shiichi Uncle and Harue Auntie set the urns into a small wooden box, the box placed on a shelf in the temple.

On the day we left for Hiroshima, Reverend Hara came to my room to deliver a letter of introduction and the address of a friend, a Reverend Seki, who lived in Teramachi, the City of Temples. He handed me an official-looking envelope addressed in artful calligraphy.

"Just mention my name. He'll know," Reverend Hara said. "He might be able to put you up for a few days while you look for a place." He left me with these last-minute instructions as if I were his daughter. I felt a surge of warmth for him.

Our family said our good-byes to Reverend Hara and the boys who had become our friends. Soon, the boys, too, would be leaving the temple to go off to war, for in the end, Reverend Hara had been unable to hold them back. The boys sent us off with a lot of bowing and patting of the children's heads. Teruo said to the girls, "Study hard when you go to school, and pay attention to what the adults have to say. Keep warm, wear your sweaters, and watch your step. Move sure-footedly—with grace. Try not to pick up a cold wind in your lungs."

"Yes," the girls said in loud, clear voices of obedience. With so much faith in their small but stout hearts, nothing seemed to bother them at this moment, as if they had everything to look forward to. That's because they are young, I thought. But soon and surely enough, they would feel the weight of the world upon them, for I could already see changes in Sumie, a sullenness, a sudden brooding, a dark cloud gathering above her brow.

As we pulled away from the temple buildings with our rickety cart, Iwao lifted his face mask and shouted, "Norio, Sā-chan, till we meet again." He then settled himself like a small bird into the nest of his coughing.

Fire had changed everything. Fire had altered the shape of our world. My father, my mother, Miyo, Akira, Norio, most of all Sā-chan—all existed in other dimensions because of fire. They had been spun, out of sight, into some other life and universe by flames.

I looked back to say my last good-byes. From the road I saw Reverend Hara leaning over the brushwood gate, waving us on until we turned a corner and could no longer see him. Cries of the boys' good-byes filled the air and tugged at our chests.

Harue Auntie and I pushed the cart toward the railroad station. Shiichi Uncle's breathing labored under his mask as he shuffled behind us, looking back at the temple, then at his feet. Teruo came along to give us a hand with the cart that we would leave with him; I noticed for the first time that he was walking more and more like Reverend Hara who walked with a quick, shuffling gait.

PART IV

HIROSHIMA
June 1945 – 1949

Nirvana is beyond all concepts.
—from the Teachings of Buddha

24

Leaving

A little more than three and a half years had passed since I left Hawai'i. Congregating at the railroad station with the other lean, dark-clothed passengers, we were now headed south like a flock of migratory geese. I sat with the children, away from Uncle, Iwao, and Auntie, and as we pulled out of Kyoto Station in the soot- and steam-mingled air, I watched the countryside pass, slowly at first, until the train picked up speed to race past a monotony of low country houses built of bamboo and mud and thatched roofs. Sumie nodded off to sleep on my lap while Yuki-chan pressed her face against the window, her hair that I had cut the day before swaying unevenly on her back.

As Norio had said in his first letter, with everything so peaceful in the countryside, you would never have guessed that there was a war going on. But, if you scrutinized things, you could see how run down everything was due to the government's neglect. You could see it in the shabby, dingy un- painted walls of the railroad station, in the measly food carts, in the people with broken teeth and foul breath. People looked tired, bedraggled, life's spirit whipped out of them. Hungry. Japan was war weary and sick, but the people gave nothing away, their faces inscrutable as ever, everything locked up inside. Ragged clothing sagged on skeletal frames and, like broken ap- pendages, umbrellas hung limp and tattered on their arms. No one wore decent shoes, Kazuo's mother the only person I had seen with a decent pair during my time in Japan.

Under the steady clackity clack of the rails, I looked over at the girls, both asleep. They looked so frail, pale, and skinny that a strong wind could bear them off. When I bathed them, it was easy to imagine the bones of their ribs being played on like the bars of a xylophone. It was apparent that they didn't have enough milk, and Yuki-chan had been complaining of late about pain in her joints.

Everywhere they went the girls carried their dirty old dolls with them. They cuddled them with the fondness of real mothers, and I often heard them singing sad-sounding lullabies:

Nen nen koro riyo oko roriyo	Go to sleep my child
Bōya wa yoi ko da nenne shina	You're a good boy, so go to sleep.
Bōya no omori wa doko e itta?	Where has the boy's nurse gone?

Sleep was the magic answer to their hunger. When they played mothers, the children fed their dolls mud pies and mashed leaves in their stone soup. Food, food, food, that was the only thing any of us could think about. We moved closer to real starvation each day; maybe soon we would join the ranks of what Uncle called the walking dead. Although we had more to eat at Reverend Hara's temple than in Tokyo, and Kazuo's mother had shown great generosity toward us, our diets had still been deficient.

I knew that my family back home would be struggling, but I also knew they would always have enough fresh fruits and vegetables from the garden and fish from the ocean. Saliva rushed into my mouth just thinking of the abundance. I pined for the warm, rich volcanic dirt between my toes and dreamed of what that dirt could grow. Thoughts of food back home made me feel dizzy, a bit crazy.

After nearly nine hours on the train, halting at almost every stop along the way, with small maintenance problems to attend to and passengers to take on and drop off, we arrived at Hiroshima Train Station. Shiichi Uncle's younger brother, Hide Uncle and his wife, Chiemi-san, greeted us on the platform. "This is Hi-chan, everyone," Shiichi Uncle said, introducing the children and me.

"Ahhh, you look just like your mother," Hide Uncle said, smiling, with Chiemi-san in the background nodding in acknowledgement. Our introductions and greetings were brief as we had little time to make connections for a local train. Rather than speaking to each other, we kept bowing as we walked.

Hide Uncle, who looked very much like Shiichi Uncle save for his thick crop of black hair, was tall and lean and had a pleasant face. Chiemi-san, stocky but pretty, stood aside shyly in deference to or in fear of her older sister-in-law. I sensed that Harue Auntie's tongue had been here before and had done its share of damage.

We proceeded northeast of the city on a smaller line of the National Railroad System. The train was in obvious disrepair like others we had ridden and moved with little steam. We followed the Otogawa River until we came to the base of a low range of mountains, billowy high clouds piled on their tops. From there, we caught two taxis packed with all of us for a short distance to the house. Sumie, Yuki-chan, and I rode with Hide Uncle and Chiemi-san. Little was said.

Mama often described the place where the family home stood as rustic, the place much like an old Japanese wood-carving print of a farm scene—not unlike Hide Uncle's two thatched houses that were pinned against a wooded hillside, the clearing around the houses terraced in rice and vegetables, faceless workmen bent over the dark water.

"We'll be safe here," Iwao said, after making a quick survey of the area as we walked toward the house. "If the Americans bomb Hiroshima, it won't be way back here. They'll probably attack the docks."

Sumie and Yuki-chan remained outside to acquaint themselves with their new cousins, Hide Uncle and Chiemi-san's children, while Chiemi-san showed the rest of us into the larger of two houses. "Please do come in," she said in the Hiroshima dialect that had a distinctive cheerful sound in the running together of words, and using her hands like a hula dancer, she lifted her palm upward to show us the way to the living area—the house large and spacious unlike in Tokyo—after which she quickly retreated into the kitchen to get us refreshments.

Settling down in a circle, Shiichi Uncle, Harue Auntie, Iwao, and I faced an apologetic Hide Uncle, who bowed repeatedly with his head touching the floor. "This place is very country," he said. "Hi-chan and Iwao, you must be disappointed to see these backward conditions after having lived in such a busy, modern place as Tokyo."

"It doesn't matter to me," Iwao said. "At last, we have a permanent place to stay and rest. Hi-chan has a boyfriend now, so she's the only one who will be suffering, living way out here. Right, Hi-chan?" Iwao teased in a voice that had grown deeper.

I shot a glance at him and smiled.

Hide Uncle and Chiemi-san then voiced their regrets about the deaths of Norio and Sā-chan, as was customary in such a reunion. "It has become lonely without them, hasn't it?" Hide Uncle said.

"Yes, it has," Shiichi Uncle said, suddenly overcome with grief. He looked at the floor and took his sleeve up to his face to wipe his tears. It took me considerable effort not to break down and cry.

Turning to me, Hide Uncle said, "You and Sā-chan were so close in age. It must have been like losing a sister."

I nodded and lowered my head in my deception; I had never considered her as a sister.

After a while, making sure that I had acted properly, spending the requisite time and doing the small talk with the family, I excused myself to go outside. I wanted to see what it was like, this area my parents' place of birth, the place they had come from before emigrating to Hawaiʻi. Once outside and looking upward toward the mountain in back of the house, I saw the family burial ground, the tall dark headstones of our ancestors seeking the sky, as in the photographs Mama had stuck in the family altar.

I remember my parents talking about their former homes. Rice farming had been both their families' livelihood for generations, and before emigrating, my parents had planted rice-grass shoots in the muddy waters of the paddies like the men and women I had seen on the way up to the house. As far back as the Muromachi or Ashikaga Periods—600 years or so ago—their families had worked this land.

Born with the stain of its mud on my feet, the green of the rice grass on my hands, the sound of the temple bells in my chest, the fires of the braziers in my soul, I had one foot staked in this ground. This was the land of my ancestors, their first water, their first salt, their first names, their first fires, their first pride. Papa's name, an auspicious one, was, in fact, Mizuho, which was taken from the phrase Mizuho no Kuni or Land of the Rice People.

Although my father had told me that working in the rice fields was no different from planting cane and that work was work, there had to be a difference. He had made a choice; the need to go to America had been powerful enough that he uprooted himself. America held promises that Japan did not, but had that choice truly severed him from these deep ties?

The sun had just set and pulled its low weight of light over the hills. Braced against the mountainside, Hide Uncle's house had but a narrow view of the city. I could see in the far distance the long-reaching finger of the Otogawa River, a silver thread in this light, weaving its way in the basin. I was drawn to the city fast disappearing in the blackout with only a handful of lights. Iwao was right. Living alone in the city meant that the chances of seeing Kazuo were greater. Kyūshū was not far away, and I was sure that he would find a way to come to me once I knew my address.

Hide Uncle and Chiemi-san took the smaller cottage in the back with their three children and our family settled into the main house. It seemed odd to me that Hide Uncle and Chiemi-san relinquished their own, much larger farmhouse to us but, preoccupied with my own situation, I never thought to question their move.

"I guess I can't do anything to stop you," Harue Auntie said, folding her hands over each other a few days later at breakfast, as I discussed my plans to leave and find a place of my own in the city. "Well, good riddance is all I can say."

I avoided her eyes and said to my uncle, "I'm leaving in two days. I intend to go to the city to find work, and because you and Iwao can't work, I thought this was the best way for me to help out. I'll send you money as soon as I find a job. Somebody needs to help Hide Uncle."

"You can't fool me," Harue Auntie said. "You're not going to the city to work, you're going there to see Kazuo. You must be having an affair with this man that you can forget us like this. Your vagina is heating up and you can't stand it. See how you sit, rubbing your thighs together?"

"It's not like what you say. You have a dirty mind," I said, flatly.

"Ha, a dirty mind eh? If it's nothing, then why are you going? We don't need you to find a job in the city. There's plenty to do here! You can help in the rice fields, you can help with Uncle and Iwao." Part of the truth, so, was

218

out; she wanted me to stay back to help her.

"Harue, let the poor girl be," Shiichi Uncle said. "It's best for Hi-chan to go on with her life. She needs to get away from you, and I don't blame her. If you were nicer, she might want to stay, understand?"

"On her side again, eh?"

Uncle shook his head and began to cough. Harue Auntie shifted her position and shuffled on her knees to get to where my uncle sat in order to rub his back.

Iwao mumbled from his sleeping mat on the floor, "We're all tired of your grumbling, Okā-san. We have no peace when you start."

"Quiet. You know nothing. Your mouth is too big for your size!"

"I'm no longer a child," Iwao snapped, brave these days in answering back.

"Don't listen to her," my uncle said while struggling for breath. "You go ahead. And keep well."

"Thank you, Uncle." I was so glad when he was around, able to take charge.

"No, thank *you*. You've been like a daughter. I'll miss you, but don't worry, we'll be fine. You need to be on your own."

Harue Auntie looked as if she wanted to say something, but my uncle ignored her and continued talking, his body moving back and forth as she rubbed his back.

"The government is drafting all available young men. Right now, I feel sorry for Japan, because there's no way she can end the war without losing face. Maybe we'll all be killed before Japan admits she's wrong," Uncle said.

"How can you talk like that?" Harue Auntie said.

"It's bad, isn't it?" I asked.

"I think, very bad. But there's nothing we can do. By the way, I'm giving you some of the household money for you to make a start. The rest, I'll give to my brother."

"Who said you can do that?" Harue Auntie said.

"This is part of Hi-chan's money. She's the one who saved it from the fire."

Harue Auntie snorted.

"Be reasonable," my uncle said to Harue Auntie. "It's time we let Hi-chan go. This is something you've wanted for a long time."

A few days later, on a cloudy Thursday morning in the second week of June 1945, I packed Sumie's and my things in a willow suitcase Chiemi-san lent me and left on a bus for the city. Obstinate, Harue Auntie did not come out to say good-bye. Uncle and Iwao stood at the doorway and waved with slow hands, both of them still in their kimonos, hair wild from sleeping, faces gray from illness.

As soon as we were on the bus, Sumie began to question me in her precocious way. "Why is it that Harue Auntie did not come outside to say good-bye, Mama? What happened? And why did she tell Yuki-chan not to play with me? Yuki-chan said she can't be my friend anymore."

"Is that what Yuki-chan said? I'm sure she didn't mean it. The next time you see her, everything will be fine."

"Do you think so?"

"Yes, I think so."

"Maybe Auntie is angry at you." Sumie screwed up her face in a pout and held her breath.

"You're not to worry about what the adults do and how they behave," I said. "You keep on being Yuki-chan's friend, understand?"

"Yuki-chan will *always* be my friend," she said

25

The Interrogation

The City of Temples Street was wide and busy with many bicycles weaving in and out, the riders driving like drunks, ringing their strident bicycle bells when they wanted to pass us or simply, I thought, for the pleasure of making the noise. The herd of pedestrians and bikers had to maneuver around the derelict buses and cars left in the streets. People left their vehicles on the road when they died of engine failure or ran out of fuel. No one bothered to remove them.

When we finally reached the address that Reverend Hara had given me, I had been so unsettled by the traffic noise that I almost missed the place. With my introduction in my hand, I rang the bell, and when no one answered, I rang it again. I was just about to turn away when I heard someone in a high voice shout, "Yes, I'll be right with you. Please wait. We're busy at the moment."

The entryway seemed connected to a covered walkway and, at first glance, the high walls gave no indication as to the size of the compound. While it appeared similar to Reverend Hara's temple, it was much larger, I concluded, seeing the length of the walls on both sides of the entrance. Sumie became restless as our wait lengthened.

"Let's go. Please, Okā-chan, I want to go home where Uncle and Iwao and Yuki-chan live."

"You remember what I told you? We're going to live by ourselves for a while."

221

"I don't want to live like that. I want to go home," Sumie said and began to cry.

"Sumie, help Mama? Be a good girl and stop crying. Your crying makes it hard on me."

"Is this because we're going to meet Otō-chan?"

"You mean Kazuo-san. Perhaps, but not right now."

"If we're meeting Otō-chan, then maybe it's all right," she said, her face brightening.

"Sumie, you cannot depend on Kazuo-san to be your father. He is *not* your Otō-chan! I don't want you calling him that."

"I don't have a father, so I want Kazuo-san to be my father."

"But you have a father. He lives far away . . . and you'll meet him, someday."

"Why can't I see him *now*?"

A pretty girl suddenly came to open the gate and rescued me from having to answer Sumie. I immediately saw that the girl had some of Sā-chan's exuberance but had none of her uppity manner. "I'm sorry for keeping you waiting," she said. "I was holding a ladder for one of the reverends all this time, and we were trimming a tree branch when I heard your voice. There would have been a lot of trouble if the reverend had fallen—like Hum-pu-ty Dum-pu-ty—wouldn't there?" she laughed. It was unusual for someone in Japan to know this rhyme, which made me pay extra attention to her infectious laughter that put Sumie at ease and lightened her mood. "Oh, I'm Ito Takako," she said, grabbing Sumie's hand and leading us to the temple office. "I'll be right back with some tea." She skipped away before I could thank her.

Dressed in black, summer-sheer ceremonial robes and a purple surplice, a man shuffled in his socks down the hallway as if he were sliding across the floor. He wore a blue tie jammed against his Adam's apple; my left hand went up to my neck, automatically.

"I hope you didn't have to wait too long," he said, patting his forehead with a handkerchief in the inescapable humidity. "I've been busy doing funerals."

I introduced myself, bowed, and handed Reverend Hara's letter to the man. He wiped his forehead once more before he sat down, his face puffy, especially around his eyes. "Yes, yes," he said with a serious look, nodding as he finished reading. Looking up at Sumie and me, he removed his glasses and rubbed his eyes. "Of course you can stay here for a while," he said and gave a wide smile of gold. "I have a room for you, but remember, just for another couple of weeks. After that, I'm afraid you will have to make other arrangements."

"I'll try to find another place to live before then," I said. "And I'll help out as much as I can while here."

"That's good, then it's settled. As a matter of fact you can assist me with the next funeral service. Go to the kitchen and help serve the tea. The other ladies will tell you what to do."

"But what about Sumie, my daughter, and my bag?"

"Mmm, Sumie. You can just keep her with you. That's no problem. It's enjoyable to have young children around in a time of so much death." His eyes moved to a line of mortuary tablets on the shelf. "And you can leave your bag here." Looking at Sumie, he said, "It's nice to have you here, young girl. Please help yourself to some candy." He pushed a blue dish toward her.

"Say thank you, Sumie," I said.

"Thank you." Sumie ran up to the dish and plunged her hand in. She retrieved three pieces of candy.

"One is enough," I said, embarrassed.

"I'm saving the other ones for Yuki-chan . . . and Sā-chan," she said in after-thought.

"Go ahead," Reverend Seki said. "Take all you want—for anyone you want. It's not good for me to eat candy."

"Please excuse my daughter, but she hasn't had sweets for the longest time, and I'm afraid she has forgotten her manners."

"It's not a problem for me. It's only a problem for you," he said, a flicker of a smile running across his face.

I was startled by his frankness. Not everyone was as straightforward. I knew I was going to like this man.

Over the next week and a half, I assisted in so many funeral services that I lost count of them. It was hard for me to study the photographs of some of the older soldiers who had left wives and children behind but harder still to look at the photographs of the strong and handsome young men who, like Norio, never had a chance at life.

Thinking about Norio made the possibility of Akira's death fill me with great sadness. He may have died, never having seen his daughter. I prayed for him to be safe, for Kazuo to be safe. I prayed for everyone to be safe with no one dying at the hands of another. Though I said to myself *don't ask for the impossible, because you can't ask,* I asked, fervently. Asked for *all* lives to be spared and for everyone to come home safely.

Sumie accepted the new place, because it reminded her of Reverend Hara's temple and there were other children there to distract her. I could plunge into my work with Reverend Seki without feeling guilty about having taken her away from the family.

When the date neared to vacate the room that Reverend Seki had lent me, an advertisement on the church bulletin board led me to make a hasty application as a housemaid for the Japanese Army Base Headquarters on the grounds of the old Meiji Castle in the city. Although Takako had mentioned something in passing about a job opening where her mother worked, I had ignored it, the pay better at the castle. I also didn't think I knew Takako well enough to impose on her; too, my being American felt remote to me by this time, I rarely thought of it as a detriment. But my applying for the job at Meiji Castle proved to be a careless move. I was rejected immediately as a security risk.

The day after I received notice of my rejection, Sumie and I were in Reverend Seki's office where I was preparing for the day's services with him. There was a loud knock on the door. I turned as Reverend Seki went to it. Three very short and skinny men in uniform entered the small, already crowded room, two of them with guns.

"Hey, you just can't barge in like this!" Reverend Seki said.

"We're looking for Aoki Himiko," a deep voice said, full of command.

"There'll be no guns in here," Reverend Seki said, moving behind his desk, both arms extended with palms facing out. "This is a temple." Both men quickly lowered their guns, took off their hats, and made quick bows.

His eyes surveying the room, the man in charge said, "Take her away," pointing at me.

"You can't do that!" Reverend Seki objected.

"We have orders."

Sumie ran up and clung to me. "Stay here with Reverend Seki," I said gently, kneeling down, prying her hands off my kimono. "I'll be back as soon as I can."

She began crying. "Okā-chaaaan!" she screamed when the man grabbed and jerked my arm to pull me up and push me forward. I pushed her toward Reverend Seki, and before I could say anything more, I was hustled out of the temple office to an awaiting car, my long hair flying in the wind during the hurried car ride.

At Meiji Castle, I was led to an empty room with a desk and chair, the high white walls broken by broad, dark, ancient beams that were elaborately curved. Two small locked and out-of-reach windows looked down on me like eyes, and they afforded the only source of light. I waited alone for several hours, and I tried to sleep on my hands. It was late June, but the room was cold and I shivered in my kimono, the chill flowing upward from the floor.

The interrogator who came into the room that afternoon was a young, slim, officious-looking man, immaculate in his uniform, who throughout the initial interview did not look at me but at the wall across the room. Hair that was slicked back when he first arrived soon fell to the sides or forward into his face in well-oiled strands, as if they couldn't be restrained from returning to their natural state because of the poor oil that he used.

He immediately began circling me as if I were prey. He fired questions in sharp barks, one after another, so quickly that I wondered if he even heard my answers. "Where are you from?" "Why did you apply for this job?" "Are you working for the Americans?" "Are you a spy?" "Why did you come to Japan?" On and on he went, kicking the same questions at me, hoping to trick and trip me into confessing something for my downfall.

The next two mornings, I was awakened by a very young, embarrassed soldier, fed a meager breakfast, and later, led to a stinky outhouse, after which the same intense interrogation began. My answers: "I told you before . . . I told you before . . . I told you before. . . ."

On the fourth morning, once back in my room, I walked around it to warm myself, and having nothing to read or to do while waiting for the interrogator, I chanted a sutra of praises and gratitude to the Buddha that I had learned during my studies at Reverend Hara's temple. The chanting lightened my mood and I saw that I could remain optimistic despite my dire circumstances.

"Cut that out. How can you think of smiling and chanting when you're in big trouble?" the young interrogator asked. I had not heard him come in. "There's nothing for you to be grateful for."

"Oh, you know the 'Song of True Entrusting?'" I blurted, surprised.

"I do—we all do . . . but what are you trying to do?" He may have barked these words, but I thought I heard a softening, a reluctance about what he was asked to do, a shame creep into his voice. Later, after the ritualized questioning, he didn't stop me from further chanting when he took a smoke break and paced in the back of his desk.

> . . . *Ses-shu shin ko jo sho go, i no sui ha mu myo an . . . the light of compassion that grasps us illumines and protects us always; the darkness of our ignorance is already broken through; still, the clouds and mists of greed and desire, anger and hatred, cover, as always, the sky of true and real entrusting.*

After smoking one cigarette, then another, as if his heart were no longer in the interrogation, he sat down slowly, opposite me at the table. He stroked his hair then covered his face with his hands.

"Is anything the matter?" I asked, as he dragged his face downward with the palms of his hands and looked at me with angry tears in his eyes. After a while he got up in a whip snap and walked out of the room without a word. I wondered what set off his strange behavior.

Five days after the soldiers had come for me, Reverend Seki came to the castle to speak on my behalf. He assured the officer that I was not a spy. "She's but a young girl who's been living with relatives since the war started. She's not to blame and she means no harm."

After Reverend Seki's appeal, the interrogator asked me, "So tell me, again, why you applied for this job?"

I answered once more. "Because I'm well qualified to do it. There's no other reason. I have been taking care of others ever since coming to Japan."

"While I think that you are a traitor, I'm letting you go," he said, but I sensed that by this time he didn't believe that I was a threat and saw too that I was not intimidated; he knew that I was neither frightened nor cared what he could do to me. "What are you?" he finally asked.

"I'm nothing. Just nothing," I said, and my humble expression appeared enough to satisfy him. I bowed as low as I could and silently promised that I would never make the mistake of forgetting that I was still a foreigner. No, not ever again. On the seventh day of my detention, I was released.

Sumie had a haunted look on her face when I returned. She ran up to me and buried her face into my clothing. "Okā-chan, don't ever leave me again!"

An apologetic Reverend Seki let us use his office while I looked for a place to stay, for I had made up my mind that there was no going back to Harue Auntie.

Not long after my interrogation, a hesitant Takako stopped me to say, "I don't know what your circumstances are—I had heard you were detained—but my mother's factory needs another sewing person. I was wondering if you still needed a job." I could hardly speak and barely nodded.

She smiled and went on to describe how the women worked on the first floor of a large home. "The factory is farther inland—you'll have to catch the bus—and it used to be a geisha house," she explained in her talkative manner. "My mother said that the Boss Lady was once a famous geisha and when the government closed the geisha houses, she transferred her talents to keep up with the times. Also, my mother claims that the work isn't hard but the hours are long and the pay small. Still, it's enough to get by in this day and age. You can also bring Sumie to work if you like. Boss Lady is generous that way. By the way, I was also wondering if you found somewhere to live? I know it sounds like a coincidence, but my mother and I are looking for a tenant, our tenant having left abruptly."

"You are? I do need a place to stay. The arrangement would be perfect for me and my daughter." I could hardly contain my joy.

"It would be perfect. Wait until I tell my mother. She'll love having you both. With a small child around, it'll be livelier. I'm so happy," Takako said, her hands fluttering in childish excitement. She was already making plans to move us in.

Takako and her mother did not live far from the clock tower of the Shimamura Watch Shop in the Hondori area of the city where a myriad

227

of small shops, restaurants, and houses intertwined. The clock tower, with its arched doorway, reminded me of a miniature version of Big Ben from a child's picture book I had seen in elementary school. Since I had no watch, having lost it to Sā-chan, I liked the convenience of looking out the window for the time, and Sumie liked watching the hands move.

Happy to have my own room, my first ever, I bought an inexpensive lace doily for the low table, and Takako's mother lent Sumie and me bedding decorated with storks in flight on a blue background. At the black market, I found a modestly priced but chipped Kutani vase into which I stuck wildflowers and grasses that I had picked in my wanderings along Miyuki Bridge not far from where we lived. Reverend Seki gave me a five-inch statue of a standing Buddha that I placed next to the vase, the Buddha's hands formed into the mudra of heaven and earth. Of completion and cycles.

Reverend Seki did not accept payment for my short stay at the temple. "You have more than earned your keep by helping me with the funeral services. I will even pay you if you would come on Sundays or on your days off from the factory. Perhaps, an occasional evening. I will send word with Takako," he said. Although Reverend Seki had an assistant, he was still short-handed, more and more bodies coming home for burial.

Takako, the same age as Sā-chan, had quit school to keep herself and her mother going. As I had done in Tokyo, she went about scrounging for food and fuel, the task made more difficult that summer by even tighter food restrictions. Because of her dealings, she knew Hiroshima City well. When I told her that I needed to send a letter to my family in Hawai'i, she knew exactly where to obtain the necessary documents, and before I settled down in my work at the sewing factory, she took me to the Hiroshima Red Cross Hospital for an application and special postcards to use.

> Dear Mama and Miyo,
>
> Please forgive me for not writing sooner. When I received your letter, almost six months had gone by since you had sent it. We were in an awful state at the time, having lost everything in the fires of Tokyo. We then decided to move to Kyoto, and stayed there with a kind reverend, until Uncle and Iwao grew too ill

to stay there any longer. We are now in Hiroshima where I am living and working in the city. Please write me at the Itos in Hondori.

My daughter, Sumie, is fine and I wish you could see her.

Hi-chan

When she first opened the factory, Boss Lady had taken out the shoji doors, the dividers that had lent a semblance of fragile privacy for intimate drinking parties. She had opened the place into one enormous room, but the space remained shadowy because of the dark grain of the walls and small windows. At times, while working on the rudimentary men's clothing, I imagined the music of the shamisen, the singing of women, the kick of delicate white feet across the mats, and the swish of kimono coming through the old walls.

I started as a folder on one of the long tables, and not long after, I advanced to a sewing position vacated by another worker. The steady whir of the machines fed by feet on treadles became the monotonous accompaniment to our work, our only form of music.

Fortunately, I managed to pick up a used bicycle, upon which I put a basket seat in the front for Sumie, and set off to work each day. I often walked my clumsy bicycle because tires had become difficult to find, and I didn't want to wear down what little tread mine had. At the factory, I placed a quilt on the tatami in one far corner for Sumie to play and sleep on; I brought her toys and books from home. Three other children also came to the factory with their young mothers.

Sumie didn't seem to mind the long hours. She played school or house with the other children, the one boy always the baby or the father. "I like the shop, but I don't like the mosquitoes and the rain, Mama. I wish Yuki-chan were here, Sā-chan, too." Whenever she mentioned Sā-chan I felt a lurch in my stomach and had to be glad that Sumie's complaints were small, though it saddened me that she always had to include Sā-chan whenever she mentioned Yuki-chan.

The other children, all slightly older than Sumie, played with her as if she were their younger sister. They were on the quiet side, their laughter more subdued than most children their ages. Sumie, too, was growing older, more reticent; caution began to dampen her toddler instincts and enthusiasms. Watching Sumie and the other children, I felt sorry for them, for they had seen and known more than they should with little understanding of what war was all about. One thing for sure, I could see that they were not as carefree as they should have been; they were born at a bad time in the history of human affairs, their souls old before their time.

Having finally settled down in Hiroshima City, I had Takako write a letter for me in Japanese to Reverend Hara in Kyoto.

My honorable teacher,

Thank you so much for your referral to Reverend Seki; he has been so helpful and kind. Sumie and I are doing well, and we are now living in the city where I have a job in a small clothing factory and Sumie can accompany me. I live in Hondori with the Itos, a mother and her daughter, and hope you are able to meet them someday.

I wish to apologize for having to put you out of your way, but would you please give my address and the enclosed note to Kazuo's mother? I don't know if she still lives in Kyoto, so I think it might be necessary to trouble you even further by having you send it to Kazuo's father if his mother is not around. I have never met the man before so I hope he doesn't think me forward, sending his son a note and my address in this way. I regret having to put you through so much trouble.

Enclosed is a drawing of a sparrow by Sumie. She said she wanted you to have it for it reminded her of the Sparrow School teacher—suzume no gakko no sensei—from the song that you taught her. Like me, she's been homesick for your temple.

In reverence,
Hi-chan

26

The Ogawas

About a month after I left, I went back to visit Shiichi Uncle and the rest of the family. Shiichi Uncle walked out of his room to greet me, appearing frailer than the last time I had seen him; Iwao, however, looked much better. Upstairs, Harue Auntie was seated in a corner of the living area with sewing on her lap. As soon as they heard I was there, Chiemi-san and Hide Uncle came running from their cottage over to the main house to greet Sumie and me.

I had caught the family by surprise, Iwao's hair still mussed up by sleep and Uncle in his sleeping kimono. Although Harue Auntie had a scowl, looking as if she could peck out my eyes with the beak of whatever grievances she still harbored, I did my best to ignore her.

Yuki-chan and Sumie couldn't have been happier to see each other. My strategy of using surprise seemed to have worked in the sense that I hadn't wanted Harue Auntie saying anything to Yuki-chan beforehand to spoil the girls' fun and friendship. The girls played with each other as always, and upon seeing their faces, I knew I had done the right thing in circumventing Harue Auntie's intervention.

While the children played, I took my tea with the family. Chiemi-san did the serving and kept smiling and nodding at me but said very little in Harue Auntie's presence. Seldom looking up, Harue Auntie continued to sew a child's piece of clothing.

"I also came to return the household money you gave me," I said to my uncle.

"There's no need to do that."

"I have a job now, and I want to return something."

"I won't accept it. You're embarrassing me."

"But Sumie and I don't need much."

"Take it!" Harue Auntie said. Earlier, she had crept up to the table to better listen to our conversation, and by now, she was at my uncle's side. She sideswiped his arm with a back sweep of her hand, the force of her slap almost knocking his thin body down. "She owes us and don't you let her forget it. She took away from our own children, remember?"

"But she more than made up for it by all the help she's given us."

"Otō-san's right," Iwao said under his breath. "Give it up, Okā-san."

Harue Auntie turned to Iwao and hissed her fury. "Be quiet, Iwao!"

"It's okay, Shiichi Uncle, here, take this money." I pushed a money envelope forward on the table.

"It's bad luck to take it," Shiichi Uncle said.

"It's bad luck if you *don't* take it," Harue Auntie snapped. "Take what people owe you!"

With a slow hand Shiichi Uncle accepted the money that lay on the table between us and slipped the money into his kimono sleeve—a paltry sum, considering I owed and wanted to give so much more. I saw, in a flash, Harue Auntie's hand fish out the money from Shiichi Uncle's sleeve that lay at his side and slip the envelope into the front of her kimono. "Oh," Shiichi Uncle said, but he let her go. A look of satisfaction smoothed the wrinkles on my auntie's face. Keeping his eyes on Harue Auntie, Shiichi Uncle swept his arm and sleeve across his chest.

As I was about to leave, Iwao said, "Hi-chan, when I get better may I come and stay with you in the city? I want to join one of the Middle School Service Corps demolition teams. I'll arrange it so I can be with my age group. I heard they're not too particular about who goes. The students are assembling in the city to do this—in early August, I believe—to help with the firebreaks. They're even coming from schools deep in the country."

"Sure, you may come, but only if you're better. Take a few more weeks to gain strength. I'll be waiting to hear from you."

Air-raid warnings picked up in pace, the short time Sumie and I had been in Hiroshima, but in most cases they were quickly canceled by an all-clear signal. Some days, American planes drizzled paper leaflets on us, all of them warning of dire consequences, but the people in Hiroshima were unconcerned about these warnings in the same way that people in Tokyo had been before the firebombing. Rumors flew, but like the leaflets that fell from the sky, they were treated as mere annoyances.

Women at the factory often voiced their opinions about the war as they worked. One of them, Asayo-san, more vocal than the others, said, "I personally don't think the Americans find our city a good target, other cities more important, although we do happen to have Ujina Harbor, a potential target. Besides, not many troops are left in the city."

Whenever the women discussed the planes and bombs at work, second thoughts about living in the city entered my mind. I did not want to be part of another firebombing. For Sumie's and my safety, I should have considered moving back to the country, where the odds of being bombed were less, but every time I thought of Harue Auntie's face, her scoldings, grumblings, accusations, I knew I could never live with her again. It was better for me to be on my own and take my chances.

"Hi-chan, telephone," Takako called out one humid Saturday morning, dust motes swimming in the streaks of sunlight. We had been cleaning the temple. "Long distance. I hear a man's voice on the other side," Takako said, pointing at the phone, giggling as she covered the mouthpiece. "Hurry."

I took the phone from Takako. "Hello, hello," I said.

"Hi-chan? This is Kazuo." The operator left the line with a loud, solid click.

"Kazuo, but where . . . in Hiroshima? How did you find me?"

"Hold on . . . right now I'm in Kyoto. However, I've been assigned to work at the Meiji Castle Army Base Headquarters in Hiroshima as a temporary courier for a few days. I called to let you know that I got your short note, your writing much improved. My father had it delivered to me in Kyūshū. Reverend Hara suggested that I leave a message at the church where you worked, and he gave me your number. I'm so happy I caught you." He paused and I could hear his breath quicken. "I've missed you, Hi-chan."

"I've missed you, too. When will you be in the city?"

"Not soon enough. Probably next week. Are you keeping well? How's Sumie?"

"Sumie and I are fine. She misses you."

"I'll call you again, when I know more about my assignment. Until such time, good-bye."

"Yes, good-bye," I said and saw Takako clapping, tears in her eyes.

A few days after my conversation with Kazuo, as I was helping to prepare the evening meal, a thick, solidly built black limousine arrived and parked in the narrow lane in the front of the Itos' home. Takako's mother and Sumie were playing with beanbags on the floor when there was a knock on the door.

"Yes, who is it?" Takako's mother called out.

"I'd like to see Aoki Himiko," a deep voice answered.

"I wonder who it can be, Hi-chan?" she whispered.

"I have no idea," I whispered back.

"Stay here. I don't think it's the police, but we can't be sure."

Takako's mother went to the front door, her reluctant feet moving on the mat as if she were walking through thick grass. I heard her conversing with a man before she popped back in.

"What seems to be the problem, Okā-san?" asked Takako.

"No problem." Takako's mother said, looking to me. "The man's name is Dr. Ogawa and he came to talk to Hi-chan. But seeing that we are about to have dinner, he said he would come back later."

Kazuo's father, in Hiroshima? "It's the father of the man I've been seeing," I said. "I hope nothing has happened. Did he say anything else?"

"No. He looks stern, doesn't he? A bit frightening."

"I've never met him. I can't imagine what he wants."

We ate in silence, and as soon as dinner was over, Takako and her mother took Sumie upstairs to put her to bed. I cleared the dishes, changed my clothes, and waited. I was beginning to nod off when I heard the front door slide open.

Half groggy, I got up, my legs numb and full of needles. "Oh," I exclaimed, surprised to see Dr. Ogawa already in the house and walking towards me into the living area. I bowed in greeting. "Please . . . have a seat."

He sat down without hesitation on the zabuton. A tall, well-dressed man in a pinstripe suit, he looked very much like Kazuo, except for a carefully trimmed mustache and graying hair. His skin was sickly pale, and he carried the faint odor of cologne, or—was it expensive liquor? Somehow, probably because of his age and status in the community, he had not been called to war like most doctors.

Before I could ask him if I could serve him some tea, he dispensed with the usual formalities of polite discourse and said, "I don't have much time, so I'll come straight to the point. I know you've been seeing Kazuo, but I have someone else in mind for my son to marry. This girl comes from a good family and is best suited for him."

"I'm not sure I understand what you're trying to tell me."

"Most people would have understood at once."

His distaste for me flashed in his eyes. In his voice I heard something of Kazuo's earlier tones—of arrogance, of dismissal, of easy disdain. *Don't let this man bully you,* I told myself. *Hold your ground and don't grovel like a person of low position.*

"Let me make it as plain as I can. I don't want you seeing my son again. I don't want you interfering with my plans for him."

I said nothing but stared straight into his gaze, forcing him to continue when I said nothing.

"Let's just say that you're nothing in my eyes. You're an American, and in our society you don't count for anything. You have everything going against you, and I need to protect my son. I understand you have a child and that you're not married? I'm sure you want a father for this child, and I suspect this is what motivates you."

Swallowing my anger, I said, "I'm leaving it up to Kazuo. If he wants to see me, I will see him."

"Is it money you want? I'll give you all the money you need." He removed a bundle of bills from his wallet and tossed it on the mat. "We can start with this."

"I don't want your money. You can't bribe me to stop seeing Kazuo."

"What do you mean, *bribe*? Go on, take it. You can live comfortably for a change. You can feed your daughter better. Don't you need clothes for her? Some milk? Maybe medicine? Why, you're nothing but skin and bones yourself. With this money you can buy good things to eat and have all the pretty things you want. Perhaps your daughter needs new slippers. You can buy her a new pair, or perhaps she needs new clothes. For a price you can get anything at the black market."

"I don't want or need your money." I slid the money across the mat, back toward Dr. Ogawa.

"Money is money. Everyone has a price."

"Not me. All the money in the world isn't going to change the way I feel."

"You're making it hard on me . . . and on yourself."

"I don't think we have anything more to say to each other, so please leave this house. You'll never get your way with me; I refuse to listen!"

"We'll see about that. You'll regret going against me!" he said, standing up and stomping out.

Though I shook in fury, I had thwarted his actions for the time being.

Two days later, to even greater surprise, Kazuo's mother paid me a visit. I had just arrived home from work, and Mrs. Ogawa was already sitting in the living room with Sumie, who had come home earlier with Takako's mother. I wondered if she was also there to plead with me to stay away from her son.

Sumie came running up to me with a wooden puppet rocking in her hand. When I moved into the room, I saw more toys strewn across the floor along with articles of children's clothing. It was as I had expected—another payoff. Kazuo's mother, however, was far more subtle; she was using my child to get her way.

"Look what Obā-chan brought me!" Sumie's face glowed with excitement and pleasure.

"Grandmother? Sumie, you know better than that. Mrs. Ogawa is not your grandmother."

Takako and her mother shifted their bodies on their zabuton, uncomfortable with the sharp tone I had directed at Sumie in front of a visitor.

"It's all right," Kazuo's mother said. "I wish I *were* her grandmother. I asked her to call me that. Please don't be upset."

"You're confusing my daughter and me, too. You come into my

home . . . I don't know why you are here." When she said nothing, I felt compelled to go on. "But I guess I *do* know why. You, like your husband, want me to stay away from Kazuo; only, you're using different tactics to get what you want."

I sat on the floor, less agitated now. I was not going to be pushed around by Kazuo's parents. I might lose to them, but at least I would maintain my pride. Upon seeing the nature and course of the conversation, Takako and her mother signaled that they were going upstairs. They quietly ushered themselves out, dragging a reluctant Sumie between them.

"I know Kazuo's father came to see you," Kazuo's mother said. "What a foolish man. I'm guessing that he was talking about his plans for Kazuo."

I stared at her, suddenly unsure of my footing.

Kazuo's mother reached out with her hand and placed it on the floor. "You asked why I'm here," she said. "I'm here to give you my blessing."

I looked into her eyes and saw the sincerity there; it was unmistakable.

"As I said before, my husband is a foolish man. It gives me pleasure to foil his plans. He has to have his way, you see, and I don't want to give it to him."

"I don't want to be caught between you two because of your differences."

"But you're already involved. Besides, I believe in what you Americans call *love-u*."

"You mean falling in love?"

"Yes. And as you can see, my husband has no idea what it means."

She looked down at her white hands folded in front of her in two large petals. "I want you to keep on seeing Kazuo. Don't let his father tell you what to do."

"I never intended to."

"Good, I like that. You have spirit." Leaning forward and speaking quickly and earnestly, she explained that she wanted her son to follow his heart. "Things are going to change in Japan once the war is over, even how and who people marry. The American way. And for me, I will have a ready-made granddaughter in Sumie. I'll have someone to spoil. I can't tell you how nice that would be. She's such a beautiful child."

But it was still a set-up to me. "Maybe you and your husband don't understand. Kazuo and I don't know each other all that well. Our relationship is at an early stage."

She smiled, reached out, squeezed my hand that sat on my lap, and said, "Things happen with great speed in wartime." Compared to when I first met her in Kyoto, she did not appear to be as stiff or mechanical. I was even surprised that she touched my hand. I could still see her, backed up to the door in the backseat of her sleek, black car, her thin body braced against the frame, giving me a slight nod of greeting.

"I just want Kazuo to be happy," she said.

"I want him to be happy, too," I said.

After a brief silence, Kazuo's mother rose, and like me, bending over significantly because of her height, headed out to her car. "Please wait," she said. "I'll be back in a minute." She returned with her driver who carried an armful of packages. He placed them on the floor and left.

"Gifts, for all of you," Kazuo's mother said. I was ready to protest, but she quickly interrupted me. "Please don't hurt me by refusing."

"But I feel indebted . . ."

"Nonsense!" she scolded.

Reluctantly, I called Takako, her mother, and Sumie downstairs. My daughter came bounding down like an animal let out of its cage and leaped into Kazuo's mother's arms in her anticipation of additional gifts.

Kazuo's mother gave Takako and her mother handkerchiefs, writing paper, and dried persimmons. She gave me a brand new dress with silk stockings and a pair of matching flats. Of the new dress she said, "For the next time you're with Kazuo." I could only look down, feeling embarrassed and somewhat manipulated.

After opening her gifts, Sumie asked, "What about Yuki-chan? And Sā-chan?"

"Please Sumie," I snapped. I did not want her to grow up thinking that Kazuo's mother was nothing more than a gift giver, but Sumie was not humbled an inch and Kazuo's mother winked at her, as if they already had secrets of their own.

As she played with Sumie, I studied her with quick, covert glances. She looked stunning with her jet-black hair and her alabaster complexion, yet I sensed that she was also lonely and starved for company. It was almost six o'clock, close to our dinner hour, yet she showed no inclination to leave.

27

The Proposal

One day in late July, Kazuo walked into the factory I worked at, wearing a white work shirt and white linen pants. He looked brilliant, dressed in summer whites, and I lost my line of stitching, the cloth I was working with running beyond the machine's needle on the stitching plate. I also dropped my marking bone and thimble onto the floor in the involuntary jerk of my elbow. I had never expected that he would come to my workplace.

"It's Otō-san!" Sumie jumped up from her place with the other children and ran over to greet him. Kazuo swept her into his arms, and he whispered something to her that made her giggle. She gave me a wide, toothy grin that squinched her face.

"Shhh!" I gestured, wanting to say that he was not her father.

"He *is* my Otō-san," she said in anticipation of my scold. "He's come to take us away."

The sewing place, dark and drab, brightened when the women saw Kazuo, and a rushing sound of voices spread through the room. Embarrassed and flustered by his boldness, I couldn't look at him straight in the face, my clumsy hands fumbling all over my sewing. He seemed so sure of himself now, no longer the uncertain young man who whispered his feelings for me among the cherry trees in Gion.

After he put Sumie down—I saw this from the corner of my eye because I didn't dare look up—he went straight to where Boss Lady sat at her desk. He whispered something to the woman, his hand shielding his mouth and her ear. After a moment, Boss Lady cracked a huge smile, her face crinkling like a paper bag. Leaning in toward Kazuo, she nodded repeatedly at whatever he said. "That's fine, perfectly fine," I heard her say, slapping her thighs for emphasis.

After she talked to Kazuo at length, Boss Lady walked over to me and said, "Hi-chan, you're dismissed for the rest of the day. Let Takako's mother know if you're not going to be here tomorrow. Or the next."

"Outside, I'll be waiting," Kazuo signaled and took Sumie with him.

I gathered my things, feeling foolish and giddy at the same time. At the sudden entertainment being played out before them, my fellow workers smiled with such abandonment that it made blood rush to my face. I babbled something incoherently and rushed out of the room.

Once outside, I shaded my eyes to look for Kazuo's face, which seemed bright as the midday light. My feet were suddenly no longer under me and I felt myself drifting, walking from lotus blossom to lotus blossom.

When I finally met up with Sumie and him, he said, "I arranged it with Boss Lady to give you a short leave of absence." He grinned and whispered close to my ear, "I also told her that I was going to marry you."

"You said that?"

"My actual words were, 'I'm going to marry that girl.'"

"Oh, I don't know about that . . . what to say."

"Say that you'll marry me. That's enough."

"I'd like to marry you, Kazuo, but how can we? There's a war going on, yeah, and I'm still an American citizen. They'll never let us get married as long there's a war between our countries."

"Then we'll wait. The minute the war is over, we'll get married. So, come on, show me the city. Let's make it another holiday as we did in Kyoto. I've never been in Hiroshima before."

Going toward Hondori, Kazuo walked my bicycle with Sumie seated in her basket. He looked at her and said, "Sumie-chan. How would you like me to be your father?"

"You, my Otō-chan? I would like that." Turning her head toward me, she said, "See, Okā-chan? I told you."

"I guess you did."

We braved the summer heat and dawdled along the way—stopped in a little café first, then later on for tea in a sweet shop—before heading home, Sumie playing contentedly at our side. I suggested a boat ride during Kazuo's stay, and he suggested we go to an Obon Festival Dance and later to a nightclub. According to Kazuo, he had fixed it with Boss Lady so that in the days that I planned to be out, Takako's mother would watch Sumie for me at the factory.

The boat ride up the Motoyasu River on our second day together transported us into the life of the city. The heat toward the end of July was humid and stifling, but we were too preoccupied to care, all too many things streaming through our minds. We started the ride at the river's wide sea mouth and moved inland like a herd of alligators with other sightseeing ferries and small boats topped with merchandise.

In spite of the war, people still took time off to enjoy moments of leisure. We passed under bridges where men and boys were fishing, women washing ginkgo nuts or long stretches of dyed material, the areas above us teeming with people and merchants. To Kazuo, I pointed out what landmarks I knew: Ogon-zan Hill, Hiroshima Municipal Building, Motoyasu Bridge, the ubiquitous shrines.

We leaned backward or forward on the rails of the slow-moving boat to enjoy the air—my hair flying, my new dress billowing like a parachute, and the whimsical winds playing with Kazuo's dark, silky hair. Sā-chan would have thought this ride upriver so romantic, and her eyes haunted me when I looked into the murky water below, eyes colored by the darkness of hurt and betrayal. A chill passed through my body, and I quickly turned away from the water.

The ferrymen wove their oars back and forth to guide the small boat, and one of the men hummed a strong, melancholy tune under his breath: "Song of the Seashore." Wearing only a short gauzelike shirt with a loincloth to cover himself, he looked purple around his lips and eye sockets that years in the sun had created.

"When this war is over, after we marry, would you like to live in Tokyo?" Kazuo asked.

"Why Tokyo?"

"I want to go back to school, go into medicine like my father."

"That's fine with me."

"But I'm afraid that when the war is over, maybe you'll change your mind and would want to go back to America."

Hawai'i. Home. Mama and Miyo. Everything felt so far away. "No," I said, "this is the only home I have. You and Sumie."

"If there's an invasion, as many people believe there'll be, I'll have to fight until the very end. That's when I'll see my enemy eye to eye. Where will you be then? What will happen to you . . . to us?"

"I don't know," I said. "I haven't thought that far ahead."

"If I get through the war alive, perhaps your feelings for me will change."

"I don't think so. I like you terribly much."

"For you . . . me too," he said, and clasped his hands and bit his knuckles. Silent for a while, he finally said, "Hey, let's stop this nonsense. Why are we spoiling our time together? This is supposed to be a holiday. We should be enjoying ourselves. From now on, there'll be no talk of war."

After the boat ride, we took a leisurely walk through Asano Park. Sea winds had pushed back the clouds to reveal blue skies; oak and pine trees, large and shady, covered the walkways that school children streamed across in play. We ate a late lunch of udon at a roadside stall; the noodles, coiled in a thin broth garnished with pieces of seaweed and thin slices of shaved bonito, loosened the belt of hunger cinched around my stomach. On the other side of the river, above its bank, the thick rice grass was heavy with grain, while cicadas all around us cried in a deafening roar. From the bank, young boys jigged for frogs in the streams, their bait flashing in the sun as we watched, amused by their earnestness.

The next evening, Kazuo took a taxi to the Hondori Watch Tower where we met. From there, we walked over to the largest temple in Teramachi to watch the Obon Festival dancers celebrate the time of year when spirits of the dead come back to Earth. The celebration was one of the first to be held that season. I bought a red lantern and had one of the priests on the long tables write my father's, Norio's, and Sā-chan's names on the lantern with his brush, and I lit the candle inside.

"Do you want them to string it up?" Kazuo asked.

I nodded. *Yes, string it up. Let it float in the air to call their spirits. Let it show them the way home.*

The stringer hung the named lanterns on ropes that were strung across the eaves from one building to the next; these lanterns lit up the temple yard. Strips of white paper with names of temple donors were also hung from the lines, and they flapped *plap, plap, plap* in the erratic wind to create their own forlorn music.

I followed the light of my lantern in the hands of the stringer who would place it on the rope line after a precarious climb up a ladder. The candle no longer flickered but burned with steady intensity even when a strong breeze of uneasy spirits passed through the temple yard and made the lantern sway. Other lanterns, bordering mine, burst into flames and dropped from their strings, like flares, their sparks trailing showers of light.

"Papa, Norio, Sā-chan, take this beacon. Use it to rejoice in what had been your lives. What is ours." *Sā-chan, maybe this is the only way I can make it up to you.*

The Obon dancers sang, clapped their hands, pointed their toes, raised their voices to the beat, and swayed their bodies in the lanterns' firelight to dance to the harvest moon. Dancing in the night shadows they made lovely motions and twisted their hands in joy—*arya sa, korya dokkoito na*—and their booming voices were lifted to the heavens.

The story goes that Mogallana, one of the Buddha's disciples, had rejoiced by dancing when he saved his mother from the Hell of the Hungry Ghost through his good deeds. This was his dance of happiness; he danced and danced, and others, mesmerized by his dancing, had followed him in and out of the lanterns' light, into this night.

Leaving the dancing throng, we walked out into the street where Kazuo summoned a taxi. Consulting the driver while following some written directions, we arrived at a fancy building in Hachibori, a shopping district not far from Hiroshima Train Station. The building had two tall floors and we climbed up to the second level. Polished marble, as if in a wash of small pebbles in a stream, glossed the floor, and our steps echoed down this hard, cold hallway. I had had this feeling of spaciousness in a building only once before in my life, and that was in the Territorial Courthouse Building in Hilo where Papa testified for a friend in a sugar cane land dispute. Space, like everything else, was a luxury in Japan. I looked up at the gold-leaf designs on the ceiling, my lower jaw dropping at its opulence.

"We're having dinner at this club," Kazuo said. "My father's a member."

"Your *father*?"

"Anything the matter?"

"Oh no . . ." I said.

Kazuo gave me a puzzled look but said nothing.

Inside the dining room, long stems of hanging lily chandeliers swayed from the ceiling, pushed along by fans. A big band played as couples in elegant clothing swayed on a floor of mirrors. Sleek men in vanilla suits and agile women in long gowns of wandering silk chiffon, skimmed the dance floor in the haze. Somehow, they reminded me of the faces of those Shiichi Uncle called the walking dead.

The Japanese could never rid themselves entirely of foreign influences. While most of the tunes were Japanese, I heard a version of something by Glenn Miller—"Moonlight Serenade," one of Miyo's favorite tunes—being played, the trumpet players rising and using cups to mute and open sounds coming from their gold horns. The music filled my heart with a piercing ache, a longing for home, a yearning for stability in my life, but I didn't want to spoil my evening with Kazuo and pushed such thoughts aside.

Someone in a dark suit showed us to a table near the dance floor.

"Would you like a drink? Some wine, perhaps?" Kazuo asked when we sat down.

"I've never had wine in my life except for my uncle's pig wine—his bakudan. That's what the neighborhood people called it."

"His bomb?"

"They called it that because of its big kick."

"In China, after coming home to the barracks after a long day of watching the citizens in the city, I could have used a strong drink like your uncle's bomb," he said.

I wanted to question Kazuo about China but was afraid to ask; I might have learned something I didn't want to know. His world as a soldier held shadows and secrets. I sensed they were solely his, not something I could possibly imagine, and not for me to share or to be a part of.

Continuing, Kazuo said, "My grandparents had a house in Hakone that they left to my father," he said. "It has several springs on the property. Legend has it that one of the springs, the largest, has healing powers, and people from miles around come to drink the water or use it for their wine. Maybe someday, I'll give your Uncle some of this water to make his wine. My father goes there every so often to bottle this potion, this elixir, to use in his medical practice."

I sipped the wine in my glass, and it tasted metallic, like blood.

High-ranking officers of the Imperial Army and Navy bedecked with ribbons and medals on their sashes stood in listless posture among the crowd. Kazuo nodded to men here and there. Rich, lean businessmen sat around the perimeter with women, whom I suspected were not their wives, and sipped drinks that were unfamiliar to me or lit cigarettes for the women they were with, the women blowing the smoke out in long white streams from the sides of their full, red mouths. Dancers dipped and floated their partners across the floor in long graceful strides, arms extended. Strong, expensive perfumes lingered in the clandestine atmosphere, which was mixed with cigarette smoke and expensive liquor. Here, everyone was lean but not because they were starving. Looking around me I felt inadequate and uncomfortable among these people. My dress was not long enough, and I was too dark and too starving in a real way.

When the waiter brought us our food, I watched Kazuo use his utensils—how he cut his meat, how he delicately guided food onto his fork. I hoped that I wasn't revealing the fact that this world was totally foreign to me and that I lacked an education and social skills and graces.

Midway through the meal, I spilled water on the tablecloth. "Please excuse me," I said. "I apologize for being so clumsy."

Kazuo laughed at my embarrassment but had mistaken the source of my discomfort. My discomfort? I didn't belong in his world. I felt a wave of revulsion for these people who lived and ate so well, when all around them people were emaciated and dying. I could almost smell the ugly leanness of their decay.

Nonetheless, my wanting to be with Kazuo, coupled with his charms that overpowered the truth I saw before me, made me go on smiling despite the ghostly figures that moved up to dance around us, none glowing with health but with the sickness of decadence.

They *were* the walking dead.

28

Stepping off the Bus

Sumie and I saw Kazuo off at Hiroshima Train Station the day he returned to Kyūshū for the anticipated invasion of Japan. My mood turned inward and darkened once he was gone. Sumie kept asking if she would ever see her father again, and even as I reassured her that she would, I had misgivings.

The day I returned to work at the factory, all the women in the sewing room stopped talking and started clapping their hands. They giggled, covered their mouths, and nudged each other gently. I had grown fond of them, these tiny, diligent sewing women.

"I'm so happy for you," Boss Lady said in greeting. "I hope you and that fine young man get married soon. Have many children. Japan will need a lot of boy babies to take the place of all who have died."

"Don't rush her," said Takako's mother. "If she gets married, I will have to find another tenant. We've been happy these past few weeks. So don't spoil it. Hi-chan and Sumie bring joy to me—better than a man."

Everyone roared. While I bore the brunt of their jokes, I was also the recipient of their kindness—in the form of their wedding gifts—gifts for a wedding that had not been seriously discussed. This did not stop them, however. One of the ladies had hand-sewn a silk handkerchief and embroidered some cherry blossoms in one corner; another gave me a small jewelry pouch. "I'm sure he's going to give you some pearls," she said as she handed it to me. "Think of me whenever you take them out."

A pair of chopsticks, a small hand mirror, a tea bowl, and a small blue dish appeared at my workstation. The women had so little themselves, yet they found something to give. I cried at receiving each gift.

"Now, now," Takako's mother said, coming up to pat my back.

"How am I going to repay all of you? I don't even know when I'm getting married."

"Have a good life. Make a lot of babies," the pearl-bag woman said.

Later that morning, a pair of silk panties, which had been passed across the floor, appeared. As I picked up the panties tied with a ribbon, I looked for the gift-giver's name when the woman, Asayo-san, slid across the floor to my side. "For your wedding night," she said and winked. Before I could thank her she slinked away into her corner like a city cat. After that, she never looked up at me, so I couldn't catch her eyes long enough to acknowledge her present.

Just then, some planes flew over Boss Lady's shop. "They're here again, Okā-chan," Sumie cried out and came running over.

"Don't worry," I told her. "Sirens would have sounded if there were an air raid. Look, no one else is afraid, and the other children are still playing. Why don't we go to the window and see if we can spot the planes? I'm sure there aren't many."

As I thought, just a couple of planes were in the sky. Moving up to the window beside Sumie, I watched them fly toward us. One plane flew lower than usual, and as we watched it, it veered down and let loose a belly full of leaflets. The other plane, an escort, flew high and we could hardly see it, the plane skimming the cloud line. In the background we could hear the occasional *boom, boom* of anti-aircraft guns, but the retaliation was sporadic and futile because the Japanese could never touch the American planes, which were too fast and high-flying.

"See? You didn't have to worry. They're only dropping paper."

"Can I go outside to pick them up?"

"Sure. Let's see what they say."

Takako's mother walked out with us to see what was written on the flyers. Dated July 27, 1945, they were general statements of doom for the Japanese people. I had seen them before. Takako's mother translated: the Americans listed several cities that were in danger—Hiroshima, Kokura,

Niigata, Nagasaki—but they didn't say what they proposed to do. We could do little at this point even if we knew. Most of us had no place to go and would have to take our chances if firebombing devices rained down on Hiroshima, as they had done in Tokyo, Tokuyama, Kure, Nagoya, Yokohama, Osaka, and a number of other cities on Honshu. This list of bombed-out cities was growing longer, but people continued to rely on the old invincible Japanese luck. We had heard these warnings before, and so far nothing had happened to our city.

"Just more scare tactics by the Americans," Takako's mother said. "They're good at making us scared."

"I don't know about that," I said. "Some of them are good people."

"Excuse me," she said, and changed the subject because of our mutual discomfort.

Sumie had fun gathering the papers, picking them up like leaves to be burned. She moved this way and that like a circle of wind. Somehow, picking up these sheets of paper made me teary-eyed; I felt an overwhelming sadness. I didn't want Japan to be bombed again.

That afternoon, I received a short note from Iwao that had been delivered to the Itos.

> Dear Hi-chan,
>
> I'm coming into the city to help in the Student Mobilization Service Corps. I'm feeling better so I want to give it a try. I'll be joining the students out at Honkawa School not far from Hondori.
>
> I also want to let you know that my father is going into a tuberculosis sanatorium close by, because Okā-san wants a rest from his care. My father thinks that his going to the hospital is the best thing to do. Yuki-chan is suffering from malnutrition, and he doesn't want her to catch his illness in her weakened condition. My father plans to go in after I return from the city . . .

In the rest of his note, Iwao asked if Kazuo had come to see me and how Sumie was doing. In a bit of gossip he said that no one was getting paid for their vegetables and the rice crops, and that Hide Uncle killed his last cow to help people in the village. He closed, saying that they had had several clear days, which helped his father, being that the earlier, unexpected rains had caused him to suffer greatly.

A few days later, an exhausted but healthier-looking Iwao appeared at the Itos' doorstep. Takako and her mother set him up in a small corner of the main room downstairs.

"Now, you're the man of the house," Takako's mother told him.

Iwao, happy to be doing something in the city, worked on two different days to tear down houses for firebreaks with a group of boys and girls his age. "I like being here. It's a good change from the country," he told me. Not wanting to tire himself, he decided to stay for a few more days before going home. I planned to accompany Iwao to the country and visit Shiichi Uncle at that time. I had to see for myself how Yuki-chan was faring and how my uncle was doing.

That August in 1945, on the morning of the 6th, a Monday, I planned to go home with Iwao. The night before, Sumie and I had slept badly, tossing about like stream fish out of water. She had cried in her dreams, and I had to carry her around the room and pat her back to soothe her fears.

We had already eaten breakfast and I was dressing Sumie for our trip when the air-raid sirens went off. The sirens were for the usual weather plane that flew over at that time in the morning. I was unconcerned about it and glanced at the Shimamura clock tower outside. The time: 7:10 a.m.

"Hurry, Sumie," I said, irritated at having to coax her.

"I'm tired. I don't want to go anywhere," she whined.

"Not even to play with Yuki-chan? Shiichi Uncle will be there too. He'll see you from the doorway."

"Yuki-chan and Uncle?"

"Remember? I told you yesterday that we were going to the country with Iwao. Don't tell me you've forgotten."

"If we're seeing Yuki-chan, then it's all right. Uncle too."

"We'll have a fine time. Look how sunny it is. The sky's a perfect blue."

I hoisted Sumie up in my arms to see out; she had grown heavier despite the poor nutrition.

"There's only one plane in the air, so we have nothing to be afraid of,"

I said.

"Mama, I'm not afraid of anything if we're going to Yuki-chan's house to play."

The city sounded the all clear, no other planes seen. "See, what did Mama tell you? No more planes."

Just at that time, Takako came upstairs to bid us good-bye. "Have a nice trip," she said. "And come home early!"

"How come?"

"Because I'm planning a special meal to celebrate your wedding. And I have a surprise."

"Wedding? It's too early, you know."

"You have a surprise?" Sumie asked. "I like surprises."

"That's my girl," Takako said and patted Sumie's head.

"Has your mother left for work yet?" I asked.

"No. Let me call her." Takako hollered, "Okā-san, please come to Hi-chan's room before you go. She wants to talk to you."

"What happened?" Takako's mother said, running into my room. "Takako, you scare me when you shout like that."

"I'm sorry, there's nothing the matter," I said. "It's only Takako's exuberance. I wanted to say good-bye before you left for work. Sumie and I are going home with Iwao for the day."

"Well, take care and send my regards to your family. I hope your uncle gets better. It's not a good time to be ill," she said and left.

Takako helped me button the back of the same dress I had worn the last time I was with Kazuo, the one his mother had given to me as a gift. I did not wear the summer kimono that Takako's mother had lent me.

"This is such a pretty dress. Someday, give it to me. If you marry Kazuo, he'll give you many nice things, so you won't be needing this again."

"But my clothes are too big for you."

"I don't care, I can take them in. My, you're so tall, Hi-chan," she said as she backed away to look at me. She then stepped around me and pressed her back against mine to measure herself.

"You and Kazuo must look like the giant guardians of the temple gates—Fujin, the wind god, and Raijin, the thunder god. People must stare at you all the time, the rest of us so small."

"I do have the feeling that people stare at us."

"Look at yourself in the mirror. See how beautiful you look? A regular glamour girl."

"You're silly, Takako," I said.

She giggled into her hands. "Let me walk you to the bus stop," she said as she watched me comb my hair and clip a pin in my hair. "I'm going to the Street of Temples and to the market after that. It's a short walk to the bus station, so I'll keep you company."

"It's always nice to have your company. Sumie would like that."

"It's such a nice morning, but already too warm. Such a bother, the heat." Takako stretched herself out of my window to look at the clock. "My, it's only a quarter to eight!"

Downstairs, Iwao looked unusually tired, but he said he could rest once he got home. Elated by his visit and the work he had done, he couldn't stop talking about it. He made plans to come back.

"Don't get a relapse," I cautioned.

"You worry too much," Iwao said, as I picked up my purse and Sumie's sweater before leaving the house.

The walk to the bus station, north toward Yokogawa Station, took only ten minutes. Takako sang with Sumie along the way, the two of them holding hands and swinging them in time to the tune:

Oteete tsunaide	Let's hold our hands
nomiichi wo yukeeba	as we walk together
minna kawaii	and let's all become
kotori ni natte	cute little birds.
hareta misora ni	Under the clear sky,
kutsu ga naru.	our shoes will resound.

"Take care of yourself," Takako said when we reached the station.

"You too."

"Don't forget—I have a surprise for you."

Takako looked so pretty, standing against the dull walls of the station platform in her indigo summer kimono, her geta, and small blue handbag that she flipped with her wrist as she walked.

"I can't imagine what your surprise could be."

Takako clapped her hands. "Good. I'm not saying anything more." She pursed her lips and put a finger to them.

Sumie, Iwao, and I boarded the bus after a short wait and began our journey to the country. "Good-bye," Takako shouted, walking alongside the rolling bus until it gained more speed. "Good-bye," we shouted back through the bus window and waved at her receding figure. I watched until she turned to walk toward the city.

"Takako should have come with us," Sumie said, settling back in her seat.

"Yes, she should have. That would have been nice. Maybe next time we'll invite her to come along. Today she has business of her own."

"She said she has a surprise for us, Okā-chan. I wonder what it could be?"

"I don't know." I looked through the back window to see if I could still catch a glimpse of her.

"I'm sorry I'm not going to be here for the surprise," Iwao said as he leaned forward from the seat behind us, adjusting his face mask.

We went along until I remembered I had forgotten the gifts for the family, on the table in my room. "Ara!" I said and looked around me.

"What's wrong, Okā-chan?"

"The gifts, I forgot them."

Copying me, Sumie put her hands on her hips and clucked her disapproval.

The bus had gone as far as to the sewing factory. Sumie waved to the building as if she could see the women and children inside. I decided we could get out at the next stop and walk back to the factory; I could leave Sumie there with Iwao and Takako's mother and borrow one of my co-worker's bicycles to retrieve the packages. It would take less than an hour.

I pressed the buzzer to signal our stop and walked to the front of the bus to pay our fares. Iwao got out first. He turned and extended his arm for us. I took Sumie's hand into mine. I looked down to secure my footing.

I stepped off the bus as a bright light became the world.

29

Death in Dying

My breath and heart pulled out of me, the world grew terribly dark. A strong wind rose, howled, lashed, and fueled the fires that swept the city's basin. Then a rain began—a thick rain, a heavy black rain. Even the rain couldn't be clean. It brought the ashes of bodies, trees, houses, animals, and cars back down on us in large, ugly, *angry* drops. I shielded Sumie's body with my own and quickly found a wide piece of metal roofing that must have been part of a warehouse. With what little strength I had left, I dragged the iron roof and leaned it against a crumbling brick wall. I propped it up with boards and bricks from a collapsed house left unburned in the morning fires and crawled under it with my child dangling from my arm. Iwao was nowhere to be seen. *I was stepping off the bus when . . .*

As soon as I had erected my shelter, a small, compact woman crawled in next to me. "Thank you, thank you," she repeated, her hands together in praying mantis fashion. Unharmed, her clothes still intact, only the wild blooming of hair around her face indicated that she had been in the blast.

"Help me," I said. "I need to go back to the bus stop . . . my cousin."

"You crazy? There's no station, no bus stop. No one there is alive," she said.

"But my cousin, he's resourceful and strong. Surely, he would have lived through this. I've got to find him." I began arguing, but quickly tiring, I stopped talking and fell into an exhausted stupor.

Fujin, the wind god, Raijin, the thunder god, I was just stepping off the bus when . . . What happened?

When a young man crawled up to my little shelter and tried to slip in beside us, the woman began hitting him with her slipper. "Get out!" she yelled above the sound of the rain beating against the iron roof. "We don't have room. Can't you see?"

"Leave me alone," he said, weakly.

At first I thought it was Iwao and, were he injured like this young man, I would have wanted someone to help him. Looking around me, I saw that my makeshift shelter could hold one more person. I moved over. "Let him stay," I whispered to the woman. "It's all right."

"It's your shelter," she said and shrugged her shoulders.

"Thank you," the man said with so much gratitude that I wanted to scream.

The woman moved in closer, pressed herself against my sticky thigh, and reluctantly made room for the man. I tried to cover myself as best I could. I was almost completely naked, but neither the man nor the woman seemed to notice. I rocked and held Sumie against my body until she closed her eyes; she had had them on my face continuously, and they had never wavered since the light came down on us.

We all fell into a drug-like sleep. When I awoke, the sky was gray and filled with smoke, ashes, and wind. Fires burned all around us and the energy had nowhere to go. But we were safe for the moment, our bodies under the roof, our backs against the wall. Sumie took deep breaths and shuddered in my arms, the sight of the burns and wounds on her head causing me more pain than my own injuries.

The woman next to me sighed in her sleep and the man shifted, pulling his burned jacket closer to his neck. His whole back had been burned, his bodily fluids draining, puddling where he sat. The liquid gave off a foul odor. I thought I could see the shape of the charred bones of his ribs and hips.

A fierce burst of wind suddenly tore the roof away from over our heads. I ripped a piece of what was left of my shredded slip and lay Sumie's head on it. When I rose to retrieve the roof and gather more bricks to secure it, the pain from my burns and the wound on my thigh from a flying piece of glass made me cry out with every step.

Hearing me drop bricks and grate the roof across the ground, the woman got up and, noticing my near nakedness for the first time, she draped her outer coat on the side of my body that had not been burned. It no longer mattered, my own nakedness no longer bothering me; we were all of us naked in this new, flaming world.

When the woman and I tried to get the man to move so we could fix the shelter, he refused. We worked around him.

"What a useless man," the woman grumbled. "You want shelter, but you can't help?"

"I told you before . . . leave me alone. Let me die in peace." In the same breath, he called out: "Please, water." He said this while gripping the woman's arm with such strength that she stopped in her tracks and tried to peel his hands off. When he let her go, he hugged himself for comfort and dropped his head between his knees. His face was ashen; he looked close to death.

"Oh, all right, I'll find some water," the woman said, peevishly.

"What's your name?" I asked as she prepared to leave.

"Setsuko!" Her voice was too hearty for the terror that had descended on us. "Sumida Setsuko."

She clattered out of our makeshift shelter, her loose kimono fluttering around her legs, and disappeared into the haze. Not long after she left, the man began vomiting, whatever poison he carried eating at him from the inside out. "Thank you for letting me stay here," he whispered.

"It's all right."

He cried to himself and sniffled into his torn jacket sleeves like a small child. "Ueda Mikio. That's me," he said, gasping between sobs. "I have a name . . . I'm only twenty. I'm somebody, right?"

"You are, somebody," I reassured. "Do you know what happened?"

"Don't know. This morning I came into the city . . . from the country where I live . . . with my mother. I came early . . . had lots to do."

He explained to me that he was a draftsman for the government, and that his conscientiousness proved to be costly. The bombing occurred while he was walking to his office. "I'm not sure," he said, "but I think it was a bomb . . . just one bomb. The light so bright . . ." When he turned around, he said, he got burned on his back and flew into a building, which saved him from being completely burned. "Maybe, better . . . to have died, instantly."

After the bombing, he told me, he wandered around, dazed, trying to escape the fires, then he saw my little shelter.

"I wanted somewhere safe . . . to die."

"You're not going to die," I said.

"We're all going to die. . . . Maybe not now . . . but I know you're going to die . . . your child's going to die . . . I'm going to die. The Americans planned it . . . don't you see?"

"Are you sure, it was just *one* bomb?" I asked. It had taken hundreds of bombs to do similar damage in Tokyo. If this was one bomb, the Americans could wipe out the human race with just a few bombs.

"I'm sure . . . a bomb . . . one bomb, that's all it was . . . a powerful phosphorous bomb . . . the sky was so blue . . . a fireworks festival . . . . Did you see it? . . . It was beautiful."

"Try to rest, Mikio."

"Not going to make it . . . too sick . . . Here, my jacket . . . my money . . . my card . . . Tell my mother . . . in Mukaihara . . . if you get out alive . . . I trust you."

"If I make it, I will go to see your mother."

He then stripped off his jacket, its two sleeves held together by a collar, the back gone, and gave me this tattered remnant of himself. I draped his jacket across my lap. Maybe Iwao could use it when I found him.

Mikio put his head between his knees to vomit once more, his insides sounding as if they were being ripped apart, and with his body no longer able to contain itself, he shat in his pants.

"Is there no dignity?"

"There's nothing to be ashamed of," I said.

Without another word he slid his reeking body out of the shelter and crawled away from us.

Setsuko returned with some water. She saw that Mikio was gone from our shelter and spotted him among the rubble. She walked over to him to give him a few sips, which only caused him to vomit again. In agony, he thrashed his body among the broken bricks.

"At least he had sense enough to move away from us," Setsuko said.

She chirped with the confidence of someone untouched by this sudden and total devastation. After a time, she went over to Mikio to give him more water. She also took a handkerchief from his shirt pocket, the front of his shirt flapping like a bib, though I didn't know if she had asked his permission; then with the handkerchief in one hand, she came back to Sumie and me.

"How come you have his jacket?" she asked.

When I didn't answer her, she wet Mikio's handkerchief with water and wrung out some drops with her fingers into Sumie's mouth—Sumie who swallowed the water with little birdlike movements of her throat.

"I found water from a pipe that's still working," she said, "but I'm not telling anyone where it is. It's my secret."

She went off again.

The air was cold and cut into my bones. I shivered. Blood and hope had drained out of me, and in their place, fear and helplessness, anger and anxiety had transfused my body that shook with waves of uncontrollable spasms. I curled up tighter with Sumie and pulled Mikio's jacket up to my neck. By this time, Sumie's head wound and my wounds had begun to produce a strong, sour, slightly vinegary smell—a strange smell, Mikio's smell. I must have fallen asleep again for when I woke up, the bright cloudiness above me made me think that the sun was still out. I may have slept a long while; I may have slept but for a moment. Time felt warped, free of all restraints. Winds gusted once more, and they spun the roof of my little shelter and other debris into the emptiness of the world, the whirlwind of dust and ashes swirling in a vortex of energy. I tried to cover Sumie and myself as best I could, make our bodies inconsequential, small, hollow, for the wind to pass through, but ashes stuck to where we had been burned, making us look like the concrete structures along the rim of this new landscape.

That night, I watched Mikio's shadow—a figure of suffering in the surrounding vapors from the mist, ozone, and flickering flames that had all but spent themselves—and crawled over with Sumie to where he was crouched. I sat next to him, to comfort him, if only to rest my burned hand on his palm.

"I'm sorry—putting you through trouble," he said. "I apologize for dying. . . ."

"I will stay with you."

When morning came, his hand slipped away from under mine.

As soon as she was certain that Mikio was dead, Setsuko stripped off his watch and rifled through his empty wallet, not knowing he had given me his money, which I hid in the torn lining of his jacket. She put his glasses into her pocket, which I noticed was filled with money and jewelry that must have come from other dead bodies. While I was sleeping, she had been pilfering from the dead.

"What did you say his name was?" she asked.

"Mikio. Ueda Mikio."

"How can anyone not have money in his wallet? That's so strange. He must have buried it some place around here before he died." She went about poking the broken bricks and kicking them aside near where Mikio lay dead. Afraid of her, I said nothing.

I didn't ask her age, but Setsuko looked several years my senior. She was chatty and talked incessantly about herself. "I'm a seamstress and I was about to go to work when this happened. I was lucky because I was still inside the house when the blast hit. I must have lost consciousness for a while, but that was all, my burns and bruises minor. All in all I'm in no worse shape for my ordeal. Once I recovered from a little dizziness, I picked myself up and went out to see what had happened. My oh my, what I saw was terrible!"

She showed me how light her flash burns were around her hefty, robust arms and legs and exposed her long fleshy torso, which had been left untouched, to the air. "New skin will grow over this quickly," she said, patting her rice-cake thighs. "I've lived by myself for many years, and I'm glad I have no living relatives. This way, I don't have to worry about anyone; no one needs to worry about me. What about you?"

"I have family living in the country," I said.

Orphaned while in her teens, alone most of her life, Setsuko said she had scavenged her way through difficult times, until she got a job sewing uniforms for the Japanese Imperial Navy. "Before that," she said, "I worked for a little while in a bar as a call girl but wasn't pretty enough so the head hostess threw me out. Besides, some of the men treated me like dirt." She spat in the warm dust. "I have some pride left, you know," she said, laughing. "And forgive me for taking things from the dead, but the way I see it, they no longer need their earthly goods. They don't need their watches; there's no time where they're going. They don't need their money; there's nothing to buy. Only the living need to keep on going," she said with certainty. "We can use these items to trade for food. Isn't that so?"

"Yes, I suppose so," I said.

Later in the day, she returned with a small paper bag. "Here, eat some of this. People from the outside brought these millet cakes to the railroad station for victims to pick up and eat. They don't want to give them to us in person. What do they think we are—poison? Try some. They're good."

I reached for a cake. "Thank you," I said. I made a small ball and put it into Sumie's mouth, which she began chewing, mechanically. Setsuko handed me some water, which felt gritty in my mouth, but at least it was water. I then thought of Takako. Did the bright light blind her too? I could only guess. I let out a cry, swollen with grief.

Mikio had been dead now for several hours, his body slumped over itself, smelly and charred. Setsuko decided we should move out. "We need to find a doctor for both of you," she said. Startled by the sharpness in her voice, Sumie gave a faint whine. "I know, I know, but you're going to be all right," Setsuko said to Sumie.

We stumbled away from Mikio, over the gravel, the pulverized bricks, cement blocks, splintered boards, and piles of burnt body parts. When the pain from my burns became so excruciating that I almost dropped Sumie, Setsuko swiftly took her out of my arms and glared at me for my lack of forbearance. And yet from the moment Setsuko began carrying Sumie, I sensed a change in her. Before this, the woman had been too busy going through dead bodies or yelling at me to move along, but now, with Sumie nestled in her arms, she was quiet, as though she realized for the first time the enormity of what had happened to us.

In our wanderings, we saw that people piled into any remnant of a building, already full with those needing a place to heal or die. We walked up to several of these broken-down buildings, but they overflowed with the dying and there was no one with time, energy, or resources to tend to Sumie or me. The only other possibility was the Red Cross Hospital that loomed like a citadel across the city from where we stood.

Setsuko, who wanted her kimono jacket back, the one she had draped on me, found a pair of loose pants and a blouse, which she insisted I use to cover myself. She suddenly seemed protective of my nakedness and didn't care if it hurt to have something touching my burns. She also found me a hideous pair of large, boat-like shoes to wear, skin from someone's feet adhered to their hulls.

Flies swarmed and followed us everywhere, moving in humming, roving masses. They attached themselves to my burns and Sumie's fleshy scalp. I screamed, swatted them off, and reached for pebbles on the ground to pound them away from my burns as they crawled up my sleeves, up my legs, up my back. I couldn't believe that the bomb, powerful as it was, hadn't killed them all! Flies laid their eggs on Sumie's head and on my burned arms in yellow patches like bunches of summer grapes or ripening clusters of yellow cherries. "It's terrible!" I cried out. At first, disgusted, I had flicked them off with my fingers but the flies were too numerous and, after a time, I became too tired to fight them. Soon the eggs would hatch and the maggots would weave in and out of our flesh.

Most of the dense smoke had lifted on the day following the light that changed the world, the fires having spent themselves in their fury. As I looked around me, I saw almost nothing was left in the irregular circle the bomb had created, the crater bigger and wider than the volcano at home. A two-mile radius of nothing. Only the frames or walls of a few concrete buildings remained standing along the rim, sporadic fires still igniting here and there, their smoke trailing like lost souls in the gusting wind.

I followed Setsuko from one area to another. Once I must have cried out something, what it was I don't recall, but I do remember Setsuko saying to me, "So it's done. You can't do anything about it, so stop your crying!"

Looking cold and heartless, she walked faster.

"But the people . . . the thousands who disappeared . . ."

"So what about them? You can't bring them back. Come on, we have to find you a doctor."

She started walking even faster. "Hurry and don't look around. There's nothing to look at. They're all dead. Hey, I have things to do. Don't be so slow!"

I needed to trust her; she was the only person I could rely on, the only chance I had to stay alive. I knew I was alone and couldn't do this by myself. She could get angry, slap me down, push me away, leave me to die, just as I had done with Sā-chan, but I had to stick close to her. She was my only link to survival.

Takako. Takako's mother. Reverend Seki. Iwao. I didn't know what had happened to them. Takako probably had been walking to the church or to the black market when the bomb fell; Takako's mother would have been working, sewing part of my assignment for the day; Reverend Seki would have been chanting the morning sutra of gratitude; Iwao had been by my side. I cried out in anguish, gripped my side, and stumbled to the ground when I thought of him.

"Why are you acting that way?" Setsuko said, shifting Sumie to her hip. She scrambled back toward me and pulled me up to my feet.

"It's Iwao, I lost Iwao."

"Who's this Iwao you've been whining about? What's so special about him?"

"He was with me. A nice-looking, skinny boy—my cousin. Did you see him? He had a mask covering his face!"

"I didn't see him, and he's probably dead."

"But . . ."

"But what? He's dead, dead, dead! Don't you understand?"

I then thought of Shiichi Uncle and the rest of the family. I wondered if they were all right and looking for Iwao and me.

"In your wanderings, did you pass the Shimamura Watch Tower?"

Setsuko nodded. "The tower is on its side, the building collapsed. Everything is gone in that area. What was left burned."

"Do think there were many bombs?"

"How would I know? One bomb, many bombs. They're all the same. Your guess is as good as mine." I wondered if Kazuo was caught in this disaster as well, over in Kyūshū. I had no idea how large the bombing was.

The City of Temples district, far off, looked flattened. We scrambled toward the Red Cross Hospital over crumbled stone and cement that were once buildings and walked over body after body. An incredible stench rose, and thick gas-like smells laced our nostrils and coated our tongues.

Everywhere the dead. Everywhere the smelly corpses. Everywhere the pulverized. Everywhere nothing, the emptiness of nothing.

I stopped. "I can't go any farther. . . ."

"You crazy?"

"I'm too tired."

"I'll leave you here, then!" she threatened, but she didn't leave me; instead she made circles around me like a madwoman. "C'mon. Think of your daughter!"

All I wanted to do was go into a crawl space, lick my wounds, and die like an animal. *Go ahead. Push me away like I did Sā-chan. Leave me to die.*

But Setsuko remained steadfast and clever. She kept me going by saying and doing things that angered me. "Oh, look, how ugly they look," she said and laughed at the corpses, the size of their genitals, the twist of their bodies. While she waited for me to catch up with her, she searched the dead bodies for goods and made sure I saw what she was doing. Since I was too tired to yell at her to stop, I followed her, obsessed with the idea that someday I would get even. It never occurred to me that she may have needed me as much as I needed her.

I hated Setsuko, I hated the flies, I hated the smells, I hated my life. My legs dragged like water-filled logs and I felt as though I were sinking.

I was going mad.

Along the way, I searched for people I knew among the burned faces. "Takako, Iwao, Reverend Seki." I found my voice growing louder as I called out their names. I yelled to people carrying their flesh like clothing on their arms. "Hey you, did you see them?"

"Shut up!" Setsuko said.

"Iwao, he would know what to do, he would know what to do!" I was screaming like Harue Auntie.

"Shut up, you're crazy!"

The nearly dead stretched their hands out for help but we walked on by, past their distorted puffed-up faces, past eyes that hung out like Sā-chan's. "Marshmallow, marshmallow, popcorn face," I automatically chanted, the rhyme buzzing and circling my head like the flies. Setsuko, not understanding English, looked back at me with scorn, for truly, by this time, I was in shock. In and out of my mind.

As we moved closer to the Red Cross Hospital, I could see that it had all but crumbled with only a few walls intact. The hospital was crammed to capacity with the dying, but we stopped there and stayed, my legs unable to carry me any further. I cried out something I don't remember and just stared at the lines of people waiting politely for treatment, the people sprawled on the cold cement corridors slimy and shiny with diarrhea, vomit, blood. A depository of flesh. I wanted to scream at the victims, no one saying anything about the injustice of it all, or the wait, or the horror, no matter what pain they had to endure. People around me died silently, dropping off, as if to sleep, or drifting like cherry blossom petals in the wind. In one day, the mound of dead in front of the hospital grew high as a small building.

How lonely the people must have been, not knowing what had happened to them, not having anyone to talk to and no one to help them in their dying. As Setsuko explained, "That way, it's good. Nobody places the burden of their deaths on anyone else." It was a Japanese idea—shikata ga nai—the awful but powerful resignation, full of dignity, acceptance, a go-as-you-are reality that was difficult to understand, but ingrained in the Japanese heart. *Anshū was different. It struck at the heart through sorrow and reached out beyond resignation. It cut wider, deeper, was darker.*

Once in a while, above the drone of the constant sutra chanting, I'd hear a cry of anguish for a loved one, but the dying did not cry much. If they grieved for themselves, they grieved in silence. People just died. Then they were picked up and hauled away like rubbish. I was not as stoic; I couldn't help but moan.

Because Setsuko was healthy, other nurses, from outside of the city, recruited her to help with the patients. She liked her new role. She came by to check on Sumie and me several times during the day, and she told me with a bright smile, "Maybe I'll become a nurse after this."

At night, she came to take Sumie from my arms. "Go to sleep," she said. Lifting Sumie like a sack of ginkgo nuts, Setsuko carried her away, and later I would hear her singing to my child, her voice deep and wonderful, and I was as astonished by her voice as when I first heard Iwao sing. Her voice echoed through the open corridors, through the open wings, into the night:

Odoma bon-giri	Only during Bon season,
bon-giri kara	only during Bon.
Sakya orando	After Bon she won't be here.
Bon ga hayo kurya	If Bon comes quickly
hayo u modoru	then she'll return quickly.

The song was about poor and young country girls sent to their families' landlords' homes in order to help pay their families' debts, the girls watching the young children of the household and growing attached to them, as did the children to the girls. I wondered if Setsuko, who sang the song with so much empathy, had been sold to her family's landlord by her parents.

The attendants at the hospital had some ointment and Mercurochrome to work with, but little more than that. Once, Setsuko came back with some ointment and gauze for Sumie's head, but it was useless—we had to get rid of the maggots first before we could successfully treat her wounds. Off Setsuko went again, looking through the damage for useable items. At other times, she slipped out into the streets to search bodies for items of worth, and by now, her kimono-jacket sleeves and pockets bulged, having nowhere else to put her loot.

After one of her searches, she brought me some alcohol she had found. I soaked a piece of dirty cotton with it and touched the maggots burrowed in Sumie's scalp until they died and then I scraped them away, but I couldn't kill them all. I did the same with my arm, gritting my teeth at every spot I touched, the alcohol burning my open wounds. Many of the larvae remained in our bodies.

Another day passed before an intern could see us. Sumie's breathing had grown shallower and she was eating and drinking very little. The maggots continued to be a bother—most of all, watching them wriggling in and out of our burns. The only good thing about them was that they were eating away the pus. When the young intern, recruited by this necessity out of medical school, came to look at Sumie's scalp, he shook his head and simply grunted. He killed some of our maggots with Mercurochrome and tended my burns by putting some oil on my shoulder. He looked at the right side of my body, my face, and my feet and placed some loose dressing on the bad areas. Only when he pointed it out did I realize that some of the toes were gone from my right foot. I was aware of a soreness and had been limping, but that was all. The young doctor seemed more shocked about my missing toes than I was.

That evening, word spread quickly through the hospital that the young doctor who had treated us had hanged himself from an exposed rafter, upstairs. Setsuko said, "That's what happens when they get them so young. Still schoolboys, they can't handle the suffering." Another nurse talking with Setsuko didn't agree. "It's because too many mothers make their boys softies."

On the fourth morning, Setsuko brought me a change of clothing. Helping me to dress, she whistled at the extent of my burns in the same way the doctor in Kaiwiki had whistled at my father's wound. My burned arm, having been held out for so long, had frozen in that position, which Setsuko took and rotated like the bamboo propeller wind toy that Iwao had once made for me.

My entire body had broken into a cold perspiration from the intense pain caused by the rotation. "I can't thank you enough," I whispered as she wiped my brow.

"Nonsense," she said, refusing to give herself over to any level of sentiment. "Just shut up."

Victim upon victim slept in the hospital corridors, but the numbers lessened as the days went by. Such that it was, even the stench grew more tolerable. People who came to help from areas outside the city gagged at the smells, but those of us who had been there from the beginning did not mind them at all. We welcomed the stink. Bad smells meant life—that we were still alive.

Sumie hung on to her life like the petals of the flowers she loved to pick, and I sensed that it was only a matter of time before she would die. On the sixth morning after we had stepped off the bus, the sixth morning after the blast, the sixth morning after Iwao evaporated, the sixth morning after the black rain, she flicked open her eyes wider than a doll's and, as if she had seen more than she had ever seen before, she locked her eyes on my face, drew me into her, packed my image into her young soul along with the colors, the sunlight, the air, her hopes and small dreams. It was as if she was seeing the whole universe—everything and nothing—then she was dead.

Setsuko took Sumie's death surprisingly hard. She sat on her legs, put her hands on her thighs, collapsed her shoulders, and began crying, her whole body shaking soundlessly. She tried to hold back her cries, and when she could not contain them—her body jerking in resistance—she fell forward and wept into Sumie's soft but lifeless hands. I was too stunned to cry, my sorrow dark, deep, unfathomable.

Later, her emotions more settled, Setsuko took Sumie out of my arms and laid her on the mat beside me. She let us lie together the whole day without reporting Sumie's death. Later, a woman sleeping next to me in the corridor complained. "You shouldn't be sleeping with a corpse," she said, "even if it *is* your child."

"You're right," I said. Only then did Setsuko make a report and help me take Sumie's body out of the building. I thought of Kazuo, of how receptive he was of her being his daughter, and Sumie, of him being her father. I rolled Sumie in a buckwheat mat Setsuko had found, and we carried her to the nearest riverbank where families were burning bodies brought out of the hospital. Setsuko left me to my sorrow and disappeared into the haze of human ashes.

30

The Surrender

Where I stood waiting for an open pyre to cremate Sumie's body, I heard the bickering of the scavengers, who, like Setsuko, had taken things off the very bodies I watched burn around me. But Setsuko was right. We had to go on living. Possessions were merely possessions, and they meant nothing to the dead.

"How much?" I asked the coffin man.

"The burning is free," he said. I was just about to put away the gold necklace Setsuko had given me in case I needed it, when the man saw it and said, "But I'll take that," and reached out for the gold chain, fondled it, and let it drain into his shirt pocket. The man's face was a weary mask, and he didn't look at me directly, afraid I suppose of what he might see in my eyes.

I gave him some information about Sumie, which he wrote in a tablet. "I want her burned alone, and may I do it?"

"You sure?"

"She's my daughter," I said. The man nodded for me to go ahead, still avoiding my eyes.

For Sumie's cremation, the coffin man made sure that he cleared the hole of other bones and skulls so as not to mix the ashes, then poured oil, the color of sweet tea, onto the wood. I placed Sumie on the mound the man made for her pyre and struck the match to set it ablaze. Despite the ashes in the air and the devastation all around me, I looked up and saw that it was an achingly beautiful night, the stars out behind fast-moving clouds, the darkness of the sky behind them darker still. I began to cry—a cry of such depth, that I became almost breathless as I sank into it.

"Himiko?" Lying near the fire, having exhausted myself from crying so long, I heard someone call out to me. "Himiko, is that really you?" Hallucinating—that's what I thought I was doing.

I looked up and stared into the darkness but couldn't see anyone. Then I recognized the frame—the bowed legs, the thin, long neck—that moved up into the light.

"Oh, I'm so happy to see you," I said, recognizing the figure.

I tried to stand to greet Reverend Seki but got up only as far as my knees. At last, I knew someone from my life before the strange light and the fires that had destroyed the city.

In a spontaneous move Reverend Seki fell to his knees, took my unbandaged hand, and dropped his head into it. "I was beginning to think no one I knew was alive. I lost my whole family and many people in my congregation." He named people we knew mutually and asked if I had seen any one of them. I kept shaking my head between hiccups and the shuddering of my body.

"And you lost Sumie. How terrible."

"We'd been staying at the Red Cross Hospital until she died early this morning."

"What about Takako? Do you know what happened to her?"

"The last I saw of her, she was walking away from Sumie, my cousin, and me at the bus station. Those on the streets were said to have had little chance. I doubt if she survived."

"There's no mercy in this life."

"Truly no mercy," I whispered.

"But I found you and that's a miracle."

"Yes, it is."

"It doesn't make up for Sumie, however," he said. "You'll be lonely without her."

"Why did this happen?" I asked, looking up at him.

"No one knows. There are no answers to death, the hearts of men, the will of countries—the way of the world. We can only accept things as they are in a tragedy like this."

"But what happened to us, to Sumie—everyone—is difficult for me to accept. Aren't you the least bit angry?"

"I understand the anger, but anger carries with it a different kind of destruction. It will eat at your heart if you give in to it—to no avail. It will only leave you unhappy and troubled."

"I guess I don't understand anything."

He pitched gravel in front of him. "Don't misunderstand me. I have to struggle with what happened like everyone else. I came here to look for familiar faces even among the dead. All these days, I've been performing the last rites of the pillow after last rites of the pillow, funeral after funeral, and still more people come to receive the words of the Teachings. But how can I help these people when I can't even help myself?"

We did not talk for a while and just watched the fire. "Where were you when the bomb hit?" I finally said.

"I was at the temple and sheltered by a thick old wall I flew into. Not hurt, I dug myself out just before the firestorm burned the place. But my whole family is gone. My wife had been walking the children to school and they were burned beyond recognition . . . nearly to ashes. I found them on the sidewalk holding hands not far from the temple. I knew it was my family because of a gold pendant of hers that my wife clutched in her hand." *Sā-chan did a similar thing.*

With the cremation fire burning down, Reverend Seki chanted a sutra to save all sentient beings. "I think it's the best sutra to chant, the sutra for the lonely and lost, the Bodhisattva Dharmakara giving his blessings, sending his name resonating throughout the universe so that all may hear and receive his great compassion that is, in fact, always with us. Thus we offer our praise and gratitude." Reverend Seki then said, "My life through the Inconceivable Light and Life, and Name," bowed, and closed the ceremony.

In the raging fire of cremation, I had imagined Sumie raising her arms in the fire as if she were raising them for me during one of the countless times I had picked her up to dress her or to soothe a hurt or to rock her to sleep or to sing to her. Her arms burned and fell off like the branches of trees on fire. As the fire roared around Sumie's body, it curled into itself and lumped into a ball until all the flesh was burned away. The bones under

Sumie's sizzling flesh emerged white—as Sā-chan's bones had done—then crinkled, and fell through the burning logs.

I waited for the fire to die and cool before I took the coffin man's long, steel chopsticks and retrieved the leftover bones—my child's soft and young bones that had burned so easily. I then took out Mikio's handkerchief, tied the pieces into the square cloth, and slid it into my pants pocket, the bones making a small, warm bundle against my thigh.

Looking up at the sky through the haze, I thought of Norio, Sā-chan, Iwao, Sumie, and all that had happened seemed unimaginable in my sorrow for them.

We soon had to make way for another family. "Where are you staying?" Reverend Seki asked, helping me along as we walked away from the burning bodies.

"I've been sleeping in the corridor of the Red Cross Hospital. But I should be moving on. I'm not as hurt as some of the others."

"Stay with me until you can find something more permanent. The temple has a small summer cottage for guests outside the city west of here that is not in use. We can go there. I will see too that you get someone to help you with your burns." The fingers of my right hand had begun to fuse; I was afraid I would lose them without proper treatment.

Already Reverend Seki was making plans to write to Reverend Hara, Shiichi Uncle and Harue Auntie, even my mother and sister back home. "We need to let people know that we're all right. They'll be worried." I was glad that he felt up to making the notifications. I had little strength to do much more than reel through each day's pain and sadness.

Before leaving the area, I said, "Excuse me, Sensei, but I have a friend, Setsuko, at the hospital. I am greatly indebted to her, and I have to ask her about her plans before I can make my own."

"Tell her to come and live with us, too," Reverend Seki suggested. "We can help each other."

After a slow walk back to the hospital, I found Setsuko on her knees in one of the open-air corridors, spooning drops of water into a dying child's mouth. "Setsuko, I found a place for us to stay—with Reverend Seki, a friend. I want you to come with us."

"I can't leave here. I'm needed."

"I know you are, but—"

"You go on ahead. I'll come to see you later."

"You promise?"

"Of course!" She shot me an irritated glance, but I felt it was more in play than real. "It's about time you learned to trust me."

I gave her the address, which she slipped into her kimono cleavage; she didn't even look up to say good-bye.

That night, Reverend Seki decided that he should go across the peninsula to Miyajima Island and buy some urns for his family and Sumie before doing anything else. We walked south, away from the devastation and spent the night near the railroad tracks that led to the docks. As soon as it was light, Reverend Seki left me where we had stopped, continued following the tracks, and went on to the island by boat. While waiting for Reverend Seki to return, I sat with thousands of others who rocked in their misery. I slept intermittently, nightmares pursuing me. Once, when awake, I saw that someone had come and left the victims a large bucket of water, and crawling over to it, I took the clear water into my hands to clean my face and rinse my mouth. I must have been hallucinating at that time, the separation between my body and the water unclear. In the early afternoon, Reverend Seki returned with some urns and a small cart he had found. We packed the urns into the cart with whatever else we had salvaged from our existence and walked westward to wind our way up toward the house in the hills, the walk slow and painful for me. We spent another night on the road before we arrived at our destination the following day.

The gates to the house creaked as we walked through. The windows of the house facing the city had been blown in, but the house itself looked sturdy with no other noticeable damage. Scavengers had not gotten to it and, save for a layer of dust due to the blast, the house was airy and livable.

We settled in quickly with our meager possessions. With Reverend Seki's help, I started a small fire in the stove, put on the teakettle, and broiled some edible mushrooms from an overgrown vegetable patch Reverend Seki found in the back of the house. I took the room that opened up to the garden and put Sumie's urn next to my bedside. I felt nothing again; my sorrow was too dark, frightening, and dangerous for me to even consider.

271

On the far side of the house, Reverend Seki set himself up in a room that resembled his old study with its small lacquered desk and reading lamp. I placed weed flowers from the garden in an alcove at the end of a short hallway and wiped the scroll that hung on its wall.

"The human spirit is wonderful," commented Reverend Seki the night we settled in our new home. I didn't ask him how he could think that it was so, not fully understanding his cheerful optimism. Dispirited by my injuries and demoralized by Sumie's death, my outlook remained bleak.

Nine days had passed since I had stepped off the bus and into the end of the world. Mr. Toda, who lived next door, persuaded us to listen to the radio at his home, the emperor scheduled to make a speech at noon. Speaker boxes had been erected throughout Japan for those who had no access to radios, and the entire country waited to hear the voice of the emperor, for it was said no commoner had ever heard him speak before. I knew that my relatives who were safe in the country would be listening too. I also learned at this time that a bomb had hit Nagasaki six days after Hiroshima. Nagasaki was in Kyūshū—had Kazuo been in it? *Where was he? Was he looking for me?*

In the Toda's small home, Reverend Seki and I sat with our neighbors on the floor around the radio like children, eager to hear the emperor's voice, and while we waited, Mrs. Toda served us some tea and seasoned ropes of seaweed cut into bite-sized pieces. She had prepared them in a sugar-shoyu sauce, something I ordinarily enjoyed. "Please eat," she offered. "You need to get strong."

But I was afraid of the mounting nausea that I had been feeling since the day I stepped off the bus. The smell of the sauce made it worse. I sipped my tea and waved away the food with barely an appreciative smile.

"Himiko-san, you must keep up your strength," she scolded, her bony fingers stiff, metal-like against my good shoulder. "You're way too thin. How are your burns today?"

"They're better, but they open up every time I grow weak. There's much pain from them. But that's not the only thing. It feels like I have the worst flu that won't go away. The nurses aren't sure what it is. They don't have a name for it."

"Whatever it is, I hope they find a cure."

"It's annoying to be sick every day. Reverend Seki is strong. Even if he feels sick, he doesn't give in to it."

"That's just male pride," Mrs. Toda said.

"On the contrary," said Reverend Seki who had been listening to our conversation. He had on his usual white shirt and tie but had grown much thinner, his collar hanging loosely around his neck. "There's just a lot to do, so many others in worse shape. I *have* to be strong."

Like me, he had come down with the same general physical malaise that so many victims of the bomb were succumbing to. Although tired, he continued to work—he wrote letters and conducted endless funeral services. He was already working to replace the old temple, which had been flattened, envisioning a larger one as though to accommodate all the suffering of the war.

"That's true, but you should rest," Mrs. Toda said and scolded the reverend. "Give in to your sickness a bit. Later on, you'll be sorry. You might even collapse, as others have done."

As the radio whined, seeking its wavelength, we moved closer and lowered our heads. The emperor was about to speak. Then we heard, in the most formal Japanese, the surprisingly high voice of the emperor himself. I could only understand bits and pieces of what he was saying: "After pondering deeply . . . to effect a settlement . . . by resorting to an extraordinary measure—" And he went on. Although Mr. and Mrs. Toda strained to listen to his words, only Reverend Seki seemed to understand fully what was being said. He had his eyes closed and nodded to affirm the emperor's words with an intermittent "Yes, yes . . . that's right, that's right." When the speech ended, Reverend Seki brought out his handkerchief and took off his clouded glasses to wipe them.

The emperor of Japan had declared an end to the war. It was August 15, 1945. The Japanese people, the Empire of the Sun, had been defeated and had surrendered to the Americans. I felt neither triumph nor defeat for the country, only a throbbing dullness.

Outside, a thrush cried out and leaves rustled in a breeze.

A few days after the emperor announced Japan's defeat, my legs gave way. I was working in the garden, turning over the soil to plant some late-season vegetables when it happened. Reverend Seki summoned Mr. Toda who said, "I don't know how far I can help you carry her. She's such a big person."

Once in bed, I was certain I would never get up again. Soon after, I began having bouts of severe vomiting and diarrhea, like Mikio, and could not keep anything down. Deeply concerned, Reverend Seki called a doctor's assistant to check on me. The burns that had begun to heal opened up into watery fissures.

Some days, I wanted to end my life. I thought of ways to kill myself—by fire or water or hanging or seppuku, driving the cold steel of a knife into my stomach, or plunging it into my heart, or slitting my wrists, or perhaps drinking a vial of poison, arsenic, or torikabuto, or herb. Mixed in with soup. I would end the cycles of my existence and non-existence and find satori, enlightenment.

An incredible thirst and fire churned in my body, and my sleep brought me little rest. I drenched my futon with perspiration. I was desperate to climb out of my nightmares. Every night, I faced the guilt over Sā-chan and the heartache of losing Iwao and watching Sumie die. I was prodded by the devil's foot and fell into Jigoku, a bottomless dark world, a nightmare world, the darkest of realms. Dead faces surrounded me; people laughed at my naked body; I didn't know where to hide. The dead faces called out my name, and when I responded, their faces and bodies melted like dripping candles, or they exploded like ripened melons falling from their summer vines, their insides soft and mushy. They came after me, headless, like all the dead people I had seen in the streets.

My head burst open and oozed like the pus from the fissures of my disfigurement, but none of this delirium was enough to kill me. I screamed, pounded on my futon, tore off my bandages, and cried to be left alone. "Let me die!" I moaned and thrashed about. A nurse that Reverend Seki knew came by at his request and gave me shots to quiet me down. Reverend Seki repeated the recitations of gratitude for my life and death. *Namandabu, namandabu, namandabu . . .*

And one day, *they* came without my calling for them and fought my ailments and the Demon Anshū, who threatened to overcome me. *They* took over my body, my life. I had no idea who *they* were. I still don't for I could see nothing. I could only sense their presence. *They* were not the usual doctors or nurses or priests. *They* were different. *They* had strong hands. *They* had come with quiet purpose—a resolve to save me. I had to trust that *they* would not hurt me or laugh at me. I had to trust that *they* would not look with disgust at my burns or my thinness. I had to trust that *they* would not turn away in revulsion at my smells. My body no longer my own, I gave it up to *them*.

Their hands tore away the buckwheat pillow from under my head and pulled me out of bed and dragged me to the bathhouse to wash my hair, scrubbed me down with mineral water, and dressed my wounds with smelly, sticky homemade ointments and salves. They rubbed my useless muscles, and pounded my body to improve circulation. They did this day after day without complaining, without sound, except for the sound of constancy in giving me their care and mercy to make me well. Helped me to fight the Demon Anshū every day!

They exposed my wounds to the moist air and covered them up again. They peeled off the dead skin, they forced me to sit up and drink the hot rice wine in the sake cups they placed in my hands, and with their hands soft but firm over mine, they tucked me back into bed. They kept a vigil at my bedside, burned incense and lit candles, and at night, they dropped mosquito nets over me to keep me from escaping. They kept me in a drunken stupor for days in a rotation of baths, wine, oil, and mineral water. My mind reeled. Flames from the eastern shore seared my body along the white path while the water from the western shore lapped my body, to put the fires out.

Gradually, my body began to heal; my burns improved, my infections subsiding. Although my scars felt rough and lumpy in their flow down my body, they were dry when I touched them. I was beginning, once again, to breathe the air of the living. I drank the tea, ate the boiled rice and salted plums, even nibbled the fish that was served. I sniffed and tasted in small bites. But the illness was relentless and continued. I had many relapses. Weakness, fever, and night sweats were the realities of my daily life. Often, sickness threw me back into the hold of the *President Coolidge* and sailed me across the Pacific Ocean. Other times, I felt almost well.

One day, feeling strong enough, I went down to the black market near Hiroshima Train Station. I could not rely on Reverend Seki and the Todas to keep on helping me forever—the bathing, the laundering, the cooking, the shopping for goods—so I began doing as much as possible for myself. Reverend Seki had his own malaise to deal with, and what the Todas had done for me far exceeded what could be expected of neighbors.

More than anything, I wanted to live now. There was so much to do. I had to find out what happened to Iwao, Takako, Takako's mother, and the other women at the factory. I had to find out what had happened to Kazuo.

During the time I was struggling for my life, Reverend Seki told me that in early September, Japan had formally surrendered to the Allies on the battleship *Missouri* in Tokyo Bay. I had no recollection of that historic event.

31

Hibakusha

The mirror in my room in Nishi-Hiroshima—part of a small paulownia wood dresser—had been covered with a white rice bag cloth to keep the dust from accumulating on the glass. I had never taken the cloth off, the cloth like an early fire Mama had warned me not to touch, while every bone in my body had ached to touch it. For several weeks after moving into the house with Reverend Seki, I left the cloth on the mirror. Sometimes, as I passed by it, I would reach out and touch the cloth without actually removing it, but I knew that one day I would have to look at myself. Would have to know what the light had done to me.

After my bath one evening, I went over to the dresser. Summoning courage, I leaned forward and gripped the covering with my good hand. I took a deep breath, as if to jump off a rock to meet the cold water far below, and before I could change my mind, I snapped the cloth away, lowered my body, and sat down on the zabuton in front of it. This was the first time I had seen my face since I stepped off the bus. Had he seen me, Kazuo would not have recognized me. My face appeared to be a hundred years old, whereupon I let out a soft cry. From that moment on, no one would call me Hi-chan again.

On the right side of my head where the scalp had been burned, a thicket of hair had grown in white as Norio's snow. A raw-looking red keloid scar on that side of my face clawed its way toward my eye and cheekbone, the lines of red skin tapering into my face and gripping it like the talons of a falcon. I slipped off my kimono. I let it drop off my shoulders and saw that the burns on my neck had not healed entirely, the flesh hardening, becoming crusty as cooling lava on its run to the sea, a flow that moved down the body. The sweep of my hair may have hidden the scars near my eyes and cheek, but the burns on my neck, arms, and hands could not be readily concealed. The biceps of my right arm had little flesh; the worst burns were along the shoulder, my back, and the soft part of my upper torso down to my lower stomach. One breast was practically gone, and no hair covered the burnt side of my pubic bone; there was only a white fleshy mound of keloid tissue. White flash-burn marks covered both thighs down to my knees. My forearm was charred in spots, my elbow melted down, my right hand webbed like a pintail duck's foot. I had trouble bending my right arm as well as some of my fingers, and I had lost three toes on my right foot. Areas of my body still oozed a smelly pus where the skin was broken, and the only wound that had healed was the one on my right thigh where a shard of glass had pierced. *Sā-chan had been burned beyond recognition. I was lucky compared to her.*

I was napping in my room one day and heard footsteps walking into the house of my dreams. "Sorry for disturbing you," the voice said, and Dr. Ogawa entered the room in the same way he had walked into the Itos' home the first time I met him. I straightened myself and turned my face away in the otherworldly light, not wanting him to see my scars. I saw myself groping for the bed covering in order to bring it to my face—to cover its unsightliness.

Dr. Ogawa sat on the floor next to my futon and glanced several times at my scars and reached over with his hands to touch them. I resisted, but he managed to turn my face toward him. Firm against my skin, his hands felt dry and warm. Observing the two of us from above, I saw that I was looking at my own hands, seeing the difference between his smooth ones and my own.

"It's a nice day, though humid, wouldn't you say so? Soon it will be the peak of the typhoon season." He studied my scars.

"I've hardly noticed the weather these past few weeks."

"I can imagine you haven't." After a long silence, his head down, he continued. "Himiko, I came today to apologize—to say that I'm sorry about what I said to you."

I forced myself to look at him and was surprised to see kindness in his eyes.

He continued. "Also, please understand. I do not wish to interfere in your life. From now on, I will let you and Kazuo alone." *So Kazuo was alive.* "Maybe Kazuo's mother is right. I want my son to be happy. Seeing people hurt from the bomb and this war has altered my thinking, radically."

"We have all changed," I said. "And you don't have to apologize. I don't think Kazuo is going to come to see me, so that releases you."

"Kazuo is back in Tokyo with his mother and has left the army." He then slid a white envelope across the floor. "From our family—for Sumie, a small monetary offering." My dreaming body fought accepting the envelope that Dr. Ogawa handed me, but I remember finally taking it and placing it next to Sumie's urn.

"I'm not a religious man, but isn't it a miracle how the body can heal itself?" he said.

"But there's nothing much left of me, only a scar-faced woman, a ghost woman."

"Not so. You look more real to me than anyone else. Don't you know you are lucky? Not in the sense that you got hurt, but in the way your face is divided into a clean and scarred side. Your afflictions are there for the world to see. They make you whole."

"You're just trying to make me feel better. I know what I am. Hideous. There's no other word for it."

He didn't answer but moved to open his bag. As he lifted the catch, I followed the deft movements of his clean, white hands. He worked with the precision of a tea master as he removed solvents, alcohol, ointments, and soaps, and took out beautiful monogrammed handkerchiefs, folded them, and placed them on his thighs in great ceremony.

"Bandages are scarce; I looked for the best material to use on you." He then uncorked an old ceramic blue and white water flask filled with water. "It's from our spring in Hakone. People say it has healing powers." He wet the cloth and dabbed my face.

"When I was a young boy, I often went to my grandfather's home," he said, talking steadily as he worked. "I loved going there." He wiped down the good side of my face then proceeded to the bad side. I placed my good hand on his and we worked like this, going over my burns together, the water feeling cool and astringent like witch hazel.

"My grandfather called it an eternal spring, and he warned me not to play near it. My grandmother, who watched over me during the day, was especially worried that I might fall in. She didn't know how to swim so there would have been no one to save me should something have happened. I would have had to save myself." He lowered his hands to my scarred neck and shoulder.

"And I was an only child, solitary and contained. My parents were too busy for me, and I was very lonely. I never had playmates or pets. I would often cry out of loneliness. In spite of my family's warnings, the spring became a place for me to go. I don't know why, but the sorrow I felt as a young boy I can still feel in my heart." He changed to another cloth and soaked it with the water. He wiped my hands.

"I guess we come into this world lonely and spend our lives struggling against it. We must cry for ourselves sometimes. We may have everything in life, and it still isn't satisfying. When I would go to the spring, the water would hold my face in its reflection and absorb my tears. That always made me feel better. Fish in the pond, as though blind, would nibble at the drops, thinking it food." He smiled at the recollection, and his face faded into my sleep.

When I awoke the following morning, I looked for the white envelope but realized that I had only dreamed about Kazuo's father. I dozed off once more, and when I woke up a few hours later, Mrs. Toda brought in a tray with an abundance of oranges, grapes, apples, persimmons, and figs. "I had some extra money," she said sheepishly, embarrassed by her extravagance. "And I bargained for the best. We . . . I want you well. I don't have children, you see. . . ."

After Mrs. Toda left, I sat up to eat the wonderful fruits of the end of summer. How was it possible that the body could accept such richness again? I picked up the thin slices of figs and early persimmons; I looked at their color; I let the sweetness, the coolness of the slices linger on my tongue. I never thought my body could accept fruits of such beauty again.

I had existed on dried bracken and weeds and gutter water. This was almost *too* rich.

A few days later, the weather began to change, the heat of early September abating, the clouds gathering, the days shortening and getting cooler.

One day, I heard someone outside the gate pleading, the voice raspy. "Please open up," the voice said. Sick as I was feeling that day, I went outside to see who it was. It was Setsuko, sprawled on the roadside by the gate. I was surprised. Hadn't she been the sturdiest of us all? Now she could hardly walk or speak; gravel was smeared on her face and lips. I helped her crawl into the house, dusted her clothing, and wiped her mouth and hands before I put her to bed. She had several small, blue, bite-sized bruise marks, little hemorrhages on her skin. Her hair was falling out. I called in Reverend Seki's nurse friend, who was now working with the American doctors, to administer to Setsuko's needs in the same way that this cheerless woman had come to administer to mine.

As if to further test the people's spirit, a huge typhoon passed over the basin of Hiroshima at the end of the month. Wind and rain howled; the rivers overflowed and held the city's head under water, sweeping bridges away, washing out roads, and blowing away signs. Fallen trees and mudslides blocked access to roads and made travel difficult, if not impossible, during the storm. Houses slid down the mountainsides.

More dead people, more flies, more bodies to burn beyond the hundreds of thousands who had already died or disintegrated.

"Doctors from Kyoto?" I heard about the tragedy in passing when Mrs. Toda mentioned that there were doctors who had come to help after the bombing whose home had been swept away during the night in a mudslide caused by the typhoon.

"Yes, here, let me read the article to you," she said. "It's a shame when people want to help others and die themselves." Among the dead listed in the Hiroshima *Chugoku Shimbun* was Dr. Ogawa.

At the end, even if it were only in a dream, in a change of heart he had been kind to me, and I could forgive him. *Out of compassion he had been embraced.* Now, he could return as a little boy to his grandfather's eternal spring in Hakone. As I recalled in my dream, he was drowning in his own sorrow, so much so that the river had to take him away and carry him back to his childhood pond. He would find peace there and serenity in that pool of healing, miraculous water.

By mid-November, the Americans were trucking in supplies and food in abundance and people in Hiroshima materialized as if from out of the ground, like cicada larvae. The dullness of war erased from their eyes, they moved with new purpose, calling out for a can of meat or a rope of seaweed. Many of the victims, having no place to stay, moved to the rim of the circle of the bomb like animals to a circle of fire. Dozens of new shacks had sprouted since the day of the bomb.

Down at the black market, lice-infested, orphaned children swarmed around me. Tugged at my clothing, and made demands: "Have you seen my mother?" "Hey lady, got some sweets on you?" "Here's a nice locket for your daughter." "Please, I need money for a train ride to go to my sister's home." To the little boy in short pants, a bonze haircut, and an oversized kimono covering his small wiry frame, I gave money to catch a train so he could go to his sister's. He swept the money from my hand into his grubby one, bowed in reflex if not respect, and ran off.

Near the makeshift market area at the train station, the words of bargaining filled me with nostalgia; I could hear the voices of Norio, Iwao, and Sā-chan resounding from the stalls. It occurred to me that people like my Harue Auntie, safe in the hills, couldn't possibly understand what it was like in this city as it struggled to return to life.

People trading from pushcarts had driven the prices high, as there was still little food to be had. I bargained like never before, exhausting all of my skills; I found I could lose my self-consciousness in the marketplace. At first, people stared or looked the other way to be polite, but before long they forgot my scars, seeing me only as an adversary across the counter. I bought some green tea, moldy dried squid, an apple, some noodles, and old, sour tofu. Wary of pickpockets, I held the jewelry and money that Setsuko had given to me in my bodice and tucked next to my good breast.

That day, as I wandered about the market place, I saw them for the first time. They had come into the city at last, these tall white American soldiers in their army khaki uniforms and peaked caps who studied the damage and sifted for matter in the ground. I learned they were American Strategic Bombing Survey officers and soldiers. The two I saw up close that day could have been no older than I was, one light haired and fair, the other darker with wavy hair—the first, English-looking; the second, Portuguese-looking—like boys I had known in Hilo. They stayed close to their tall, straight-backed superior officer, who knew how to speak some badly accented Japanese. They had been discussing something about the water system of the city and taking ground readings with clumsy instruments. I lingered where they stood and listened to them talking to each other.

The English language sounded strange to my ears. I couldn't catch all the words they said, as though a fog had entered my mind, but as I listened, my ears became accustomed to the rhythms, the words beginning to sound more familiar to me, until I wanted to speak the same way, the same words. I wanted to speak out to these men, but the torrent of words was backed up in my throat as if I no longer had the voice, the heat, the courage, to say them. When the men soon moved farther up the street, I moved with them, eventually passing them. Then I turned around to face them from afar and to watch them in their easy-going manner, their self-assurance as victors. One of the boys was speaking in a drawl. I wanted to go up to talk to them, offer words of submission and surrender, to say I was one of them, but I was afraid they would laugh at me.

I had had but limited association with white people back home. I had been shy even then. They had nice cars and big houses, soft, light-colored hair, and they spoke good English. Unlike the rest of the local children, they always wore shoes. They were polite to us in school, but they never invited us to their birthdays or Sunday afternoon parties. They were strangers to me. Other than the patent leather shoes their children wore, the cars they drove, and what they ate, I knew little about them, and what little I did know came from the Japanese servants who serviced their parties and worked in their big plantation houses with wide verandas.

On the way home, I saw the boy who had asked me for money to buy a train ticket. "Hey wait!" I called out. "Why aren't you on your way to your sister's?"

The boy, who could not have been more than nine, gave me a look of disgust as he laughed from the side of his mouth and with a swing of his head spat on the ground like an adult. "Home? What home? I bought my-self some bean cakes," he said, taking out a toothpick from the bottom of his kimono sleeve to poke at his decayed and crooked teeth. "Stupid lady. What do you take me for? Go away—you, you *Hibakusha!*" Saliva sprayed in contempt from his mouth.

The word he called me took me by surprise and I rushed after him, wanting to know what it meant. "Don't you dare touch me," he said, jump-ing back when I tried to keep him from running away.

"No one can tell if I was in the bomb," he said. "But you—you are a scar-faced woman. You've been branded like a cow. Everyone knows who you are. You carry the mark of the burning devil!" He ran off, his long kimono dragging behind him.

Hibakusha. So now I was Hibakusha, survivor of the atomic bomb. Victim.

When I told Reverend Seki what the boy had called me, he shook his head at the boy's response, but what he said surprised me. "All of our lives are interdependent, and in a way we are complicit to all that every other human being has done or does in his or her life. Countries at war all carry a heavy karmic debt, the causes and conditions wrought and interwoven in and out of our lives, creating this huge net that had been cast upon us where no one is innocent or exempt. Yet, at the same time, remember, it is not retribution. It is simply random, the way it is. *Such-ness.*" Everything in life was more complicated than I could ever imagine it to be.

That night, I made a nourishing broth of seaweed and began to feel a bit more settled in my understanding of what had happened. Without much talking Reverend Seki and I slurped the soup I had fattened with tofu and garnished with green onions. The only sounds came from Setsuko who vomited whatever she ate into the wooden bucket placed at her side.

"It's no good, Himiko," she said when I helped her into bed, her spirits falling. "I don't know why you even try to help me. The doctor's helper says I should drink a lot of fluids, so I drink the fluids, but what's the use? What I drink comes back up. They say I have to rest, too, but don't they know I'm stuck in this bed by weakness? Kill me, Himiko. I beg you. Save me that way. This is worse than dying."

I wiped her face and put a wet towel on her forehead and pushed back her tacky hair. Some of it came off in my hands. Dark pimples grew in spots on her scalp.

"You must keep on trying," I told her. "You have only this one life, this unrepeatable life, as Reverend Seki says."

Setsuko smiled as I said this. "It's unbecoming of you to preach to me. I'm miserable." Even when she dropped off to sleep, her teeth continued to chatter.

I wanted to take her into my arms, hold her, and console her, but there was no room for this display in our lives. I could only show how much I cared for her in other ways and replicated what *they* had done to me—the bathing, the wiping, the feeding.

"No matter how hard it is, you have to try. If your body didn't want to try, it wouldn't struggle so much," I scolded. The first days after the bombing, she had been so strong; now she was thin and weak, no different than I was. Looking at her drawn face, I remembered how kind she had been to Sumie.

I continued to improve, my red blood count up, so one day I caught the train to Mukaihara in search of Mikio's mother. It was a tiny place in a wooded but tranquil area about an hour or so by bus from the rim of the blast in the city. The house sat sturdy as a daruma doll in a wide but shady grove, a window for one eye. I liked it at once.

I knocked on the cottage door. A woman opened the door, peered through a crack, and stared at me. "Hello, my name is Aoki Himiko," I said to the eyes.

She stared at my ruined face without embarrassment. "Do I know you?"

"I met your son right after the bomb hit. I promised him I would come to see you should I live through my ordeal."

She opened the door wide and showed me in. The woman was almost doll-like in how fair and small she was.

As we drank tea in the dark, quiet house, I passed her his glasses and the money that Mikio had given me before he had died.

She took the glasses but rejected the money with a shake of her head.

"Mikio wanted you to have it. Take it in his memory." I finally persuaded her to take the envelope. She reached out, took it from my hand, and placed it on her chest, while murmuring her thanks.

"Did Mikio suffer? Was he badly injured?"

I lied and said that he died in a matter of minutes. I didn't tell her how badly burned his back had been. She didn't need to know the details.

"His face remained untouched," I said. "Don't be unhappy about his death. He was dying for the emperor and his cause. It was something he wanted to do. He died peacefully."

"Was he burned badly?"

"No," I lied again.

"Then what did he die of?"

"It's difficult to say. Like so many others he got ill from the light."

"The bomb was powerful, I hear. He *must* have been in pain."

"If Mikio was in pain, he didn't show it. He was very brave."

"I'm glad he died quickly. I've been hearing about this dreadful illness, but the newspapers say very little."

She grabbed my good hand as weeping racked her body. "He was such a good son. He did nothing mean in his life. The fireflies he caught, he let go, the fish he caught, he let go. He didn't deserve to die."

"No, he didn't."

I asked her about Mikio's life, and what I found was that he lived such an ordinary, filial life that it filled me with a special sadness because it could have been so complete.

"How powerless most people are in time of war. We really can't control what happens to us. It will be lonely for me now that he's gone," she said.

Before leaving Mikio's home, I offered incense, placed white chrysanthemums in front of the serious face of his photograph on the family altar, and rang the bell in reverence for his short life.

32

Healing: Spring 1946

Her health improving with medication and treatment by the Americans, Setsuko began to work at restoring the temple with Reverend Seki, their temporary office near the train station where most businesses had congregated for the time being. I took care of the house and the gardening. Doctors back from the war and practicing at a clinic for Hibakusha told us that Reverend Seki, Setsuko, and I had survived because we had been shielded from the full impact of the bomb's rays—the distance of the bus from the point of impact and my being blown back into the bus, its cab shielding me; and thick walls protecting Setsuko and Reverend Seki. My physical condition, however, made it difficult for me to find work, and while I learned to write a little with my left hand, my penmanship was a childlike scrawl, and my right hand remained useless, rag-like, most of the muscles atrophied by burns and disuse. I applied as a salesclerk at several shops, but when shopkeepers took one look at my dangling arm, they found polite excuses to turn me away. I walked from one establishment to another, hoping to find any job that I could do.

"Surely there must be something," I said to Reverend Seki. "It seems nobody wants to hire people like me. They are finding that shoppers are afraid of the Hibakusha. I'm useless anyway, I can't write or read Japanese very well in the first place."

Outsiders, those from neighboring prefectures or men home from the war poured into the city and took most of the available jobs while we

Hibakusha stayed in our homes and hid. The few companies sympathetic to people like us had long lines waiting at their doors each day. Some people could easily hide their condition, but those of us with visible scars could not hide what we were. Months passed and I saw fewer and fewer scarred people on the streets. Many had died, some had killed themselves or gone into hiding.

And people stared. On the trolley I once caught a man peering above a book he was reading; he couldn't take his eyes off me. Our bodies stank and people whispered about our disfigurements. Some believed that what we had was contagious; others said it was a spiritual defilement. The more superstitious believed we carried the evil eye. In the streets, children teased us and jumped over our shadows so as not to have our dark forces go through them. Sometimes I wanted to touch someone on purpose. One child at the trolley station called out to me and taunted: "Show me your face!" I frightened the boy by going after him with my burned arm extended, and I lifted my hair away from my face with my good hand to show him the red claw that gripped it. "I'm a ghost. I will haunt you," I said, rolling my eyes up. The crowd of children with him scattered, and although I laughed at them, it gave me no satisfaction.

That same day while walking toward Reverend Seki's temporary office near the train station, I bumped into Asayo-san.

"Oh my goodness," she cried out. "Is that you, Himiko—really you?"

"Asayo-san, I'm so glad to see that you're all right."

"Yes, if you can call this being all right," she said, pointing to her eyes. One of them was a hollow socket. I also saw that she was missing her right ear, several of her teeth, and most of her hair.

"I should be thankful that I can still see something. The others were not so lucky."

"Do you know what happened to Takako's mother?"

"She died in the fire when the factory burned down. Many of the women had been pinned under the cypress beams of the entertainment hall. I was lucky to escape," she said. "Ahh, but her daughter—poor girl was badly burned on her face."

"Takako's still alive? I thought she was dead. Where is she?"

"Oh, it is awful what happened to her. She lived, but the scarring on her face is so bad, it's hard to look at her. The last I heard she went to the coalfields in Chikuho to work in the mines. When she went, her burns weren't healed and she was still feeling sick."

"Chikuho? I can't believe she would go there. I hear it's horrible."

"Those scarred like Takako, with no relatives to help them—that's where they go. No one cares about their scars; there, they don't have to care how they look."

I thanked Asayo-san, and though we made plans to meet again, we knew that we wouldn't. I watched as she walked away from me in perfect posture, nodding to everyone she passed. She didn't notice or seem to care about how they stared.

I put myself into debt by going down to the black market and borrowing money from the loan shark, Mr. Nigai Uri—Mr. Bitter Melon—the nickname people had given him.

"You have a year to pay the original amount, plus the same in lending fees," he said.

I would worry about that later. I had to go to Chikuho to bring Takako back to Hiroshima. The afternoon I left, Setsuko packed me some rice balls, a piece of fish, and cucumber slices for my journey. "Take care. I heard the place is rough with rowdy men," she said.

I caught the train and crossed the isthmus to Kyūshū. For a time along the way, the train followed the coastline inland and later headed toward the mountains of Saga Prefecture. After a long, slow, winding ride I got off at a dirty station in a dirty, nameless town, coal dust in the air coating the buildings and darkening the sky. In an inn close by, I heard shouting and cursing where a fight was in progress; men spilled out of the door in only their loincloths, pummeling one another with their fists and kicking wildly. I continued to walk down the street to a place called the Gokuraku Inn and inquired about a room.

"If you're looking for work in the mines, be at the entrance early in the morning. They start at five," the clerk said, noticing my scars.

I wrote my name in the registration book, the first time I had written something official with my left hand. "Where's the entrance to the mine?" I asked, after I was done.

"You Hibakusha are not only scarred, sometimes you're stupid," she said with lazy cruelty. "Didn't you ask your recruiter?"

"I came by myself."

"Oh, so you heard about the place, eh? I don't know what they can do for you, seeing that your right hand looks in bad shape. The most you can do is to sort coal, the worst job. Start walking up the hill and over the bridge. You can't miss it. It's like a woman's dark hole." Her voice and face cracked in laughter at her own crude joke.

"Is there a dormitory where women like me can stay after we get a job?"

"The company will give you a room. Or, you can stay with some of the families around here—those who take in workers."

Early the next morning, I made my way to a long, low, ramshackle building at the base of a hill, which fit the description of the dormitory. I climbed a flight of stairs and saw women dashing about in men's undershirts. I stopped one of the women and looked into her scarred face. "Oh, I'm sorry," I said and made my way down the hall.

I stopped another woman in the building and said, "Do you by chance know of a girl by the name of Takako?"

"Takako? Let me see. Sorry, but I don't know anyone by that name. Some new girls have come in, but I don't know who they are. We keep to ourselves here," she said and backed away.

I went through another hallway with large, dirty windows on one side. The narrow corridor went all the way to the other end, but I saw no one who looked like Takako. By that time, many of the women were filing toward a back door to pick up small wooden lunch boxes. Outside, women were climbing the hill in the back, which led to what must have been the entrance to the mine. I knew my chances of finding Takako would be better if I stood at the entrance to look at the women before they went down the shaft or rode one of the coal cars, so I walked up the hill as fast as I could to catch up with the first of them. I stood there, scanning faces. Many of the women turned away or looked down as though they were afraid to meet my eyes, afraid to be recognized or seen.

"Hey," a woman called out. "If you're looking for a job, you should just wait where you are. The superintendent will come up later to see what other workers he needs."

The last of the women passed by. Somehow I had missed Takako. I was about to leave when I heard a thin, high voice yelling from a coal car filled with people going into the mountainside.

"Please take me back," the muffled voice begged. It sounded like Takako. When the woman cried out again, the voice was unmistakable. I heard a disgruntled male voice above the whine of a coal car making its way back.

"Takako!" I said and waved. "It's me, Himiko."

I tried to move up to the car but a surly guard stopped me, pushing against my shoulders with his hands. With no hesitation, Takako climbed out of the car and walked up. We grappled to hold each other's upper arms.

"I'm so happy to see you," she said and began crying. She let go of her hands on my upper arms and slumped to the ground on her knees.

"Look at me," she said, looking up, pushing aside her veil. Takako's face had been blistered like roasted pig skin from the blast. "I ducked behind a wall but not before my face caught the heat. I was walking toward the center of town after I left you. Where's Sumie, Iwao?" I shook my head.

"Oh no! I'm so sorry. Iwao, Sumie, too? . . . I can't believe it."

I recognized Takako only in her eyes; they remained alive in the center of her scars, and they still smiled, despite what had happened to her. Something of her cheerful self remained.

We traveled back to Hiroshima the next day, only after burning her clothes from the mine in an open field near the dormitory. We watched her coal miner's pants and faded indigo shirt burn up with the paper we had gathered as fuel. She turned her face away from the fire when the wind shifted and drove the heat our way. "Heat hurts my face," she explained. "One good thing about the mine shaft, the damp and cold is easy on the burns." Takako straightened the thin, gauzelike covering over her face and drew the ends closer around her face near her mouth. I couldn't describe the extent of her injuries, they were so bad.

When we reached the house in Nishi-Hiroshima that evening, Reverend Seki and Setsuko welcomed us, and after a quick introduction, I put Takako in Setsuko's and my room and laid out a futon for her to sleep. "This is good," she said that first night and quickly fell asleep.

Soon after Takako joined us, we learned that the temple's headmaster had assigned a new reverend to come to Hiroshima and Reverend Seki was being transferred to a sister temple in Kobe. His dreams of building the new temple in Hiroshima would not be realized, at least not by him. "I'm afraid you can no longer stay in this house," he told me. "The new reverend will be living here with his young family, until new quarters on the temple grounds can be built."

Setsuko had decided to go with Reverend Seki to Kobe. She would find a job there and work for the temple as his helper. It was a good arrangement for her and the Reverend; nobody would know that they were Hibakusha, which would ease their transition into a normal life. The general feeling for many at the time was that it was better not to admit you were a victim of the bomb. As for me, I wasn't sure what to do with myself. "Come with us," Reverend Seki said. "We've been together all this time. I'm sure you can find a job in Kobe."

"You've been too kind as it is, Reverend Seki. It's time I made my own way. Besides, I have Takako to think about. She's like my sister and I want to take care of her. I also need to see my family. Maybe Shiichi Uncle and Harue Auntie will take me and Takako in for a while. I must also think about going back to Hawai'i. My mother and my sister must be worried about me."

"Please promise to come and see us in Kobe if you decide to leave Japan."

"Don't worry, I will."

Later that week, before I saw Setsuko and Reverend Seki off at Hiroshima Train Station, I sat beside Takako's bed and held her hand. When her body began to heave because she felt nauseated, I rubbed her back and hummed softly to her.

"I'm sorry about your face, Himiko," she said, looking up at me after her vomiting had subsided.

"I'm sorry about yours."

Our eyes met and we began to laugh.

"Oh, you look so pretty," she said. "What a pretty pin in your hair. Oh, and I'd like to have your white dress." I rolled on the floor, and we laughed even louder.

That she did not bring up Kazuo was a relief. Without asking, her intuition probably told her what had happened.

Just before she fell asleep, I said, "Will you promise to tell me what you and your mother were going to make for supper the day I stepped off the bus?"

"I will, but not right now . . . too tired. Yes, my surprise . . . I'll tell you, tomorrow."

Setsuko, Reverend Seki, and I cried as we waited on the platform for the train that would take them to Kobe. We stood apart from the waiting passengers and there was no need for many words, and because we had been through the same hell, we knew one another's pain.

I did manage to tease Setsuko, however, by saying, "My, how you have changed. I hardly recognize you anymore."

"I guess no one goes through something like this without having their crudeness knocked out of them and replaced by humbleness," she said and smiled broadly.

When we parted, we waved long, slow good-byes.

Before returning to the house, I went to see Mr. Bitter Melon to borrow more money from him. "You sure?" he asked with a sly look. "You can't run away from me, you can't hide. I will find you." His assistant sat on a chair and looked up at me while cleaning his nails, making short, curved sweeps with the hard edge of a knife.

"You won't need to find me."

"I will add this money to your first loan and expect it during the fall equinox."

"Why, that's in less than a year!"

"Take it or leave it," he said.

When I returned to the house I called out to Takako: "You want some tea? How are you feeling? I'll be there in a minute."

I washed my hands and wiped my face and neck. The day was extra humid and it felt like rain. I opened all of the windows in the house and walked to our room where Takako lay on her side, sleeping. I moved to the windows and opened them a bit more to brighten the room. I continued to talk, and it was when I asked her a question and she didn't respond that

I turned around and realized she was dead. A soft light fell on her rough, crusty face. Beside her hand, on the side of her bedding, lay an open cloth bag, a worn pencil, and an unfinished note: "Thank you for everything," it said. "Everyone should have a clean, quiet place to die. I'm glad I didn't die in the mines."

33

A Return to Kyoto

A few days before summer, I caught a bus to Asagun where I got off near Hide Uncle's home. With Sumie's urn tucked firmly under my good arm, I walked up the road with a small bag of possessions and a package of roasted peas for the family. I was returning to this house in defeat, like the Japanese soldiers who had come back from the war, and while I dreaded facing Harue Auntie, I had no choice. I had to swallow my pride and humble myself before her. I needed a place to stay and would have to learn to live with her again.

I saw Chiemi-san working in the rice fields along the way up to the house, overturning the soil for planting. She was wearing a white hood and apron with pants rolled up to her knees, the water up to her ankles. In the fall, the family would be harvesting this rice.

"Chiemi-san," I called out, waving hard, happy to see her.

She looked up, dropped her gloves, and came running down the pathway. She began sobbing before she reached me. "I am so heartened to see you," she said, choking on her sobs with every word as she dabbed her eyes with her sleeves.

"I'm fine," I reassured her. "I got burned, but I can do almost everything by myself now—so many others in worse condition, yeah? Where's Hide Uncle?"

"He's been sick. It came upon him ever since he went to Hiroshima to look for you, Sumie, and Iwao."

"Oh, I'm so sorry, I didn't know that." I paused, not knowing what to say. I then asked, "Was Iwao ever found?"

Chiemi-san shook her head as she helped me with my packages.

We walked toward the family compound. As we made our way up the slight hill, I could see Harue Auntie looking down on us from the main house. When Yuki-chan saw me, she came dashing out. She shouted something unintelligible with a wave of her hand, then ran down the shallow hill as fast as she could to meet us.

"Big sister!"

She looked so grown up since I had last seen her. Before reaching us, she stopped, made a full bow, fell to her knees, and began crying into the lap of her school uniform. Her body jerked as she talked and cried. "I'm so happy to see you!"

"It's wonderful to see you, too," I said as I walked over to her crouching body. I pulled her up to me. "You don't need to cry. I'm fine."

"They said you were badly scarred. I want to see your face," she said with the clear, frank curiosity of someone young. She took my face into her hands and studied my scars. "Sā-chan was worse!"

"Yes, she was. My burns are nothing compared to hers. Hey, you'd better get up before you dirty your school uniform."

"Right, and before my mother gets angry," she giggled, whereupon Chiemi-san and I broke into smiles. Yuki-chan got up and skipped ahead of us.

Inside the main house, everyone talked at once, wanting to tell me their stories of what happened to them on the day the bomb fell—all except Harue Auntie. Throughout the talking and drinking of our tea, she sat glumly, far back in a corner, as far away as she could from me. She stared at the scars on my hands and face. She said little, probably hating the attention I was getting. Several times she lifted the corner of her mouth in a snarl like a dog's, and I was unsure if she was about to attack and bite.

"The bomb made a horrible sound," Hide Uncle said. Bald as a Zen priest now, he had come from his cottage to greet me. "I thought for sure it was the end of the world. The gods were angry at us."

Chiemi-san added, "I thought my body, my ears, were going to burst in the blast."

According to Hide Uncle, the police in the area advised them to stay where they were until they heard more news, but as he explained, "I was hardheaded and went down to look for you in spite of the warnings. I searched the area where you lived for two days but didn't find anything."

"I'm so sorry about your illness; you jeopardized your life for us."

"Shiichi, your uncle, wanted to leave the hospital to search for you, but it was a good thing that the doctor and Harue Auntie discouraged him from making the trip."

Harue Auntie gave one of her derisive snorts.

"It was a time of anguish for my brother, not knowing what happened to you and the children."

"I'm so sorry about Iwao," I said, dropping my torso and head to the floor.

"Iwao was not your fault. We're just happy you're alive and well. We're also deeply sorry about Sumie. Yuki-chan was inconsolable when we received word from Reverend Seki that she had died," Hide Uncle said.

I also learned from Hide Uncle that Mama had written to them twice since the end of the war. She was alive after all these years. Whatever she had had not been fatal, so it was not an incurable cancer as I had imagined through many sleepless nights.

Hide Uncle read the letters out loud for me, the first letter dated April, 1946.

> *My dear brothers,*
>
> *Although the war has been over for many months, there has been an embargo on correspondence, and those in Hawai'i were permitted to send out parcels with letters only recently. I sent some sugar, so please divide it accordingly.*
>
> *But my first concern is Himiko. Have you heard from her? I've been so worried. I haven't heard from her all these years. Please let me know how she is and what has happened to her and my grandchild.*
>
> *During this time, although we lived with some anxiety in Hawai'i, it was nothing we couldn't handle. We always prayed*

for Japan and for your safety. When we heard on the radio the
sad and pitiful news that Japan had to declare the end of the
war because of the atomic bomb, we fellow Japanese in the is-
lands cried in sadness. At the same time, we were relieved.

The Japanese in Hawai'i were not despised by the whites
here and had kept a good relationship with them, so we have
been lucky. Please let me know more about how you are.

Small Sister

"I wrote back, informing your mother that we were all okay, but that Sumie and Iwao had died in the bomb," Hide Uncle said.

In her next note, Mama said:

My brothers,

How sad to hear that Sumie died because of the bomb.
I will never get to see her. Was Himiko badly injured? She
must have suffered. Please let me know more about her condi-
tion. Miyo and I will also try to send what we have to share
with you. You should be soon receiving the box of clothing and
canned goods I sent.

We're all getting old, aren't we, my brothers? My hair is
white and my teeth are false. I'm also always complaining
that my feet or back hurt. Miyo is not married so she helps me
around the house. My strokes have made my left side useless so
she's been a big help. At least I can write some. Again, please let
me know more about Himiko.

Small Sister

Hide Uncle studied me as he folded the letters and placed them in their envelopes. "It's been a long journey on a difficult road for you, hasn't it? From Hawai'i to Hiroshima."

"Yes, a long journey."

So, Miyo never got married. I wondered if my taking her money to go to Japan had anything to do with it.

Moving to face Hide Uncle and Chiemi-san directly, I said, "I'm sorry to burden you again, but I need a place to stay until I can arrange to go home."

From where she sat in her corner, Harue Auntie suddenly cleared her throat and said, "You're asking the wrong people, Himiko, and the answer is no. I can't have you in the house, especially with your uncle due home any minute. He's weak and I can't risk his catching what you have."

"Harue-san," Hide Uncle said. "I probably have the same sickness as Himiko. You can't turn her out on account of that."

"I don't want to burden you, but I need your help," I pleaded and swung my body around on the mat to face Harue Auntie.

"You don't have the right to stay here. You left when we needed you most." Glaring at Hide Uncle, she added, "We can't have any more sick people around here. I will not stay in this house if she comes to live here, so Hide, Chiemi, if that comes to pass, you will have to move out of your cottage."

I was confused. "Please, I'm sorry, but I have no place else to go. I have very little money."

"Look, you've been assuming the wrong things. Hide Uncle does not own this place."

"Oh?"

"This whole place belongs to Shiichi Uncle, so everything that sits on this land is *my* property. I can do as I please when your uncle is not here. Hide-san and Chiemi-san just helped to work the fields that your grandparents left to Shiichi. How could you not have known that? Humph, you missed it because you were too busy thinking of yourself!"

That explained why Hide Uncle and Chiemi-san relinquished the main house for the smaller cottage when we first arrived from Kyoto. *How stupid I'd been. I was thinking too much of Kazuo and myself!*

"Please, Harue-san," Chiemi-san said from her husband's side, speaking in a soft, deferential tone, "you can't turn Himiko-san away."

"It's not for you to say, Chiemi-san. You don't know what this girl brings with her, and you don't know how unkind she's been to me. She's nothing but trouble."

"This is extremely cruel of you," Hide Uncle said.

Harue Auntie ignored him and looked straight at me. "I want nothing to do with you. Stay away and don't come back!" She got up and walked into another room, sliding the door with a bang.

"I apologize for her hard-heartedness," Hide Uncle said after an uncomfortable silence. Chiemi-san sat with her head down, sniffling.

"Okā-san can be so unfair," Yuki-chan said.

"It's okay. You just be good and listen to your mother. Study hard and do what she says."

"It's still not right." I smiled at Yuki-chan's adult-like perception.

I got up, walked to the doorway, and picked up Sumie's urn. "I should be going then," I said.

"I feel terrible," Hide Uncle said. "If there's some way we can help you, please let us know."

Before I left, Hide Uncle gave me some condolence money for Sumie and something extra for myself. I did not refuse the "something extra," which would have been proper. I also asked for the address and name of the sanatorium where Shiichi Uncle was staying.

On the way back to the city, I dropped by the Blue Sky Sanatorium to look in on Shiichi Uncle, by luck the place within walking distance of his home. When he saw me, my uncle's lips trembled with emotion. "I'm just so glad you're alive, Himiko-san."

Shiichi Uncle looked much better and seemed to be on his way to recovery. He had put on some weight and no longer looked like one of the walking dead. "The doctors are trying a new drug on me, brought in by the Americans," he said.

"I'm happy for you. Soon you will be strong again." I went to sit by him and held his hand. "Thank you for everything," I whispered.

I didn't tell him about my visit to the house and what transpired there. It was at that moment, while I was talking to him, that I knew what I had to do. "I've come to say good-bye, Uncle. I'm going back to Kyoto."

"Kyoto?"

"Yes, Kyoto. I want to place Sumie's ashes in the temple—with Norio and Sā-chan. And Uncle, about Sā-chan . . ."

"Shhh. There's nothing more to be said."

"But, you don't understand."

"Oh, but I do. There's absolutely nothing to explain."

It was as if he wanted to spare me from making a confession, and while it meant that sharing what I knew would have eased my burden, my anshū, it would have placed more suffering on *him*. He was right. It was better for him not to know, and since this was the way he wanted it, I had to honor the wishes of this man I had grown to love as a father.

Reverend Hara had just finished raking the courtyard leaves into a pile and was about to strike a match to the leaves when I approached him from the back. He turned, the sun shining into his face as he looked up. He blinked and shaded his eyes.

"Hah, Himiko-san!"

"Sorry, I didn't mean to startle you."

"Oh no, on the contrary. I was just thinking about you, but the last thing I expected was for you to actually appear. Here, come away from the sun."

He led me into the shade. "Let me look at you," he said. Feeling uncomfortable under his gaze and scrutiny, I looked to the ground. "Don't be embarrassed. You haven't changed a bit. Yes, a few scars here and there, but your good nature is still with you."

"I haven't always been as proper or good as you think. I've had my moments."

"Who is exempt? No one. Being imperfect is human, being foolish is human. But your eyes are still strong and full of life."

"You can tell all that with just one look?" I teased.

"What I can tell is that you've been through a lot. Your scars—they are the marks of distinction—the story of your survival as a victim of the bomb." I hated the words—*victim, survivor*—but these words described exactly the person I had become.

"I wish others felt the same way; Hibakusha are treated like outcasts."

"People are afraid of what they don't understand. In this country, being different is looked upon unfavorably. But your difference has always been part of your strength."

Reverend Hara and I walked over to the small reading room to talk and catch up on our lives. Teruo and two of the other novices were still at the temple, and seeing we were rapt in conversation and had forgotten the time, they brought our meals, smothered the candles in the compound, leaving the ones in the room we were in to taper in long shadows across the wall. Reverend Hara and I talked late into the night.

"I knew you were alive," he said, "but I never expected to see you in Kyoto."

"I had nowhere else to go."

Reverend Hara nodded, reached over, and patted my shoulder affectionately. In our conversations, Kazuo's name was never brought up, and I was afraid to ask.

The reverend provided me, once more, with a place to stay and gave me back my old job as cook and housekeeper. I showed him my fused hand, a small rice paddle now, and told him that I didn't know how useful I would be.

"Don't worry. Anything is better than our present situation. We've been rotating as cooks again."

"I also have these frequent, vague illnesses that plague me."

"The novices and I will take over when that happens. A one-armed and sickly Himiko-san is better than any number of novices," he said, smiling.

Of the five boys who had been at the temple when I was there, one had died of unknown circumstances; the other had decided that becoming a Buddhist priest was not his life's calling. Three others had come back after brief stays in the army, including Teruo, who had been shot in the left arm and had undergone surgery to fix the shattered bone. He bowed deeply when he saw me. "I'm glad you're back," he said.

"The boy is like my own son." Reverend Hara later said.

On the day I was to hold a service of inurnment for Sumie, Kazuo's mother appeared at my door, a bunch of white peonies in her arms. She was thin and elegant in a black dress; being a widow became her. I observed that she looked relaxed, and not particularly mournful.

"Please do come in," I said.

She slipped off her heels, crouched down, and sat on one side of the zabuton I provided. She placed her small, black handbag on her lap, white petal-like fingers draped over it, and I could hear the faint slide of strands of her expensive pearl bracelet when she moved her hands. I excused myself and went to the kitchen across the way and brought back some green tea with wheat wafers on a tray into my room.

She ate the wafers in small, thoughtful bites while she sipped her tea, eyes lost in concentration. We had only our thoughts between us as we sat in silence.

Finally, putting her teacup down and looking straight at me, she said, "My deepest condolences. Sumie was like a granddaughter to me."

"Thank you for your sympathy. My condolences too, upon your husband's untimely death."

She opened her bag and removed an envelope, which made me think about the envelope her husband had given to me in my dream. After sliding the envelope toward me, she prostrated herself upon the floor in a bow and slowly pulled herself up.

"I appreciate your sentiments," I said, "but I can't take anything more from you."

"Please accept it—for the joy Sumie brought me."

With this, what could I say? I put the envelope into the folds of the front of my kimono.

"And Himiko, about Kazuo . . ." Kazuo's mother said.

"I'm going home to Hawai'i soon," I said, interrupting. I was afraid that I could not discuss Kazuo with his mother and keep my composure.

But she continued. "Although I came to offer my condolences, I also wanted to talk to you about Kazuo. It's important that you know how he has agonized over you these past months."

"He has? I'm surprised. There's been no indication he felt that way, so tell him I'm doing as well as can be expected, and that I'm soon going home to be reunited with my mother and sister."

"What you say doesn't help me. I need to talk about Kazuo. I've been concerned about how unhappy he seems without you."

I took a deep breath. *Kazuo unhappy? He betrayed me! I was in love with him and thought he felt the same. Weren't we supposed to get married? He never made an effort to find me.*

"Perhaps if he came to see you . . ." she finally said.

"See me? I don't think that is possible."

"If you could just say something to ease his pain, then."

"All right, if you insist. Tell him that I release him, forgive him. Wish him all the happiness in life."

"I can carry that message back to him?"

"Yes, definitely."

With that, she looked relieved. A few minutes later she left my room.

In the spring of 1947, Kyoto newspapers showed the wedding pictures of Kazuo and his new bride, I presumed the one his father had picked out for him. She looked retiring and shy and her wedding gown was beautiful, white, and obviously very expensive. Kazuo appeared in a white day coat and a top hat in his hands. He looked resigned. Like so many modern couples, neither of them was smiling; they already seemed bored with each other. Looking at the picture, jealousy and anger burned the residue of any goodwill I had for him.

Later that year, the season of harvest festivals of the white moon arrived to find me feeling run down. The humid weather had brought back my illness. Reverend Hara found me walking in the churchyard late one night, searching for Sumie. I was walking as if through the light that had changed the world, my burned hand extended. I was walking through the fire along with all the others, like hungry ghosts, without the prospect of a miracle to cool or soothe our unbearable pain.

"What are you doing?" Reverend Hara said.

In my delirium, I vaguely remember telling him, "I'm looking for Sumie, for Kazuo. Why am I still living? How did I survive? Where's Iwao, Norio, Sā-chan . . . Sumie?"

Some time later, still with a fever, I lay in bed and looked around me. Cut flowers in a careless arrangement stood in a vase by the window of the small room, and Teruo, who was soon to take his tonsure, his first ordination, sat nearby practicing a chant in his melodious baritone. He had on a white shirt over a dark pair of pants, a sutra book open in his hands.

"I thought I had fallen into a field of blossoms," I said and looked up at the flowers. "I thought I was dying, with you saying my last rites."

Teruo smiled and pushed open a window.

"It's a beautiful day out," he said. "It's good to see you awake, Himiko. You've had a high fever for the past several days. The doctor had to drain several blisters that formed on your scar tissues and gave you a transfusion."

I felt the bandages on the right side of my body, which was in line with the window.

"How many days?"

"Four. Your fever went down a bit yesterday. Reverend Hara will be relieved to find that you are much better. He couldn't be here today."

"Where am I?"

"At the hospital. Ogawa Hospital."

"Ogawa Hospital?" *Oh no, Kazuo's hospital.* "Listen, I can't stay here. I can't pay the bills. Please take me back to the temple."

"I can't, but I'll give Reverend Hara and the doctor your request." Teruo bowed out of the room.

I fixed my gaze on the overly sweet-smelling flowers. I couldn't tell what they were. Their vibrant petals had a waxy coat to them that I imagined, if ignited, would burst into a million colors.

The sun moved farther up the window. In a sudden shift of the angle of the rays, a searing stab of light flashed across the room, seemingly having burst from the flowers; I shielded my face with my left hand. Out of the flash, I saw someone enter the room. It was Kazuo.

"Himiko?" he said and pulled up a chair. Though looking as handsome as ever, he appeared older, harried, and thinner, his white coat hanging from his body.

"Have you been here before—to see me?"

"No, I knew you were here, but I didn't know what to say. I came today because I heard you were getting better and would be going home." From where he sat on my left side, he could only see the good side of my face, so to him I must have looked unchanged. "I've been running the hospital since my father died. In addition, I've been studying to pass my medical exams. They're more grueling and competitive than I imagined they would be. But today, I wanted to see you and . . ."

I didn't respond. We talked little between the long silences. For me there was nothing to say, for I didn't want him to know anything more about me—my hurt, the betrayal I felt, my injuries, my fears, my guilt, my sorrow. I looked to the flowers and the threads of light that wove through the thin curtains. When I noticed that I had my burned hand out, I quickly hid it under the sheet for I didn't want him to see the bad side of my body. After a while, Kazuo pulled his chair closer to the bed. "Himiko," he began, but faltered. "I'm so sorry about Sumie."

"Thank you."

"I also wanted to say . . ."

"You needn't explain," I said, my eyes straight ahead, on the flowers. "What you do is no longer my concern." It was true that right after the bomb I did want him to come and see me, but that was no longer the case. Didn't I tell his mother to inform him that I had released him? "I wish you would leave the room. I don't want to see you again!"

"Please, Himiko. I came here to apologize."

"There's nothing to apologize for."

"I was wrong, Himiko. Terribly wrong. You don't understand how wrong."

Anger welled and almost overcame me, but what I felt was left unsaid in its futility: *What right do you have to come into this room to ask for my forgiveness? How selfish of you, caring only about your own discomfort and guilt!*

I swept my legs off the bed and let them dangle. In what was now the heat of insurmountable anger, I turned my body directly at him and said, "Look at my face, Kazuo." I made a dramatic sweep of hair away from the bad side of it. "Take a good look. See my neck scars, too!" I turned the burned side of my neck towards him and pulled down on my kimono at its collar. I then slid off the bed. I took a few steps toward him, to stand in front of him, but he scrambled like a cornered cat to get out of his chair. I startled him further when I reached out and grabbed one of his hands.

"What are you doing?" he said, trying to pull his hand away.

"I want you to feel my scars."

"Why are you doing this?"

"Why?" I gripped his hand tighter and guided it to my neck. "Because I thought you came to see me. I am my scars, you know. There, don't you like what you see and feel? Don't you want to make love to these scars, to me?"

This time, I forced him to touch my face. "In all this time, weren't you the least bit curious as to how I looked?" He averted his eyes from mine. "Is that all you can do—pull away?" But I could see that while he was repulsed, he was also fascinated. Finally, stopping his resistance, he tentatively made a move to touch my face.

306

I wanted him to feel these scars that I had to feel every day. I wanted him to know what I lived with, what all the Hibakusha lived with—every second, every minute, every hour of every day of every month of every year, of every hundred years, every thousand years, every hundred thousand years, every kalpa, a million kalpas, time eternity, time immemorial. I wanted, too, for him to know what it would be like for him to live and die with my scars. *Feel.* Most of all I wanted him to understand why we could no longer be together.

I released his hand and dropped the kimono off my right shoulder. "Look at how my burns caress the mound of my breast," I said. "I no longer have a nipple on this side. And look at my keloids, the redness and the roughness of the designs." I dropped the kimono off my left shoulder and cupped my good breast. I draped my useless right hand around his neck and pulled him toward me.

"Himiko, don't do this," he said. "Please let me go!"

"You can't go yet," I said, not knowing where my strength was coming from in restraining him on his neck. "Here, kiss my shoulders and feel my lumpy skin on your lips." I pressed my body as close as I could to his. "Whenever you kiss your wife's soft smooth shoulders, think of mine. Feel me instead. I don't want you to forget, ever, how I feel to you, understand? So kiss me."

His breathing quickened. As I moved in closer, he tried to move back. "Why do you want to do this?"

"Am I that repulsive?" This time, he started toward the door, almost dragging me with him. "Oh, don't leave now," I said, coyly. "The sideshow has just begun." To block him, I quickly moved my back to the door.

"Himiko, I don't want to see any more or kiss your scars!"

"But I'm not done yet." I unwound the dressings that covered my midriff with my good hand and brought it up to his face. "Smell this. Remember it," I said, and using my wrist, I circled my webbed hand tighter around his neck and pushed his head forward, and down. "Smell my dying!"

"Please . . ."

"I want this smell to follow you for the rest of your life."

"That's enough!"

"Enough, why? Because it makes you uncomfortable?"

"It's not what you think."

"Then what?"

"I don't know." He peeled my hands off him and put both of his hands up to cover his face.

While he may have given up, I wasn't about to. I took his hands away from his face and moved up to him once more. I took off my sash and dropped my kimono to the floor. I stood naked before him and pressed his hand against my bare pubic bone. "Feel this and remember it all your life. Go on, feel it!"

"All right, all right, you win. You've made your point. I hate your scars. I wish this had never happened to you!"

"But it did, don't you see?" I said, cooling down, suddenly feeling deflated. Defeated. "I'm still Himiko."

"No, the Himiko I knew is dead!" he said and quickly left the room.

34

True and Real Life

Not long after the incident with Kazuo, I noticed an ad posted by the General Headquarters of the occupation forces at Kyoto Train Station where I had gone to deliver a message for Reverend Hara. "Translator Wanted," it read. I applied for the position at a small office nearby and ran up Horikawa-dōri and back to the temple on Takatsuji. I found Reverend Hara in his study and did not wait for him to tell me to sit down.

I bowed and said breathlessly, "Sensei, today I applied for a job with the Americans as a translator. You think I can do it?"

"As a translator? Of course you can. I hope you get the job."

"I'm so excited—have never been so excited! I know I can do this if given the chance. But do you think I even qualify? I have no education. The only advantage I have is that I can speak English and know Japanese fairly well, but oh, I hadn't thought about this—what if they want me translate their writings? Then I'm doomed. I'm practically illiterate. What am I to do in that case?" I was talking faster and faster.

Reverend Hara laughed and said, "Now, now, calm down. I'm sure it will be fine. I see all kinds of jobs posted around the city by the Americans asking for workers. If they can't use you as a translator, at least they can use you for something else."

I waited for an immediate answer from the U.S. Army, but none came. After two weeks, just when I was about to give up hope of being called, a hasty message came to the temple, requesting an interview for the following morning at nine. Since I didn't have anything decent to wear, I borrowed one of Teruo's old kimono and wore that. I figured that the Americans would not know the difference between male and female patterns, so I could wear it with impunity. Japanese people would stare and perhaps talk when I passed by them, but I was used to people staring. Didn't they stare at me in any event because of my scars?

When I entered the office near the train station ten minutes before my interview, the kindly, polite young white officer, who seemed not to have noticed my scars when I first applied for the job, was not there. Instead, there was a short, cigar-smoking, sloppy looking gentleman behind the desk whose mouth fell so wide it looked as if he were opening his mouth for a dentist.

"Uh-hum," he finally said, grabbing for thoughts. "Captain Peterson will uh be with you in a minute. You can sit there," he said, pointing at some chairs. "You uh one of those—you know?"

I ignored him, but not before I narrowed my eyes at his curiosity and forced him to look away.

Captain Peterson was a tall, erect man who stood up when I entered and leaned forward on his desk, as if from the front of a small boat, looking through a fog. "Please," I said, waving my hand, "you don't have to bow to me. I'm an American."

"So I see from your application," he said, looking down at the paper work before him, then holding out his right hand for a shake instead, his hand feeling rough and dry when I took it. Licking his index finger, he used it to turn the pages of my application and quickly skimmed through it. "I'm sorry, but I didn't get to review this until now. I also see that you are a victim of the bomb?" If he stared at my scars, he was polite about it.

"Yes, I am."

"I was in Hiroshima before coming here, so I've seen the devastation. I'm sorry you got hurt. You know that all your medical expenses will be taken care of, right? It was bad, but I guess it was the only thing we could have done."

Only thing? How dare you! Even a firebombing would have been better. I felt a sudden surge of anger that nearly catapulted me from my seat. What saved the captain from my wrath was my practicality. Exercising gaman, I held back what I really wanted to say. I was in desperate need of a job. If I had a romantic notion that I was going to be rescued by the Americans once they came into the city, I was quickly disabused of the idea. There was going to be no rescuing; I had to do things on my own, in my own way, in my own time. Although I was corresponding regularly with Miyo and Mama at this time, and Miyo had offered me boat fare home, I had declined her generosity. I had used her money once, and I couldn't do it again. I also didn't want to leave Sumie behind.

"Would you please describe what I have to do?" I asked, getting back to Captain Peterson.

"Oh, it's simple. All you have to do is to ride with the officers and translate for them, that's all. You think you can do that? Not many English speakers here know as much Japanese as you do. Also, I need someone to give Japanese oral language lessons to some of the officers and their wives."

"I can speak Japanese, but I can't read or write much of it."

"That doesn't matter," Captain Peterson said. "At the language school, all that the career officers and their wives require are some of the basic stuff—hello, good-bye, counting money—just to get around until they are transferred. You think you can handle that?"

"Of course I can," I said, boldly.

"Okay, you can start tomorrow, doing translations. I will let you know about the language school. See the clerk outside about getting a clothing stipend for the PX. He will give you details."

From then on, I worked with a variety of officers and their drivers, my job consisting of showing them where to find this and that for their building projects in and around the city. While curious about my scars, the men and the Japanese we worked with quickly forgot about them once we began negotiating for supplies.

About a month after I secured my job as a translator, I began teaching Japanese. Although the students, mainly high-ranking officers of the occupation and their wives, were glad to have someone who spoke English to teach them the basic words of Japanese and who wrote words on the board in a rudimentary but understandable informal, my-own-kind-of-Romaji way, these officers, who came to a school near the train station for three nights a week, proved to be more challenging than my translation duties.

When I first went to class, the men and women stared at me, which I had anticipated, the women more than the men curious about what had happened to my face. Initially what shocked them most, however, was that I was an American citizen.

"How come you're in Japan?" one of the women asked, which opened a barrage of other questions. "How old are you?" "From Hawai'i huh? So you weren't interned." "Did the Japs put you in jail here, because you're an American?" They were very insensitive in asking their questions. Without revealing much, I tried answering them as plainly as I could, explaining that I had been trapped in Japan during the war. While I disclosed very little about my personal life, I just wanted to let what I could say out in the open and out of the way.

"Are your scars on your face and neck what they call keloids?" a woman asked.

"Yes, but mine are not large."

"Eeeyewww," she exclaimed and cringed behind her husband's shoulder.

That first session, I was glad that they soon became less concerned about my scars and went on to talking about other things, only occasionally glancing at me.

These officers and their wives, who came to my oral-language classes two nights a week, lived in a housing facility that had been constructed at the Kyoto Botanical Garden, the army providing me with transportation to and from the temple. The wives, especially, acted as though they were on vacation, needing the language only for the duration of their stay, so what we went over one evening was easily forgotten by the next session, for they could hardly wait to get out of Japan, the facilities not to their liking, many of the conveniences of home lacking, and the food challenging. The men were also bored, talking more about their projects in the city than listening to me; they all acted as if my class were one large social club.

After a month of teaching, as I was trying to deliver an oral lesson above their chatter and because no one was listening, I picked up my things and simply walked out, tired of their entitled lives, their insulting looks, rude questions, and general disrespect.

"Will you go back to teaching the class?" Captain Peterson asked when he learned that I had quit. "The men and women are very sorry about their poor behavior. You've been the best they've had, and they are quite contrite."

"I'm afraid not. You will have to find someone else. I will, however, continue translating for your officers, but I'm not going back to teaching those, those . . ." I said and walked out of his office. *Slobs! Jerks!*

The spring of 1948 brought more good news. Setsuko wrote, announcing that she and Reverend Seki planned to get married. "Will you and Reverend Hara be able to attend the small wedding and reception in Kobe?" I wrote back to say that I was coming. Reverend Hara declined the invitation but sent a gift with me.

For their wedding, I gave Setsuko and Reverend Seki some money and an American toaster from the small PX in Kyoto. Setsuko winked at me when I gave her the gift. She asked: "Are you still dealing in the black market?" We laughed together like schoolgirls.

Reverend Seki and Setsuko lived in a small but comfortable apartment in Kobe close to the temple, and I could see how much of a steadying influence Reverend Seki had been for Setsuko. "You're becoming too *dignified* for me to recognize you anymore," I said to Setsuko.

The couple had immersed themselves in work for the temple they were assigned to and planned to adopt a child orphaned by the bomb. They had already picked him out, which was one of the reasons they were in a hurry to get married. They showed me snapshots of their Sadao taken at an orphanage in Hiroshima. The four-year-old—a cheerful, happy-looking child—was to be released right after their wedding.

The evening I left, I took Setsuko's hand in mine and said, "We made it, didn't we? We managed to survive."

"Yes, together, we managed . . ."

We bowed to each other, unable to hold back our tears.

The Allied Occupation Forces paid me well for my duties as a translator. Every month I saved a small amount for Yuki-chan's education and deposited it into a post office savings account for her. While the sum was small, the fund would help her in the future. It was my way of paying the family back without giving money directly to Harue Auntie.

With additional savings, I took a train to Hiroshima one day, before the swell of summer, to visit Shiichi Uncle and the rest of the family. While in Hiroshima, I thought about my debt to Mr. Bitter Melon in passing and decided I would get to it some other time.

Since I had left, there was much more activity all around the city. In taking the short train ride to Asagun, where Shiichi Uncle and Harue Auntie resided, I also saw more people working in the fields than ever before. When Shiichi Uncle first saw me walking up the roadway toward Hide Uncle's cottage, he hollered from the main house: "Hi-chan, welcome back!" and came rushing down to meet me on the road. Chiemi-san too came running out of her cottage. After greeting me, Chiemi-san excused herself and went out to help in the fields. Drawn and frail looking, Hide Uncle stood at the doorway until Uncle and I came up to the cottage, but feeling tired, he soon retreated to his bedroom. He had been fighting leukemia, the result of his search for Sumie, Iwao, and me after the bombing.

Unlike his brother, Shiichi Uncle looked well and had put on some weight. Just before going into the lower house, I saw, in a flicker, Harue Auntie peeking out from between the door curtains of the main house, but she did not come out to greet me. I knew that I would never have any real engagement with her for the rest of my life, which suited me just fine.

"I want to apologize for Harue Auntie—the way she put you out," Shiichi Uncle said, once we were seated inside Hide Uncle's cottage. "If only I had known at the time. But everything worked out better than expected, didn't it?" I smiled and nodded. "In the end, that's what it's all about, that things turned out well. And look at you."

Uncle wanted me to stand and turn around; he nodded his head in approval. "You look very American in your stockings, white blouse, and black skirt. High heels too! You look like your mother—in a picture I had of her in American clothing."

For a while we talked lightheartedly about this and that, but the weight of my guilt about my cousins was something that I could not shake off. I suppose, looking back, it was just another shallow attempt to ask for my uncle's forgiveness in a need to expiate my guilt. "Uncle, about Sā-chan, and Iwao, too . . ." I began.

Shiichi Uncle's eyes suddenly darkened and turned so cold that I stopped saying anything more. While he had stopped me verbally the last time I broached the subject, this time it was his piercing eyes that did it. This time, there was no mistaking the accusation in them, and I knew that he knew I had something to do with Sā-chan's death, making me realize that my involvement had been painful to him all these years. How cruel I was in bringing it up, again! I imagine that he had often intervened on my behalf because of Harue Auntie's suspicions, that now it seemed he could do no more for me. He had been holding back all this time, and had I not said anything it would have been fine, but to him, right at that moment, he had found that perhaps I had not learned that some things were best left *unsaid*.

"I'm so sorry. I didn't understand," I said, realizing my ignorance, the hold of my ego, and most of all knowing that after this, my visits and his regard for me would be limited.

I went back to Kyoto feeling sad about the whole matter. Had I still not learned anything, after all that I had been through—while vainly thinking I had? Was there no *true* realization?

With another Obon season ending that year in August, all of Kyoto had been darkened for the Daimonji Fire Festival. Long streams of people with lighted lanterns made treks to different vantage points in the city. I caught the bus and went to the area of the Heian Jingu to watch the burning of the ideograph for "dai"—"great"—on the mountainside of Higashiyama. I intended to watch the fire from along a small canal near the temple.

A man and woman, who looked like Kazuo and his wife, walked out of the reflection of this fire, their faces glowing in the flames of the lantern lights all around us. I didn't expect the feeling of Kazuo to be so near. I looked up at the man and he returned my stare without flinching. I couldn't tell from his expression if he felt anything because he had no idea who I was, but whatever he was feeling made him pull his pregnant wife farther into the crowd and away from me—most probably reacting to my scars.

I noticed that, as a couple, they looked neither sad nor happy; they looked like an ordinary couple on an ordinary holiday in the city, and I wanted so much of that ordinariness in my life.

Just then something happened to me. I had to go back to Hiroshima. I wanted to be among the Hibakusha, my own people. I realized that if I didn't go back, I would always hide from the truth, for it was easier to feel normal among people who were normal. I needed to be reminded, daily, about what and who I really was.

"I had expected that you would eventually want to go back there," Reverend Hara said when I told him of my plans the next morning. "Very often we need to go back to the place of our deepest anguish. It's only natural. You must go to your life."

"Yes, and be grateful for it," I said. "Strange to hear that from me, isn't it?"

"No, it isn't. If we don't change and grow, what is life for? Will you be okay?"

"Yes, I'll be all right. I've learned to write again—with my left hand. I can walk without much of a limp. I wrote in a poor hand to a dead friend's mother— her son, Mikio, someone I met during the bombing—and have asked to stay with her in Mukaihara."

"The mother of the young man who died?" I nodded and Reverend Hara continued saying, "And not your relatives?"

"No, they have to be free of me, too. Clearly, my way is not with them."

I obtained a transfer from the U.S. Army to work in Hiroshima, and on the day before leaving, after the last noontime meal that I had prepared for Reverend Hara and the boys, I returned to my room and the fragrance of spring flowers that the boys had cut and brought to my room as a farewell. I took the bouquet up to my nose and thought of my days in Kyoto, about Kazuo and the times we spent together in the city, then stuck the flowers into an old temple vase to place on my low table.

I couldn't help thinking that the flowers were like the daisies and lilies that Sumie and Yuki-chan held in their hands at Nijo Castle. I remembered that, on the day at the castle, Kazuo and I could have been an ordinary couple of an ordinary family, the girls picking the no-name flowers while we watched in natural happiness. Perhaps we would have talked the talk of families, gone home that evening, eaten a simple meal, put the children to bed, and turned to each other to make the ordinary and natural love of a husband and wife. Perhaps a child would have been conceived out of that naturalness, in life's longing for itself. That was all there is to life, I thought.

I wondered if Kazuo would be a good father, a good provider, a good husband, happy in the mundane celebrations of anniversaries and birthdays and deaths. Could he be ordinary, unlike his father and mother? As for me, although I had worked through most of the fire of hate and anger I felt towards him, I still had to fight my way through it in order to get to the fullness of an ordinary life. Could I leave aside my resentment of his betrayal because of my pride? Thinking deeply about our circumstances, I felt I had progressed in how I saw him. I could not begrudge him the small moments of happiness that he would encounter, nor the balance he was to have in this life, which I hoped would be good and sustaining. I could not for a moment be unhappy about the warm, manageable fires in the ordinary place in his ordinary life and his marveling at their steady glow. I didn't want him to ruin all that he had by taking on a lover and hurting his wife. I wanted him to be a good husband. I wanted the best for him in his life—for what I would never know or have.

The flowers would wilt by late afternoon. Though a residue of hurt remained, at least I was no longer as sad as I had been about what had happened to Kazuo and me. It seemed that our situation had been settled, and had the war not come, things might have been different; I could see that. The day I saw him, my anger was so large. That I reacted so harshly was my one regret, for it left no room for us to ever meet again—not even to say "hello."

I continued working for the General Headquarters as a translator in Hiroshima. Four years after I stepped off the bus, the city began renewing itself at a furious pace. Wide new streets were being planned and the place was becoming unrecognizable, considering the devastation that had hit it. With help from the Americans, more buildings and businesses were being built, the circle of devastation growing smaller. It seemed as if the more that was built, the more the bomb receded from the people's minds. We could begin to live again.

Unfortunately, a year or so after I began living with Mikio's mother, she fell terribly ill with a disease doctors knew little about. Her sister and I began caring for her over the months, her condition becoming progressively worse as the days went by.

"Himiko, I feel so obligated," Mikio's mother said as she sat up one day. "You don't have to stay. You should leave for work."

"I will, as soon as your sister is here."

"But aren't you going to lose your job? I don't want you losing your job on account of me."

"You don't have to worry. I won't lose my job."

"I'm so glad you're here. I feel very secure when you are around. You are so patient. You never get angry."

"I wasn't always like this," I confessed.

Strangely, it felt as though I had been waiting all my life for the bomb's light, so that I could be at Mikio's mother side in her illness. All the time I had spent in cooking for the family, bathing the children, washing my hair, going to school, dancing, singing a song, climbing a tree, raking a fire, kissing a forehead, scratching a knee, or going to sleep, I'd been heading toward the light and this place on the earth. The moxa burning upon my back, the holiday at the beach, Papa's fireball, the cane fire, my fights with Auntie, my rejection of Hamada-san, Norio's death, Sā-chan's death, Iwao's death, my relationship with Kazuo had all brought me to that hour, that minute, that second, that moment. And into the light.

Then, back into Mikio mother's room to care for her—to do what was good and in its own way very ordinary—what families do—caring for their children or the elderly in the cycle of life and being happy in whatever circumstances befall you.

"I will bring you some tea and your pain medication. You should take the pill before your sister arrives," I said. "I will leave when your sister gets here."

"I wish you could stay with me all day," she said and took my hand before I could stand. "I like that you are kind and quiet, not over-emotional. When something happens, like a seizure, my sister gets close to hysteria."

"But remember, she's the only one who can make you laugh."

"That is true!"

"And that is good."

"Yes, good, but I like you because you are serene. You aren't fussy about little things. You never raise your voice."

"You wouldn't know it to look at me now, but I had a bad temper. I was also very vain. Ha, look at me now."

"Mmmm. We learn as we go on living, don't we?" I went to the cabinet and got down her pills. *Yes, we learn as we go on living, and I learned the hard way how devastating an uncontrollable temper or vanity could be.*

"Shh, take the medicine and rest."

"You are also too serious," she said and smiled.

I had reason to be serious. I understood what it meant to suffer. I understood what it meant to be in a war. I knew what anger and reacting to anger could do. I understood what it meant not to have enough to eat. I knew what it meant to want peace and security so much that it hurt. I knew what it meant to be disfigured and in constant pain. I knew what it meant to lose a child. I knew what it meant to kill someone. I knew what it meant to be a liar. My anshū may have been *my* anshū, but a part of it was now deeper and broader. While I was carrying the weight of my life—my guilt over the children, and other members of my family—people I loved and hated—I was also carrying the weight of countless others, and in the end, all of humanity!

In the years after the bombing, visiting American doctors and physicists from the Economic and Scientific Bureau set up a clinic for the Hibakusha. When I began living in Mukaihara, I went there for treatments and had my body and scars examined.

Doctor Jameson at the bureau liked me because I was frank and immodest and submitted myself completely to the doctors' scrutiny. "Go on, do anything you wish," I said when they examined my body.

Doctor Jameson always commended: "You are a good specimen for our follow-up studies about the effects of the bomb on humans."

The U.S. Army Surgeon's Investigative Team had come as early as the first week after the signing of the treaty. I had seen them at the hospitals or in the city talking to victims, their notepads in hand, taking their calibrations of people's scars. They were fascinated by the size of people's keloids. Almost four years later, they were still recording and keeping track of the victims, including me and Hide Uncle whom I had placed into the program.

I sat naked in the team's examining rooms. The bright light hung over me, and I was like a teru bōzu doll, released and naked in the wind. I hung there in the white light of the white room while the doctors in their white frocks examined my body. I felt no shame that they did this over and over again; I could hum the songs of home or flip through magazines while they treated me. I let them scrape my keloids, I let them look into every orifice and measure every crevice, every limb; I spread my legs; I let them puncture and drain any abscess for cultures without succumbing to pain, this probing of no consequence to me because I was what I was.

This was the body I would carry with me to my grave. It was neither ugly nor beautiful, good nor bad, and I was no longer attached to this mere vehicle of life as I had been in the years of my vanity. I could give it up to the doctors as an offering to their studies. I moved when they asked, opened or closed my eyes when asked, lifted or dropped my arms when asked. I was not ashamed of the stains I left on their white sheets or how I smelled. I took their medicines and used their ointments, and I submitted my body to their tests. It was like running through the cane fields once more, kicking the cans, biting into the bitter blades of grass. Accepting my disfigurement.

The army photographer, who I only knew as Joe, was appreciative whenever he came to photograph me and my scars. "You make it easy on me because you're always perfectly calm," he said. "You never cry and that's good. I can take these pictures without you complaining." A white flash, another white light, made negatives of my body and I was suspended in that light. "You are a model patient," he said, and soon word of me spread from Hokkaido to Okinawa and later the wider world. Photographs that came back to me showed the landscape of my body, places I had been—the fields of pāhoehoe, the rainforests, the long beaches, the swirling eddies. I had picked my way through the susuki and the elm trees and the hanging spines of matsu, the whips of willow, the wisps of blue flowers. "The photos," Joe said, "are works of art," but I didn't know about that. To me they were mere documents of my reality. Some say they had an eerie quality about them or looked mysterious. Again, they were nothing like that.

One day, while examining me, Doctor Jameson said, "I would like you to write your story to accompany the photographs we have taken of you." I protested at first, but when he said, "The narrative will shed light on the horror of an atomic bomb. I think that's a good thing. Perhaps, people will look at the pictures, and instead of engaging in war, look toward peace as an alternative." I agreed. How could I *not* write this story?

Gradually, I became free of every insult and injury, every bad name. While I accepted my body, I was also free of it. It was a curious but wonderful feeling. The doctors, photographers, the viewers of these pictures had nothing to do with how I felt, for I felt no contempt or sadness, no joy or desire, no jealousy or hate. My body was neither sublime nor profane, but whole, conceived of oneness. This body, absolute, was mine and theirs, and now an object for the world to see. In all reality, I no longer owned my body. It was no longer mine but part of the elemental heat and light. From then on, I was simply living my true and real life.

Despite my failures and regrets, I began to live in a kind of freedom I had not known before. I could gradually see myself for what I was and became more aware of the true nature of life itself. My taking responsibility for all that I did without blaming others made it slowly possible not to be lonely or afraid. *In this burning house, it is the natural working of the Inconceivable Light that promises to save us all.*

Although I was accepting of what I had done and had become, my most personal and darkest sorrow was not far from the edge of my memories. At times, I would dream fierce and terrible dreams about those I had wronged or about bombs and fires, but nothing stayed with me for long, save the one I had of Sumie:

She looks at me and touches my face, and her eyes never leave mine. Her look is one of infinite trust, that I would make things right. She gazes into my eyes with so much love and with so much sadness that it breaks my heart. She opens and closes her mouth to breathe, but watching her becomes unbearable, so I press my face to her cheek, my heart against her heart.

The fireball lifts itself back in a climbing roar of suck, dissolving everything in its center, and pulls upward to the heavens a radiant heat of flaming air—of houses, people, fences, horses, bones, flesh—everything that stands in its eye. There is nothing but its power, its terrible, incredible power that I am in.

Then a great silence descends. Out of this silence emerges the undiminished wailing, something that will stay with me all my life—the cries, the screams of people trapped, burned, or buried alive.

Sumie continues breathing short, shallow breaths, but close to dying, she makes no other sound. I touch her cheek and in a valiant effort she tries to smile. "Okā-chan," she finally whispers.

"Everything is going to be all right," I say to her. Young as she is, she knows

that she is going to die, soon.

Large tears slide from the corners of her eyes. Her teardrops fall into my burning hand, and, for a moment, they cool my palm like spring water.

Acknowledgments

A book as long as this was in the making acquires many friends along the way. Many people have been part of this project and I have been humbled and blessed by their generosity. I extend my affection and gratitude to all.

I wish to thank the following organizations for their financial support in making the publication of this work possible: the Cooke Foundation, the National Endowment for the Arts (NEA), the Hawai'i State Foundation on Culture and the Arts, and the Mayor's Office of Culture and the Arts. I also wish to thank the NEA and the US/Japan Friendship Commission Creative Artist Exchange Fellowship, which allowed for my stay in Japan when I first began this project.

I also wish to extend my deepest thanks to the following individuals: Sam and Mary Cooke for their friendship, grace, and perpetuation of Hawai'i's culture; Eric Chock and Darrell Lum for their insights and suggestions; Joy Kobayashi-Cintrón for her generous heart; Wing Tek Lum for keeping us in line; Cathy Song for her help and support; the late Reverend Toshio Murakami and the late Mrs. Yoko Murakami for Shinjin and my language and tea lessons; the members of the Bamboo Ridge Study Group for the many hours; my teachers and friends of Jodo Shinshu for my lifelong appreciation for what is difficult to achieve in its simplicity and for keeping me on the path; Lani Uyeno, Niki Landgraf, and Gayle K. Sato for their early readings; Fay Shimizu and Kazuko Ioroi for some of the Japanese; Mutsuyo Unger, Kathy Meyer, and Yuma Totani for their assistance; Mary Tahan and the late Jim Ellison for their encouragement; Rowen Tabusa for his tireless work in creating the cover; Milton Kimura for his "good eye"; Normie Salvador for uncovering the facts; Stephen Little for the white spaces; Reverend Eijo Ikenaga for the calligraphy; Darius Kono for his perseverance; and David for his library and, most of all, his love.

For their help in Japan, my gratitude to Tomoyuki and Hiroko Kanakogi and family, Keiko Niho and family and the late Satoru Niho; Yoshio and Toshiko Satsukawa and family; Naoko Shimamura of International House in Tokyo; Professor Masami Usui; the late Professor Kazuko Watanabe; Reverend Gene Sekiya; and Reverend Masako Sugimoto.

About the Author

Anshū is Juliet S. Kono's first novel. Her previous publications include two books of poetry, *Hilo Rains* and *Tsunami Years*; a collaborative work of linked poems with three other poets, *No Choice but to Follow*; a collection, *Ho'olulu Park and the Pepsodent Smile and other stories*; and a children's book, *The Bravest 'Opihi: How Two of Hawai'i's Smallest Sea Creatures Saved the Day*. The recipient of several awards, including the US/Japan Friendship Commission Creative Artist Exchange Fellowship, she has been anthologized widely, most recently in the *Imagine What It's Like: A Literature and Medicine Anthology*. In 2006, she won the Hawai'i Award for Literature.

Born and raised in Hilo, Hawai'i, she now lives in Honolulu with her husband and teaches composition and creative writing at Leeward Community College.

KON Kono Juliet
Kono, Juliet S.
Anshu : dark sorrow

DATE DUE			
9.13.21			

2019